THE UNSWORN

AN UNBOUNDED NOVEL

BOOKS BY TEYLA BRANTON

Unbounded Series
The Change
The Cure
Protectors
   Ava's Revenge
   Mortal Brother
   Set Ablaze
The Escape
The Reckoning
Lethal Engagement
The Takeover
The Avowed
The Unsworn

Other
Times Nine

Imprints Series
First Touch (prequel)
Touch of Rain
On The Hunt
Upstaged
Under Fire
Blinded
Street Smart
Hidden Intent
Checked In

Colony Six Series
Insight (prequel)
Sketches
Visions
Travels

UNDER THE NAME RACHEL BRANTON

Lily's House Series
House Without Lies
Tell Me No Lies
Hearts Never Lie
Your Eyes Don't Lie
Broken Lies
No Secrets or Lies
Cowboys Can't Lie

A Town Called Forgotten
Kiss at Midnight
This Feeling For You
Reason to Breathe

Finding Home Series
Take Me Home
All That I Love
Then I Found You

Other
How Far
I Don't Want To Eat
   Bugs
I Don't Want to Have
   Hot Toes

THE UNSWORN

AN UNBOUNDED NOVEL

TEYLA BRANTON

WHITE STAR PRESS

This is a work of fiction, and the views expressed herein are the sole responsibility of the author. Likewise, certain characters, places, and incidents are the product of the author's imagination, and any resemblance to actual persons, living or dead, or actual events or locales, is entirely coincidental.

The Unsworn (Unbounded Series #9)

Published by White Star Press
Kissimmee, Florida

Printed in the United States of America
ISBN: 978-1-948982-34-4
Year of first printing: 2022

In memory of my father, Kenneth,
for giving me his gift of writing. He was a great father
and always my best editor. I am grateful for all the books
we worked on together, mine and his, and for everything he
taught me about writing. Dad, though my heart is
broken without you,

I

know

you are

proudly

watching.

♥

LOVE YOU FOREVER!

Chapter 1

THE OCEAN CHURNED WITH A FURY THAT WOULD HAVE SUNKEN the nearby battle ships if they had not retreated from the epicenter. Small geysers became huge columns of icy water jetting hundreds of feet into the frigid air as if each battled to be first to escape the monster lurking in the depths below. I watched from the deck of a cargo vessel, hands gripping binoculars, my breath caught in my throat.

Reduce speed by eight point two three percent. I took the thought from an Avowed scientist watching from a nearby sub and relayed it to Keene McIntyre, who obeyed instantly. Levitators, scientists, shielders, chemical manipulators, and more all worked together to raise Sinalta and its four million residents from beneath Antarctica's South Ocean where it had hidden from the rest of humanity for thousands of years. One mistake would be one too many.

Sinaltans had long ago lost the knowledge of how to raise their city, and it was only Keene who now made it possible. With his ability of synergism, he could identify the patterns in anything, not to see how they worked but instead to change and increase the efforts of others. His was a force similar to an atomic reaction and with every bit as much potential power.

This meant he was possibly the most dangerous man in the world. One slip, one variation from what the scientists directed, and all would be lost. Yet without his help, Sinalta would have remained underneath the water and become a vast, frigid, watery grave.

So far we'd been lucky. Though Sinaltans could not raise their failing city alone, their Avowed scientists, like our Unbounded ones, understood the patterns of how things worked, and they had agreed that Keene's ability tipped the scales toward success. Sinaltan's ruling families knew this was their only chance to save their people and retain a national identity, so they had agreed to our terms of aid.

For our part, we Unbounded—along with the rest of the world leaders—understood that helping Sinaltans raise the city, despite their grave crimes against humanity, was the only way of avoiding nuclear war with an enemy we couldn't reach or outgun.

Keene had been on a Sinaltan sub—or transport as they called them—for most of the last week, helping them directly, but he currently stood at the railing of our massive cargo vessel a short distance from me. I was his only connection to the Sinaltan scientists now as he received much-needed physical support from one of the Unbounded healers we'd brought in from Emporium Headquarters in New York, who constantly repaired and eased the aches in his body.

Despite the help, Keene's face was worn, his brown hair lank, and sweat poured from his lean figure. His skin had roughened and burned from exposure, as his extreme efforts impeded his normally rapid healing. All of him screamed exhaustion, but this was most apparent in the way his hands jutted out rigidly in front of him, palms up and fingers curled, as he enhanced the power of the twenty-one Sinaltan levitators who were on other transports and ships. He claimed his hand contortions helped him maintain control, but from the stage of his mind, it felt painful to me. In the past day, his hands had begun shaking.

With my ability to channel others, I'd helped Keene over the past weeks with both raising the city and easing his pain, but I couldn't keep up with his constant effort because I had another, more important life to worry about.

"We need additional support in quadrant sixteen," an Avowed scientist said aloud—unnecessarily, as I could see all the details from his mind. He and his friends had unwillingly given me permission to be inside their thoughts for the duration of the lift. As if they could stop me.

Using my sensing ability to channel both the Avowed scientist and Keene, I found the exact spot where the scientist calculated that we needed more support. *Got it,* I put in the scientist's mind as he finished detailing his order. I usually tried to let them finish their explanation so they would feel I completely understood. They couldn't know how much words actually got in the way.

I directed my borrowed synergism that way, sending Keene the pattern of what I was doing. One tiny boost in the wrong direction meant we'd lose the control we barely maintained. My fingers tightened on the binoculars until they were probably as rigid as Keene's.

Behind me, Ritter Langton stepped close, his body meeting mine with a familiarity that made all my senses sing. "Erin," he murmured, his voice like a caress. I leaned against him, wishing I could stop long enough to absorb his anxiety, but this was the moment of truth, and I needed to pay close attention. His arms wrapped around my body, and through our mate connection it was my anxiety, not his, that ratcheted down a notch.

"Almost there," I assured him, and also the other members of our original Renegade cell: my younger brother Jace Radkey, our cell leader Ava O'Hare, and Mari Jorgensen, who was Keene's girlfriend and who stood at his side.

No one responded, but without trying I felt their nervousness. I also felt Mari preparing to shift all of us away if the worst happened. Gathering power, calculating numbers. When I channeled Keene this way, everything around me was clearer.

At last, the shooting column in the middle disappeared and a small half circle began to emerge amidst the roiling mass of water, almost invisible even through the binoculars. Then, gradually, other water columns fell and didn't rise again as Sinalta's dome grew above the surface. Four long weeks, it had taken to get this far, plus two weeks before that to prepare for movement. The preparation wasn't all that we'd wished for, of course, but with the clock ticking for the four million people in Sinalta's ten square miles of engineered city, it was the best choice.

Water sluiced off the sides of the dome, slamming into the columns of water on the circular edge like a huge mystical sword chopping through ice. Spray shot forcefully in every direction.

Three seconds more thrust. I put the words into Keene's mind, as calculated by the scientists. *Two. One. Stop.*

The vertical water spray cut off instantly as the rest of the dome settled above the surface, leaving only huge swells crashing violently back and forth with a force that would have sent tremendous walls of water throughout the city if the dome and electronic shield hadn't been in place. The tension around me released like a verbal sigh, and a small cheer went up from the crew of our cargo boat.

"Well, it didn't blow up," said Jace, his voice mocking.

I lowered the binoculars and gave my younger brother a glare of disapproval. His short white-blond hair spiked with the wind coming off the ocean, but his eyes, the color of the clear sky overhead, were triumphant.

He was right. Not one or two, but all of the city's three nuclear power plants had taken turns overheating during the past weeks, but they hadn't exploded, then or now, so we were definitely ahead. Keene also hadn't collapsed, and no one had miscalculated. Even with the extra week we'd tacked on with the angled rise to avoid icebergs and certain underwater formations, we'd succeeded in bringing Sinalta safely to the surface. The city was now moving northwest toward Australia—albeit slowly at the moment without Keene's help—with the intention of continuing on to the southeast coast of Madagascar, where it would come to a rest, at least temporarily. Negotiations regarding a final resting place were ongoing as the world's major political powers wrestled with the advantages or disadvantages of having the city in or near its jurisdiction. I secretly suspected that the Sinaltans still expected the world to hand over an entire country and its mortal population for their use. We'd already let them know that South Africa and the continent of Australia, rumored to have been promised to them by the ousted and imprisoned former leader of the Emporium Triad, were off limits.

"Nicely done," Ritter murmured, giving me a brief hug before offering Keene a congratulatory slap on the back—a light one, I noticed thankfully since Keene looked ready to collapse.

"Whoa there," Ritter said as Keene did choose that moment to stagger back from the railing. Ritter put a hand on his arm and guided him to a lounge chair Mari had set up for him earlier. With a groan, Keene stretched out, his eyes closing instantly as the gray-haired healer placed his hands on his forehead.

Ritter moved away to talk to Ava and the ship's captain, a former Emporium employee, but now our employee since the merge, like the cargo vessel that Ava officially commanded. There were no longer Renegades or Emporium factions, only Unboundaried, or Unbounded for short, who ran the massive Emporium conglomerate. And now there were also Avowed, who lived two thousand years, like the Unbounded, and could only be killed in the same manner—by severing the body's three focus points. They claimed that all Unbounded and Avowed originated in Sinalta before its submersion, and they were probably right. Unfortunately, they placed next to no value on mortal lives, and with each day that passed, I grew more worried that the Avowed would be a worse enemy to the world than the Emporium Triad had ever been.

Turning back to the water, I studied Sinalta's semi-transparent dome, arching high into the air above the tall buildings that crowded the outer third ring. I hadn't visited that part of the city yet, but even from this distance, the overcrowding among the poorer Sinaltans was clear.

"I'm going over there to look for Dimitri," I muttered to Jace, gripping the railing to steady myself now that larger waves had reached our position, rocking our boat. I took a deep breath to fight off nausea. "I need to know he's okay." Dimitri Sidorov was more than a friend and Ava's second-in-command. He was my biological father.

Six weeks had passed since we'd left Dimitri in Sinalta and three since we'd heard anything from him. Three long weeks of silence. It was our punishment for Ava's refusal to conduct more electronic—rather than in-person—interviews with the kidnapped Unbounded descendants, called embryos by the Avowed. These embryos had been taken from topside and assimilated into Sinaltan society in an effort to expand their gene pool that was suffering from insanity. Thirty-six hundred years—give or take a century—of interbreeding and killing all those who didn't Change hadn't occurred without consequence.

Our deal to help raise Sinalta had included freedom for the kidnapped, if they wanted it, yet not a single one interviewed expressed a wish to return home or to leave Sinalta, even when we promised their children would be part of the deal. One hundred percent refusal among former street children or throwaways might be possible, but there were several hundred people still alive who had been taken from loving homes, some as recently as earlier this year. Something stank, and only a sensing Unbounded like myself or Ava could determine who was lying and why. But only in person. After Ava had announced that she would not accept the electronic interview results, Dimitri had suddenly been too busy to report to us.

"You sure Ritter is going to allow you back into the city?" Jace asked. "I mean as op leader, of course."

I shifted my gaze to where Ritter stood talking, his legs apart, his bulk perfectly balanced on the deck despite the rocking ocean. His black hair tangled in the wind, and his sleeveless shirt made him resemble some kind of pirate—hard, unmovable, and mean. But the link we shared since our marriage showed me the man underneath, and I softened my usual smirk as he glanced my way. I knew how much I meant to him—no, how much *we* meant to him. Our daughter and I, the former being only three months along inside me. He'd waited most of his two hundred and seventy-four years to have a family, and he'd give anything to keep us safe.

I looked back at Jace. "As long as Mari comes with us, we can shift out at any moment." Ritter still might object, but he wouldn't stand in my way. No one would, not even Ava. I wouldn't let them. "I have to interview the former embryos anyway," I reminded my brother.

Ritter strode toward us, and I raised the binoculars toward the dome again, steeling myself for the pending confrontation with the Avowed. Would they lower the dome and the electric shield that protected it?

The dome, which contained lighting, air conduits, a false sky, and whatever else the ancient Avowed had determined necessary for life under the water, was unnecessary now that the city had surfaced, but there had been arguments in favor of keeping the dome up while Keene and the others continued to move the city to its eventual destination. With the imminent electronic shield failure, most agreed that doing so wasn't a good idea because once the electric shield failed, the weakened dome itself would be a danger to the entire city. Of course, I wanted the electric shield down for other reasons. With it activated, I couldn't mentally search the city for Dimitri.

"We need to find him," I said in a low voice to Ritter after he returned to my side. I glanced over to see him staring out over the still-undulating ocean, his jaw tight, his black eyes filled with emotion he normally kept well hidden. For a long moment, he didn't speak, and I could sense his fury—not directed toward me, thankfully, though it wouldn't be the first time I had angered him. I was plenty willing to push back when I had to, though I was softer now since our marriage because I knew how much he'd already suffered and how it still affected him.

"They'll have to bring down the dome and the shield," he said finally. "Mari can take us then." He locked gazes with Jace. "You come too. Because we still don't know where Scala and Tsaousiss are, and they might cause trouble."

Jace gave a sharp nod. "It's why I came back from New York. I've been wanting to find Scala and that other douche bag since they imprisoned us and ordered our deaths." He rubbed his left arm where he'd been shot while imprisoned, though even the scar had long since disappeared.

I knew it wasn't the only reason he was here. Without Keene there to help him run the corporation and solidify our take-over, he was drowning in paperwork and physical inactivity at Emporium headquarters. Jace and Keene were the biological sons of former Triad members, so it fell to them to provide continuity, and at least one of them had to remain in New York at any given time. Pure torture for Jace, who was gifted in combat like Ritter—and like his imprisoned biological father.

"We shouldn't have let the Avowed keep Dimitri," Jace added, his brow furrowing.

Ritter frowned. "We didn't have a choice."

I wasn't so sure, but it had certainly been the peaceful way out. The Sinaltans had wanted leverage to make sure we didn't blow the hidden explosives I'd asked two discontented Avowed to place on the electric shield, leverage I'd needed to prevent the ruling families from executing my team. As far as I knew, neither the explosives nor my contacts had been located.

"What if he's not okay?" It was Mari who voiced the concern, leaving her vigil at Keene's sprawled form to join us. "Maybe his silence is because he's hurt and not because they're punishing us for basically accusing them of threatening the embryos into staying."

I frowned and my next words came out as a growl. "Oh, it's a punishment, all right, but they've reached the end. Dimitri is coming home tonight, or their seer will come back as my prisoner." I lifted my chin in challenge, but I should have known better. Mari's dark eyes glowed with excitement, and Jace's eager expression told me he was all in. Like me, they were recently Changed, and I was the first to admit that we sometimes acted before we considered all options.

"Really?" Ritter said, lifting a brow at me. "You had to encourage them?"

"Yes, Your Deathliness." I smirked as I used the nickname I knew both irritated and pleased him. "Let's get ready now so we can shift the instant the shield is down. They won't expect us that soon."

"Maybe not, but they will be vigilant," Ava said, stepping away from the railing where she'd been standing after finishing her conversation with the captain. Obviously, she'd kept tabs on the conversation like a good leader always did. Her steel-gray eyes bore into me, strong and unyielding. As her fourth great-granddaughter, I'd inherited those eyes, along with her blond hair, which meant we could pass as sisters. She might look thirty-three, but she was over three hundred years old. Maybe because of our relationship, I pushed the boundaries, or maybe it was simply that my recently activated Unbounded genes wouldn't allow passivity. Either way, I was doing this, but it would be easier with her approval.

"Before you say no," I hurried to say, "remember it's because of Mikyn Zenos and his foretellings that they are able to justify their murders. *Of babies.*" My hand went instinctively to the swelling below my abdomen. My mind also touched the presence there, and I felt a distinct contented acknowledgment.

"Oh, I'm very aware of that." Ava's tone stopped just short of rebuke. "And now that we have other healers who can trade off, Dimitri is no longer needed there. We *will* get him out."

Her words reminded me that no one wanted Dimitri back more than Ava, and I was perhaps the only one who knew why, including Ava herself, and it wasn't because she'd suggested the compromise that left him behind in the first place.

"Now that they're above water," Mari said, "we can get past the electronic shield underneath the city. It's not like the shield over the dome itself since Keene and their Avowed are no longer enhancing it. After all, they always have ships coming and going, right? So they can work and communicate with us. They have to open their subgates periodically to do that." She bounced a little on her toes, like a prize fighter awaiting her next bout. With her hair drawn back into a single braid, her quarter Japanese blood was more apparent.

"The bottom shield is still too reinforced from the lift," I said. "And their scientists are planning to keep that going until they get to the Indian Ocean or wherever they end up. There's no danger of a crumpling dome to deal with down there." Then another thought occurred to me. "Even if they take down the dome above, they might try to leave the top electronic shield up for as long as it holds. From my understanding, the dome itself was never designed to keep the water out. That's accomplished only by the electronic shield and its thousand-plus generators." I learned that there was more than one kind of electric shield generator. In fact, after the past six weeks of being inside the Avowed scientists' minds, I knew more than I'd ever cared to about their infamous shield.

"No." Ava folded her arms. "With the imminent shield failure, it would be ludicrous to keep it up. Especially since they can simply shoot any ship that approaches the city and have nuclear options to retaliate if any country tries that route. They'll feel safe, which is why I insisted we keep Mari's ability a secret, so we can enter the city at any time without their knowledge. Otherwise, they might have scrambled to create a lesser electronic shield like the kind we use. Those may not keep out tons of water or reflect a nuclear attack, but they'll still block Mari." She leveled a stare at Ritter. "Enough talk. We've kept our bargain and brought them up. It's time they keep theirs. Choose your team and gear up. I'll make sure they get that shield down."

"Will do." Ritter's voice sounded like a salute.

Ava turned on her heel and strode away, walking every bit as easily on the ship as Ritter. Was I the only one ready to lose my lunch over the railing? And I couldn't contribute all of it to morning sickness, though without Dimitri around to ease my symptoms, it was far worse than I'd ever expected as a semi-immortal.

"Do we need to use a ship to get closer?" Jace asked Mari.

Mari rolled her eyes. "No, I don't need to get closer. Didn't I just shift you here from New York?" She turned and started back to where Keene lay, saying over her shoulder, "Let me know when it's time. My gear's ready." She patted the hilt of a knife sticking out of her black bodysuit, which was not only bulletproof but had custom pockets containing emergency equipment and various weapons. Most of her bulges were of the steel variety and testified of her unique fondness for knives.

"Since when can't she take a joke?" Jace scowled after her.

I grinned. "Did you bring your gear?" I asked, eyeing his white button-down shirt and black dress pants—clothes he'd always avoided before his forced leadership role at the Emporium.

He snorted. "Left it here. Not much going on at headquarters."

"You think that's a good idea?" Though things appeared calm at the moment, I didn't trust Stefan Carrington, the soul-less Triad leader whose genes Jace unfortunately shared, even though I'd seen for myself that he was locked up in our prison compound in Mexico. "You saw how determined Stefan was when we visited. We have no idea what backups he has in place. And that Avowed woman who escaped in Mexico knows where we're holding him. If he somehow gets free, we are all in big trouble."

The amusement drained from my brother's face. "It's been months since the takeover. He needs to stand trial."

"I agree, but until Keene officially takes his father's place in the Triad, it can't happen." And until Stefan was officially convicted, Jace's appointment in the Triad couldn't be made permanent either. "Besides, we've all been a little busy with this Avowed thing." The boat rolled, and I bit back an increased surge of nausea.

Jace put a hand on my shoulder. "You look green."

"I'm okay," I said, all too aware that Ritter was with us. I wasn't about to give him a reason to take Ava to Sinalta in my place. My sensing abilities were stronger than Ava's, and she couldn't channel others' abilities the way I could. In fact, I hadn't yet met another sensing Unbounded who could, though I believed Mikyn Zenos, the Avowed seer and top leader of one of Sinalta's ruling families, might be the exception. He had somehow inherited both his parents' abilities, which was unheard of in either of our races. This dual ability was the only reason he held so much power among the Sinaltans. Foretelling if an infant would one day Change had completely altered their society and drastically lowered the value they gave mortal life.

"I'm going to suit up," I said, taking a step away from them. I might fight to release Dimitri, if that's what it took, but I would also protect my child. The body armor I'd borrowed from Stella, another member of our cell who was also expecting, was like a bodysuit on steroids. It was nearly impenetrable, which was the peace of mind I needed. While the Avowed were strangely reverent of all expectant women and their babies, at least until after the birth when Mikyn predicted the baby's future, I wasn't about to trust that goodwill. Any race who murdered their own babies just because they were mortal couldn't be trusted.

"I'll be down in a minute," Ritter said, grabbing my hand and squeezing it. "There's something I need to do."

"Okay." I waved a general goodbye and hurried off to my

quarters below deck before I embarrassed myself and threw up everywhere. A stop at the galley for some crackers and a special Sinaltan tea made from a certain seaweed would also go a long way to setting me to rights. Apparently, even though I was constantly absorbing, my body still wanted a reserve sitting in my stomach. I'd learned the tip from my Avowed informant, who sadly was still missing, along with his wife. Their young daughter, currently my ward, was with my older brother, Chris, and his two children back at our Fortress in San Diego, but every time we talked, I had to break her heart yet again. For all I knew, her parents had been found and arrested by the Sinaltan Senate. It was one more reason to go to Sinalta.

Mouth full of crackers, I sipped my warm tea on the way back to my quarters. Ritter was probably already there, waiting for me.

A slight noise ahead made me reach out mentally, but my ability didn't show me any life force besides those in other areas of the ship. Which meant it had either been the groan and creaking of the ship or an Unbounded who could block me completely—not an easy feat these days, even for the most skilled.

Even so, caution drew me to a stop in the narrow hallway. I listened, poised for action, though there could be no danger on this boat, not with Sinalta's shield still up and considering that we were smack dab in the middle of the South Ocean. The only near thing I could sense was an unshielded mortal life force somewhere to my right in the next corridor. Probably one of the sailors.

Shaking my head at my overactive imagination, I took another long sip before stuffing several more crackers into my mouth—completely unhealthy white crackers, which were already working an uncanny miracle in my body, easing the nausea. It was almost embarrassing.

I'd taken only three steps when something fell onto the floor in front of me. The glint of black metal barely registered before I kicked out instinctively. The gun went flying. At once, the slender, black-dressed figure was on me. A woman. I could see her life force now, faint but still there.

I tossed my cup at her, liquid and all, but it wasn't hot enough to do damage. Dodging a jab, I sent a punch to my attacker's face. She grunted as her head snapped backward with the blow.

That was when I recognized Brenna Dabney. I nearly laughed. The Avowed might be able to form an impressive mental shield, but she was no match for me. I had half a foot and twenty pounds on her. And better training. I slammed my fist into her face again, stepping back to avoid her kick. Blood dripped from her cheek.

The life force from the nearby corridor was coming up behind me now, the glowing so mentally bright I didn't need to look to see the person coming. It might be a sailor who belonged on board, alerted to the fight, but I didn't believe in coincidence.

I sent a twisting roundhouse kick to the woman's stomach, and she stumbled back, slamming into the wall as I'd intended. Then, whirling, I faced the second opponent. He was big and mean-looking, but he was mortal, and all my genes begged me to fight him. To toy with him and show him that his power was no match for my superior training. Even if it meant I broke a bone or two in the process. Jace would do it. Ritter would not. That siren of confidence was one of the main reasons Ritter forced us all to train as hard as we did. I couldn't let that confidence take over. Not with the baby at risk. I had to be absolutely careful.

Cursing under my breath, I reached into the man's mind. He had no mental barrier, not even the flimsy one mortals learn to use. It wouldn't have mattered. I sent a flash of light into the sand stream of his mind, brighter and with more force than I intended because the woman was on me again. He collapsed with a huge crash.

I spun away from the woman, realizing she'd taken out another weapon that looked suspiciously like a spring-based ballistic knife. "I'm pregnant!" I yelled, though the knives were notoriously hard to aim, and I was confident I could dive the right way before she hit me.

Just in case, I pushed out a mental barrier to protect my torso. It wouldn't withstand much more than a bullet or two before breaking, but I could make another one so powerful around the baby that not even Dimitri could trace a healing path there. It was a habit now to put it in place whenever I was threatened or worked out with the others. However, it wouldn't remain if I died—even temporarily died—so I needed to protect myself.

"You're with embryo?" Brenna blinked. "Then stop moving, so I won't hurt you." Her voice was strong, honeyed with hypnosuggestion.

I gave a mocking snort and feinted at her, pulling away at the last moment. "That doesn't work on me."

Her face flushed a deep crimson. Like most Sinaltans, she had blond hair and blue eyes, though her skin wasn't nearly as pale as those who had lived all their lives under the sea. "I will kill you then," she growled. "I don't care about your baby."

She was lying. She'd been raised in Sinalta, and though leaders might give lip service to their reverence for potential embryos, Brenna did not. I could feel her turmoil on her surface thoughts, her upbringing battling with her more recent selfishness. This was a woman who'd spent fifty years tracking down and kidnapping descendants of Unbounded, sending them to Sinalta, where they would breed if they Changed, or if they didn't, to work and die in their underwater mines.

I faked to the right and then lunged left, grabbing her knife hand. With a final yank, I sent the knife to the ground and snapped her wrist.

She howled and began retreating, but I grabbed her shoulders and hit her against the wall.

"Who sent you?"

"I just want to get to Sinalta now that it's topside!" Her face crumpled with the words.

A lie. "Do I have to get it from your mind?" I could hear footsteps now, pounding toward us. My people coming to my rescue. "I broke through it last time, so it will be easier now. Or you can just tell me." I pushed on her broken wrist.

She sucked in a noisy, high-pitched breath. "Okay, okay," she panted. "Stefan Carrington sent me. I helped him escape."

My world tilted. If she was telling the truth, my worst nightmare—and the entire world's—had just come true. Stefan Carrington, former leader of the Emporium Triad and Jace's biological father, was loose again.

Chapter 2

I SHOVED BRENNA AGAINST THE WALL SO HARD THAT ONE OF THE clips in her tightly pinned hair clattered to the metal floor. "What do you mean, you *helped* him escape?" I snarled. If it was true, Stefan was probably already halfway toward devising a plan to take control of the American government, beginning with retaking the Emporium.

"He sent me after you and your brother Jace." Brenna's nostrils flared as if annoyed at the forced explanation. "He says he'll need your help for what he plans to do for us in Sinalta. I decided to go after you first instead of your brother because he's combat." Her eyes strayed to the mortal I'd taken out. "Stefan didn't tell me you could do that."

"Stefan didn't tell you I was expecting a baby either, did he?" I retorted. Last I knew, Stefan had thought me gifted in combat like him, and even if he'd since learned the truth from Brenna or someone else who knew I was sensing, he couldn't know the depths of my control.

Brenna didn't answer, but I could sense betrayal leaking from her surface thoughts.

Before she could answer, Ritter rounded the bend down the corridor, coming toward us fast, the edges of him blurring. Coming to the rescue. It was one of the things he did best.

But he wasn't the first to reach my location. Close to me, out of Brenna's line of sight, Mari shifted into appearance with a soft *pop!* She touched my arm, her knife in hand. "Step back. I got her covered."

Brenna jerked with surprise while I opened my mouth to protest. Then I thought of the baby and stepped back to let Mari take over. But I still had questions.

"Who else is with you?" I demanded as Ritter reached us. Because Stefan couldn't be stupid enough to send her alone, could he? I didn't count the mortal as help and neither would he. More likely, the man was a paid henchman Brenna had picked up along the way. With her ability of hypnosuggestion, any mortal and even many Unbounded would follow her to the ends of the earth.

Down the hallway, Ava came into view, sprinting. When she spied us, she slowed to a fast walk before bending down to check on the sprawled man, and I realized how dim his life force had become.

"He's going to need a healer," I said. Silently, I added through her surface thoughts, *There wasn't time to be careful.* Guilt ate at me now. Some might argue that the man had made his choice when he joined Brenna. But had the choice really been his?

Ava nodded at my silent addition. "Why didn't you call us? When Ritter shot off, we realized something must be wrong."

I met Ritter's gaze and saw the same question in his eyes. He'd felt my upset through our mate connection because I hadn't tried to hide it, so he couldn't complain that I was being secretive. I could block him if I wanted, and he could block me for the most part, though I could always feel him in some way if we were in range.

"For her?" I thumbed at Brenna, scorn lacing my words. "I didn't need help. It's not like she's combat, and she broadcasts every move she makes. I was fine. But I doubt she's here alone."

Ava's jaw tightened. "You could be right. I just got off the satellite with Stella, and she had some bad news. Terrible news, in fact, especially coming now. Stefan Carrington escaped the Mexican compound sometime in the night, and his escape wasn't noticed until now. We're not sure how, but he had help."

"Apparently we have our old friend here to thank for that." I gave Brenna a fake smile with too many teeth. "Where are your accomplices? On this boat or waiting elsewhere?"

Brenna glanced between Mari's knife and Ritter's scowl and rushed to say, "They aren't here. It's just me. I was going to grab you and then entice your brother to come save you."

I was offended at Stefan's thinking so little of me that he'd only sent Brenna. But during our takeover, some of Stefan's memories had been permanently removed, including the memory that I was supposedly his daughter. His people had filled him in, though, and he apparently believed them. Later when Jace made himself known, Stefan had tested Jace's DNA himself, and that only solidified his belief that I was also related. Letting Stefan believe I was his daughter ate at my gut whenever I thought about it, but it was better than allowing my brother to face that burden alone, even if Jace knew the truth. I couldn't help Jace run the Emporium in any real way because I couldn't pass a blood test, but my support was key among the Emporium soldiers who still believed me to be Stefan's offspring and his first choice to take his place in the Triad.

"Turn around," Ritter ordered Brenna, fury leaking from his voice and showing in the knotted muscles of his neck. He patted Brenna down, finding another knife, a grappling hook, and two syringes with needles.

"Stefan knew she'd be caught," he said in disgust once he

saw the poor display. "She's nothing more than a message." When Brenna started to protest, he spoke over her, "Face it. You are expendable." With a jerk, he zip-tied her hands together behind her back.

I was beginning to understand. "Stefan knew we wouldn't kill her." Because we weren't like his old Emporium soldiers.

A snarl twisted Brenna's lips. "You don't know what you're talking about." Despite the brave words, the resignation in her eyes showed that reality was setting in.

"Bring her to the deck," Ava said, turning on her heel. "We can get a signal there, and we won't be overheard by the captain or his men. We need to contact the compound and see what progress they're making with reacquiring Stefan. They are understaffed with the recent incarcerations, and we may have to go after him ourselves. She'll be our best bet to find him."

Ritter's hand closed around Brenna's arm. "When she doesn't return, he'll know we figured it out."

"Maybe," Ava conceded. "Or maybe enough of his brain was tampered with that he just isn't that smart anymore."

The man Jace and I had seen at the prison compound hadn't shown any sign of incapacitation, even after I finally managed to break past his strong mental shields. My bet was that he was simply taking advantage of Brenna, and we had to act fast before he managed to undo all the good we had done in the Emporium since our takeover.

"I know where he is," Brenna said. "I'm supposed to take you to him."

"Shut up," I told her. "I'll see for myself what you know when we get above deck." Too bad we couldn't interrogate her in the bridge, the command center of the ship, where we had comfortable seats and the latest technology. But the captain and crew had worked for the former Triad, and it would be better for us if they didn't know Stefan had been our prisoner.

"Have you searched the ship for life forces?" Ava asked me.

I paused, sending out my thoughts. "Nothing that wasn't here before, unless they're good at blocking. Not many are," I added. "Especially her kind." Avowed, I meant.

Brenna snorted with offense but didn't speak.

Ava gave a short nod. "Same here." To Ritter she added, "Alert the crew just in case."

"Will do."

I didn't wait until we reached the deck before starting work on Brenna's mental shield. Hers was particularly strong for a Sinaltan, as it had once been reinforced by Statesman Tsaousiss, a powerful Avowed hypnopath, and she'd apparently maintained what she'd learned in the process. But I'd broken through once before.

Blunt force while she was distracted was my best chance at breaking into her shield, and she was certainly distracted as Ritter dragged her through the corridors and up onto the deck. I drew my talisman, a mental version of the machete I'd been gifted by a mystical native who lived in the Mexican jungle, and began my work.

Ritter stopped outside the bridge to inform the captain of the breach, and then we continued to the railing near where Keene appeared to be sleeping. Mari paused to check on him.

"I'm finished here for now," the healer said to Ava, moving toward us with the sureness of all Unbounded. The graying of his hair gave him about sixty-five equivalent human years, which put him over fifteen hundred actual years lived. There weren't many of the old ones left after thousands of years spent fighting, but they did exist, especially in several smaller countries less involved in the fight to protect humanity.

"Anything we should do for him?" Ava asked.

"He just needs rest. I gave him a dose of curequick, but I

don't recommend any more for at least two days to avoid the chance of addiction."

"Thank you, Eurand. You should take a break now and call your family from the bridge. I'm sure they'll have been watching the raising on the news and will want to hear how it went firsthand."

He grinned. "They will. Thank you."

We moved past Keene and gathered along the railing where the buildings of Sinalta, still protected by their dome, towered above the water. The city and more than two dozen ships like ours that flanked her were moving northwest toward Australia, though at a pace indiscernible to me at the moment. Whether the slow speed was only because Keene rested or because the Sinaltans were debating what to do about the dome, we couldn't know.

I felt the tug of the city on me. Somewhere in that maze Dimitri waited for release, and I yearned to free him. But first I needed to find out what Brenna knew.

A crack began in her shield. One more hit was all I needed, and I was in, leaving a thread to secure a tiny opening so Ava could follow when she was ready. I stood on Brenna's mind stage, watching the sands of her memories rush downward past me to somewhere beyond my feet where they vanished. It was a bit like being close to a highspeed freeway at rush hour times a thousand. There were no signs of the constructs I'd cleared from her head the last time, which meant no sensing Avowed—or empath as they termed it— was preventing her from showing me the truth about her current mission. I suspected Mikyn Zenos had been the creator of those constructs, and the fact that he could do it so well was one more reason to fear him.

I nodded at Ava to let her know that I was ready when she was.

Ava drew out a satellite tablet and called the compound manager in Mexico. After a brief delay, Irwin Stafford's ruddy face appeared on the screen. "Please report," Ava commanded.

Irwin grimaced, running a hand through his thick blond hair. "No luck on finding him yet. We've got everyone we can spare outlooking." He frowned. "It looks like he vanished into midair. He must have had help."

The word *help* set off a series of rapid memories in Brenna's mind. Faces and places skidded by in her sand stream, too tumultuous to decipher without questions to focus her thoughts.

"From inside?" Ava demanded.

He gave a sharp nod. "And out."

"Well, keep on it. Let me know if you pick up his trail." Ava stabbed the off button and his face vanished.

Next, she called Stella, who was at the Fortress in San Diego. Stella appeared quickly as if she'd already had the connection open and waiting. She wore her neural headset, and the furiously blinking lights told us she was busy sifting through the internet for information.

"Sorry," she said. "No sign of Stefan yet. What about Dimitri?"

"Nothing so far," Ava began. "Wait," she said as a message popped up in the corner of her screen. "I just got word that the Sinaltans will be lowering the dome. We'll be able to search for Dimitri then."

I exchanged a look with Mari, who had rejoined us, and we both grinned in anticipation.

"Good." Stella's pale, heart-shaped face, complimented by dark, slanted eyes that were enhanced to perfection by the nanites she instinctively controlled in her bloodstream, nodded at the announcement, but her next words showed her most pressing concern. "So about Stefan. Chris is fueled up and ready to go if you need a plane. Should I have him start flying to meet you in Mexico? I'd come, but I can do my work better here, and it's not like I'm much use in the field right now." Her eyes dropped briefly downward, though we couldn't see the swell of her baby, nearly seven months along. The baby would be my nephew since my older mortal brother, Chris, Stella's current husband, was the father.

Ava considered a moment, then shook her head. "No. We'll get something here, if we need it. Time is of the essence. But make sure he keeps Anina inside the Fortress at all times. No leaving the property for the time being, no matter who she's with, even our security guys. We don't know yet who is behind Stefan's escape, but at least one Avowed is involved, and that means Anina could be in danger from those searching for her parents."

I felt a rush of anger at the idea. Anina Padovan was my ward, entrusted to me by her Avowed parents, who had helped me and betrayed their people because they wanted a life for the daughter who their seer, Mikyn, had deemed would not Change and whose only future was to be a servant or die in the underwater mines like her two older brothers.

"Will do." The screen went blank without Stella making any physical movement that I could detect. It was always disconcerting to me when she did this.

Ava turned her gaze to Brenna, but before she could speak, Jace came toward us, excitement registering in his quickened steps. "I heard what happened from the captain. They're still searching but so far have only found an Avowed sub secured to the side of our ship."

Which explained how Brenna had arrived here.

"Your turn to talk," Ava snapped at Brenna, joining me in the Avowed's head, following the thread I'd left for her. "Where is Stefan?"

Also ask her who is helping her and where they are, I said to Ava. *When Irwin said Stefan must have had help, she had a strong reaction, but it went by too fast to see exactly what.* For me, this was even more important than where Stefan was because it meant we might all be in immediate danger from her allies, whoever they might be.

This rapid private communication took place before Brenna could begin talking, and when she did open her mouth, a shout from Mari halted the interrogation. "Hey, look! The dome is coming down!"

Sure enough, the physical dome over Sinalta was in motion. Everyone stared in fascination as the sections near the top separated with a huge V and began slowly moving first to the side and then collapsing inside each next lower ring.

"The power that takes," Mari muttered, and I knew she was using her mathematical ability that made her shifting possible. The computations would be clear in her mind, as clear as the sands in Brenna's thoughts were to me.

A slight grinding accompanied the movement of the shields, but in all I judged it to be nominal, given that they had not moved in over three thousand years. The rings continued to collapse, folding slowly into a massive open trench surrounding the edge of the city that had to also extend for hundreds of feet below the water. I could see that eventually, once the shield was down all the way, it would form a fourth, albeit smaller ring for the city, made up of the vertical pieces of the semi-translucent material.

"That is incredible," Jace murmured.

"They still have the electronic shield in place," I muttered, sending out my thoughts and trying to get inside the city itself. The electronic shield, powerful enough to protect the physical dome from tons of water and thousands of years of corrosion, made the electronic grids we put up look like child's play.

The level of engineering involved made my mind clog with formulas I wasn't gifted enough to understand except to know that as long as it was there, I couldn't search for Dimitri.

"My guess is they wanted to protect the inhabitants and the buildings from any accident that might occur while taking down the dome," Ritter said. "But as soon as it's low enough, they'll release each section." He met my eyes knowingly. *Be calm and wait,* the look told me. Instead of making me angry as it might have in the old days, I understood that he meant wait like a lion ready to pounce, not in defeat because I was too weak.

As difficult as it was to tear myself away from the mesmerizing display, I refocused on Brenna. Ava conceded to my silent plea with a brief, *Go ahead. She's all yours.*

Relieved to have something to focus on, I faced Brenna. "Who helped you get Stefan out of prison? Tell the truth. I'll know if it's a lie. Don't leave anything out."

"I have nothing to hide," Brenna said, her mouth forming a sour pout. "I was sent here to tell you the truth."

"Then talk," Ritter growled.

Brenna shot him an uneasy glare. "It was easy enough to get one of the kitchen employees to give us information. Once we knew where Stefan was being kept, it was a simple matter of planning and compelling people to help." With her ability, she meant.

"No way," I said. "The employees are all Unbounded, and they are taught to resist hypnopaths. There's no way you could have forced them. Who helped you?"

Brenna huffed, her nostrils flaring wide. "Okay, it was Statemen Tsaousiss and Scala. They did it. I was responsible for hiring mortals for distraction and for our transportation."

Mari gasped, and Ava frowned. "So that's where they've been," she murmured.

"And it explains their success," Ritter added.

Harren Tsaoussis was a master hypnopath, much better than Brenna, so he might have made headway with some of the newer employees at the prison compound. Fortunately, even if he was on the boat now, he wasn't much of a danger to us, or even to our mortal crew, as long as Ava and I were vigilant. Turleen Scala, however, was a levitator and might be able to do everyone real damage.

"They talked their way past the shields and lifted him right out of the compound," I said, seeing the thoughts clearly now in Brenna's mind. "Scala killed a dozen guards by tossing them into the air."

"Reset," Brenna corrected. "Or temporarily killed as you call it. They'll recover. Seriously, it was too easy."

It hadn't been, not from the thoughts in her mind. Scala, Tsaoussis, and Stefan had all been shot, Stefan multiple times. Only Brenna in the escape helicopter had avoided physical injury.

"You should have been prepared for such an assault," Brenna mocked, her eyes going back to Sinalta and the ongoing folding of the dome, which was near midpoint now.

She's right, Ava said to me.

We haven't seen levitators in centuries, I protested, tightening my fists at my side so I wouldn't punch Brenna's satisfied smirk.

Yes, just as they haven't seen a shifter like Mari. She is their weakness as she was for the former Emporium Triad. We should have learned from her appearance.

Ava was right, but there was no going back now.

"Aren't you going to ask me where he is?" Brenna asked.

My turn to scoff at her. "Brazil is a big place. It should say something that he doesn't trust you enough to give you his actual location before I agree to meet with him."

Her lips pursed. "Maybe so, but given your empathic abilities, maybe it was smart of him."

"Most definitely." I glanced at my brother, but he appeared mesmerized by the collapsing dome. I wanted him out of here, far from any mention of Stefan. The man had too much charisma.

"So why does he want to talk to Erin?" Ava demanded. Irritation dripped from her surface thoughts, though I realized her upset was more because of the electronic shield that still kept her from Dimitri than for anything else.

Brenna shook her head. "I don't know. But he and Tsaousiss and Scala are in agreement. Adamant, in fact. Stefan says it's a matter of life or death."

Jace whirled, as if he'd been listening intently all along. "*His* life and *his* death," he growled, "because this time he is not going to survive."

I wanted to add my outrage to his, but that would only fuel my brother's impetuousness. All the paperwork and physical inactivity at the New York headquarters had made him ripe for action. I reached out and touched my brother's arm, and instantly his mental shield dropped. I was honored by his trust but also worried at how exposed it made him. His trust was based on our relationship. Didn't he see that he was also vulnerable to Stefan because of their relationship?

Easy, I told him. *We'll have our chance.*

We should never have imprisoned him. He should have been executed.

I agreed, but he wouldn't know that unless I put the words in his thought stream. I formed my response carefully. *Right, but I need to hear what he has to say. Then we'll figure out how to deal with him.*

A tumult of emotions passed through his mind, familiar to

me because they were nearly identical to my own. Except his also held a hint of longing regarding Stefan that scared me. I needed to remind him that we had a father—the good mortal man who'd raised us with our mother. But not now.

This flash of communication held so much meaning that I was surprised to hear Brenna barely responding to Jace's statement, which for her still hung in the air.

"Stefan means that it's a matter of mortal lives," she explained. "All mortals. That's all I know." She glanced again toward the city, her emotions fluctuating. Though she had shown a great reluctance to return to Sinalta and her people, she was conflicted about it.

"You could go home now," I told her. "It's no longer under water. Things might be different."

She gave a sharp shake of her head. "Sinalta isn't big enough for all of us as it is. If our other city hadn't self-destructed, maybe things would be different. Anyway, I have to take you to Stefan and the statesmen. That's my job now, and I'm getting an awful lot of money for it. Stefan is even better at incentives than Sinalta's ruling families."

"So that's why you're here? Money?" I should have known.

Her smile didn't reach her eyes. "Always."

"How do we find Stefan?" asked Ritter, always practical.

"As Jace stated earlier, I have a transport, currently attached to the side of this boat. I'm supposed to take Erin and Jace to a bar in Rio de Janeiro, and Stefan will contact us there." Brenna purposefully didn't say which bar, but I saw the information in her mind.

I met Ava's eyes. "First we get Dimitri." I stared out over the ocean at Sinalta. Over two-thirds of the city's rings were tucked away. The grinding sound was louder now.

"They'll leave at least a hundred feet of the physical shield up to protect the buildings from waves," Jace said.

"It'll be more like six hundred feet," Mari said as another section disappeared. "Storms at sea can get pretty rough. In fact, it's almost there."

"Can't they leave up part of the electronic shield?" Jace asked.

The question was for Mari, but I answered. "They don't even know if they will be able to do that, but we only need a crack."

Even as I spoke, the movement of the dome sections ground to a halt, and I felt the entire electrical grid go down. It was as if someone had shattered an aquarium and all the water had burst out, only instead of water, it was the glow of life forces, thoughts, and activity. At once, Ava and I were searching for Dimitri, and so was Mari, who could find people not through thoughts but through their color numbers. Four million people. It was a lot of data to search through, even concentrated into a ten square mile radius.

"I can't find him." Ava's eyes locked onto mine. "But I don't have your range."

"I can't reach all the sections, either, especially down into the sublevels." I glanced at Mari, and a subtle shake of her head told me she hadn't found his color number.

"We've got the population of Los Angeles crammed into a space less than half the size of Manhattan," Mari said. "It could take time."

"What's going on?" Brenna asked.

Ava ignored her. "Jace, take her to the brig. We can't afford distractions right now."

"I'll be right back." Jace pulled out a gun and pointed it at Brenna. "Walk," he ordered, "or we'll go to Rio without you."

She took a step and balked. "Maybe I can help if you'll tell me what you're looking for."

"Move it!" Jace waved the gun impatiently.

"Wait," Ava said, facing Brenna. "It's our healer. Mikyn Zenos took him prisoner to assure our cooperation. Is there a place they would hold him in Sinalta that we can't reach with our minds?"

Brenna shrugged. "Not unless it's shielded. And that's not really hiding him, because if you find a place like that, that's where he'll be. But I think you should really be focusing on Stefan right now, don't you?"

Ava waved her hand in dismissal and turned back to the railing as Jace marched Brenna away. Once, the Avowed had cut off her own hand to escape us; this time she wouldn't have the chance.

"Take your time," Ritter said to us. "He has to be there."

Closing my eyes, I sent out my thoughts, tracing paths in the life forces as I tried to find the one I knew. Thoughts assaulted me, roiling and pushing and vying for attention. It was an impossibility.

"Mari," I began.

"Yes, you can channel me."

I slipped into her mind and began using her ability. The life forces I saw abruptly fell into an organized whole that I could easily keep track of, even with the addition of the thoughts she couldn't detect. *Wow,* I told her. *I forgot how easy numbers are for you.*

She laughed. "His color number is brown," she reminded me, showing the exact shade we were looking for. I remembered it now, as if I'd seen it in a dream. Together we searched, going through each section of town methodically.

Dimitri was nowhere.

"I don't see any places that are shielded either," Mari said. "Though I can't see the far section under the water, where you say there's all that engineering equipment."

"We have to ask Keene's help," Ritter said. "I'll wake him."

I looked at Mari reluctantly. "He's right," she said. "It's not like he has to do anything. You can channel him and me at the same time."

"Okay." We watched as Ritter crouched next to the lounge and called to Keene without touching him. It was the safest way to wake any Unbounded, but I didn't like that it took more than a few seconds for Keene to blink his eyes open. Ritter gestured for him to remain lying down, and I almost wished I'd broken into Keene's thoughts without his permission, which shouldn't be hard in his weakened state, but I immediately felt guilty at the thought.

The moment his shield dropped, I dived inside his mind, releasing the thread I'd left connected to Brenna because it was a distraction I didn't need with two people and three abilities already to keep track of.

Instantly, the glow of Sinaltan life forces increased tenfold, and even with Mari's color numbers and control, I almost gasped. Instinctively, I checked the mental shield around my baby. It was as strong as ever, and I breathed an internal sigh of relief.

Everything settled into a strange clearness. I could sense each inhabitant of the city, their emotions and thoughts. I saw weeping, arguing, laughter, and lovemaking. Color numbers that moments ago seemed nearly identical were now infinitely different. Hundreds of different blues and yellows and reds. I peered into the spacious mansions at the center of the city and into the tiny high-rise compartments where people lived in sanitary but overcrowded conditions. I saw underneath the city in the vast corridors and rooms crammed with equipment. I moved with people over the walkways that spanned the buildings and drove in their numerous transports that could travel by either land or sea. Suddenly those transports, both public and private, had a combined number of nine hundred and six thousand, and the part of me using Marie's ability exalted at the knowledge, though the count wasn't high when you considered the four million inhabitants.

"Easy," Ritter whispered in my ear, and only then did I feel myself shaking.

Nodding, I dialed back on the intensity, focusing only on finding Dimitri.

He wasn't there.

A tear squeezed from the corner of my eye and rolled down my cheek. "He's not in Sinalta," I forced out from a suddenly dry throat.

"Impossible!" Ava's eyes flashed anger.

"We need to go over there and talk to Mikyn," I declared.

"We'll force him to tell us where Dimitri is!" said Jace, who had apparently returned from depositing Brenna in the brig while I'd been concentrating on finding Dimitri.

Ava turned from our hot declarations and studied the city. "No," she said, her own voice now controlled. "First we'll deal with Stefan." Her eyes shifted to Ritter. "Gather whatever you and Erin need to have a chat with Stefan. I will deal with Mikyn Zenos and the Sinaltans. Jace will return to New York to make sure Stefan doesn't ruin it for us there."

"No!" Jace flushed a deep red. "I'm going after Stefan." But his defiance melted under Ava's steady gaze. "Please," he added. "I have to."

"I understand how you feel," Ava said, "and I am not unsympathetic. Normally I would have no issue with you being on the team. However, right now you're needed in New York. We cannot lose our foothold at headquarters. That must be your priority."

For a long, moment Jace didn't speak. Finally, his mouth opened, but before he could utter his reluctant capitulation, another voice resounded over the deck: "I'll go to New York."

We turned to see Keene on his feet. "We've brought the Sinaltans up as promised," he added, "and until they give us back Dimitri, I am under no obligation to continue helping them. Besides, with my father's death made public, supposedly killed in our battle with the Avowed, it's time I made my position in the Triad official. That way Catrina Silvaski and I will be able to maintain a majority even if Stefan recants the transfer of power we faked for Jace."

Catrina Silvaski had taken the place of Delia Vesey, the former Triad sensing Unbounded, and she had been miraculously on our side from before Stefan's imprisonment. She was beautiful as well as kind, and Jace had a semi-secret thing for her but had been hesitant to pursue a relationship because she was forty years older than his twenty-nine—our mother's age—though Catrina's early change put her physically at around twenty human years.

Ava studied Keene. "Are you sure you're up to it? If Stefan makes trouble, he could possibly find witnesses that prove you were the one who killed Tihalt." Which was true, and though he'd acted after Tihalt McIntyre had killed Keene's brother, those who still believed in the old Emporium wouldn't care. The Triad members had been considered gods who could do no wrong.

Keene snorted a laugh. "All those who witnessed that battle who weren't from our cell are either dead or still at the prison compound in Mexico. It'll be my word against Stefan's. And dealing with the Emporium will be a breeze after the hell I've been through these past four weeks."

Ava's head tilted as she considered, looking at Ritter for input the way she'd once turned to Dimitri. "It's the best idea," Ritter said. "Having Keene there will make our position stronger with Stefan once we catch up to him."

"I agree. This situation with the Sinaltans will have to wait while we take care of other business." Ava's voice was cool, but I sensed her regret like a stab in my chest.

I wanted to protest, unwilling to leave Dimitri behind. My heart ached with the idea of him remaining in the hands of the Avowed, who cared nothing for anyone except their own advancement. And Jace needed to be as far away from Stefan as possible. Yet knowing my brother as I did, he would eventually go after Stefan no matter what any of us said, which made him unfit to stabilize the Emporium conglomerate in the first place.

Then there were also Brenna's cryptic words about Stefan's business being a matter of mortal life or death. Sometimes being a guardian to the mortal world meant putting aside our own desires. Jace might not be able to do so, but I understood my role.

"I'm not happy about any of this," I said when Ava and Ritter looked at me, "but it does seem like the best plan. However, before we leave, give me five more minutes with Keene's ability, and I'll have the name of every kidnapped embryo who has been coerced into remaining in Sinalta, as well as the reason for their decision. No need for personal interviews."

Ava's gaze sharpened. "How many have been forced to say they want to stay?"

I gave her a solemn stare. "Nearly every one of them."

Chapter 3

AFTER A SHORT DEBATE, WE OPTED NOT TO BRING BRENNA TO Brazil, as that would only mean one more enemy to deal with. I had the name of the bar and Mari had the coordinates, so Brenna was no longer necessary. She'd remain in the ship's brig that was equipped with an electrical shield and a sound barrier to prevent her from using her ability on the ship's crew.

Leaving Ava to find Dimitri on her own was harder than I anticipated. Dimitri hadn't been the man who'd changed my diapers and watched me take my first steps. He hadn't taught me how to drive, grounded me, or stayed up late when I was on a date. He hadn't taken me to see any sports games, picked me up at school, or driven me to the store.

He had never wept over my grave.

Still, we shared a bond I could never share with my mortal father who had done all those things with me. I admired Dimitri's vast store of knowledge brought by a millennium of life, the elegance of his manners, his kindness, the thoughtful gifts he gave to those he loved, and how he kept calm under fire.

I loved how he let me channel and explore his healing ability. Most of all, I loved how willing he was to simply sit and talk.

It no longer bothered me that he'd given up his opportunity to be a part of my childhood. I understood his watching from afar was the same sacrifice too many Renegades had endured to give their posterity a normal life. I hadn't been so self-sacrificing after my Change, and that had nearly cost my family's lives. Emporium soldiers had almost killed Jace then, but lucky for me, he'd Changed. The father who raised us would have died if I hadn't been able to donate a heart to him and regrow another for myself. My older mortal brother, Chris, had been luckier, but only in that he and his children had survived; his first wife, Lorrie, hadn't.

In short, I loved Dimitri for who he was and the sacrifices he'd made.

I'd always assumed that Dimitri and I would have time together, to make up for the beginning, but what if we never had the chance now? I bit back bile and stood with the others as Mari opened the shifting coordinates in Rio and folded them around us, leaving Ava behind with the ship's captain, the healer, and our two mortal guards. Keene went with us for now, but he and Mari would continue on to New York immediately after dropping us off in Brazil.

My last glimpse of Ava's face as we shifted was her staring over the ocean at Sinalta. No doubt she was experiencing similar emotions about Dimitri and the fact that we had no clue as to his whereabouts.

Which meant . . . what? Was he dead, or had he somehow left the city while it was still submerged?

Mari shifted us not to the bar in Rio, but to a Renegade safe house there, checking to make sure no one was waiting for us in the apartment before we completed the shift. It took more effort for her to fold the new place around us, but it meant we didn't spend any time in the *in between,* which was disconcerting for some. I actually liked it, especially enjoying how Mari's numbers ran through my mind, perfectly in control. Perfectly predictable. Because I could channel Mari's gift, shifting of any type was usually a little thrilling for me.

Except this time, I immediately ran for the bathroom and began losing what little I had in my stomach. Ritter was with me before I'd finished, patting my back somewhat awkwardly until I sank into a miserable little heap next to the porcelain goddess.

"Bad shift?" He gathered me in his strong arms.

I frowned. "It's never affected me that way before. I think I'm upset because of Dimitri."

"We'll find him."

"Maybe. But we lost Cort." Cort Bagley, Keene's half brother, was the first Unbounded member of our cell that we'd lost since my Change, and his permanent death had made the possibility too real. Many of us had died temporary deaths, but we'd always come back. Cort would never come back now, and the five hundred years he'd lived suddenly hadn't been enough.

"Dimitri has value to them," Ritter reminded me.

"Right." I had to pull myself together or Ritter would leave me behind when we went to meet Stefan. Ritter might be my husband, but he wouldn't allow me to endanger the mission or put myself in peril because of my distraction.

Ritter's hand dropped to my stomach, where I maintained the shield protecting our baby. I let the shield melt away and sent out a mental probe, receiving back a sense of contentment that would soon become real communication. I knew already that our daughter was fearless, not startling at anything but eager to learn about its cause, and I didn't know if that was because she was confident in me or in her own self. It seemed strange when she was so tiny and so completely human that she could be entirely unperturbed. I yearned to trace all the paths of her little body as I had before with Dimitri to make sure everything was still all right and growing correctly.

And yes, I was tempted more than I admitted to anyone to see if she had the spark that meant she would one day Change or if I'd have to bury her before I'd physically aged another two years. I couldn't search for the spark on my own without developing a second gift like the Avowed leader Mikyn Zenos, but I believed it was possible for me to channel a healer and combine my gift to learn the future written in my daughter's DNA. But to what end? Knowing wouldn't change the facts, though it could alter the way I saw my daughter.

Out of habit, I pushed back the familiar agony the thoughts caused. I'd thought I'd come to terms with knowing I'd live for many lifetimes after my older brother, Chris, and his two children were gone, but since becoming pregnant and learning of Mikyn's foreseeing, my conflict had resurfaced. It was different when it was your own child in question. How had my people endured watching their loved ones die for so many years? It put Dimitri's choice about my childhood into perspective.

"I'm all right now," I said. Except for a bit of remaining nausea.

"You and Jace check in with Stella while I talk to a guy I know. It's four hours later here than on the ship, and I know where he might be during the lunch hour."

I stared at him. "What do you mean, talk to a guy?"

"He's one of us. Or he was once. He may be able to give us local backup that Stefan won't be able to detect. If it comes to it."

"Okay then." I knew better than to protest because Ritter was the best at what he did.

Keene and Mari were already gone when I returned to the sitting room, where Jace paced. "All good?" he asked.

"Almost." I left Ritter to explain his plan while I made my way to the kitchen to find something to ease my nausea.

All our safe houses were filled with cans and dried foods, items that endured. There would be cash, electronics, medical supplies, and all kinds of clothing, which might come in handy as long as I could use my body armor under them.

I opened a can of black beans, grabbed a spoon, and forced myself to eat while I called Stella on a tablet. Beans were almost as good as dry toast for me. Somewhere nearby I could smell bread and some kind of meat. I would absorb molecules of those too.

"Hey, Stella," I said, settling at the kitchen table as she approved the connection.

"What happened? You look awful."

"Dimitri wasn't there."

"Oh, no."

"Right. I'm sure Ava will fill you in after she talks to Sinalta's leaders about Dimitri, but Keene and Mari went to New York to install Keene officially in the Triad now that we've declared Tihalt dead, in case Stefan reappears there. And we're in Rio for a meet with Stefan."

"I don't like that idea."

"Neither do I, but we have to recapture him at some point, and it might as well be now." I just had to do it while keeping Jace alive.

"You have my body armor?"

"Of course."

Her outgrown armor was only minorly inconvenient because of my greater height. Even using our thin armor technology, this super armor was three times thicker than what we typically wore under our bodysuits or had incorporated into our single-piece combat suits.

"I know you're worried about Dimitri, but I don't think you look green because of him," Stella said, her voice sympathetic. She waited for an answer, so I conceded the truth. "I am a little green, but I'll be okay in a bit." I waved a spoonful of beans, letting my annoyance show. "What I don't understand is that even though our metabolism is sped up, why isn't pregnancy sped up more than two months? I don't pierce my ears because it's a pain to keep making the holes, and my hair is always long, whether I like it or not, unless I want a daily haircut. I can heal from a gunshot overnight and from burning seventy percent of my body in only a week, and grow a new heart in a mere three days. In light of all that, having to be pregnant for more than a month seems unfair."

"Our bodies repair things that are wrong," Stella said. "A pregnancy isn't a wound or disease, it's nature, and while we often deliver two months earlier than mortals, that's only true fifty percent of the time. Sometimes it's only a month or a few weeks. The baby isn't Unbounded, after all, so it progresses at a fairly normal rate despite our bodies' efficiency at growing it."

"Then why do they come early at all?"

"Better blood flow, optimized organs and hormone levels, coupled with the perfect intake of sustenance through absorption. But it's better that you prepare for the entire nine months because those more recently Changed like you sometimes go full term. But don't worry. Once it's over, it'll have gone fast."

"Easy for you to say since you're almost at the end." Less than a week, if the seven months held true. "I think what you don't want to admit is that we're evolving into something other than human."

"Ya think?" Jace said, appearing in the kitchen doorway. He rolled his eyes and sprawled in the chair opposite me. "Isn't that the whole issue?" When I stared at him, he shrugged. "I couldn't help but overhear your conversation. Keep in mind that some of the more drastic healing we do is because curequick speeds us up even more. Come to think of it, maybe you could use that to help you deliver early, but your kid would probably act like a crack baby."

My turn to roll my eyes. "I don't think so." He had a point, though, and it was one of the reasons I was staying away from curequick, even after a particularly taxing workday.

"So is there any chatter here about Stefan?" Jace asked Stella. "Especially centered around a place called *Bar do Tio Alberto.*"

I felt guilty that Jace had to be the one to bring us back to business.

"Just a minute, and I'll check." The lights on Stella's neural headset blinked more furiously than before, but in less than a few minutes she shook her head. "Sorry. There's no chatter. Either he's keeping a low profile, or he hasn't had time to ruin anyone's life yet. Keep me apprised, and let me know if you need anything. I have to go—Ava's calling." The screen went blank before I could reply.

I sat back in my chair and regarded my brother. "Look," I said, "I'm worried about you."

"What's to worry about? We'll get the bastard and go back to the ship."

"It's not that easy. I know how confusing it is to have him as your father, but remember he isn't really your father. Our real father is the man who raised us, the man we respect and who taught us his values. Just because Stefan's manipulated sperm was present at your conception doesn't mean you're like him."

Jace flushed a deep red. "I know that. But manipulated or not, it doesn't change the fact that his blood is flowing through my veins, and even though I believe nurture is stronger than nature, there is still a drive inside me that has nothing to do with our parents. I joined the Army because of those urges. I exulted in my Change. And a very large part of me wonders if he'd raised me, would I be like him?"

"No," I said immediately. "You'd be like Keene. He was raised by a father in the Triad who was every bit as evil as Stefan, and Keene came to our side anyway. His brother Cort chose good as well."

Jace wasn't convinced. "Keene was a second-class citizen among the emporium soldiers. Despite being Tihalt's son, he was nothing until he finally Changed. If he'd Changed when most of us do, who knows what he'd be like? And wasn't Cort part of the Renegades before he knew about his parentage?"

My brother had a point, but he missed something huge: I knew his heart. "You have always fought for the underdog," I reminded him. "That's why you went into the Army. To fight for your country and to help others. That is also why you reveled in your Change. Besides, I trust you." I swallowed hard because what I said next wouldn't be easy, and it took away a little bit of the trust I'd just proclaimed. "But you've got to realize something. Stefan has charisma like I've never seen before. When I was first taken to Emporium headquarters, I hated him with everything that I was. Yet at the same time, I wanted . . ." I shook my head. "I guess I wanted him to be proud of me."

Jace looked down. "Well, I'm going to kill him." He spoke the words quietly, and they tore at my heart because my brother wasn't a killer. Yes, he'd killed when we'd taken over the Emporium, but that was different. That was like being in the Army and fighting for the whole world.

"Jace," I began.

He shook his head. "It's better for one man to die than to lose the world and everything we've worked for. He is not innocent."

I couldn't disagree. Stefan had killed far too many innocent people for his own gain. "Okay," I said. "I have your back."

But I had seen how Keene was haunted by killing his father, and I needed to protect Jace. That meant I would have to kill Stefan myself.

Chapter 4

WE STARTED FOR THE *BAR DO TIO ALBERTO* WHEN RITTER returned from leaving messages for his contact, as he hadn't been where Ritter expected. We'd debated going in disguise since Ritter was in every Hunter and Emporium database in existence, which meant anyone looking for him would recognize who he was. Jace and I were less noticeable and on fewer databases, but Stefan would know who we were, no matter the disguise, and he was our only immediate concern. So in the end, we went to the bar undisguised and in full body armor, with swords on our backs and weapons in every special pocket in our suits.

The place fell silent when we entered, as bartenders and patrons alike stared. With less than six months since the announcement to the world of our existence, that was to be expected. Of course, we might be worshippers from the Church of the Unboundaried, playing dress up, but the reluctance of the mortals to take their eyes from us was a hint to the more perceptive that we were the real thing.

The smell of beer, spiced meat, and stale sweat permeated the air. Even at one in the afternoon the bar held more people than I expected. Maybe because it was Friday and people were starting the weekend early. Most of the patrons sat before plates full of rice topped with some kind of meat and bean stew, likely a specialty of the house.

So not just a bar, I thought, upping my rate of absorption. I tasted a hint of pork and beef and beer on my tongue. My body would only absorb what it needed, and doing so would prepare me for any confrontation, though my mental perusal of the bar had already told me no Unbounded were currently inside. Just a lot of mortals with bright life forces.

Ritter paused before the bar without sitting, one strong fist on top of the black granite. A large, swarthy bartender rushed up to him. "What can I get you, sir? Would you like to hear our specials?"

"I'm looking for someone," Ritter said. "A man named Stefan Carrington, though he might not be using that name." He gestured to Jace, who drew out his cell phone and presented an image of Stefan. "Also two others." I showed my phone with the statesmen's photos on them, given to us by Mikyn himself six weeks ago when they'd first gone missing.

The bartender paled. "They came in last night. Said someone would come in asking. I-I'm supposed to call them." He sounded apologetic at the idea.

"Better get to it then." Jace gave him a predatory smile.

The man looked at Ritter before muttering, "Yes, yes," and hurrying away.

Jace grabbed a handful of peanuts from the bowl on the bar and began shelling them. "I can't remember when I last saw a bar with peanuts like this," he murmured.

Ritter's gaze panned the bar, snagging on a squirrely guy by the door.

"He's about to leave," I told him. "He's anxious to tell someone we're here."

"Guess we're leaving too then." Ritter led the way as we followed the Brazilian out the door.

"Let him get a little bit ahead," I said. "I've got him. He's not even trying to block."

We trailed along slowly as he scurried through the streets, dodging people strolling along the sidewalks. Five streets and five turns later, he finally stopped in front of a mansion with a beautifully manicured lawn that was protected by a white wooden fence. A wide, covered porch held several wicket armchairs. A sign near the fence read *Bed and Breakfast,* and under that was a *No Vacancy* sign.

"Nice digs," Jace commented.

Ritter nodded. "Stefan must have access to his funds or at least some of them."

"Or the statesmen do."

"Right. All that slave-mined gold." Without warning, Ritter burst into motion, sprinting up the cobbled walk to the porch to reach the front door before the Brazilian did.

The man gasped and threw a punch. Ritter blocked it, then twisted the man around, locking his arm around his neck. "You're going to walk away and not come back," he said. "And it might be best for you to leave the city for a while because you won't be able to complete your business and your employer doesn't reward failure except with punishment or death."

The man mumbled something in Portuguese, his voice rising in panic. Ritter let him go, and he darted away even faster than he'd come.

"This looks like a good place to stay," Jace said, grinning up at the balcony jutting over the porch. The white wooden railing around it matched the fence we'd passed to come up the walk. "I like the breakfast part. Did you get a whiff of what they were eating at the bar? It smelled heavenly."

"It's *feijoada*, and it tastes as good as it smells," Ritter said in the same casual tone, though tense excitement radiated from him. He was not the only one who'd chafed at the downtime.

"That's all you smelled at the bar?" I guessed I was the only one who smelled the sweat. Probably thanks to my condition.

Ritter joined us on the stairs in front of the porch. "How many?"

I knew he was contemplating the risks of confronting Stefan here and now or returning later after talking to his contact. I studied the life forces inside the house. "Four," I said. "No mental shields, so it's likely they're all mortal, though I'd have to lay eyes on them to be sure. No sign of Stefan in their thoughts." Something on my right registered. "Wait. Incoming life forces to our right, dim and blocking. Coming fast!"

"Move!" Ritter growled, gesturing to my left, even as he leapt for the balcony above, hauling himself up and over so he could get the drop on whoever was headed our way. Jace moved just as fast, melting into the brush in the flowerbed, no doubt having pulled on a metamaterial cape. As it only bent light, the metacape wasn't perfect in broad daylight, but it was deceptive enough with the addition of the foliage. I had no time to don my own cape, however, as the newcomers appeared before I could disappear around the house.

"Looking for something?" asked a male voice.

I turned to see six men coming through the open gate. "Just going to ask about staying at this bed and breakfast," I said, eyeing their casual jeans and button-down shirts that were left open at the neck. They could have been any tourists—except for the overkill of automatic rifles slung around their necks. "Do you own it?"

"No, but we have one where you will be more comfortable," the same man said without a trace of an accent. In fact he sounded as American as I did. He had dark hair and eyes like many typical Brazilians, but he was Unbounded, and the way he carried himself and the shield over his mind said he was a trained soldier, no doubt gifted in combat. He'd known exactly where to find me, so he'd also know that I wasn't alone. His subtle glances at the door and to the sides of the house told me I was right. Something had triggered their appearance, and my guess was the bartender had reported that we'd followed his customer out the door.

"No thanks," I said. "I like this one."

"I'm afraid I have to insist." His smile was confident, but his five companions looked around, clutching their rifles uneasily, as if disturbed by my friends' absence. My guess was they were not as experienced as the first Unbounded, though they still knew how to use mental shields.

"I'm actually waiting for my father," I said. "And you don't want to cross him. He has a tendency to murder people who get in his way." This had the desired effect of making the soldiers more uneasy, except for the man in charge, which I supposed was why Stefan had chosen him as their leader.

The soldier smiled. "Well, lucky for you, then. It just so happens that I know where your father is." He leveled his automatic rifle at me. "So, if you'll come with us, I'll take you to him. And maybe call your friends too."

I gave him the same smile I'd given Brenna—the one with too many teeth. I knew what was expected of me, by both my people and theirs. I was supposed to go along, and since I wanted to see Stefan, that wouldn't be all bad.

Except I didn't trust that murderous snake. We needed the meet under our control, not his.

All at once, everything around me seemed to slow. I could sense Ritter, now preparing to strike from the roof, or wherever he was hiding, his life force almost non-existent. That I could sense it at all was only because of our mate connection and the likelihood that he was leaving a crack in his shield in case

I needed to channel him. Jace was moving behind the men in the shrubs, his life force dim but still apparent to me, and more easily accessible to my mind.

I didn't reach for either Ritter or Jace but solidified the mental shield I had been building between the men and me in case someone decided to go crazy and start shooting. I would heal, but the baby wouldn't. Had Stefan told the leader I was expecting and to take care? Possibly. Or Stefan might not care about his grandchild since he likely had many others over his thousand years of life. Besides, he might say that I could always become pregnant again.

I should wait and let Ritter and Jace make sure of my safety. At the very least, I should step back and cause a delay. But I felt instinctively that these men wouldn't hurt me. I also knew which way the leader would move and that Ritter would take him out and also the man to his left before I would be able to act. This wasn't a feeling born of long practice together but came from something I couldn't explain. Not my gift. It felt like Ritter's, though I wasn't in his mind.

With an eager grin, I stepped forward. "Well, sure. I'll come," I said, lifting one shoulder in an obvious tell that Ritter and Jace would both recognize. A knife released into my hand with the motion.

I threw it.

Motion exploded around us. The leader dodged as a throwing star grazed his cheek. The man on his left collapsed when a second star sliced fatally into his neck. My knife sank into the throat of the man behind the leader, and a fourth man fell with a silenced bullet hole in the side of his head. Then Jace was on the fifth man, his metacape shifting and revealing his outline in the bright sunlight.

Still in motion, I twisted, jabbing my boot into the ankle of the leader, who was still slightly off balance. He stumbled at the impact but recovered quickly. Definitely combat Unbounded from the way he anticipated our moves. I silently cursed the fact that I hadn't kicked him harder and higher, but doing so might have left me exposed, and I had to protect the baby.

I threw my own star as his knife shot toward my chest, hovering in the air for the briefest of instances as it hit my mental shield and fell harmlessly to the grass. My star sliced into his eye. That he merely reached up and pulled it out was a testament to his experience.

Even as I sidestepped a punch to my chin, a blur that was Ritter flew through the air from the building behind me and slammed into the sixth man, whose life force winked out under his blade. Without a single grunt of satisfaction, Ritter leapt in front of me to confront the leader.

Except I was no longer there. I was behind the man with my gun pressed to his neck.

"I'm pleased to let you accompany me to my father," I growled. "However, I don't exactly want him to know I'm coming. Are you going to tell me where he is? Or does my husband here get to convince you?"

We both looked at Ritter, whose face was flushed with a crazed madness I recognized as so far beyond anger that the man's permanent death wasn't an impossibility. Ritter, who had lost so much, would die—and permanently kill—before losing me. And the baby. An overreaction since I hadn't really been in danger. This man hadn't been tasked with killing me.

Ritter roughly plucked the assault rifle from the leader's neck and pointed it at the man. Jace slipped into full view from behind his cape, glancing up and down the quiet street before bending to check our victims.

"My orders were to take you without serious injury," the man said. "This was completely unnecessary."

I folded my arms and gave him a placid stare. "Then you

don't know my father very well. If you don't tell me, I will break through your shield and learn the truth anyway." I smiled. "Better yet, I'll wake up one of your companions and ask him. They don't seem quite as experienced."

"You'll tell us, or you will die." Using one hand, Ritter pulled his sword from his back sheath with a ring that echoed loudly despite our open surroundings.

Behind him, I saw a curtain flutter inside the bed and breakfast, but the brief glimpse of a face immediately retreated, so I wasn't worried about interference. Local police, however, were a different story, and likely they were being called.

"You have thirty seconds," I said. "Make your choice. We can either leave you in pieces for the local police, or we can stash you somewhere mostly intact. That way you'll have time to run. I promise we'll keep Stefan occupied while you do."

The man's nostrils flared. "I'm not running. Stefan told me I wouldn't best you, but I'm to tell you where he's at. He's waiting."

He'd obviously not believed Stefan's prediction about his loss. I'd been disgusted that Stefan had only sent Brenna after me, but now I didn't know what to think of this latest revelation. I certainly wasn't going to feel satisfied that Stefan apparently knew we would best his men. Would the information the man give us be a trap? I looked at Ritter for a clue, but he didn't meet my gaze. Anger still poured off him in waves.

"Start talking." Ritter's voice was guttural. "Jace, get a tranquilizer ready."

We left the men in the side yard behind a small stand of bushes and trees. Each was unconscious but still breathing, except for the one Ritter had taken out on his jump from the roof. He'd take a day or two to recover from his temporary death, even without a dose of curequick, which I wasn't about to waste on him.

We saw no sign of the local constable, and I was beginning to think that maybe Stefan had paid whoever was in the house not to report any strange goings-on. If so, that was better for us. According to the leader of the men who attacked us, Stefan was holing up not at the bed and breakfast but in a house down the street with a considerable number of trained soldiers. In light of this news, we went back to the safe house to talk things over. I was all for walking up and knocking on the door, but Ritter overruled me.

"We can't meet on his terms," he said. "I'm not taking you into the lion's den."

"You heard what the man said. Stefan isn't going to hurt me."

Jace snorted from his sprawled seat on an easy chair. "I think 'serious injury' are the key words here, and as you're so fond of pointing out, there are worse things than death. Besides, it's not like we're going to start believing that murderer now."

"We'll send him a message for a public meet," Ritter said. "Where he has as much to lose as we do."

I plucked at the arm of the couch where I was seated. "I don't want to endanger innocent people."

Ritter glared at me. "It's about time you started thinking more about yourself."

I jumped up from the couch where we were sitting, my hands clenched at my sides. "What on earth are you talking about? I was careful today. I knew exactly what he was going to do."

Ritter also stood, a vein popping out on his neck. "That man threw a knife at you. You could have been hurt! Same as when Brenna attacked."

"No way. I knew what he was going to do next. And her too."

Whatever Ritter was going to say died on his lips as Jace rose and headed toward the door. "I'm going out for some of that bean and meat stuff. You guys let me know what you decide. I'm not getting in the middle of this lover's spat. But don't forget that we have a time crunch here. Remember Dimitri?" With a little roll of his eyes, he left the apartment, slamming the door behind him.

I studied Ritter. Anger still leaked from him, anger and something more. Uncertainty. I tilted my head, taking him all in. "What's really bugging you?"

My words deflated his anger enough that he sat again on the couch. He patted the seat next to him, but I settled sideways on his lap, twisting slightly to place my right arm around his neck. His arms encircled me as I kissed him deeply, exploring his mouth with my tongue until more of the anger was gone and another emotion took its place.

"You are so predictable," I said, injecting a little laughter into my voice. "Are you sure what you need isn't just a little private time? Heaven knows there hasn't been much for us lately. I'm feeling it too."

He allowed himself a tiny smile at that, but when he spoke it had nothing to do with my words. "How did you know what they were going to do? Were you channeling Jace? I think if I knew for sure that you were, I might not have been so worried. My gift tells me you are more at risk now, and I admit, it's hard dealing with that."

"You've never cared before that I've chosen to channel Jace over you," I said. Not only was Jace's mental shield easier to get into in a pinch, but our relationship was also far less complicated than the one I shared with Ritter. For much of our relationship, Ritter and I had battled as much as we had flirted. It was part of our courtship. Besides, with our mate connection, any danger I faced already could put him at risk of distraction, and I didn't need more of that on my conscious. Jace wasn't aware of when I was channeling him unless I spoke silently in his mind.

Ritter's mouth stretched into a semblance of a smile. "You've never been pregnant with my baby before."

Therein lay the difference. With our marriage things hadn't changed all that much between us, but once he'd found out about the baby, everything changed. He had waited centuries to be a father, to open himself to someone—to me.

"I didn't channel Jace," I admitted. "I didn't feel I needed to."

His eyes narrowed, and he relaxed his hold on me, his right hand falling into my lap, his left supporting my back. "You were stronger during the confrontation. I could still see the baby and that vulnerability, but you were strong. If you weren't channeling Jace, you had to be channeling someone. Because if you weren't . . ." He lifted his hand and stroked my cheek, his fingers gliding down to my neck in a trail of fire. "Erin, during that fight, you were combat Unbounded. You moved too fast for anything else."

"Okay. Maybe I was channeling Jace, but I didn't realize it." I hadn't been, though. I was pretty sure. Or had I? "Look, we need to leave this discussion for later. But we can't keep having this conversation. You have to take my word that I was careful. You saw the knife fall after hitting my shield, right? I was safe. And even if it had hit me, Stella's body armor would have protected me. Believe me, it's uncomfortable enough to be secure."

His knuckles rapped the armor over my breast, and the *clunk* sound testified to my words. "Point taken."

I leaned my side against the crook of his arm, beginning to feel a bit uncomfortable sitting sideways on his lap, despite his larger bulk. Probably because of the baby pushing on my bladder. "Anyway, what are we going to do about Stefan?"

His arms tightening once more, he pulled me even closer, his lips softly nibbling my neck. "I think we meet him near the Copacabana promenade. My contact owns a hotel right on the beach, and there will be enough people to allow us a safe meet, especially if my contact comes through like I expect him to. Let's send a messenger to Stefan and set it up."

I'd written out an invitation and sealed it in an envelope by the time Jace came slamming back into the apartment. His face was bloody and the sleeve of his black bodysuit torn.

"Stefan?" I asked, reaching for my gun and looking at the door, expecting at any minute for people to burst in, even though the surveillance monitors on the wall showed no one out there.

He frowned and shook his head. "It was Hunters. And apparently, here they're just as mean and hate us all as much as their counterparts in America—plus, the local cops seem to be on their side. If it weren't for a couple of believers who offered to buy me a beer, things might have ended worse than a few broken limbs."

"Hunter limbs?" I asked hopefully.

"Uh, no." He grimaced. "Cops. And they may be looking for me. I think I'll probably need a disguise to get around while we're here." He gave me an apologetic smile, but he didn't sound upset. In fact, I suspected he was on another high from his second fight in one day.

Ritter swept up the envelope from the coffee table where I'd tossed it. "I'll check in with my contact and get this delivered." He leaned toward me, casting a glance at Jace. "Keep an eye on him."

"I will."

Chapter 5

AT FIVE-THIRTY THAT EVENING, WE WERE SEATED IN THE POOL AREA at the Copacabana Palace, courtesy of Ritter's contact. The price of a stay was three to six hundred a night, depending on the day of the week and the time of the year. Overpriced in my opinion, though it was one of the more spacious hotels on the street, which was crowded with tourists even in July when the temperature of the water was ten degrees lower than in January or February. The sun was on its way down, but still in the seventies, and the Friday nightlife was just beginning. Dance music added to the festivities around the pool.

We debated whether Jace and I should go in alone, with Ritter and his contact lurking on the perimeter, but in the end Ritter came with us. Hundreds of years dealing with Stefan gave him experience we simply didn't have.

This time we didn't dress like Unbounded. I was still wearing my armor, but over it I wore a lightweight, fluttering dress that hid the black material—and made me look rather larger than usual, something I would have to get used to during the next few months. Ritter and Jace wore the lighter version of body armor underneath snug slacks and fitted button-down shirts that made the most of their muscles, giving them the air of runway models without any of the gag-me-on-femininity so many men seemed to portray these days. Ritter's longish dark hair shone glossy even in the fading light while his beard-brushed face could have been chiseled from granite. Jace, with a shadow on his chin, newly black hair, and concealing brown contacts, could be his brother. It was unlikely that anyone looking for the man who had broken the nose and arm of two different police officers would recognize him. I suspected the real reason for Jace's disguise, however, was because he was anxious to look as unlike Stefan Carrington as possible. Our clothes from the safe house closets contained the usual hidden pockets for weapons, but the one thing we'd had to leave behind were our swords. We wouldn't be using them here, and they would only make us stand out.

Oddly enough, there were mortals wearing swords around the pool, dressed in dark clothing with their eyes outlined in black and their hair spiked like some kind of gothic Unbounded wannabes. Likely those were adherents to the Church of the Unboundaried who believed we were angels come to save the mortal world. For many centuries we had been just that, although most of our exploits would never be made public. But we'd also done harm to the world, most notably in withholding medical and scientific advancements, though that blame was more properly laid at the door of Stefan and the former Emporium Triad. For every advancement we passed on to mortals, a dozen more were squashed by his minions.

Despite our "normal" disguises, eyes followed us as we settled at a circular table nearest the poolside bar, translating our Unboundedness into what mortal minds comprehended as beauty. But that wasn't the only interest we attracted. Ritter briefly locked eyes with a dark-haired, olive-skinned

Unbounded man behind the bar. I also noted a coffee-skinned waiter with a buzzed head and a tanned, slender woman with straight black hair picking up towels, both unblocking mortals, who were very interested in our little party. I didn't know if they were Stefan's men or belonged to Ritter's contact, but as they were only watchful and not oozing animosity, I assumed they were with us. I only hoped they could stop Stefan from hurting anyone else if something went wrong.

So far, the evening was peaceful. I could smell the ocean and taste salt on my tongue. Gulls winged across the very blue sky over the beach across the street, but the music drowned out their lonely cries. The ocean, so blue and perfect, called to me.

Soon, I promised myself. *When the mission is all over and Dimitri is safe.*

I absorbed more salt and molecules from the foods around me, positively drunk from the array of tastes. For once, I didn't feel nauseated.

We didn't have long to wait. Stefan walked into the hotel from the street side, let in by someone who apparently had access. He looked much as he had the first time I'd seen him: tall and well-built, his short hair blond enough to cover any gray, and the magnetism in his sky-blue eyes palpable. Fine lines showed on his face, giving him character and experience. He wore tailored black pants, and the first three buttons on the blue shirt under his khaki dinner jacket were open, revealing blond chest hair. Even for our kind, he stood apart. Conversations died as he passed the mortals on his way to us. He showed no signs of the gunshot wounds I knew he had sustained in his escape, which likely meant he had access to a healer and injections of curequick. Whatever pain he still experienced was masked completely.

I recognized the two people with him instantly: former Sinaltan Statesmen Harren Tsaoussis and Turleen Scala.

Tsaoussis limped slightly while Scala appeared undamaged. Both looked significantly different from the last time I'd seen them before they had fled an impending Senate punishment. Obviously Avowed, with their tall figures and overly pale, nearly translucent skin and blond hair, yet instead of the typical Avowed clothing of robes and togas, they now wore regular slacks and shirts. Tsaoussis had traded his mythical bearded lion god look for clean-shaven skin and short hair. Even his formerly caterpillar eyebrows were clipped politician short. It was his left leg that was giving him issues after his role in last night's escape, I noted, in case it became important. Scala was still wearing jewels but no longer dripped in them, and her hair was flat and modern instead of teased to enormous heights and accentuated with hairpieces and circlets made of precious metals. Either statesman could pass for Unbounded instead of an Avowed from an advanced underwater city whose fashion had been stuck in some ancient Grecian era.

Next to me, Ritter tensed with readiness, but Jace looked amused. "Well, look at that. He's certainly not hiding his relationship with the statesmen who tried to murder us. That should tell us something."

"He'll have guessed that Brenna already told us about them." I studied Stefan's face as he approached, noting that he didn't appear worried. He radiated the confidence of a man on top of the world instead of an escapee from a jungle prison. Of course he hadn't exactly been tortured there, and he'd had nearly a day to recover from his incarceration. For us, that was enough.

"Erin," he said, smiling and holding out his arms. "Thank you for joining us here." As if he'd sent us the invitation to the Copacabana Palace and not the other way around.

Reluctantly, I stood, but I did not step into his proffered hug. Instead, I shook his hand stiffly. "Stefan," I said, nodding stiffly.

Jace and Ritter also stood to greet our guests, and almost immediately Stefan's gaze shifted from me to my brother. "Hello, son," he said. "Nice to see you again."

"Not for me," Jace ground out. "You should be in prison. You haven't finished paying your debt to society."

Stefan laughed. "Even with all the years I have left in this world, I wouldn't be able to pay that debt."

"But then who's trying, right?" Jace gave him a scowl. Despite the disguise, I saw how much he looked like Stefan, and it hurt my heart to see the resemblance.

Ignoring him, Stefan extended a hand to Ritter. "I hear congratulations are in order, both for your wedding and for your pending fatherhood."

Ritter's fist clenched at his sides, a sure sign he was fighting the urge to hurt Stefan. "Why don't we cut the small talk so you can tell us why we're really here? In case you hadn't heard, we're a little busy saving four million people—even if most of them are Avowed whose atrocities make them unworthy of being saved." As he spoke, his eyes came pointedly to rest on Tsaoussis and Scala.

"Right, right, and a very good job you've all done." Still playing the host, Stefan gestured to the table. "Please, let's sit before we begin our discussion." After taking the seat closest to me, he signaled the waiter with a wave of his hands. "A round of *caipirinhas* for everyone, please. Plus an extra Scotch." He indicated me. "And coconut water for the lady." He gave me a smile that caught me off balance, though I knew how charming he could be. I refrained from glancing at my brother to see how he was taking the act.

I glanced at Tsaoussis and Scala, then back at Stefan. "Why are they here?"

"Statesmen Tsaoussis and Scala are allies," Stefan said.

"When they learned of my incarceration, they were kind enough to help me escape."

"They are fugitives from their own people," I retorted.

"Yes, but unfairly so." Stefan tented his hands on the table, tapping the tips of his fingers together. "There is more to the story than you know."

I couldn't believe his audacity. "I was there. They tried to kill us when we went to help. By doing so, they almost sealed Sinalta's fate, essentially betraying their own people."

Stefan cocked his head at me. "You have to understand where they're coming from. Their world is not like yours. Or even mine. They did the best they could with the situation given them."

"They set themselves up as gods," Ritter growled. "They kill their own children. That is inexcusable." He paused, his eyes narrowing. "Of course you would know all about such things."

"Sacrifices are required for the good of the whole." Stefan's voice was calm, but I could see the anger burning behind those blue eyes. If so much hadn't been riding on this meeting, I suspected he might challenge Ritter here and now. Having fought with Stefan and trained with Ritter, I really couldn't say who would come out the victor. "Regardless," Stefan continued, "Harren and Turleen are the rightful rulers of their people, not the pretender who is there now."

I gave him a fake smile. "Ah, but Mikyn Zenos is a statesman and leader of a Sinaltan ruling family, just like they are. And it was the entire Senate that voted to remove them."

"Mikyn Zenos has used his position to undermine us," Scala injected, speaking for the first time. "He is a murderer."

A statement I couldn't refute, though I doubted my reasoning was the same as hers. As far as I knew, the fact that Mikyn could not only test babies to see their future but could mess with a child's DNA was something he'd kept from his peers.

I exchanged a look with Ritter and Jace before saying, "We would agree with you on that."

Tsaoussis leaned forward, his fingers splayed on the table. "What do you know? How exactly is he killing our people?"

His wounded tone incensed me. "You know exactly why people are dying," I spat, leaning forward to confront him. I had to force my hands away from my weapons because every part of me wanted to haul these two statesmen to justice. "Do you expect me to believe that you suddenly care about your mortal offspring? Regardless of what Mikyn is doing, you and the other prominent families have consistently chosen post-birth murder rather than raising a child destined to remain mortal. The children of lesser families who choose not to kill their babies are sent to the mines or forced into servitude." I paused for a quick breath. "And on top of that, you stole *our* children to widen your Avowed gene pool and mortal work-force. That makes you every bit as guilty as Mikyn."

"We were desperate!" Scala's face flushed with passion, her accent more lyrical than her colleague's. "With every decade that passed, the Zenos family gained more and more Avowed while our families"—she indicated Tsaoussis—"and the other two ruling families' posterity declined at noticeable rates. Even those not in the ruling families at least remained steady."

Tsaoussis nodded vigorously. "Though there are witnesses to the embryo ceremony, there is concern that Mikyn's decisions about the embryos—our embryos in particular—are no longer accurate."

"You mean the babies," I countered, tasting gall. "They are not embryos once they are born. Surely you can agree with the rest of the world on at least that much."

Tsaoussis's mouth stretched in the thinnest of smiles. "You

know our laws. Families have a month to accept the birth. A month before or after makes no difference."

I was about to tell him where he could stick his ridiculous laws when Scala rushed on, "Additionally, we began having more and more issues of mental instability, which make us dependent upon Mikyn's treatments." She saw my surprise and nodded. "Yes, we know he has some healing abilities that are somehow connected with his seer duties. And we believe he is directly responsible for the mental decline in our families. We've had to euthanize too many of our elderly before their time. That's also the murder I'm talking about. The murder of our families."

They could be right on both accounts. Mikyn might be refusing care for the elderly, and he might be lying about their babies' futures, thus allowing them to be murdered by their parents. And he also might not try to alter their children's DNA, though they wouldn't know that. But as Tsaoussis had said, there were mental witnesses to Mikyn's testing, and I didn't believe he could do too much without being caught. I'd realized what he was doing after witnessing a single testing. As the lone Avowed healer, and a very aged one at that, was it possible that Mikyn was simply overworked? Yet either way, his actions had resulted in the murder of too many innocents for me to ever trust him. He'd make good company for Stefan and the statesmen when they were all behind bars.

Jace grinned mockingly, and I could tell he thought fate was at work on the ruling families, or perhaps some deity like the Avowed pretended to be. Ritter, however, looked grim, as if being with Stefan and not killing him was painful.

The drinks came, and Stefan downed his first Scotch with barely a gulp before starting in on his *caipirinha*. He couldn't get drunk on this regular alcohol, but if he consumed enough, he might get a temporary buzz, which was apparently his goal.

I guessed he'd missed his favorite whisky while at the Mexican compound.

My coconut drink came in nothing other than a real coconut, but inside wasn't straight coconut water. It tasted more like creamy, sweetened coconut milk made from the flesh itself. It was fantastic.

"What do you want from us?" I asked Stefan, annoyed with myself for liking anything he'd ordered. I wanted to add that we planned to return him to Mexico, but I would reserve that tidbit for the time being. "And please don't say you want your place back in the Triad. Even if you were able to gain enough supporters, which I highly doubt, with Keene and Catarina both in the Triad, we will maintain control."

Stefan waved a hand. "I am no longer interested in being part of the Triad, and I don't even need the funds I'm sure you've confiscated. I have plenty stored elsewhere. What I want is your support in removing Mikyn Zenos from the Sinaltan Senate so we can bring stability to the city and guide their growth into the country they will become."

I stared at him for a moment in silence, working hard to hide my shock. He actually believed we would give him Sinalta? And Scala and Tsaoussis were going along with the idea? My gaze shifted to them. "You have no idea who this man really is."

Tsaoussis's smile was thin. "His ideals and ours are in line. This is why we've worked so well together for the past fifty years."

Using other mortals, he meant, and less powerful Avowed. "No," I said, "we won't help you. Mikyn Zenos might be a monster, but he is less a monster than Stefan Carrington."

"Come now," Stefan said, the amusement in his voice taunting. "You barely know me."

He was pushing my buttons, but I didn't care. "It's you who've forgotten me since your memory was erased. I remember all our time together very well." Including how much he liked Scotch.

"I know you're my daughter and that you are much like me." He cocked his head to study me very much the same way Jace did.

"You know? Or is that what you were told?" I mocked, knowing the dig would wound him. He'd allowed a raider, a man he'd thought his friend, close enough to mess with his mind, and he would never get those memories back.

He only inclined his head. "I trust my people. Interestingly enough, I was told by men incarcerated with me that you are gifted in combat and that I was impressed with your ability, but Brenna claims you are sensing and can break through mental shields."

At this the Avowed exchanged a wary glance. They knew I was sensing from our last encounter, but they apparently hadn't discussed their knowledge with him. I was also guessing they now suspected Mikyn had lied about his ability to see past their own shields.

"What am I to believe?" Stefan asked me. "What have you been hiding?"

"Maybe someday I'll show you." It was a threat, but he only laughed and glanced down at the arm I had wrapped protectively about my middle. For the second time that evening, I had to work hard not to reach for a weapon. Baby or no, I bet I could put my ballistic knife into his chest before he could react with the gun he'd have stashed inside his jacket.

Ritter gave a miniscule shake of his head, pulling me out of my mindless wrath. What was wrong with me? He'd warned me before our shift to Rio about letting my emotions take over. He'd never had to do that before the baby.

Stefan signaled the waiter. "Another round," he called. "And two more Scotch."

"You told Brenna our meeting was a matter of mortal life or death," I challenged. "Was that a lie?"

Stefan smiled. "With Mikyn Zenos out of the way, mortals will be saved. That is no lie."

But it was a falsehood because even if the children survived to mortal adulthood, they would be worse than second-class citizens.

I focused on the statesmen. "Why would you want to share your power with this man?"

Tsaoussis's eyes shut momentarily before opening, as if tortured to have to deal with someone so inferior. "As you can see, at the moment we have no power. We have all played into Mikyn's hands exactly as he has been planning for decades."

"Mikyn was the one who preserved your peace," Jace said. "And for the record, he's the only one of the ruling families who didn't try to kill us."

"Yes, but we were all played!" Scala's voice rose with frustration, drawing the attention of several swimmers lounging nearby. She took a long swallow of her drink as if to calm herself. Lowering her voice, she started again in nearly perfect English. "We are not asking you to reinstate us with our families. We have that part under control. What we want is your help in returning to Sinalta and in replacing Mikyn with one of his descendants once we get there. Part of Sinalta's agreement with your government, and with your leader in particular, was that we'd be imprisoned, and baring that, permanently exiled. We simply need you to retract those requirements and allow us to peacefully pass the ships you have watching the city. Then together we will remove Mikyn."

It appeared so simple and inviting, especially since getting rid of Mikyn was something I longed to do, yet I sensed deception leaking from Scala's surface thoughts. Which meant it was time to break into one of their minds to see if I could determine their true intentions.

Of the two, Tsaoussis's mental shield was stronger, so I chose Scala. I drew out the imaginary version of my machete.

"And how does that help Stefan?" I asked. "As I understand your government, the five ruling families fill the seats in the governing branch of your legislature. The leaders from each family—the statesmen—make the laws in your Senate, while your executive branch, consisting of a magistrate and his cabinet, administer the day-to-day. So unless you're going to create a new ruling family, that leaves Stefan out."

Tsaoussis glanced at Stefan, as though asking permission. I hadn't known the statesman long, but letting others call the shots didn't seem his style. However, Stefan must have given him some sign because he continued. "We will vote him in as our magistrate," he said. "Of course, we'll work together with him much more closely than we do with the current magistrate."

Now it was making more sense. In theory, the Avowed legislative and executive branches of government were supposed to have equal power, but in actuality the executive leader was at best little more than a figurehead and at worst a gopher for the ruling families. Was it possible Stefan didn't understand the way it worked?

"And in turn for your help," Stefan said, "I will officially turn my Triad seat over to my son." He nodded at Jace before meeting my stare again. "Or even you if you prefer, though I assume that is not your wish, or you would have been running things there already instead of allowing your brother to take my place. I'll sign any documents you bring to Sinalta once we are there, and you can bring whichever witnesses need convincing." His grin was compelling and infectious. "You will forgive me, of course, if I do not travel to Emporium headquarters to do these things."

Because we would imprison him.

"So you're seeking asylum in Sinalta?" Jace asked.

Stefan inclined his head. "In a manner of speaking."

Something was off about the entire deal, and I renewed my efforts on Scala's shield to find out what. I was extremely doubtful that Stefan hadn't done his homework on the Sinaltan government. Which meant something else was going on, something Stefan wasn't telling us—and perhaps the statesmen as well.

I broke through Scala's shield as the waiter arrived with the next round of drinks. In the rushing sands of her thought stream, I could see she indeed planned to limit Stefan's role in Avowed affairs, mostly using him as an ambassador to interact with the world in order to be assured that the families could continue their iron-fisted rule as they had before rising from the depths of the ocean.

So not going to happen when infanticide and enslavement were legal in their city. As long as I and other Renegades existed, we would protect the mortals from the Avowed just as we had from the Emporium.

Scala wasn't really concerned about what happened to Stefan after he helped them remove Mikyn Zenos. He might have diplomatic immunity through Sinalta, but if he disappeared, she wouldn't weep over him.

Feeling Stefan's stare, I looked in his direction. I had the strange feeling he knew I was inside Scala's head, plundering her thoughts. What was his plan? He had to know the duplicity in the statesmen's hearts.

Tentatively, I stabbed my machete into his swirling mental shield, but it was much stronger than the last time at the prison compound, and far stronger than either of the Avowed statesmen. Given time and concentration, I could break through and take him down mentally. But how many of the smiling faces around us belonged to him? I sensed at least four blocking life forces who had arrived when Stefan had, people I was positive didn't belong to Ritter's contact. There could also be mortals lounging around the pool and others out of sight. Unfortunately, the meeting place protected him every bit as much as it protected us. Maybe more so because we cared about the innocent mortals.

"Well, what do you say?" Stefan's eyes rested on my brother almost tenderly in a way that turned my stomach. "Working together, we Carringtons can help the Avowed *and* put everything right with the mortals born there."

Put everything right? That was something I was sure Stefan had never concerned himself with. I hit his shield again.

It was Ritter who answered. "We'll talk to our people and get back with you."

I couldn't resist adding, "We don't usually negotiate with terrorists." I widened my gaze to include all three of them. "Even if we allow you to reach the city, who's to say they won't throw you immediately in jail?"

Tsaoussis's blue eyes barely stopped short of a condescending roll. "The warrants issued for us are Mikyn's doing. Without him, our families are powerful enough to reinstate us, as Turleen has already indicated. And now that our city is above water, we'll have adequate mental health care as well as an influx of Unbounded blood from those who follow Stefan. As we build our new country, our guidance is needed there more than ever."

Stefan leaned back, eyeing the fresh drink in his hand as lovingly as he'd stared at my brother. "Take all the time you want. But realize that in the meantime, Mikyn will continue to test and pass judgment on babies."

I took a long drink of my coconut water, using the cover to send another mental blast at Stefan's shield. The barrier barely gave a dim shimmer at the pressure. He'd likely asked Tsaoussis to command him to keep his shield strong, which meant there wouldn't be time for me to break in tonight.

I set down my coconut and addressed Tsaoussis and Scala. "One more thing. If Mikyn was going to hide a prisoner, where would he put him? Is there a place inside the city where they can hide someone from a powerful mental search?"

Tsaoussis regarded me, his blond eyebrows raised thoughtfully. "That depends. Do you mean a search from one of your regular sensing Unbounded or one that includes the man who helped raise our city, the one with the gift of synergism?"

Obviously, they had been keeping informed of what was happening inside Sinalta. "With Keene's help," I clarified.

He considered a moment before shaking his head. "There is no place that I'm aware of. There are remote rooms in engineering below the city, but I don't think they would withstand such a search. You would have at least sensed the existence of an electronic shield. If we were still near the underwater mines, there would be plenty of hideaways that would be easy to shield, but those are too far away now."

"Why do you ask?" Stefan tore his stare from his second Scotch, or maybe it was his third. "Did you lose someone?"

I debated whether or not we should mention Dimitri. My gaze drifted toward Ritter, and I could see the same conflict in his eyes. Anything they knew might help us. On the other hand, it was not entirely impossible that they themselves had something to do with Dimitri's disappearance and planned to perhaps hold him as leverage if we didn't agree to their requests. But wouldn't it be better to know such a thing now?

"Our healer was in Sinalta during the raising of the city," I said, making a decision. "However, it's been three weeks since we've heard from him." I watched them carefully as I spoke, paying close attention to the memories rushing past me on the stage of Scala's mind.

I saw no deception in her as Tsaoussis said, "Our need for a healer is great. They would not hurt him. Something else must be in play." He paused. "Or someone else. But once we're back in the city, I personally promise to find your healer and return him to you."

Ritter leaned forward, one elbow bent on the table, his eyes digging into the statesman. "And you think our helping to remove Mikyn will pave the way to peace?"

"Yes. The others are afraid of him," Tsaoussis said with a firm nod.

"But without Mikyn as your seer, how will you know if a child will Change or not?" Jace said. "Your entire hierarchy is based on knowing before the first month is over."

Scala's lips pursed. "Stefan has helped us see that there are other ways we can deal with our mortal offspring, and now that we will have the space, we'll be able to investigate those options."

Stefan caught my gaze as if to say, "See, I'm saving mortal lives." I wanted to spit in his face.

"However," Scala said, "we do not intend to kill Mikyn and will continue to use his gift in the future in a more limited capacity."

Of course.

"You must help us," Tsaoussis said. "Mikyn is a danger to everyone. Surely you can see that."

I should be glad that their determination to remove the seer might mean saving at least some infants. Still, I wasn't convinced yet that handing the government back to them was a good idea. A lot depended on if taking over had been Mikyn's plan all along, and if he planned to continue his butchery.

It looked like it was my job to find the answer to both those questions.

Stefan finished his drink and stood to leave. I glanced at Ritter, looking for a sign. The moment of truth had arrived. Were we going to fight or let Stefan walk away?

"While you think about it," Stefan said, his grin mocking, "know that I have already begun my campaign to retake control of the Emporium. Check with your friends there if you don't believe me. The ball is now in your court."

Chapter 6

I N THE END, WE HAD NO CHOICE BUT TO LET STEFAN LEAVE THE HOTEL
or risk too many bystanders. But Ritter had asked his contact
to follow Stefan to whatever new hideout he was likely heading
to, so maybe it was only a delay in his capture.

I stayed connected with Scala for as long as possible,
reminding myself that Mari could shift all over the world,
and in theory I should be able to mentally trace Scala at least
through Rio, but I lost her within five minutes. I suspected
someone else gifted in sensing had cut my thread to her, which
gave this round to Stefan.

Jace was strangely quiet during the journey home, and that
worried me. We doubled back four times to lose the multiple
tails Stefan placed on us. I only hoped those people we had
following him were better than his men.

"Do you think Stefan could really retake the Emporium?"
I asked Ritter.

"My guess would be no." Ritter reached for my hand. "But
he could make things very difficult."

At the safe house while Ritter checked the two surveillance

monitors on the sitting room wall to be sure no one suspicious was lurking outside, I confronted Jace. "You can't believe anything Stefan says," I told him. "He doesn't plan on making the world better—certainly not for mortals."

He stalked to the couch and put his feet on the coffee table before answering. "I know, but if what they say about Mikyn is true, what he let you see inside his mind back in Sinalta might not be the whole truth."

He had a point. Mikyn had hidden much from the Avowed families, even his own posterity, but had he also hidden things from me when I'd been in his mind? After some thought, I knew the answer had to be yes. Any man as strongly gifted as he would be able to hide certain things. I'd seen the constructs he'd put in Brenna's mind, and they were every bit as powerful as the ones Delia, the former triad leader, had put in mine, except his were a whole lot sneakier. Which meant everything Mikyn showed me could have been purposeful.

But why tip his hand about altering DNA? Unless he felt the siren call of playing God would tempt me enough that I wouldn't betray him to his people.

Why hadn't I pushed to have him exposed? I'd told myself it was because he was the only half-sane leader in the city, but it was entirely possible that I wanted to learn more about manipulating DNA. So maybe in a way my silence had been bought.

"Agreed," I said, pushing the thoughts aside. "He might have hidden things from me. But that doesn't mean exchanging one murderer for another is going to help anything in Sinalta."

"We may have even bigger issues," Ritter said, still studying the screens. "Don't forget that Sinalta has enough nuclear weapons to take out most of the world. I don't like the idea of those kinds of weapons being in Stefan's hands."

I sank abruptly to the couch, suddenly light-headed. I hadn't been thinking of the weapons. As a member of the Emporium Triad, Stefan had not held anywhere near that kind of power, though not for lack of trying. We'd barely manage to prevent his takeover of the US government. With Sinalta under his control, he'd become far more powerful than he'd been as the leader of the Emporium Triad. No wonder he had his sights on the city.

I finally drew myself together enough to say, "That will have to be part of the negotiations then. But we should talk to Ava and Stella right away."

Ritter grabbed the tablet from the coffee table and began punching in contact codes. Jace scooted closer to me and said in a low voice, "Erin, seeing him . . . it's like . . . seeing something familiar."

"I felt the same way when I met him," I conceded. "As if I recognized him." Of course it had been Jace that Stefan had reminded me of, but I didn't see the need to tell my brother this. "But we can't allow our emotions to assign any kind of responsibility toward him. He has spent decades using people—our people."

Jace's mouth twisted as he said, "He's hiding something, some plan that will give him control of all Sinalta. We have to stop him."

I noticed this time he didn't say Stefan needed to die. Of course, part of that was because killing people wasn't who we were. But the other part was because on some strange level, Stefan did feel like family. I hated that, hated that Stefan was in any way related to my brother.

Ava and Stella's faces appeared on the two separate surveillance screens, and Ritter gave them a quick rundown of our meeting with Stefan.

"What about retrieval?" Ava asked. "Now that you know where he is, I mean."

Ritter shook his head. "We tipped our hand when we sent

the note to meet. But our intel said he had too many men there for us to take him this afternoon. He didn't show any fear of meeting with us at the hotel tonight, either. I suspect he brought enough men to start a little war."

"And now he'll move."

"Most certainly. I do have someone local following him, so we may be able to discover his new location. And they are able to provide some backup, if the numbers are right."

"What about informing Sinalta that we have locasated their missing statesmen?" Jace said, recovering a little bit of his usual cocky attitude. "They might be able to do something to stop them."

"Maybe we should hold off on that until we know if they're right about Mikyn." I was feeling nauseated again, so I consciously began drawing in nutrients that saturated the area near our safe house. My skin prickled all over with the absorption and the nausea began to ease, though I knew it wouldn't completely end until I had something solid in my stomach. The coconut juice was also pushing on my bladder, along with the weight of the baby. "I find it hard to believe that everything Mikyn showed me was an act. He seemed regretful."

Ava's gaze shifted to me. "Ah, granddaughter, sometimes acknowledgment of evil and sorrow doesn't necessarily mean someone will change their actions, especially if they see it as good for the whole. History is rife with injustices accomplished in the name of saving the many and ignoring the few. Of freedoms forever stolen in the cause of safety." Her three centuries of life showed in that statement, rife with a pain I could not fully understand, though I knew the story of how she'd Changed and how many loved ones she'd lost. "Mikyn Zenos may very well feel remorse and even sorrow, but that doesn't mean we can trust that those emotions will lead to something better."

"Statesman Scala believes he has done something to increase his family while others are shrinking in number."

"Do you think that's possible?" she asked.

I had to concede that it was. "Even if he isn't outright lying about a baby's potential, he could simply not attempt to alter the DNA of their children. A worst-case scenario might have him actually alter the DNA of the other families to eliminate the possibility of Change instead of trying to evoke it. In either of those scenarios, those children would be lost."

"I can research the statistics of the families," Stella said, "but he would need to give us access to those stats. If he's innocent or doesn't know what we want it for, he may agree."

"Or if he's faked the stats," Jace commented.

Stella shook her head. "I'm fairly confident I'll be able to tell if he has or at least if there has been manipulation of the data."

"I'll ask him," Ava said, her face set with determination. "Having more data about their people may help me figure out what to recommend to the government about placement. They cannot all stay in Sinalta—and those ghetto buildings in the outer ring will need to be redesigned or replaced. If we don't find an option for the city to expand, the Sinaltans will lose their identity as they disperse among the nations."

"Despite everything, that would be a sad conclusion," Stella said. Then her smile brightened as someone came into the room off-screen. "Hey, kids, did you have fun?" Murmurs of assent came to us as my niece, Kathy, and my ward, Anina, moved into view.

The girls were both blond and blue-eyed, but there the resemblance ended. Kathy was tanned and strong, and though petite like her late mother, she had recently hit a thirteen-year-old growth spurt, leaving her with mostly sharp angles and gangling arms and legs, even while beginning to show a few late curves. She wore an old T-shirt and ragged cut-off jeans and had her hair gathered in a loose, uneven braid she had obviously woven herself. By contrast, nine-year-old Anina was nearly as tall as Kathy but obviously still a child, slender, but with a pale, rounder face and no sharp angles. Her long hair, a shade darker than Kathy's, was twisted up in an elaborate knot that I knew the child had also created herself but with far more skill than my poor niece. Hair design, hair pieces, and adornments were important in Sinalta, and Anina had been trained well, especially because her life as a mortal servant had been ordained since her birth.

Had Mikyn messed with her DNA? Her father, Graeme Padovan, was the great-grandson of Mikyn Zenos, but that relationship hadn't prevented Anina's two brothers from being sent to the mines at age ten like most surviving mortals born to the Avowed. Presumably, when he realized she would not Change, he would have tried to alter her DNA, and failing to make it work meant she only had another ten or twelve years left to live. Could that damage be repaired? Or had Mikyn not attempted the alteration, showing compassion to her parents who had already lost two sons? I found this unlikely, but it was impossible to know. If Dimitri had been here, we might have already figured it out together and maybe come up with a way to fix whatever had been done. I was eager to try. Even if I hadn't been busy, I couldn't exactly experiment with another healer on my own, as we hadn't yet decided to spread the word of Mikyn's ability. The pressure of doing nothing weighed on me. As long as her parents were missing, the child was my responsibility.

I waved. "Hi, girls. How are you doing?"

"Have you found my parents?" Anina asked eagerly, her Sinaltan accent much less noticeable after six weeks topside with my niece and nephew.

I shook my head. "I'm sorry. But you know the city is up,

right? I'll be going over there soon to do some investigating. I just have one more thing I'm working on right now. But I believe your parents are no longer in the city, and that's a good thing." I hadn't seen them in my search for Dimitri that morning, and I would have noticed them.

"Then why haven't they come for me?" Anina's blue eyes watered with unshed tears. I knew what she wasn't saying because we had discussed this many times in the past six weeks.

"They love you and will come as soon as they can. You have to believe in them and hold onto that. And until they do come, you have all of us. Your parents knew what they were doing by leaving you in our care. You're having a lot of fun with Kathy and Spencer, right?"

Anina gave a rather solemn nod. "But they don't do very much homework. That's not allowed in Sinalta. Even mortals have to study, at least until they are ten and go to the mines."

Next to her, Kathy groaned. "I told you, it's summer. Nobody has school in the summer here. We do plenty of work when school is in, and so will you. You'll see."

We all laughed, but inside I found it hard to be amused. I felt a strong urge to tell Anina's parents about what Mikyn had done, that the early deaths of their sons had likely stemmed more from Mikyn's manipulation rather than from their captivity in the mines. But what about the rest of the Avowed? Didn't all the people deserve the same knowledge? How ironic was it that those who had chosen not to murder their babies, but rather send them to the mines or into service, had still sealed their fates by allowing Mikyn Zenos, revered seer, to foretell their futures? In that respect they had still been murdered.

It wasn't right.

Anina turned her face toward Stella. "Can we have ice cream? Volleyball is a hard sport to practice."

Kathy laughed while Stella nodded. "Of course, dear. We're having dinner late tonight, so that'll be fine."

With a shout of joy and a wave of excitement, the girls disappeared from the screen. For a moment no one spoke, and then Ava said, "She has a point, though. If her parents aren't in the city, they should have found a way to contact us on the ship or through Emporium headquarters."

"Kind of strange that it appears both they and Dimitri are no longer in Sinalta," I said. "They must have used a transport to get out at some point before the city shields went down. It's possible they are even with Dimtri, but I've been channeling Keene off and on for weeks now, and I haven't seen any hint of them."

Ava shook her head. "That doesn't necessarily mean anything. Her mother is a very good engineer, and her father is sensing. Plus, they have many friends in their underground network, so I trust they can take care of themselves. Nevertheless, now would be a very good time to find them so we can utilize that network. We have to figure out if any of what Mikyn has told us is true."

"So what do we do about Dimitri? And Stefan?" I asked, as torn as ever about the conflicting assignments.

Ava, outlined by the sky and ocean around her, considered a moment, looking around as if instinctively searching for someone. Dimitri was my guess.

In the end, it was Ritter who answered, "I'd like to check out where Stefan is holed up. If we can take him, then that part of the problem will be solved at least. If that doesn't work, the next thing we need to do is talk to Mikyn to discover what his intentions really are and where he's taken Dimitri."

"Without Keene, the Sinaltans won't get to either the Indian Ocean or Africa any time soon," Stella said. "So the ball might be in their court, but the advantage is currently ours. Which means we have a little time."

"Don't forget the nukes," Jace muttered.

Ava's gravestone eyes settled on him. "Exactly."

After disconnecting, Jace stalked to the kitchen for some coffee while Ritter returned the monitors to surveillance mode and came to sit beside me.

"You're allowing your emotions to cloud your reason." His hand went under my flowing dress and glided up my leg, his fingers moving over the bulges of weapons tucked inside the pockets of my body armor.

"Oh yeah, Your Deathliness? And what is this?" I put my hand over his, halting his upward movement, the thin material of my dress between us.

He twisted his fingers to capture my hand expertly inside the material folds. "This is me getting you to relax."

"Ha," I said. "Relaxing is what got me into this"—I patted my belly—"in the first place."

His grip tightened. "And are you glad?" His voice stretched taut. "Because it isn't like you had much of a choice."

I knew how much he wanted to be a father, how long he'd waited, never believing there would be enough peace for him to let down his guard. Because he hadn't wanted to father children only to place them with mortals to give them some semblance of a normal life, at least until—or if—they Changed.

Except things were different now. We'd altered the future, and now that the world knew about us, and we were no longer running from Emporium hitmen, families were a whole lot easier.

Yet this baby hadn't been intentional. I'd lapsed at channeling Stella in order to keep my body from ejecting the birth control nanites, so the accidental pregnancy was my fault.

And I was glad. Yes, the weight of responsibility was enormous, and while a part of me shrank from that, the me who was raised in a normal, loving home understood that families were the fabric of a strong society. I had the opportunity to make a difference in a way that was more important than anything else I'd ever done with my fists or weapons.

Pulling my hand from Ritter's, I placed my hands on either side of his face, pressing them against his cheek. "I am so glad," I told him. "This little bit of you is more a part of me than my parents or Jace. Or Chris and his kids. She is *everything*." I kissed him hard as the tension in him eased away.

"I love you, Erin Radkey," he murmured against my lips, "and I will love you for the rest of my very long life. So get used to it."

"I think I can do that."

"Good."

I glanced at the monitors on the wall, now showing the olive-skinned man from the hotel's poolside bar. "Looks like we have company."

Ritter jumped up. "That's my contact. He wouldn't come here if he didn't have information."

"Then let's go see what he wants."

We went down the elevator in the apartment building to meet the Brazilian in the dark streets. That he even knew where the apartment building was located, if not the room, told me how much Ritter trusted him. There was still so much I didn't know about Ritter and the centuries he'd lived without me. If I hadn't Changed, we would never have met. I tried not to think about that.

Jace and I did reconnaissance of the street while Ritter walked ahead with the Brazilian until we came to a little park with a couple of benches under some trees. Ritter and the Brazilian sat on one while Jace and I settled on the stone wall behind them.

"I had six people set up to follow them," the Brazilian said in near-perfect Oxford English. "Tag team, so to speak. Each lost the trail, and they were my best." He laughed. "Or almost my best." He removed a tablet from the small case he carried, the screen so dim it was barely viewable even in the dark. "Apparently, my twelve-year-old is a little more advanced. He used a new gadget I got for him—basically a drone, only much smaller and almost indetectable. No sound. He followed them right to their house. The house whose address you texted me earlier." I leaned over Ritter's shoulder to examine the image. It was indeed the same house we'd walked by earlier after eliciting the information from Stefan's men.

"It appears to be an ordinary wealthy house that is typical in these parts. Stone walls, gate, and cameras," the man continued. "But the enormous addition in the back and the men sitting in the courtyards surrounding the entire house tell me it's not. These improvements certainly don't register on the government's website, and they are far over the limit in this area, which tells me it was either built before the limits existed or that a lot of palms have been greased. I'm betting on a little bit of both because the addition does not look new. He's probably had it in place for fifty years or more. There's also an electrical grid over the house because I tried to send in a bug." He grinned. "You know, one of those little devices that look like an insect and record things. It went dead instantly."

"He went back to the same house when he knew we had the location?" Jace's brow furrowed. "That can only mean one thing."

Ritter nodded. "He's not afraid of being recaptured."

"Which means he has plenty of men," I finished. "At least more than we do."

"We can get more men," Jace said. "Mari could have them here tonight."

"And start a war in the city?" Ritter asked, shaking his head. "He understands better than most what resources we have at our command, so whatever he's created is going to be similar to our Fortress. He'll have far more men than even the ones we captured today know about."

Our Fortress in San Diego, where Chris, Stella, and the kids were now, could withstand a siege from the US military, and it had underground tunnels in the old sewers that we could use to escape to safety. While it was doubtful Stefan was connected to any undergrown sewers this close to sea level, concrete escape tunnels were likely. He'd had decades to set it up.

"I have men watching the place now," the Brazilian said, standing. "I'll let you know if there is movement."

Ritter rose and shook his hand. "Thanks for all your help."

"No problem. It was fun going undercover in my own bar. We've been out of the action down here since you guys took over the Triad." He gave us all a lazy smile. "I enjoy the peace for my children, but I'd be lying if I didn't say I missed the action."

"I'm sure your wife is grateful for the help with your ten kids."

He shrugged. "We have nannies. But my wife is mortal, and she has now pulled the plug. Little bit of relief, actually. Each pregnancy gets harder for her as she gets older." A shade of sadness entered his voice, not at the ending of pregnancies, but at the thought of losing his mortal wife, which would happen too soon, babies or no.

"Thanks again," Ritter said.

"Let me know if I can be of further assistance. I have more gadgets." His joviality returned, he nodded at all of us before turning away.

I sat with Ritter on the bench. "So now what?"

He leaned back and folded his arms across his abdomen. "We can't take Stefan here, so that means we must create an opportunity away from his entourage. In the meantime, we need to discover more details about his true agenda. Because I don't for a moment believe that he's falling in line with the Avowed statesmen. He intends to take over all of Sinalta, and he has a plan to do so. We need to find out how."

"I'll go talk to him," I said. "I'll be able to figure it out. No matter whose mind I have to hack into."

"No," Ritter and Jace said together.

I stared at them. "He won't hurt me." I wasn't too sure, though.

Ritter took my hand, his thumb smoothing the skin on the back of my hand. "There is too much risk. The baby gives him too much control over you. Over us."

He was right, and I knew it. I would do anything to protect my baby, but my love for my brother had blinded me because I knew what Jace would say next.

"If anyone goes in, it should be me," he declared. "I've done it before."

"No," it was my turn to protest. Yes, he'd gone into Stefan's den before with a positive result, but the rest of us had been there to back him up. Even as an acting member of the Emporium Triad, a position he'd taken in Stefan's absence, there was no guarantee as to Jace's safety in Stefan's stronghold. While I'd learned that Stefan did care about his posterity with surprisingly fierce pride, he had dozens if not hundreds of offspring. Which meant if Jace didn't fall into line, he was ultimately expendable, giving a decided advantage to Stefan.

"Erin's right." Ritter frowned at both of us as he considered the options. "No one goes in. We figure out something else."

Jace paced as I sat on the bench quietly, enjoying the calm weather, which was beautiful and not too warm or humid this time of year. My nose filled with the aroma of flowers mingled with food coming from the cafe across the street. Despite the late hour, two little boys were playing soccer on the pavement next to a small jungle gym and swing set, and Jace soon joined them under the lights, the cares falling from his face like a cloak. A gentle buzz had me digging awkwardly into a hidden pocket of my armor for my sat phone. Ritter chuckled at the contortions I made so that I wouldn't reveal my armor under the dress.

"Man, I hate this armor," I muttered, glancing at the message. "It's a notification from our server. I have a message."

Which was shorthand for our encrypted online accounts where we could contact team members if other means of communication were broken down or compromised. My thoughts jumped immediately to Dimitri.

"We don't know it's him," Ritter cautioned.

"We don't know that it's not him," I said, and then answered my own statement: "But why wouldn't he simply call me instead of using the server?"

"He might not have access to his phone. But does anyone else have the information?"

"You mean like Anina's parents?" I shook my head. "Just our people and my family. Could Stefan have gotten it? Maybe even cloned my information at our meeting?" The idea infuriated me.

"With our protections, I'd say it's next to impossible."

"Then maybe it's legit." I jumped up from the bench. "I'm going back to the safe house to log in." I had my passwords memorized and could access the server from here, but I wanted to have Stella tracking what I did—and a protective electronic grid activated in case Ritter's contact wasn't the only one with a spy drone.

"Agreed." Ritter's eyes went to Jace. "You go ahead. We weren't followed, so it'll be safe. I'll give him a moment, and then we'll come along. He needs to release some tension." As I left the tiny park, Ritter joined the game, making me smile.

Hyperaware of my surroundings, I made my way back to the safe house, studying everyone I passed as if they were one of Stefan's men and I might need to hack into their minds or fight to the death. But every person I passed was mortal and had no concern for me except to wonder who the beautiful woman was in the flowing gown. I was used to the notice by now, after nearly a year since my Change, and it amused me that not one of them noticed I was definitely dragging a lot of extra baggage in the form of baby and body armor under my dress.

Close to the apartment, I was followed for half a block by an old Brazilian man in a fedora and baggy dress pants, but he was only exactly what he seemed, his mind on the grocery list tucked into his breast pocket.

Who had sent the message? In the old days I'd be worrying that it was my mortal parents in danger from some Emporium hitmen or perhaps an informant watching a descendant who might Change, but it was a different world now. If it had been my parents, they knew I was halfway around the world helping with Sinalta and would have called Chris or the emergency line to the Fortress before trying the more secure methods.

Back at the safe house, I called Stella as I began bringing up my encrypted message boards on the tablet. She appeared in a corner of my screen. I quickly explained, and her neural headset went into overtime blinking. "I have no contact on any of my accounts," she said. "And Ava hasn't said anything. I don't think it's Dimitri."

It was her gentle way of pointing out that Dimitri would follow the line of authority, not start with me. Maybe I needed the reminder. "And everything looks good? No hacking? Has there been any tracing or odd pings on my phone or whatever it is you look for? I'm just worried after that meeting with Stefan. I have no idea what technology Tsaoussis and Scala brought with them."

"No, nothing unusual," she said. "If I had to bet, it would be that this is a legitimate contact from someone who is concerned about being tracked. Go ahead and log in."

I was quiet as I typed in my codes and checked both of my accounts. They had been set up by Stella originally, and she knew what she was doing, but I was still uneasy. There was a message on the second account, and I drew in a swift breath as I read the first sentence. "It claims to be from Valerine Padovan." Anina's mother.

"What does she say?"

I read the rest of the text aloud: "We have escaped Sinalta and are in a place called New Zealand, but we have been followed and are in immediate danger. Please come quickly to the address below. We have urgent information for you. I beg you also to bring news of our sweet Anina. We miss her so much."

Chapter 7

I WAS, OF COURSE, SKEPTICAL THAT IT WAS ACTUALLY VALERINE WHO had sent the message. Because to message these accounts, they had to know about them in the first place and how to log in far enough to initiate contact. Not your ordinary message board. But there had been no time at all for me to communicate this information to Graeme or his wife before they had disappeared into the depths of Sinalta to set the explosives on the shields.

In the six weeks since, they had not been found in the city, despite their law enforcement's continual searches. This failure had given me hope that they'd managed to somehow escape the city safely, which I believe had been verified now by my own mental search. But they hadn't asked for help from the nations' boats flanking the city, and they hadn't come for their daughter. If they had access to these accounts, they had somehow received the information from someone who knew me.

Someone like Dimitri.

"I can't find any reason why this wouldn't be legitimate,"

Stella said. "I'm just not sure why they're using this contact method instead of calling headquarters. That information is easy to find, and we've alerted our people to be on the lookout for the Padovans."

"Maybe they're being followed. I'll let them know we're coming. Will you tell Ava? And I'll need Mari, if she can leave Keene. A plane will take two days."

"Yes. But tell them not to contact you again unless it's dire. Valerine might not know how to cover her tracks."

"She's an engineer from an advanced society," I reminded her.

"Yes, but she has no experience topside." Stella disappeared.

Valerine had said they were in urgent danger, and already we might be too late. That had to be why they hadn't gone to our Fortress in San Diego or the Emporium headquarters in New York to seek asylum and claim their daughter.

I typed a short message: *Anina is safe. Help is coming. Refrain from contact unless necessary.* We never knew how many times someone contacting the secret accounts would be able to log on, so we got right to the point. If a location was given, we'd make three attempts at a pickup unless directed otherwise. That was protocol.

I paced the room as I waited for Stella to arrange things. Valerine's message very clearly meant for me to come, and I would go. For Anina's sake, and for the possibility of learning more about Dimitri.

I was opening a can of chicken that was only semi-offensive to my pregnancy hormones when Ritter and Jace arrived home carrying fresh bread, fruit, and huge steaks. I immediately broke off a chunk of bread and stuffed it into my mouth. It was warm, and I wondered how they managed to find fresh bread this late in the day.

"Oh, this is fabulous," I said around a chewy mouthful.

Ritter laughed as he filled the plate and handed it to me.

"I've heard stories about pregnant women," he said, "but I never believed them before now."

"And you didn't think there would be anything left to learn after a few centuries." I injected a note of irony into my statement.

"I can go grab some pickles," Jace offered.

"No, thanks." I rolled my eyes and grabbed another chunk of bread. The nausea that always seemed to lurk just below the surface retreated slightly.

As we ate, I told them about the message and how Stella was arranging things with Ava for contact. "We should go as soon as possible," I said. "Graeme and Valerine need help, and they have information. It might be something about Dimitri."

"Someone else could go," Jace said.

"They trust me. It has to be me. With Mari shifting us there, we can be in and out in no time. I'm the one who got him into this. I owe him."

Jace stalked to the cupboard for a plate and back again. "Hey, he saved our lives, so doesn't that mean *he* owes us, not the other way around? Isn't there a Chinese proverb saying that when you save a life you must take care of it?"

Ritter gave him a pained smile. "It's not really a Chinese proverb. That's western fiction."

"Well, I'm not going," Jace said, clanging his plate on the table. "I have to find out what Stefan's planning." He held up his hands to stop my protest. "I know, I know, I'm not going to his place, but I'll contact him, and we'll have a little, you know, father-son time." He grimaced as though saying the words hurt him. "I promise not to do anything dangerous. But I think I can find out at least something of what's going on, because even if he plans on taking over Sinalta, he's got to gain our approval to get to the city with the statesmen. We control who enters the city with our barricade. We also control the

Emporium, and it's a major power both politically and financially. Stefan should know—he created it. He's dangerous, and that alone makes him a priority. I want to help Anina's parents and find Dimitri as much as anyone, but they would be the first to want to protect the mortals from both Stefan and the Avowed statesmen."

Ritter's brow furrowed as he considered Jace's words. "All right," he said after several long minutes, "but you're not staying alone. I'll help you figure out what trick Stefan is trying to pull."

My protest against Jace's plan died on my lips. If Ritter remained with him, I could trust that my brother would be as safe as possible while near an insane megalomaniac. Ritter and Jace would protect each other at all costs, and Ritter's experience would guide my brother's hotheadedness.

Ritter's gaze turned to me. "You go to New Zealand, but you'll need backup."

I knew how much it cost him to say the words. He wasn't choosing Jace over me; my brother had simply taken on the more dangerous assignment.

"If Mari can't stay with me because of whatever Stefan is doing there, then someone else will," I told him. "I'll contact Graeme mentally before we even begin a conversation. I'll know if someone's stalking him."

He nodded. "I'll want regular reports."

I looked up at him from my chair and couldn't help saying a bit mockingly, "Yes, Your Deathliness."

Jace let out a huge guffaw.

Fighting his own smile, Ritter passed me another chunk of bread.

"I WISH I COULD STAY FOR THE FUN," MARI SAID AS WE APPEARED IN A grassy cemetery in Dunedin, New Zealand. "But things are heating up in New York, so I'm under strict orders to get back. Stefan has already filed an official complaint regarding Keene's Triad appointment, and I'm taking Keene to solicit support from all over the world. We're also gearing up for a physical attack in case that's part of Stefan's plan."

Which very well might be, I knew, if we didn't fall into line with Stefan's new plans—and I had no intention of doing so.

"Hey, you saved me two days of flying," I said. "That's more than I could ask."

We hugged, and she shifted away. But I was not alone. She'd also brought Blaze Vincent and Oliver Parkin to back me up.

"Erin, good to see you." Blaze enveloped me in the bear hug we hadn't had time for in Rio when they'd stopped to pick me up. It was three-thirty in the afternoon on Saturday in Dunedin, as opposed to ten-thirty on Friday night in Rio, so I'd jumped ahead thirteen hours, and the transformation back to daylight was welcome.

I took his hand in mine, holding it tightly. "You too. It's been months." Blaze was the son Ritter had adopted at age thirteen more than a hundred and sixty-seven years ago after his great-grandfather guardian had died. Of Portuguese descent, Blaze had dark hair and eyes that actually resembled Ritter, though he was shorter and his shoulders were broader. He was a roaster, or in other words, he could manipulate matter in a way that caused just about anything he touched to burst into flame or melt.

"And I'm excited to finally have a little sister," he said, gesturing to my stomach. "You barely look pregnant."

I tapped the armor I still wore. "Hear that? It's Stella's iron suit. I'm definitely pregnant."

He laughed. "Bet Ritter loves that armor."

"He actually does. I think he'd cover me in bubble wrap as well if I let him."

"Can't blame him."

"You know, you guys are making it hard to concentrate," Oliver said, his voice dripping irritation. At least there was no self-righteous sniff to punctuate the words.

Oliver Parkin, Stella's third great-nephew, was an illusionist who could create illusions that not only looked but smelled real. His ethnicity was a mixture, with African American being the most dominant, depicted in his bronze skin and short, tightly curled hair. Oliver had Changed and joined our Renegade group at the same time as Mari, and as they were both Stella's descendants, they were related, but they were little alike. Everyone loved Mari, but not so much Oliver. He was the awkward, selfish, and annoying member of our team. But his IQ was off the charts, a fact he didn't mind reminding everyone about often and at length. Fortunately, violent conflict had beaten him into shape a bit, and he was mostly tolerable these days. Plus, he'd been put to work at headquarters in New York in front of a computer, where he couldn't offend as many people.

In our current situation, Oliver was the best option for the most convincing and thorough disguises. Normally, I could channel a technopath in order to use nanites to change my actual features for a short time, but these days, I wouldn't risk changing even half my appearance, especially to a male, as men could not maintain a pregnancy. Oliver's illusions didn't actually change my body, and he beat everyone out on high-class distractions.

At the moment, Oliver was busy looking up something on his phone, no doubt using his superior brain to decide how to make us look like natives.

I held in a smile. "I really don't think it matters that much who you make us, Oliver. Just so we don't look like ourselves. They aren't all that different from us here, and I'll be able to sense Graeme as soon as he's close enough."

"It will only take me a little while longer." He squinted at the phone again. "I want to have backup disguises too. Maybe a dozen or so. And background people." For his fantastic memory, that would be child's play.

To give Oliver space, I walked a little distance between two headstones, and Blaze followed me. "And how are you with the recovery?" I asked, lowering my voice. "If you don't mind telling me." He was a good hundred and fifty years older than I was, but because of Ritter, I felt a responsibility toward him. I was his stepmother, after all.

He held up his hands. "Still clean," he said. "Been that way since that last job in Portugal. No falling back, no more curequick." Blaze had been brought to near death through his curequick addiction caused by his dedication to accepting the most dangerous missions and being wounded so often. But as valuable as curequick was for speeding up our recovery, the addiction was horrendous to deal with. That last time, he'd almost died. But he'd completed the mission as usual.

"I'm glad. Ritter said you would keep with it."

"It's always there, like an ache," he said, "but I love life more. Maybe in a century or so, my brain will forget. Anyway, Jenna wants me to pass on the message not to get me shot or anything. She wants me back in time for the wedding." He grinned. "Between you and me, a couple bullets wouldn't faze me or keep me away from marrying that woman."

"Well, let's both do our best not to get shot. I definitely want to be there for the wedding."

He glanced quickly at Oliver and then back at me, holding out his hand. "Look what I picked up." A small fire formed in the palm of his hand, hovering a few inches above his skin.

Then, abruptly, with a strange pulse, it turned into a glowing, molten mass.

I gasped, impressed. "How are you doing that? I thought you only made things get really hot so they burned. What even is that?"

"Lava," he said. "Or something like it. Just don't get too close. Can you feel the heat?"

"Yeah." In fact, I was starting to sweat under my armor where before I'd been a little chilly. It was awesome. "Doesn't that burn your skin? I know you're resistant to heat, but no one is that impervious."

"Apparently, my skin radiates a magnetic force which keeps the lava from burning me and contains it to the shape I choose. I have no idea, really, the science behind it. I barely learned this trick a few months ago from another roaster in Uganda." He flicked his fingers, and the fiery mass vanished.

"Can I try?" There weren't many people outside our core team who knew that I could channel the abilities of others, but Blaze was family so of course he knew.

"Sure." His mental shield, as strong as any I'd ever seen, cracked open slightly, and I slipped onto the stage of his mind. "Okay, show me," I said.

He began slowly by gathering bits of molecules from matter nearby. From the headstones, the grass, the trees, and even the air. It was much like absorbing nutrients into our body, except instead of drawing the atoms into his pores, he formed a ball in the palm of his hand. I did the same. As the heat increased, it rose a few inches and burst into a flame that became suddenly molten. But it didn't penetrate the invisible barrier protecting my skin.

"Ritter is going to love this," I said. "Is it wrong to hope we meet whoever is after Graeme and Valerine so we can toss a few in their direction?"

He laughed. "Not in the least. Just don't let it fall to the ground here, or we'll cause substantial damage. To get rid of it, you have to reverse the process. Slowly the first time, okay? Until it disappears. Once you have more practice, it'll be almost instantaneous."

I did as he demonstrated, amazed at how easy it was. Of course, linked to him, it was as if I'd been practicing for months.

"Does this mean you're no longer just a roaster, or that you're a roaster who can do more than start fires?"

"I don't really know. Guess I won't until I try teaching this to a few of my peers. There aren't many of us, so I haven't had the opportunity."

"Okay," Oliver called. "I've got images of some actual residents. We'll use teens first. No one will look twice at us."

As Oliver spoke, Blaze's face melted away into that of an older teen with pale skin and even paler hair. His body shrank and became almost too thin. Oliver also lost years, looking about fifteen but with a muscly physique that made me want to laugh. Classic Oliver. Blaze winked at me as I bit my lip to stop a snort of laughter.

I couldn't see what image Oliver had given my face, but I was suddenly wearing short shorts and flip-flops, and my legs were a coffee brown. "Nice," I said. "But you know it's winter here, right?" While it wasn't exactly freezing right now, the July temperature was a good twenty-five degrees less than it had been in Rio, and more than thirty degrees colder than in New York where Oliver worked. Oliver's illusion didn't waver, but long pants suddenly covered my legs, and I wore some kind of loafers. We all grew jackets, or looked like we had. With the change in temperature here, I was grateful for my real boots and armor.

We caught a taxi and gave the driver the address, which was an eatery in a shopping mall, the perfect place for a safe meet during the winter, if the parties wanted to remain unnoticed by casual observers. But it also might put innocent mortals in danger.

We made the taxi driver drop us on the opposite side of the mall. No one looked twice at us as we blended in with shoppers and walked through the mall to the eatery. Of course, thanks to Oliver, no one could see my armor or the sword I carried on my back. I sent out thoughts, searching for Graeme and also looking for dimmer life forces. A lot of teens gathered in the food court, which I wondered about before remembering it was Saturday.

It was great being in action again, and if I was completely honest with myself, it was good to leave Jace in Ritter's capable hands. Stuck on the boat, even helping Keene, I'd felt useless, especially not knowing about Dimitri. Now I was giving my Unbounded gene exactly what it yearned for.

I reached out and contacted my baby through my shield, to make sure everything seemed okay. As I did, I experienced the sensation of tracing the veins and pathways in her body. It wasn't as thorough as what Dimitri could do, or another healer, but it was different as far as my ability was concerned. Maybe it happened because I was her mother.

I refocused on the crowd as we neared the middle of the eatery, picking up at least a half dozen dimmed life forces—no, eight of them to be exact. But the blocking was poorly done, and it would be relatively simple to break inside their minds, which told me they were likely Avowed. The generations they'd been led to believe that no one could break into their minds were once again proving useful for me.

"We have a little problem," I said, my voice low and tense.

"What is it?" Blaze asked.

"Eight Avowed. Three at the table in front of the sandwich shop, two over there by that taller plant, and another near the doors, about ready to go outside. And two more . . ." I turned and pretended to look at my hand, surprised that they sported a neat French manicure. I had to give credit to Oliver and his attention to detail. Between my fingers, I scanned the large space we'd just passed, finally narrowing the dimmed life forces to a store at the edge of the eatery where two men stood behind a group of mothers with strollers. "By that baby store."

"Can you sense Graeme?" Oliver asked.

I reached out further, looking past those I could see to the back rooms of the eatery restaurants and further away in other stores. Nothing. If Graeme or Valerine were here, neither registered on my senses. "I can't find him."

"Did he ever respond to your reply?" Blaze asked.

"I told them not to."

"I always thought that was a dumb protocol," grumbled Oliver.

"Just a minute, let me see if these Avowed know where he is." I chose one of the Sinaltans and broke through his mental shield with a few strong hits. Finding the right thoughts without directing questions took more time, but they were here for a reason, and it didn't take long to discover they were waiting for Graeme.

"They don't know where he is," I said. "But they believe he will be here in an attempt to meet someone."

"How would they know that?" Blaze asked.

"They must have been watching him. Maybe even followed him here." Oliver smiled at a pretty girl who was looking covertly in his direction.

I put my arm around him as if he belonged to me. We couldn't afford distractions. "Maybe. If that's the case, they're expecting us, but if Graeme didn't get my message, he might not know we were on our way. Especially if he sensed them here and had to leave."

Blaze nodded once. "If he does show up, he'll be walking into a trap."

"I don't think he's stupid enough to get caught. He'll be somewhere close and very much in disguise." Slowly, I reexamined every single life force inside or near the eatery, in case Graeme was sitting somewhere with his mind completely open and unblocking, studiously thinking about hamburgers, paying bills, or a fake job at the local library. It was what I might do to hide in plain sight if I were desperate. Graeme was nowhere.

"He's probably not inside," Blaze said. "He'll want to see who shows up. But if he's looking for you, he's not going to recognize you."

I thought about that for a moment before coming up with a new idea. I pulled out my phone. "Okay, Oliver, I need a change. The little girl in this picture is Anina, Graeme's daughter. You go ahead and turn me into her, slowly as we walk out of here, but don't make me as young as she actually is because the Avowed might recognize her too."

We headed out of the eatery through the double doors, my mind focused on anyone with a life force. The Avowed now standing outside the door didn't look twice in our direction. He was definitely not an empath, and neither were any of his friends, or they would have already spotted us. Hundreds of cars filled the parking lot and more people streamed in, but none bore any resemblance to Graeme.

Then I spied the homeless man on the sidewalk leading into the eatery, sprawled under a mound of blankets between a statue and a garbage can. He appeared to be asleep, yet his mind, open to my probing, didn't show the typical placid lake of the unconscious. There was only an empty wasteland that distorted as if I was peering through the eyes of a drunkard.

Graeme? I sent out a tentative query to his surface thoughts, only to have my attempt bounce off the drunkenness, and I realized the man's mind wasn't really open at all but shielded to look like a drunk man—and shielded so deeply that even the surface thoughts sensing Unbounded used for casual conversation were absent. It was ingenious, and in nearly a year of working with and fighting Unbounded and Avowed, I had never seen such a thing.

I'd definitely found Graeme.

Since we'd stopped moving, the Avowed by the door was paying close attention to us as he was everyone who lingered. I looked down at my illusion body and saw that I had de-aged to about twelve.

"I found him," I told the others, "but I'm going to need a distraction to make sure we aren't noticed."

Blaze grinned. "Guy by the door?"

"Yep. But not like you're thinking. We can't make him suspicious. I need Oliver."

Oliver's hologram grinned haughtily, exactly as he would have done with his normal visage, which said a lot about what reactions he felt were appropriate. No wonder everyone thought him arrogant. "I got this."

"Back him up," I told Blaze. "I don't want anyone seeing me talking to that bum behind the garbage can."

"Are you sure it's him?" Oliver frowned. "Doesn't look like the guy in your picture with the kid."

"It's him," I said.

I waited for a few minutes as more people arrived at the entrance, all high school age. The lack of life forces told me they were illusions. Two teens began a fight, and others formed a knot around them on the sidewalk. Real mortals walking out of the eatery stopped to see what was going on.

Leaving Oliver and Blaze to watch my back, I wandered toward the drunk, who didn't move or make any reaction to my approach. I tested his mind again, calling, *Graeme, Graeme!*

No response. I pulled out my machete to break in as I had done with him once before, but abruptly one of his eyes pulled halfway open. He sucked in a gasp of air.

"Anina?" He blinked both eyes in confusion, probably to see her so grown up.

"It's Erin. I'm under an illusion. Anina is fine. But stop whatever you are doing so we can talk." I knelt down on the sidewalk next to him and watched carefully as he dismantled the odd shield, which was a kind of mental construct. Usually those hid sensitive information, but this time it hid the fact that he had a real mental shield firmly in place while appearing to be passed out. Ingenious.

Aren't you the creative one? I said as I finally felt his presence.

No answering amusement reached my senses. *They've got Valerine. They must have picked up our trail and followed us here to the meeting place after we sent the message from the café across the street. We had to go there since the transport we stole isn't compatible, and we didn't have the supplies to override the built-in safeties.* Silence for a moment before he added, the words tense with despair, *They cut her in half, right as I watched.* My stomach tensed with his anguish. His mental barrier cracked, and I saw the memories from the sand stream of his thoughts, hurtling past me in violent repetition as if I too had witnessed the horrific event.

Just in half? I asked. *Are you sure?* I had to ask because he might not be showing me all the memories. Half she could come back from, but if all three focus points were severed, there was no coming back from that.

I don't know because I ran. I knew the only way to save her was to reach you, and that meant not turning back. But they took her with them, right in front of witnesses. They covered it up somehow. So I believe she was reset and not killed. Since then, they've had this place staked out—waiting for me, I assume. I think it's their intention to drag us back to Sinalta to stand trial. All I could do was to hope you showed up. I couldn't even see if you replied.

They might be waiting for Valerine to regain consciousness and plan to use her to capture you.

That hope is all that keeps me sane. The strain in his voice echoed throughout the walls of his mind, filled with pain, loss, and terrible, mind-numbing regret. *And our daughter, of course. She really is safe, right? You weren't just saying that?*

I did the only thing I knew would soothe me at a moment like this—I showed him my last memories with Anina and other images that showed her laughing and happy with Kathy, Spencer, and Max, our dog.

Thank you. His relief was palpable.

The fight near the mall doors was dying down, and people began walking in our direction, their life forces bright. Mortals. In my young girl illusion, I poked Graeme with a stick I found on the ground as if I were curious about the unconscious man.

A woman stopped to look at us. "Hey, you 'right?" she asked Graeme with a heavy native Kiwi accent. When he didn't react to the stunted phrase, she turned to me. "He looks a bit sus, sweetie. Probably munted. You best go find your mother."

I nodded and stood but walked only as far as the garbage can before she disappeared into the parking lot. *Do you know where they're keeping her?* I asked Graeme, maintaining my distance.

No idea. I barely escaped them myself before putting on this disguise and coming back to see if you showed.

How long have you been here? Because the foul odor emanating from the blankets and the numerous flakes of dandruff in his long hair hinted at numerous days. Even a body with a fast metabolism couldn't clean the clothing it wore.

Three days. The police here chased me away a few times, but I came back. It's not like I have to go find something to eat.

But I only got Valerine's message a few hours ago.

That's because she programmed it to go after we left the cafe in case it was somehow being monitored by Mikyn's people. It was supposed to go in twenty-four hours, not three days. I've been about to give up a thousand times, but I kept telling myself that she's new to this archaic technology, or maybe your flight here took longer than by transport. He paused before adding, *It's good you didn't go inside the eatery because Mikyn sent an empath with them.*

We did go in, and there are eight Avowed in all, but I don't think any of them are sensing. At least they didn't seem to detect us. You sure it's Mikyn who's after you and not one of the other Avowed families? I was thinking more along the lines of a certain few statesmen who just happened to be hanging out with Stefan.

I thought so at first, but I recognized some of them. These are mostly my kinsmen. Pain laced his words.

That makes no sense. Mikyn promised me he would do his best to run interference for you if you were caught. But then . . . Valerine's message said you had important information. Does it concern him?

Information? I don't know what you mean. We were being followed, and we didn't dare try to find you in California with them on our tails. We couldn't endanger Anina.

That's not what Valerine's message said. Would she exaggerate to get us here more quickly?

No. If she said she had information . . . A sigh of understanding took him. *We were apart for most of the time that we were still in Sinalta. And I stood lookout while she actually sent the message here. Maybe she didn't tell me in case . . .*

What about Dimitri, our healer? Do you know about him? That might be part of the information. *Did either of you see him in the past three weeks?*

I haven't seen him, and up until you told me about Valerine's message, I would have vowed that she hadn't either. We left Sinalta nine days ago, and we've been running from these guys ever since. Okay. *Tell me the rest later,* I said. Because Blaze was signaling that five of the Avowed were coming to check out the commotion, and with all these real people mixed up with Oliver's fake ones, there was bound to be some bloodshed if they discovered us. Maybe they were already aware of our presence, if what Graeme said was true and they had an empath I hadn't detected. *Follow us when you can. We'll wait at the edge of the parking lot.*

Go to the southwest corner, Graeme directed. *We parked our rental vehicle there.* He sent me an image of a blue SUV as I began walking into the parking lot behind a group of real kids. Blaze followed me at a respectable distance, but Oliver hung back to clear out his illusions slowly.

When we joined up halfway through the parking lot, Oliver was smirking. "I bet those Avowed think topside mortals are crazy."

I wasn't amused. "Which will only add to their belief that mortals are little better than intelligent apes. Anyway, we have a problem. Graeme says they have Valerine, and she's dead."

Oliver sobered at that. "Really and truly dead?"

"I hope not, but we aren't leaving here until we find out. And we need to do so quickly." For all their advancements, the Avowed hadn't known about curequick before we'd met them, but whoever had taken Valerine probably had some by now. "If she's alive, as soon as she's conscious, they'll learn that she programmed a delay on the message and that Graeme has no clue about the information she claims to have for us. They won't stick around after that."

"Meaning we'll miss our opportunity to rescue her and capture them," Blaze said.

I nodded, coming to a halt as I reached Graeme's SUV. "Or they might kill her for good."

"How are we going to attempt a rescue?" Oliver asked. "We don't have combat Unbounded to help us. You said they had eight people in there."

"Plus at least one more." I leveled a stare at him. "Sensing like me. But I suspect that person isn't here at the moment, or he would have joined his friends during the commotion. Everyone real there had a life force."

Oliver groaned. "This just gets better and better. Don't we have a team in Christchurch we can call for backup?"

"We can't wait for them," I said. "That's too far."

Blaze grinned at Oliver. "Don't worry. Surprise evens out the odds. As long as they don't know we're here, we have the advantage. We are so doing this."

I matched his grin. "Now you're talking. We just need to find them."

"I know how we can do that," Graeme said from behind us, speaking evenly but still looking completely crazy.

I was already turning in his direction, having stayed in mental contact with him, passing along our discussion for his input. The others also turned, Blaze with the hint of a fireball in his hands that winked out immediately.

"Oh, yeah?" Oliver asked. "How?"

"Easy," Graeme said. "I'm going to let them capture me."

Chapter 8

I'D PREFER THAT YOU DON'T GET YOUR HEAD CUT OFF, I TOLD Graeme silently as we followed him back through the parking lot of the shopping center, separated from him by a wall of illusion that made it appear as though we weren't there. The challenge, of course, was to make sure that no one walked through the wall, and that the illusion remained active on both sides.

I'm sort of hoping that myself, he responded. Unbidden, I saw the image of his wife as a sword cut through her body.

Graeme currently bore no resemblance to the bum I'd found on the street, having cleaned up at the Avowed transport he and Valerine had used to come to New Zealand. The craft was berthed at a rented dock and miraculously had not yet attracted the wrong kind of attention. Aside from the fact that he wasn't wearing sailor gear or even an Avowed toga, Graeme looked much the same as when I'd first met him six weeks earlier. Only the grimness in his face and the way his pants hung loosely around his waist showed that his worry for his wife was taking its toll.

All my usual weapons made comforting bulges in their custom pockets, and Blaze carried double what I did. Even Oliver had a couple of guns and a knife, though I knew from the reports Ritter had received of our daily team practice sessions that Oliver still wasn't very good with either. We also carried extra sedatives, curequick, and more weapons in our small packs, along with a change of underwear and a listening device or two. Despite our preparations, I longed for a drone or something of that manner, but the only real technology we had were the trackers embedded under our skins, complete with the nanites that prevented their rejection, and our special sat phones, which we knew would be discovered in a moment if we sent them with Graeme.

That meant we couldn't let Graeme out of our sight, because while I could stay mentally linked with him, that link could be severed with technology or with his death, temporary or otherwise. Presumably, I would be able to mask our thread of connection from any sensing Avowed—unless they were very good, which Graeme doubted. Regardless, I wasn't going to make the mistake of underestimating my opponent. If Mikyn had sent these people after Graeme, then they were to be feared.

My mind wandered to my brother and Ritter, but I had to trust that they were taking care of each other, just as they would trust me to take care of my team and the baby.

Blaze must have read some of this in my face. "Don't forget our new little toy," he said, a grin growing as he opened his fist to expose a fireball. A rush of relief spread through me. He was right. This weapon would shock everyone, and we didn't need to get close to use it. If needed, I could channel one of the combat Avowed. The main thing was to make sure the empath didn't see us coming. Or at least not until it was too late.

As he walked into the mall, Graeme was immediately

confronted by an Avowed man near the door, and the others moved swiftly toward him. He held his hands out. "I'm not armed," he said in Sinaltan, the meaning coming across our mental connection. "I surrender. Just take me to her."

"Who did you contact?" one of the men asked, fingering what must be a weapon in his jacket pocket. "And what did you tell them?"

Graeme shook his head. "Just a topsider to tell her we were ready to see our daughter. I stood lookout while my wife sent the message, so I don't know the exact content. She's the one with the technical skills."

"Lower your hands but keep them where we can see them." The Avowed began patting him down.

This man is from Mikyn's own household, Graeme told me. *And he's related to me. Not close. Most of the others who are approaching are also distantly related. Mikyn has his own small army of combat soldiers, by the way. A couple of these men might have been hired from another family, though. Two aren't familiar to me, but then I don't know all of Mikyn's progeny.*

A ruling family? Or an unimportant one?

No way to tell. Depends on Mikyn's alliances. We are the only family with empathetic abilities in our genes, but we have other abilities as well. One of these men is a scientist like Valerine, and one is a technopath.

The mention of an army reminded me distinctly of Stefan and how for many years he had bred soldiers for combat. So many of the beautiful gifts like singing and dancing and the more rare ones like shifting had all but disappeared. The Avowed had retained more of the creative gifts, or so I'd been led to believe, but it seemed they too had bred soldiers.

The Avowed finished patting Graeme down, and a few mortals stared their way anxiously. "Hey mate," someone called behind Graeme. "You all right?"

Graeme nodded. "These are my buddies," he said in English, sounding surprisingly convincing.

"They're coming out," I warned Oliver, who'd already given us youthful disguises behind our illusion of a wall. Just in case.

Only six of the eight I'd identified emerged, which told me they were still watching to see if anyone showed up there to meet with Graeme and Valerine. I briefly thought about sending Blaze to take care of them but decided it would be better to come back later, in case they had regularly scheduled check-ins.

We followed Graeme and his captors as close as we could into the parking lot but far enough away that they couldn't detect our footsteps. Thankfully, fewer patrons were in the parking lot, so we didn't have to work that hard to avoid innocent bystanders. The Avowed piled into a large gray van at the very edge of the lot, driven by a uniformed mortal. We had to make a dash for Graeme's rental to keep up. We followed them through the traffic that was waning now as night fell. This was not exactly a popular nightlife area.

"You aren't hiding us now, are you?" I asked Oliver from my place behind the wheel. The last thing I wanted was to have someone crash into us.

"They'll see a small car with a teenager inside," he said, sitting in the passenger seat next to me. "But I'll mask us as we turn into the hotel, so watch out then for other cars."

I frowned. "I'm hoping they'll go to an apartment or house where there aren't so many people."

"Not likely," Blaze said. "I bet they don't plan to be here long."

"Can't you do your mental hocus pocus on them and make them all fall down in one swoop?" Oliver said, casting me a smile.

I came to a stop at a light and stared hard at him.

"What?" he said. "There are rumors, you know. Especially in New York. And they've been growing ever since you escaped Sinalta."

Blaze chortled from the back seat, apparently finding that greatly amusing. "She'd have to be in all their minds to make a difference, but I don't think it will come to that. We'll get a room as close as we can to them and see what we come up with. No telling how many more they might have there, but there's only six of them in that car now since they left two at the shopping center." He sounded disappointed.

"Those two might join us soon since it seems to be closing," I said.

He snorted. "One can only hope."

I decided not to remind him about the Avowed empath we hadn't yet encountered.

I followed the Avowed past the first two hotels to one that was notably larger and more expensive. I wondered briefly how they had exchanged the gold from their underwater mines for cash or credit, but then realized that after fifty years of trading with the Emporium, Mikyn probably had large accounts lying in wait. Graeme must have gathered funds also during his years as a topside agent, as he obviously didn't have problems moving in our world.

I parked in a stall far from the hotel, noting as we followed the Avowed inside that the SUV once again took on its real appearance. Oliver still held his wall illusion over us, and we almost collided with their driver, who stopped suddenly outside the hotel for a smoke. When he was gone, Oliver let the wall fade.

I held out my hands in Oliver's direction. "They probably won't rent to us if we go up to the counter looking like kids."

He aged our illusions and gave us business suits. Oliver smirked at me as I glanced at him. "Hocus pocus," he said.

I bared my teeth in a grimace, and Oliver shut up immediately. Blaze smirked as he pulled open the hotel's front door.
Ahead of us, the Avowed went into an elevator, but this time
we didn't follow. I'd get the room number from Graeme.

At the hotel desk, a too-thin young woman with straight
black hair to her waist offered us coffee and aromatic brownies
as we asked about vacancies.

"Is suite five-oh-five available?" I asked. "Or another room
in that area? We've had friends stay there before, and they
highly recommend it."

Unfazed by our request, she began searching on her
computer, and by then I was in her unblocked mind. I could
see that the Avowed had not only the room number Graeme
had given me but also the adjoining five-oh-six and five-oh-
seven, all with convenient connecting inner doors.

"Sorry, those rooms are booked," the woman said, "and we
don't have anything else on that floor tonight. But six-oh-six
on the floor above is available. The suites are exactly the same,
with two queens and a couch pull-out. That should give you
the same view of the park."

I looked at Blaze, and he gave a subtle nod. "We'll take it,"
I said.

The girl smiled. "Okay, how will you pay? And I'll need
some ID."

I fished a credit card and one of my many false passports
from an inner pocket and slapped them down on the counter.

The girl stared at it and then back up at me in confusion,
but in the few seconds delay, Oliver must have done some
adjusting on his illusion of me because the consternation on
the clerk's face disappeared.

A short time later, we were upstairs in our room. *We're in
the suite right above you,* I told Graeme as I settled onto a plush
couch that was as comfortable as it looked. *Any sign of Valerine?*

You already know I haven't seen her. His response had a slightly desperate edge. *I can feel you still here in my mind.*

I've been a little occupied. Can you feel Valerine? He should feel her faintly at least through their mate bond. All those gifted with sensing that I knew of experienced some level of that, though maybe it didn't work if your spouse was clinically dead.

Not where I'm at now. Which was on a couch with his hands and feet tied, I knew.

Well, they have taken three rooms, and I can feel life forces in at least one of them. She could be there. I wasn't about to start wading through minds until I knew where their empath was. *What are your captors doing now? Can you see any of them?*

They're arguing on the balcony. I can't hear anything. Teach me how to break through their shields. His desperation had been replaced with determination. *If Mikyn can do it, I should be able to learn as well.*

That might not be true, as there was a large variance among different people with the same ability. I'd seen as much between Ava and me. Besides, I believed Mikyn had two abilities, which put him ahead of all of us.

Later, I said. *Is the empath with them?*

Yes.

Good, that might distract him as I probe the other rooms.

Her, he corrected. *My first cousin, Lacole.*

I saw a memory of the empath in his mind, a typically pale Avowed woman with blond hair and four hundred years of experience, which put her at a century older than Ava.

Okay. Let's explore a little while she's occupied. You can tag along, but don't do anything. I have no idea if I'll be able to shield us from her. And with possibly four combat Avowed there, plus the other three, that would give up our advantage.

Slowly, I began to search outward, careful to keep on the lookout for anyone who might be watching for a mental attack.

In the next room, bright, unblocked life forces beckoned. I entered one of the decidedly female minds and saw five other women lounging around the nice room in clothes that revealed more than a little skin, which told me some of the Avowed weren't isolating themselves from physical comfort that the so-called lesser mortals could offer.

"Are they ever going to come in?" asked a buxom redhead wearing a dress that displayed her ample cleavage to advantage.

"Who cares?" muttered a blonde as she helped herself from a food service cart. "With what they're paying and all the room service we want, what's to complain about?"

"It's just weird," said another blonde. "They barely come in here, and then it's just to get down to business. It's like we're trained monkeys or something." She had no idea how true this statement was.

"I only need a few thousand more bucks before I'm out of this life for good," said a brunette with short hair and an upturned nose. "I hope they stay at least the week." Murmurs of agreement met her comment as the first blonde brought a plate of chocolate-covered strawberries to the couch, where the woman whose mind I was in gave a little squeal of delight and reached for one.

There was nothing more to see, so I carefully released an idea into the sand stream of the woman's thoughts, urging her to the luxurious bathroom where she adjusted her hair and peeked into both the large tub and shower. No one else here but the six women.

I sensed embarrassment in Graeme's thoughts at the women's presence at the hotel. *Did you really think all the children you helped steal ended up as beloved offspring in the ruling families? You had to know that many eventually became adult companions, those who were too pretty to let die in the mines.*

Shame filled him. *I knew,* he confessed. *I justified it because of Anina. It was the only way I could keep her from the mines, and after my boys died there . . . It's still no excuse.*

But I understood. Perhaps I would also do anything to protect my unborn child, and given the choice, he had betrayed his rulers in the hopes of righting their wrongs.

We need to check the third room. I couldn't immediately feel anything inside, but that didn't mean a blocking Avowed or a mostly dead Valerine wasn't there. Without eyes in the room, it would be difficult for me to determine. We'd need to convince someone to go inside the room, and doing so would make us infinitely more exposed to the empath.

I think I feel . . . Graeme began. *No, I'm sure I feel our bond.*

I focused on his thoughts and felt it then. It was extremely faint and coming from the bathroom of the third suite. *I feel it too,* I said, *but she's not currently alive.*

Reset, he agreed. *We have to rescue her.*

Of course. Now that we know where she is, we can come up with a plan.

That was when I felt another presence hovering near us: the Avowed empath who had finally noticed our poking around. *Who's there? Graeme?* The thoughts were in Sinaltan.

Respond to her, I told him.

Take me to my wife, he said. *Please Lacole. I can feel her.*

Soon enough. The woman probed against his shield, but I reinforced it. *Aw,* she said through their surface connection, *you've learned a few new tricks.*

So have you. I know about Mikyn breaking through mind shields. I suppose he has been your tutor. He's crazy, you know.

Her mental smirk was clear. *He's a genius, and you and Valerine will stand trial for what you've done. In fact, you'll be the means of reuniting our people under Mikyn.* She stopped the communication, but I could feel more threatening to burst from her.

She knows something, I told Graeme uneasily.

Can you break through her shield? he asked. *She always was a . . . how do you topsiders say it . . . a suck-up to Mikyn.*

I was confident I could break into her mind because she hadn't yet detected the tiny shielded thread that connected us, but doing so would reveal our presence. *Keep talking to her,* I told him. *She's coming inside.*

He moved, craning his neck to focus on Lacole, who came through the balcony door toward the couch where he sprawled. Her blond hair was shorn so close to her head that I could see a large black freckle above her ear, not an imperfection her genes would have eradicated, but something inherent in her biology. She wore loose off-white pants and a shirt that draped somewhat like an Avowed toga, though the pants likely would have been laughed at in Sinalta. Behind her, Graeme and I could see the others were still on the balcony—six dimmer life forces—but moving restlessly behind the closed doors and vertical blinds.

"Please, just let us go," Graeme said, struggling to sit up.

Lacole's lips twisted mockingly. "Not a chance. And even asking that shows you have no idea of the bigger picture Mikyn has for our people. But we do need to know who you contacted and how much you told them. Telling us could make things easier for you—at least until we get back to Sinalta."

"Like I already told your friends, I don't know anything about how Valerine contacted them."

"But what did you say? Did you give them information about Sinalta? What did you tell them about Mikyn's plan?" Lacole turned away as she spoke, settling in the chair by the couch.

Graeme's thoughts became weary. "We just want to reunite with our daughter. Valerine sent a message to the woman taking care of her. That's all."

Lacole's laugh was low and light. "I wish I could believe that."

She tapped the armrest with her fingers, three of which were adorned with jewels. "That doesn't explain why you didn't go to San Diego straight away. That's where your daughter is—all of us know that."

Graeme's emotions surged with an irritation he didn't hide. "Because we knew you were following us! We knew we were being hunted. We barely escaped Sinalta with our lives as it was. We didn't want to be forced back there."

"Too bad. You have to stand trial, or our people won't feel safe." She folded her arms across her abdomen. "Are those explosives still in place?"

"What? Of course not! Look, we did what was necessary to free our daughter—to free all our people. The ruling families—Mikyn included—tried to kill the Unbounded who came to help us. Valerine and I made sure they knew not all Sinaltans were like them. *We* are the reason the city is above the water once again. The Unbounded we helped were the only ones who could do that."

Lacole jumped up. "Statesmen Tsaoussis and Scala tried to kill them, not Mikyn. He made peace. And yes, Sinalta is finally topside, but maybe you don't know that we won't be given the land Triad Carrington promised us because he has been conveniently imprisoned. You have to ask yourself, if the Unbounded can turn on their own kind and imprison their rightful leader, what are their true plans for us now that we are back in their world and at their mercy? Our leaders have every right to eliminate those who attacked our alliances."

That is a screwed up view of things, I told Graeme. *Stefan was never the leader of the Renegades. We took over the Emporium to save the mortal world.*

The Avowed ruling families don't care about mortals, Graeme reminded me. *Do you think Mikyn had something to do with freeing Stefan?*

On the way to the transport, we'd filled him in on Stefan's escape, and I almost regretted telling him in case he blurted it out to this woman. *I'm not sure,* I said. *But if Mikyn is in on freeing Stefan, that would mean he's still in contact with Tsaoussis and Scala, because they are definitely involved, and if the statesmen are not wanted criminals as Mikyn claims, that changes everything between our peoples.*

Could that be what Stefan was hiding? That he wasn't only working with Tsaoussis and Scala but also Mikyn and the other Avowed families? Had we been party to raising an evil that might possibly succeed in destroying the world where Stefan had failed?

Easy. Not all of us are involved. Graeme's thoughts told me I had let more than a little of my worries reach him. *Though I can't blame you for the concern. I'll try to get to the bottom of this. But first we need to rescue Valerine.*

Right. I'll talk to the others. But I would keep an eye on his conversation as well as I could in the meantime.

"You have only Stefan Carrington's word that he will help us," Graeme was saying to Lacole as I opened my eyes and signaled Blaze and Oliver.

"We had fifty years of trading and cooperation," Lacole retorted.

Graeme had no answer to that, so I focused on Blaze and Oliver, quickly explaining the situation. Backup was too far away, and we were outnumbered. Somehow, we had to find a way to overcome the Avowed and rescue Graeme and Valerine without risking ourselves. Or rather, without risking my baby.

I was confident I could protect myself, but what would I tell Anina if I lost her parents?

Chapter 9

B LAZE AND OLIVER BEGAN DISCUSSING PLANS THAT RANGED FROM
faking room service to get them to open the doors to using
Blaze's fireballs to cut into the rooms. To my Unbounded genes,
it all sounded like excellent fun, but the mother inside me kept
reining back and plaguing me with thoughts of Ritter and Jace.

Had they been able to determine Stefan's true motives?
Surely Stefan didn't trust Tsaoussis and Scala as he had appeared
to do at our meeting. He was too savvy. Maybe it was Mikyn he
was actually working with, using the other two statesmen along
the way, just as they were using him. And us. He could very
well be planning to deliver them up to Mikyn for judgment.

My sat phone rang, and I answered, expecting Stella but
not feeling all that much surprise when I discovered it was my
husband. "You reading my mind now, Your Deathliness?" I
asked.

"So you're thinking about me."

"Maybe a little."

"Oh? And what are we doing in these thoughts of yours?"
His deep voice was half teasing, half serious.

"I'll show you later." I let the words hang flirtatiously before adding more seriously, "We've found Graeme and Valerine, but we'll be a little bit longer. We have a few Avowed to contend with."

"Need help?" Tension entered his voice.

Even if I did, he was too far away, as was the rest of our team. "No. We've got this. Blaze taught me a new trick, and I'm looking forward to trying it out. No way are we letting Mikyn's goons take Graeme and Valerine back to Sinalta to face trial for helping us escape their prison." I felt a sense of betrayal as I said the words. Mikyn had appeared to be instrumental in helping us, which resulted in our agreement to raise Sinalta.

"Well, I guess explosives targeting their electronic shield generators is a touchy subject, even if it saved us and therefore their city." His irony oozed through the connection. "My bet is that he'll somehow use them to gain more political power."

"At this point, anything is possible. Any news on your end?"

"Jace met with Stefan again, this time without the statesmen. We're even more sure that Stefan's original plan before we captured him was to deplete Sinalta's riches and possibly woo away many Avowed living on the outer ring, and then to destroy the city leaders, and possibly the city as well, if it came to it."

"But then we stepped in."

"Right. Without control of the Emporium, he couldn't do anything, especially from a prison cell. But Jace and I are sure Stefan has a new plan to dump the statesmen and gain power there."

My mind worked furiously. "The empath Mikyn sent believes we betrayed our 'leader,' Stefan, which makes me worry that Mikyn might also be involved in freeing him."

"Which would mean Mikyn might be secretly working with Tsaoussis and Scala as well."

The idea of them all working together or separately with Stefan made me ill. "The Avowed rulers and Stefan definitely share the same view of mortals."

Ritter was quiet a moment. "Regardless of who ends up in charge in Sinalta, I am more worried about their mortals than I was when Stefan alone was in control. Together he and any Avowed are a serious threat to the entire world."

"You mean we might have just brought a starving lion into the proverbial cattle enclosure."

"Exactly, though I suppose the world is a pretty large cattle pen."

The thought that we should have let the Avowed city self-destruct hung unspoken between us. In hindsight, it would have been the safer route for the topside mortals and probably for the rest of us too.

I'd seen regret in Mikyn's mind about how their mortal offspring had been treated, but as Ava had reminded me, that didn't mean the so-called Avowed seer would let his conscience dictate his actions. After all, he'd condemned hundreds of thousands of children to death or shorter lives to keep the Sinaltan government in status quo. Maybe a little regret meant nothing in his overall plan.

"We need more information," Ritter said. "This could be an attempt on Stefan's part to use the Avowed to retake the Emporium."

"I know just who to ask," I told him, picturing Lacole's face.

"Okay. Be careful."

"Always. You too." I knew the warning was his way of saying "I love you," and for the first time, it didn't even annoy me.

I hung up before I could ask him if my brother was falling under Stefan's charismatic spell. I had my own job to do, and I'd leave Jace to Ritter.

I turned my attention back to Blaze and Oliver, who exuded

excitement that immediately swept me in. Oliver even volunteered to dress up like a hotel employee.

"So what's your vote?" Blaze asked after another go-around of discussion.

"I like the idea of you and Oliver going to the room where the mortals are with a cartful of food and expensive wines." I pulled a syringe of sedative from my duffel. "One of these inside each bottle will put the mortals to sleep and dull the Avowed's senses."

"The mortals might be in less danger that way," Blaze said, "but so diluted, it'll barely faze the Avowed."

"That's where Oliver's illusions and your fireballs come in. With the goal of grabbing Graeme and the empath, if you can. She has information."

"And you?" Blaze asked. The amused flash of his eyes told me he knew I didn't plan to sit this one out.

"We'll also get a laundry cart, and while you're distracting them, I'll use one of your fireballs to get inside the room where they've stashed Valerine. Once she's in the cart, I'll push her outside to the SUV. I'll give you the word when I get there, and you can escape."

Blaze pondered for a moment before grinning. "I like it."

"Solid plan," Oliver said, with either a tinge of envy or disgust. I wasn't sure which.

"Let's go then." I leaned over to grab my pack with the additional sedatives inside. "And fast. I think they've begun their party with the mortals below, and some of them will be distracted." I could feel the life forces below moving around, and music was now coming through my connection with Graeme.

Erin? Are you there? Graeme asked as I led my team to the restaurant on the top floor of the hotel. *They're taking me somewhere. I think to Valerine.*

That's good. You can help me get her out. I filled him in on the plan, but my explanation was cut short as one of the Avowed tied a gag around his mouth and shoved him into the bathroom where Valerine lay. For the first time, we saw her through physical eyes, still clothed and lying in a stain of blood that was too small for the huge gash across her stomach, meaning that she'd bled out elsewhere, or it had gone down the drain. Her tall figure looked small in the huge bathtub, her knees bent and resting against the side. No curequick covered her wounds, and there were no empty syringes of it in the small, decorative trash receptacle, which would have increased her already accelerated healing rate by five times, but the fact that they had put her two separated ends together would at least speed up her recovery since the top half with the two still connected focus points of heart and brain had only to heal the connection with the lower half instead of regrowing it altogether. Still, without curequick, a glutein concentrate containing sugars and proteins reduced to their most usable form, it would be a long process.

Graeme began heaving at the sight. Liquid burned a fiery path up his throat as he began choking.

Calm down. I said, using all my mental strength to close his eyes. *The last thing she needs is for you to choke on your own vomit. Get control of yourself now! I'll need your help when I come for her. I'd like to bring Anina both her parents, but Valerine has information that makes her the most important, so if there's a choice about which of you to save, I will choose her. I'd rather do it with your help.*

For long moments, he struggled, eventually winning the battle but collapsing to the tiled floor. *Okay,* he said finally. *I'm okay.* His entire body shuddered. *Why didn't she trust me?* The thought was unexpected. *She didn't tell me anything.*

I wanted to say that maybe Valerine didn't have anything to tell, but Lacole's comments made it clear there was information, and that meant Valerine probably did have it, or Mikyn wouldn't have gone to such lengths to keep it secret.

She must have had her reasons. You need to trust her. Because Graeme might have experience topside as a sailor, but he wasn't a fighter under any stretch of the imagination. I knew how much they loved each other, and I was guessing she'd been protecting him.

Just hurry, he said.

I will. But you keep alert. I need to know if anyone else enters that room. I'm hoping they'll all be busy celebrating and will leave you alone, but they may not. At the moment, only two are left in the middle suite. I need to know if that changes.

The technopath is Lacole's husband, Graeme said, pulling himself up to a seated position but not looking into the bathtub. *So it's probably them. I heard her say something about contacting Mikyn.*

Okay, thanks. The technopath was a problem because if he kept nanites in his blood as Stella did, he could effectively change his face to look like any of us, but I'd let Oliver and Blaze know to be on the lookout for him.

We found a laundry room conveniently attached to the restaurant. We also found a closetful of supplies and were soon dressed as hotel employees to preserve Oliver's further illusions for the coming confrontation. After that, it was a matter of submitting a false order from the room and gathering the food and wine as it was prepared. I had to momentarily deviate a few of the regular employees so we could take the cart, but as it was near shift end, my job was easy.

We were in the elevator going down when Graeme sent me a warning. *I think the two from the shopping center are back. But they're in the hallway. Either that or there were others we didn't detect before, and they've come in to warm up.*

I relayed the information to Blaze and Oliver. "They'll be on rotation," Blaze said. "At some point someone from the room will trade with them."

I nodded. "We'd better hurry. You guys can still go in from the door. Maybe out as well, depending on how fast you are and whether or not the guards outside hear anything. You should use the deadlocks on the doors to slow their entry, just in case. But I'll definitely need a new way to Valerine. I'm thinking a ladder."

"That means you'll have to get into the room above that suite," Blaze said.

"It's empty. If it's not, I'll deal with it."

Oliver laughed. "Carrying a body up a ladder won't be easy." *In your condition* was the implication, and he might be right since Valerine was a tall woman, and she'd be dead weight.

"I'll figure it out," I told him. "Graeme will help. You just keep the Avowed out of the room until I give Blaze the sign."

"As long as it's him and not me." Oliver made a face. "I don't like the idea of anyone inside my brain."

"Don't worry. You're safe," I told him, having no desire to see what was in his self-aggrandizing mind. "With an empath around, the fewer connections I have to protect, the better."

Finding a ladder only delayed us seven more minutes but had the added benefit of giving us a universal key card, which I needed to get into the room above Valerine. Thankfully, it was still empty, and I locked the deadbolt in case the hotel rented it to another guest. Once the laundry cart and ladder were inside, we added the sedatives to the bottles of wine, and the guys set out, with me linked only by a thin connection to Blaze's mind.

As they started down to the next level, I disabled the fire alarm and began burning a hole in the bathroom floor. The tile was making it difficult, so I moved from the bath area to the sink where lush carpet covered the floor. The ball burned quickly through the carpet and underlying trusses, but I stopped before going all the way through. I widened the top part of the hole before finding a fire extinguisher in the hallway closet and dousing the area to prevent smoke from leaking too obviously from the room.

We're giving the two in the hallway a bottle of the wine, Blaze stated silently.

Good, I told him so he'd know I'd heard. The door in front of him was opening. *Don't think about me now unless you need me for something. I'm here, and I'll let you know if I need help.* I didn't want him thinking he had to focus on giving me a play-by-play. I'd see as much as I needed to, depending on what I was doing.

Right. I'll ignore that I've given you access to my brain, he promised, amusement radiating from the thoughts. I really liked my stepson. He'd make a good brother to my daughter.

Moments later, they were pouring wine, and as one woman collapsed onto the couch, that was my cue to get moving. I finished the substantial hole, lowered the ladder, and started down, jumping partway. In the bathroom, I yanked off Graeme's gag and cut his bonds.

"Wrap her up and tie her." I tossed him a stack of sheets I'd taken from the laundry room, one of which I'd cut into strips for a rope. "I'll lock the adjoining door, just in case. Then we'll get you both out of here." I'd feel better once that door was secure.

I stepped from the bathroom—and only the abrupt raising of goose bumps on the back of my neck prompted me to dive and roll. A knife whizzed past me and sank into the door behind me. I wasn't alone.

A tall man hovered in the sitting area near the balcony door, his wide shoulders rivaling Blaze's. Even looking at him, I couldn't detect his life force. I had the fleeting thought that he couldn't be Avowed because, besides Mikyn, none of them had ever been forced to learn such strong shielding, and even topside such a feat was normally reserved for the most talented sensing Unbounded. Yet this man looked as blond and sickly pale as any Avowed long starved for sunlight.

I sent my own knife flying, not at him, but at where I somehow knew he would be. I heard a grunt as it sank home, and then we were both on the move again. A throwing star hit my invisible shield, which I'd instinctively strengthened. I saw surprise on the man's lean face as he drew his sword so fast the edges blurred. No doubt that he was combat, not sensing, or he would have detected my link with Graeme. I thought about my gun, but I couldn't risk it without the silencer. Even as I pulled my own sword and parried his first swing, I knew I'd have to be smart to beat this man. No one could save me; my friends were all too far away. I leapt onto the bed to gain a little height, jumping back when he went for my legs, and then scoring a hit on his shoulder.

How had I managed that without channeling him or one of the other combat soldiers? Maybe he wasn't as skilled as I thought. He threw three more knives in succession, and each one I batted away. Confidence swelled through me, similar to the confidence I experienced when channeling Jace or Ritter.

He was still bigger than me and had the advantage of reach. I was shorter and faster, though. If I had more time, I'd wear him down to find out who he was. Or what, rather. Not quite Avowed, despite his pasty face.

"Who are you?" I asked in English.

"The person who is going to permanently end you." His response was in the same language without notable accent.

"I'm with embryo." I said it only to see his reaction.

He hesitated, and I sent a fireball at him. He moved to escape but in exactly the way I expected. The molten orb hit him in the chest, burning a hole so fast he didn't have time to scream out before he fell. I dived for the closet and the fire extinguisher that was located exactly where one had been in the upstairs room and sprayed him. His body jerked once more, but he was dead. For now. Reset.

Smoke hung in the room, and I hurried to disable the smoke alarm. As I finished, Graeme came from the bathroom. His gaze flicked to the man on the floor.

"You know him?" I asked. "He was here in the room when I came down because he was waiting for me after I left the bathroom. His life force was completely masked, but I don't think he's sensing."

"He looks familiar."

"To me too." I stared at the white-blond hair and pale face. "But most of you have the same look."

Graeme snorted. "If you were paler, you could be from Sinalta. They'll all be darker soon under the sun, even with how fast our skin regenerates."

He was right. I tossed down the extinguisher. "Blaze and Oliver are fighting now. They're outnumbered. We need to get out of here."

"Stop right there."

I turned to see Lacole standing in the doorway adjoining the suites, a pistol aimed in our direction. "So, Graeme," she said. "I see you weren't exactly honest with me."

I half expected more Avowed to explode into the room, but she came through alone, walking a few steps to her right so she could peer past us into the bathroom. Was the ladder visible? I didn't think so.

"Hello," I said. "I'm Erin Radkey, Stefan Carrington's daughter."

She spat on the carpet. "I know who you are. A traitor!" She moved a few more steps toward the door leading to the hallway.

Vaguely, I was aware that in the far room, Blaze had killed

three Avowed with his fireball and set another one on fire. Soon the fire alarm there would alert the entire hotel, no matter how many illusions Oliver called to life.

Graeme, I said through our private connection. *Get Valerine up that ladder. Before Lacole lets in the guards from the hallway.*

But your baby—

Go! With more force than I intended, I mentally shoved at his brain to make his legs move. Shock reverberated in his mind that such a thing was even possible. But we were running out of time. Blaze was facing two more Avowed, one who was so skilled that I worried about my team's success.

"Stop!" Lacole shouted. She fired at me as she leapt for the door, but I was there before her. I kicked out to send her gun flying, pulling my own and aiming it at her head.

"Bathroom now," I ordered.

"No. You won't kill me. Or if you do, I'll just wake up in a bit."

"You tried to kill my baby." I formed a fireball in my hand.

Her gaze flickered to my stomach. "I didn't sense that. You must be blocking. Funny how easy doing something like that is once you know how. Such a little thing to mask, isn't it?"

"Go into the bathroom. I won't ask again." I pushed the ball into her shoulder.

Lacole's scream deafened me. But she began to move, scrambling into the bathroom and then up the ladder. I almost expected her to bolt at the top, but Graeme was ready with a gun he'd taken from my bag. Pounding began on the door as I jumped onto the ladder, my feet barely touching a few rungs on my way up. A syringe of sedative made sure Lacole wouldn't give us any more problems.

"Quick, get them into the laundry cart." Together we dumped Lacole inside, and then Graeme gently laid Valerine's bound form on top. We covered them both with blankets.

With their ability to absorb, neither was in danger of suffocating, not that it mattered at the moment for Valerine.

I was worried about Blaze and Oliver. *We're almost to the elevator,* I put in Blaze's mind. *I can come help if you need me.*

No, we got it. You'd better hurry outside. I had to trap the last guy in a ring of fire, so the alarm went off. They'll shut down the elevator soon. But Oliver's been hit. A pause. *Wait, no. He's okay. Must have been one of his illusions. Don't tell him, but I'd have had no chance to beat all these guys without his misdirection. Even with my fireballs. We'll burn through the wall and get out from another room. Meet you downstairs.* The thoughts transferred to me instantly, before the elevator door could even open. I also felt his elation, tinged by fear, and his very real worry about Oliver and the unconscious ladies. It hadn't been an easy fight.

We pushed the cart inside and jabbed at the button. To my relief, the doors shut, and we started downward. Graeme sank against the wall and sighed. I didn't want to tell him that we weren't out of the woods yet. If the elevator stopped working, we'd be in big trouble.

"You still have that gun?" I asked.

He nodded absently, his thoughts obviously elsewhere. "You *made* me move. There was a hole inside that man's chest, and Lacole was burned. What else can you do?"

"It's complicated," I said. "But there's a lot more many of us can do, when we need to."

He considered that. "Your baby?"

"She's fine."

"Okay, but I have something to say that I don't think you're going to like."

"What?"

"That man up there?" He paused. "When we were trapped in Sinalta and they were looking for us, we saw the recordings of the Senate meeting when Mikyn took control, the one where you were given custody of Anina."

"Okay." I wished he'd get to the point because we were arriving on the lobby floor.

"That man upstairs, he reminds me of that man who was with your team. The younger one. Blond guy who looks like one of ours."

He had to be talking about Jace. "No," I said. "That's my brother." But he was right. The man upstairs didn't look like me. He looked like the part of my brother that I didn't share. He looked like Stefan.

BEFORE GRAEME COULD RESPOND, THE DOORS OPENED, AND WE emerged into chaos. Apparently, the entire hotel was being evacuated. No one paid us any attention as we pushed our cart out a side door and across the parking lot. The wail of sirens cut through the quiet of the night. On the fifth floor, we could see the glow of the fire, and I hoped the firefighters got there in time to save the women.

We had loaded Valerine and Lacole into the back of the SUV and were searching the growing crowd for Blaze and Oliver when they finally emerged from the crowd, jogging toward us.

"What took you so long?" I said, scanning the people behind him to make sure they hadn't been followed.

Blaze shrugged. "The fire got out of hand. The firemen will get there in time to save the Avowed, but maybe not the women, so we had to get them out."

I nodded. *Of course.*

Oliver pulled the SUV door open and jumped into the back seat, looking exhausted and subdued, though not a single bruise marred his face. Trust Oliver to come out of a battle without a mark. But his respect for Blaze must have grown if he was giving him shotgun without even being asked.

I was opening the driver's door when a redheaded woman in a tight dress and heels stepped from behind the SUV and pointed a gun at Blaze's head.

"Nobody move!"

Chapter 10

I DREW MY OWN GUN AND POINTED IT AT HER. "I KNOW YOU. YOU'RE one of the hookers."

Oliver and Graeme emerged on either side of the SUV, Graeme holding up his gun with a shaking hand that didn't bode well for the redhead, or anyone nearby.

Easy, I told him.

The woman stepped behind Blaze to use him as a shield. "Not exactly. I'm undercover CIA."

"Prove it." I didn't put my gun away, but I relaxed a bit. That explained why she wasn't passed out with the others.

She held a fold of ID in front of Blaze's face. "It seems to be valid," he said. "And she did help us get the other women out." His tone was light, but every part of him was tense. And was that smoke wafting up from his skin or from his shirt? I didn't envy the woman if he couldn't rein it in—which might be hard after what he'd just been through.

"Look," I said. "If you really are CIA, you might be of some help to us." I was already on the stage of her mind, looking through her sand stream, and I believed her. "What is your involvement with the Sinaltans?"

"Sinaltans?" she asked. But my question brought the answers to the forefront of her thought stream. She hadn't known anything about them. Her organization had been tracking drug dealers, and when the group had begun throwing money around and purchasing controlled substances, she had gone in to learn more. "Do you mean those people from that city they just brought up from beneath the ocean?"

"Yes," I said. "If you'll put that gun away, I'll tell you what we need you to do because those people might get away if no one knows what they are."

"You're the ones who came in with guns blazing." Her eyes strayed to Blaze, her freckled nose wrinkling. "I knew there was something suspicious in the way you stayed to serve us the wine."

"We were rescuing a captive," I told her, "and she has important information, but we need to get her medical help."

"I can't let you leave."

"You have no choice, unless you think you can kill all of us before we kill you. You feel that heat? Blaze there isn't going to be able to hold back for much longer. And unlike us, you won't come back when you die."

"You're Unbounded." The redhead stepped back from Blaze, as if finally understanding her danger. A wise choice, as anything he touched would likely burst into flame. "How do I know you aren't the bad guys?" she added when no one responded to her accusation.

"Because we haven't already killed you. If we had time, the President's son Patrick Mann would vouch for us, but for now you'll have to take my word for it." *Now put the gun away,* I said silently in her mind. I had control of her hand now, and she'd have to fight me to pull any trigger. But to make her choice more obvious, I showed her possible outcomes to this confrontation, all of them ending with her incapacitation or even death.

She jerked and stared at me. "Your abilities," she said. "I thought those were only rumors."

"Put the gun down," I repeated aloud, not acknowledging the statement. "I know you have backup here, but I also know they're too busy trying to get the Sinaltans out of those rooms before the fire takes over, and the others en route don't have your current location. We really don't want to hurt you, but we will if you don't stand down."

Several heartbeats passed as I contemplated sending a flash of light into her head or giving Blaze a signal, but abruptly she nodded and holstered her gun. "Okay, I see that I don't have any choice right now. What do you want me to do?"

"I know that they might look dead or mortally wounded," I said, pocketing my own gun. "But if you want to stay alive, you'll give them each a full dose of this every four hours until they are behind sturdy bars." I fumbled in my bag for a packet of sedative syringes, tossing them to her. "And you'll need someone versed in holding Unbounded."

"So they're Unbounded, which means you didn't murder them." Relief poured from her in a wave.

"Avowed, actually," I corrected. "But it's the same thing."

"Is the whole city like that?"

Too late, I realized that someone at the top hadn't shared the news with the rest of the world, or at least not with the commoners, which was unfair. How could any country decide to give them sanctuary without knowing the whole truth? I certainly wasn't keeping up the lie.

"Most of them." I put one leg into the SUV. "We'll have our people contact yours about specific charges that we'll be filing, but make sure your jail cells are strong and that no one gets close to them without adequate firepower. They can disarm most anyone."

"I'm aware. We have protocols in place." But she kept the syringes. "So you're not going to show me what's in the back of your car?"

I shook my head, but Graeme spoke up. "It's my wife, Valerine. They cut her in half. We need to get her to a healer." He still had his gun out, though it wasn't quite pointed at her.

The redhead paled. "Right, okay. Here's my card. If you'll have your representative call me."

Blaze took the card, which blackened where his fingers touched, but it didn't burst into flame. I considered that a win for all of us.

"We'll be in touch." I ducked into the SUV, and when the others were inside, I started driving, edging from the crowded parking lot, half expecting someone else to try to stop us. No one did, though as we started down the street, fire trucks and police cars sped past.

"Little harder than I thought," Blaze said, stretching his shoulders. "Things burn so easily."

Thinking of how the fireball had eaten through my opponent's chest, I had to agree. "Someone was waiting for me in the room," I said, glancing at him and then at the road. "Well trained. Like one of Stefan's old hit teams, but definitely Avowed. But he . . . he looked like Stefan."

"That doesn't seem to fit with what we've heard of Avowed."

"It's worrisome." I glanced in the rearview mirror to see how Graeme and Oliver were taking that news, but Graeme was facing the rear and half kneeling, his hand going over the seat to rest on Valerine. Next to him, Oliver was slumped in the seat with his eyes closed. Apparently, his witty repertoire had been exhausted.

"He did good work," Blaze said, noting my gaze in the

mirror. "Even some hand-to-hand with one of them. I thought he was shot, but he was fast enough to duck, I guess."

"I'm glad." Maybe the success would fulfill Oliver's urge to show off for a while. He usually stayed away from direct combat, but when confronted, he'd always come through for us. "Did you get the guys in the hallway?"

"Only one. The other one went into the room. He'll be caught if he tries to save any of his people."

"Then we need to focus on helping Valerine." I considered the options. "Let's reach out to the team in Christchurch. If we take Graeme's transport, that's only a few hours away."

"They're good people in Christchurch," Blaze said. "But you'd better step on it before someone identifies this vehicle as having been at the hotel."

"Hold on tight then. And while I drive, you call Ava. She'll need to run interference with the CIA."

After loading our cargo, Blaze abandoned the rental car at a nearby gas station and joined us onboard. By the time he returned, Graeme and I had secured Lacole in one of the bunks in the tiny crew quarters and had given Valerine a dozen injections of curequick.

"Isn't there anything else you can do for her?" Graeme asked, massaging his shoulder as if it hurt.

"I'm no healer," I said, "but I've seen how Dimitri traces paths in the body, and I can try looking at those. I'm not sure what it would tell me, though."

"Please try."

"What about an interior tracking device?" I asked him. "Lacole is bound to have one."

Graeme shrugged. "That's not a concern at the moment.

Valerine was able to refit this transport with an electric grid, so they won't be able to find or attack us mentally. It's our hydrogen engine I am more concerned with, even burning as efficiently as it does. Once we get to a certain speed, those can be tracked by anyone with the right technology."

"I'll let our friends in Christchurch know about Lacole's tracker," Blaze said. "They'll help us come up with a solution before we get there."

"You should do it before we take off." With a final look at his wife, Graeme stepped toward the door. "Not sure if you'll be able to get past the electronic grid. It's nothing like the one protecting Sinalta, of course, but it's strong enough. You have our destination coordinates?" At Blaze's nod, he added, "I'll get the engine started, then, while you go outside to call."

Blaze followed Graeme from the crew quarters, leaving me alone with a subdued Oliver and the unconscious women.

"Are you okay?" I asked Oliver. For a black man, he was looking awfully pale.

He slowly climbed the ladder to the top bunk without even taking off his boots. "Just tired."

"Well, no wonder. You've been creating illusions all day. Want some curequick? I have some if you don't have any." I hadn't seen his pack, so either he must have left it in the room we'd rented or lost it during the fight.

"Uh, sure." He dangled an arm. "Will here do?"

I nodded. "You haven't had any recently, right? We don't want to risk addiction."

"I'm good." He watched as I slipped the big needle into his vein. Curequick was thick and not extremely pleasant to inject, but I didn't have any of the drinkable kind on me because a needle in the bloodstream worked faster and was preferred for combat. It caused a pleasant buzz as it worked its way through the body, like a mega dose of caffeine. Personally,

I hated needles and was glad it was him and not me. He didn't seem to mind.

"You'll feel it in a little bit," I said, "but you might as well rest anyway. I'm not sure how much longer it'll be before you can return to New York." At least not until we got Valerine back to San Diego. Learning her information was the most pressing thing, especially as her information might be a clue to Dimitri's whereabouts. In the meantime, I could question Lacole when her heavy sedative wore off.

"Thanks." Oliver massaged his arm but didn't complain at the obvious discomfort. When he spoke again, his tone was haunted. "Those fireballs . . . They ate right through their bodies. I never saw anything like it. A few more, and they would never have woken up."

"Blaze wouldn't do that, not unless it was necessary. None of us would." I gave him a sympathetic smile. "But it is freaky." I sighed. "I guess we're all freaks." Without thinking, I put my hand to my stomach, though I couldn't feel my flesh beneath the sturdy armor.

"Are you okay?" Oliver asked, seeing the movement.

I laughed. "Yes. I just . . ." I wanted to tell someone about the fight with the combat Avowed in Valerine's room. About how easily violence had come to me, as if I'd been channeling not only Blaze but a combat Unbounded. Had I broken into one of the Avowed minds instinctively? I supposed it was possible, but Oliver wasn't the person to ask. "Anyway, my baby's fine, too. And I know I'm only three months along, but I can't wait to meet her."

He stared at me without responding.

"You did know, right?" I asked. "About the baby?" I was certain our whole team knew, even those currently working in New York.

"Uh, of course I heard. I was just thinking . . . Never mind.

It's been a long day." He gave me a thin smile. "But congratulations. I can't remember if I ever told you that." His affected way of speaking was more pronounced than ever. Snooty, Jace would have said, but Oliver had done well today, so I was trying to choose other adjectives.

"You didn't, but I've barely seen you since I found out. So, thanks." I paused a moment before saying, "Well, I'd better take a look at Valerine like I promised Graeme."

He nodded and lay down, sighing as if every bone in his perfectly formed body ached. Or maybe he was missing his customary designer loafers.

I crouched on the floor next to Valerine's body on the first bunk. Graeme had unwrapped her face and put a blanket over her middle to hide the blood that had seeped through the sheets. I was glad because now that my adrenaline had eased, I felt nauseated again. I needed to eat and would as soon as I finished here. At least Sinaltan transports typically carried the seaweed tea I'd been using to ease nausea.

I reached out and touched Valerine's head to make my job a little easier. What I really wanted when I'd offered to look at Valerine was to see if I could examine her thoughts. It was intrusive, but it might give us the information we needed faster than waiting for her to heal. I felt guilty not asking Graeme's permission, but I was the op leader, and it was my call.

I entered her mind, but instead of seeing a placid lake that signaled a normal sleeping or unconscious mind, which I could then dive into and find memory bubbles, her mind stage was a vast wasteland, cold and dark, with heaps of debris that might be collapsed memory bubbles. When I touched one, nothing came from it, though her brain's focus point was obviously still alive on some level, or the parts wouldn't regenerate. Apparently, the information it stored currently wasn't available, which would explain why Ava had never taught me to search the mind of a dead person.

I began instead to trace the pathway of the arteries and veins. They were working but not in a way I understood. Dimitri would be able to explain, of course, but I was the only one here. As I approached the area where she was cut, I could see accelerated activity as her body repaired itself. If only I could mentally align the veins and muscles the way Dimitri could. That would at least help the healing. I reached out and physically manipulated her flesh until it looked better, then went on to the next section. Not perfect, but it might help.

Sometime later, I had done everything I could, and I wasn't all that certain I had done anything at all. I was queasier than before and utterly exhausted. But there was still Lacole. She had information too, and she was alive, which meant maybe I could take it if I could find it. Her shield might not be strong when she was asleep. Some Unbounded lost control of their shields completely when they were out.

Unfortunately, her barrier was still strong, and I suspected she'd reinforced it through a third party. The information might also be hidden in constructs, impossible to extricate from memory bubbles, and messing with them while she was unconscious might set off a mental trap. For now, I'd wait until I was rested, and maybe even until I had backup. It wasn't long to Christchurch, and we were out of communication for a while anyway.

I stumbled from the tiny room, stunned to realize that an hour had passed while I'd worked on Valerine. I really needed that tea. As I prepared it in the small cafeteria alcove, I munched on a few crackers. The transport had a system that brought in ocean matter so we could absorb nutrients—Sinaltans knew their stuff—but the smell of the ocean was strong and did nothing good for my nausea. Still, seafood was good for growing babies, right? I left the tea steeping as I made a pit stop in the miniscule bathroom, wishing I could strip down and shower.

Finally sipping my tea, I went to find Graeme and Blaze in the control room. I was torn between going back to Ava and the boat so we could find Dimitri and checking to make sure my brother wasn't getting into trouble. But first we needed to take care of Valerine.

"What's our ETA?"

"Fifty minutes." Blaze looked up from the screen on the wall that showed not only the sonar but the actual views from different sides of the ship. "They're meeting us on a dock south of Christchurch."

"We're making good time then." The primary system of the Sinaltan transport was hydrogen derived from seawater, which meant they had achieved what the rest of the world only dreamed about. It simplified everything about sea travel, which I supposed was a natural occurrence after thousands of years living underwater.

"Yes." Graeme swiveled his seat toward me. "How's Valerine?"

"The same. I couldn't do anything more. It'll help once we get her into a curequick solution and to a healer."

Blaze stood. "I know you're some kind of wonder woman, but you look like hell. With all the time zone hopping, you're past time for rest. We all are." He looked at Graeme. "Wake us when we're on approach. I'm taking my stepmom here and putting her to bed."

I laughed. "Okay, but only because I want to be in top shape when I question that monster empath we caught."

Before we reached the hallway, an alarm on the panel sounded. Graeme muttered something in Sinaltan and put his hands on the controls. "I have bad news. We're being followed. My guess is that it's another transport."

Blaze and I went to stand behind him, noting a blip that had appeared on the screen. "I guess that guard got out," Blaze said.

"Or they have more friends." Graeme sighed. "This is probably the same transport that followed us from Sinalta. They probably picked up our trail again when we began moving."

"Are they going to catch us?" I asked.

He shook his head. "They're larger and have bigger engines, but Valerine made a few changes before we took off. My wife is a very good engineer. We'll beat them to Christchurch just like we did to New Zealand."

"What about the authorities here?" Blaze asked. "What if they see us?"

"We're within the shipping lanes already, and we have codes. It's one of the reasons we chose to come here. That and it was one of the closest land masses where we could contact you. We traveled deep until we got close enough and then radioed in so we didn't alert coastal patrols. We appear to be another large yacht with valid registration codes."

Blaze scowled. "Why does that sound like something that needs to be stopped?"

"Because it does," I said. "But as yet their technology isn't common knowledge, so we don't know what to look for." I didn't add that the White House had already put people on the alert.

"Anyway, I'm not concerned about them catching up." Graeme's fingers typed across the controls. "And now that I know they're following us, there are things I can do to get further ahead and maybe even lose them for a time. You two get some sleep. I've done nothing but rest for days."

Blaze looked at me as if silently asking if we should trust

him, but I'd already been down that road before. I might not spill all my secrets to Graeme, but I trusted him with my life. Better yet, he'd trusted me with the life of his most precious possession: his young daughter.

"Let's sleep," I told him.

Back in the crew quarters, everything was exactly as I'd left it. Blaze wrinkled his nose. "Does it smell like burned flesh to you in here?"

I shuddered. "It didn't until you said anything. But of course it does. It's probably clinging to our clothes."

"Sorry. I didn't notice it before." He climbed the ladder to the fourth bunk under Oliver, squeezing his large body into the narrow space. I guessed he'd had more than a century to fight any tendency toward claustrophobia.

My own body hit the too-thin mattress on the third bunk, and as I gave myself up to sleep, I had the distinct feeling that I was missing something important. But what? For the moment, I was too tired to care.

Chapter 11

TRUE TO HIS WORD, GRAEME HAD PULLED AHEAD ENOUGH FROM our pursuers that he was able to put the engines on low some distance before we docked, presumably causing us to vanish from their tracking monitors. He was confident they wouldn't locate his transport's position, but he locked it down just in case.

"I planned to turn it over to you anyway," he told me, handing me a small tablet. "Seeing as you left the other one we gave the Emporium back in the Antarctic somewhere."

"We were hoping you could use it to escape," I said with a grin. "But we'll try not to lose this one."

The team in Christchurch consisted of four former Renegades, who Blaze had once met when they'd joined together to foil an Emporium plot to smuggle drugs into New Zealand. Two men, Calum and Sebastian, appeared at the small dock in a black van to pick us up, and there was a lot of back-pounding before they began driving us to their headquarters—an old grade school near the edge of town that had been abandoned two decades ago.

Sitting in the back seat next to Blaze, I texted Ava to let her know we had arrived in Christchurch, and she had some surprising information. "Looks like Chris is flying here to take us back to San Diego," I announced.

Blaze blinked at that. "Even flying as directly as possible, it'll be twenty-four hours with gas stops. I know Stefan is making trouble, but wouldn't it be better to see if Mari could carve out some—" He broke off as he apparently remembered that we were not advertising Mari's ability, especially to Avowed, allies or no.

"Not going to happen," I said. "But Chris estimates eighteen hours or less. He's already in the air. Ava says everyone in New York is occupied as important leaders arrive for the voting Monday afternoon."

Triad votes were only allotted to important leaders in the Emporium, while the rest of us would watch via the internet. Normally, the voting was a mere formality, basically a swearing of allegiance, as Triad positions were chosen by the predecessor, but with Stefan free, we had to be ready for anything. Keene hadn't been his father's choice, though his realistically forged paperwork was the most recently dated, which meant he should gain the seat. Whoever was the actual heir, however, hadn't yet come forward, and we had no idea what kind of debauchery the person had committed over a lifetime that had put him in Keene's father's favor.

Once we arrived at the Christchurch Renegades' headquarters, we met the other two team members, Rose and Dean. I was surprised to learn that Dean was a mortal and that he and Rose were married. For at least six years, if the ages of the five little boys running around the school were any indication.

"They keep things lively," Rose said with a smile. "And they insisted on staying up to meet you. We don't get many visitors, and since they're homeschooled, we don't have strict schedules." While the men all looked Caucasian, she was obviously Polynesian, or Maori as they were called locally, with long black hair, dark eyes, and olive skin. She wore a bright, loose dress that did nothing to hide another tiny glowing life force inside her.

"At some point, I'm going to send Dean for a little snip," she added, casting her husband a wicked grin. "But I always wanted a large family, and now seems like a good time. But I guess you know all about being ready." Her eyes dropped to my abdomen. Encased in Stella's body armor, she couldn't possibly guess about my condition, so that could only mean one thing.

You're sensing. I easily connected with her surface thoughts.

She smiled. *Yes. You probably haven't heard of me, but I've heard of you. It's a pleasure to meet you, Erin, even if you are a Carrington.*

Erin Radkey, I stressed. Having Stefan's name attached to me grated.

Of course. I didn't mean anything by it. But now that Stefan has granted temporary control of his Triad seat to your brother, he might be able to repair some of the hatred he's engendered among us former Renegades as well as the Emporium.

In my book, that would never happen. Stefan was a danger until he was killed, especially to my brother. Fortunately, her teammate covered my lack of response.

"We have the curequick set up over here." Calum waved a hand at the long tables lining one wall of what had obviously been the school cafeteria.

"Stay here with your dad," Rose told her children in a tone that brooked no argument.

Graeme and Blaze carried Valerine over to a table next to a white body bag that zipped on the top. Unlike a regular body bag, it had a stiff interior liner filled halfway with clear, thick gel. Laying Valerine on the table next to the bag, they cut off the sheets and her clothes, revealing the ugly wound, but I was happy to see that she didn't divide in two, signaling that healing had already begun in earnest. Calum drew out a needle, though, and began stitching the wound.

"I can only do the muscle and skin," he said. "I don't know anything about the veins and such, but this should help her heal faster, especially since we'll be moving her. Don't want to tear anything that has started healing more than we have to."

Stitching usually did help, and Valerine wasn't exactly in a position to protest. As they carefully rolled her over to stitch her back, I entered the wasteland of her mind and tried to follow the veins and arteries again. I wasn't sure, but the wasteland seemed to be healing. Wetness bubbled on the ground, and the dehydrated memory bubbles were filling in.

Finally, we slipped Valerine's body into the gel. Next came the IVs in each wrist and another in her chest. I remembered how those lifelines had felt when I'd been brought back from death—like pure, cool, blissful relief.

"We'll have to replace these bags every hour or so in the beginning." Calum added a five-gallon container of curequick inside the bag so she was covered completely. "But until you get her to a healer, that's really all we can do."

"It's really good," I said. "Thank you. But let's leave her mouth uncovered." She could absorb oxygen just as she could nutrients, but once she came back to life, I knew from personal experience how disconcerting it was to suck in gel for that first attempted breath.

"What about the other one?" Rose asked. "We don't have another bag, but we can do the IVs."

We all looked at the table where Sebastian and Oliver had set down Lacole. "She's only sedated," I said. "Should wear off in another couple hours."

"That's why I put on cuffs," Blaze added.

"A good stimulant might help her." Except now that I was focused on Lacole, something didn't seem right. Her life force was so dim that it was almost nonexistent. "Rose," I asked. "How skilled are you at questioning people?"

Dean laughed, having come over to chase one of the smaller boys. "Are you kidding? She's the best. Just ask the kids." He hoisted the child onto his hip.

Smiling as he'd intended, I moved to the table where Lacole lay with a blanket someone had pulled over her. "Have you ever examined unconscious memories? I need a lookout in case of boobytraps, and Graeme here hasn't done it before."

"I'd like to learn," Graeme said, moving closer. "And three minds are better than two."

Rose came to stand across from me, regarding the Avowed doubtfully. "I don't think that'll work. Look how dim her life force is. She's dead. Regenerating, but still dead."

Tingles of unease pricked along my neck. I sent out my thoughts, and this time Lacole's mind barrier was completely gone, and in her head, only the same wasteland that had greeted me in Valerine's mind met my mental probe.

"Blaze? Oliver? Did either of you notice this?" I demanded, though I knew the responsibility lay only at my doorstep. I was the one who could sense life forces, but I'd given myself over to sleep instead of following up on my feeling that something was wrong.

Blaze shook his head, and Oliver placed his hand against her throat. "No pulse. Maybe she had one of those, uh, suicide pills."

I kicked at the table leg, cursing under my breath. "I should have examined her on the transport."

"You couldn't have known she'd taken anything." Blaze stepped toward me and put a hand on my shoulder. "And you couldn't have done it without backup."

"I had Graeme."

"He was busy with the submersible, and he's not—" Blake broke off.

"He's right," Graeme said. "If she's been studying with Mikyn, we don't know what she's capable of."

Without answering, I stalked across the room toward a long counter where foodstuffs had been spread out invitingly, not because I was hungry but because I was angry at myself, and I didn't want the others to see me so out of control. But before I'd taken even a few steps, a strange feeling of comfort enveloped me. At first, I thought it was Rose, emoting, but then I realized it was coming from inside me.

From my daughter.

Instantly, I tamped down on my anger. *Hey, there,* I said, in tight communication to her. *I'm okay.* I sent her happy thoughts, and happiness radiated back to me. Apparently, my little girl was growing and growing fast. I wished Dimitri were there to tell me how developed she was now and if everything was still perfect. She seemed healthy to me, and the healers I'd had checkups with aboard the boat said everything was all right. Still, they weren't Dimitri.

I took a white roll from a basket on the counter and began looking for tea.

"That's what always calms my stomach," Rose said with a laugh. "Strange that something so unhealthy can do that. But I have some ginger chews that also work miracles. I'll get them for you."

"Thanks," I managed to say in a voice that didn't sound too unfriendly.

She hesitated at the door next to the counter that led into the kitchen. "Um, I gather that Avowed was unconscious but alive on your way here? How much do you trust your team?"

I glanced over her shoulder where the men were seated on

a mismatched gathering of couches. Blaze, who had given his life for the Renegade cause more times than I could count; Oliver, who was newly Changed and an arrogant pain in the ass, but who had always come through when he was needed; and Graeme, who had betrayed his country to save my team. Could he have taken revenge on Lacole for his wife's reset? I didn't think so.

"They're all solid," I said.

She nodded. "It's just those suicide pills usually act fast."

"Maybe it was a slow release. Or set off later in something she was wearing."

"Sebastian will look. He's combat."

I swallow a bite of roll. "Combat, huh? And what's Calum?"

She smiled and followed my gaze to the dark-haired man. "He's a summoner."

"Really?" I'd known a summoner once, Francis Bennet, but she'd died during our takeover. "Animals, bugs, birds?"

"All of the above," she said. "The boys love it." She paused, and I waited for her to ask the question I'd been dreading. Ever since we'd learned about Mikyn's ability to detect whether or not a child was destined to Change, and even though we hadn't officially announced anything, rumors had spread. It seemed every Unbounded mother had sent in questions to the Emporium headquarters about finding out if their child would Change. Maybe it wasn't a bad thing, as long as they didn't also know that altering the outcome was a possibility. If they did, how many would take the risk? It was a moral dilemma I still couldn't reconcile in my own heart.

I would give anything to have my daughter Change. Anything but steal years from her mortal life if I failed.

But instead of asking how to predict her children's futures, Rose simply smiled. "It's really late, and I should go throw the kids in bed. Let me know when you're ready to see where you'll sleep. One advantage of living in an old school is that we have plenty of rooms, and I had our housekeeper clean them when I heard you were coming."

The tension building again inside me cranked down a notch. "Thanks."

WE ALL SLEPT IN UNTIL NOON AND THEN SPENT MOST OF SUNDAY afternoon waiting for Chris to arrive at a private runway outside Christchurch. Near dinner time, Calum, Rose, and Sebastian drove us to meet him, leaving Dean at the school with the children. Both Valerine and Lacole were still technically dead, but their life forces were stronger now, so I felt encouraged.

Blaze was in a good mood, having stayed up swapping stories with his old friends, and Graeme was also fairly jubilant as he anticipated a reunion with his daughter. But Oliver was in a foul mood, barely responding when addressed, so we ignored him. He carried himself a little awkwardly, and I suspected he had internal injuries that were painful, as he'd asked Calum for more doses of curequick. Either that or he was using illusions to hide the fact that he'd actually been shot. Doing so to save face would be classic Oliver.

My older brother Chris waved to us as he descended the plane's stairs. His blond hair was tousled, but he otherwise looked rested despite having been in the air all night. "Just need some fuel," he called, gesturing to the trucks that were heading our way.

I hugged him, then he shook Blaze's hand and nodded at Oliver before I introduced him to Rose, Calum, and Sebastian.

After the introductions, Chris went to meet the fueling guys, and Rose turned to me. "You didn't mention he was mortal." Like me, she could tell at a glance.

"I try not to think about it," I admitted.

She smiled. "Why do you think I have so many kids?" When I didn't answerww "I plan to have ten more this go-around. Dean's family carries only the latent gene, but now that we can alter his sperm, my babies have up to a forty percent chance of Change instead of twenty, so I know I'll have at least some company after Dean goes. And the others . . . well, they'll have a good life, and I'll love them for as long as I can."

"You sound like you're talking from experience."

She grinned. "Calum is my son from my first marriage fifty years ago. He's all I have left now, and he is worth it. But so were the relationships I had with my other children. I was fortunate. While so many Renegades had to hide offspring from the Emporium, I lived on a tiny island near here and loved them every day of their lives, not for what they might be but for who they were. Death doesn't happen overnight, and it's okay when it does."

I understood then why she didn't ask me how to foretell her children's futures. She wanted to keep the hope and to love them without reserve. It was something I needed to remember.

"We live in the me-me-me generation," she added. "But I think people risk too much by only having one or two children at a time. You never know when accidents will happen or other unforeseen things. I lost an Unbounded daughter to the war with the Emporium, a mortal daughter in childbirth, and a son to cancer before we found the cure. But the others lived a full life. The more family you have, the greater your chance of happiness. Life is too long to spend it alone."

"Have you always lived here or nearby?" I asked. Because life seemed simpler here somehow. "You don't speak with a heavy Kiwi accent."

"Heaven's no. I've spent the past century all over the world. I met Dean in Florida, in fact. But there's never any place except these islands that are home to me. My grandparents and parents were born in New Zealand. I'm going to have all my children here, and when the time comes, I plan to die here."

I thought about that for a moment. I'd been born in Kansas City and lived there until my Change, and I didn't feel that way about the city, not since the battles we'd fought there. Even the Fortress in San Diego wasn't quite home, and yet it was there I felt the safest. "You might have a good plan," I said, wondering what Ritter would think of having a passel of children on the remote island Cort Bagley had left us in his will. He'd probably be sickeningly pleased.

Chris returned from his chat with the fueling guys. "Won't be long now. I brought the larger plane knowing we'd need the room for your, uh, unconscious passengers." To Blaze he added, "You look like you're expecting company."

Blaze drew his gaze away from the road that also served as the runway. "Not exactly, but our submersible was followed most of the way to Christchurch. We don't think they have any idea where we are, and our friends injected Lacole with a temporary signal blocker at the dock where they picked us up until her tracking device can be removed, but you never know."

"Then let's get loaded, so we're ready when the fuel is." Chris motioned us up the stairs.

When the men had deposited Valerine and Lacole inside, we bid farewell to Rose and the others.

"We'll keep an eye on your submersible until you come back for it," Calum said.

"Thanks for everything." I took one last look at the empty runway before ducking inside the plane.

Our corporate jet wasn't a luxury liner, but it was decidedly spacious after the tight living space on the Sinaltan transport. One side of the plane held four sets of double seats and two tables, arranged so two chair sets faced one another around each table. On the other side of the aisle were two single-facing seats with a smaller table. A narrow bar with a refrigerator and microwave took up the remaining space behind the single seats, with storage space for food supplies. Beyond the two bathrooms, another section at the rear of the plane had three triple sets of bunks on one side, for a total of nine bunks, and a storage area opposite. The bunks featured metal grates to lock in prisoners we might need to transport to our Mexican prison compound. Perfect for our current needs.

Following me inside the plane, Chris grabbed my arm and pulled me into the cockpit.

"One thing before we go," he said. "I'm wondering if you'll do something for me. Well, really for Stella. But I don't want you to tell her."

Dread knotted in my stomach. I knew my brother loved Stella with a passion that maybe he hadn't felt even for his first wife, and I sometimes worried that he was on the rebound after her recent death. I also knew that part of his fascination with Stella was because she not only exuded Unbounded confidence, but she had over two centuries of experience that made her interesting. Not to mention the fact that her nanites basically enhanced her already considerable beauty. I wasn't sure if Stella loved Chris back or if she simply loved the idea of family that a widower with two children offered, a man willing to father the child she craved. Just because I'd decided to stay out of it and support them didn't mean I had stopped worrying.

"What do you want me to do?"

A shout interrupted any reply, and Blaze appeared in the cockpit doorway. "We've got company. Avowed, most likely. Only one SUV, but they have assault rifles. Calum and the others can hold them off if we get into the air now."

Shots resounded outside as Chris pushed the plane into motion. I fell into the co-pilot's seat and strapped in, my body pressing against the chair as we leapt forward. Blaze braced himself in the doorway. Moments ticked by, moments that I feared we might be hit and burst into flame. Then we were in the air, circling the area, watching as the SUV retreated under fire.

"They don't seem to be interested in staying to fight now that we're gone," Blaze said.

"No, but how were they able to track us, and if they can track us, why didn't they attack the school earlier?"

"Must not have tracked us fast enough before we got inside the school's electric grid," Blaze said. "Or possibly, they researched the airstrip as a likely target."

I considered that and shook my head. "Something is still active inside Lacole. Maybe a backup. Or even inside Valerine and Graeme, something that activated when they left Sinalta. Even so, better warn Rose and Calum to be on the lookout for visitors."

"They know. But this means the Avowed can track us once we land."

"Nope." Chris flipped a switch and turned to look at us. "We're out of range, and there is no way they can beat us to San Diego. Even if there's a super strong transmitter somewhere, we'll be back at the Fortress before they can begin to locate us."

"Right." Blaze released the doorway. "And now we're warned." He gazed at me. "You want something to drink?"

"She'll be there in a bit," Chris said. "We need a moment."

Blaze arched a brow but didn't speak as he nodded and spun around, leaving me at my big brother's mercy.

I would almost rather fight a gun battle than let Chris say what I could already feel screaming from his surface thoughts. He'd never been good at blocking anything from me.

"Okay," I said, resigned. "What do you want?"

Chris held my gaze unflinchingly. "When the baby comes, I want you to tell me if he will be Unbounded."

Chapter 12

AFTER AN EIGHTEEN-HOUR FLIGHT THAT INCLUDED ONE STOP FOR
fuel, we arrived in San Diego on Sunday afternoon at five,
which, since we'd gained nineteen hours when we crossed the
international date line, made it appear as if we'd arrived an
hour before we left New Zealand. I didn't think about it too
much, except to note that we were back on or near the same
time zone as the boat near Sinalta, which explained why I
hadn't been able to sleep for most of the day.

I was missing Ritter, worrying about Jace and Dimitri,
and furious that Lacole still hadn't returned to life. After a
long rest in a bunk, Oliver seemed to be walking better now,
but he wasn't his normally offensive self, which even Chris
commented on. He'd never really liked the guy, though, and I
suspected it was partly because Oliver was Unbounded while
Chris was not.

Since we'd taken control of the Emporium and ousted
Stefan, we no longer used the secret tunnels to get into the
Fortress. Marco, a mortal and a former black ops employee,
drove us right up to the very tall and armed main gates, where

Charles, also former black ops, let us in. The grounds took up an entire block, and the house itself was a veritable mansion with three stories, a concrete basement, and enclosed courtyard. An electronic grid ran over the house and even the courtyard, where a pool and every imaginable piece of playground equipment entertained Chris's two children, who were privately tutored at the Fortress.

It felt good and safe, but we really hadn't spent more than a few months here in the nearly seven months since we'd renovated it, so I still felt a little like I was in someone else's house. But when we used the keypad to come through the door from the garage, Max, our dog, came skidding along the hallway floors, barking with unconcealed glee. The Collie-Chow mix had long golden hair and a beautiful face without the sharpness of a full-bred Collie. Jace had found Max sick and abandoned on the side of the road years earlier when we'd lived with our parents, and now we were stuck with him. He wasn't much of a guard dog, and he couldn't even fetch, but he loved us all with a single-minded devotion, especially me, though I wasn't all that fond of dogs. Only Chris's kids, Spencer and Kathy, who were in charge of his feedings, were higher in his blind devotions.

"Hey, there." I bent to give him a good scratch. I'd made it a point to heap as much love on him as possible since the time he saved my life. My devotion was a little too late, but he never held it against me.

Stella and an elderly Asian woman I didn't know came from the main hallway, either from the kitchen or the conference room, and I straightened in surprise at the sight of Stella. I hadn't seen my sister-in-law for over a month, except online where I'd only seen her face, and her stomach had grown significantly. In fact, her once-slender figure looked stretched as far as it could possibly go. No wonder Chris was anxious.

Chris greeted his wife with a quick kiss before I hugged her.

"So good to see you in person," I murmured. "It's been too long." She was my first friend after my Change, and though Mari and I had become closer over the past few months, I missed Stella.

She was as beautiful as always, with her heart-shaped face and straight, very black hair reaching past her shoulders. Even while pregnant, her figure was striking. I was barely fitting into her armor these days, and I doubted I'd look as attractive when I was ready to deliver.

"Yes, it's been far too long." Stella bumped her fist into Blaze's and then hugged Oliver, her third great-nephew. "You too." She kissed his cheeks. "Mari tells me you two cousins have been spending time together in NY. I'll be glad when they no longer need you and you are both home again."

I snorted. "Mari's in love with Keene, so that might never happen."

Stella's smile was placid. "Oh, he'll follow her. It's not like she can't shift him to work every day, right? It's Oliver who will be hard to convince. He loves New York, don't you, nephew?"

He nodded and smiled. "Yes, I do."

"Oh, but where are my manners." Stella motioned now to the Asian woman with her long graying hair swept up in an elegant twist. "I'd like you to meet Hoshiko Kita. She's a healer, so she'll be able to care for our Avowed guests." She gestured to the two rolling tables Blaze and Graeme were pushing through the door from the garage.

"That's fantastic," I said to Hoshiko. "We really need them to wake. Thanks for coming. I know you've probably journeyed as far as we have to get here, but I hope you're rested enough to look at them as soon as we get them to the infirmary."

"Oh, I'm quite rested," Hoshiko said in perfect British English. "I flew in from Japan two weeks ago."

"Hoshiko is here to deliver my baby in Dimtri's absence,"

Stella explained. "She's my fifth great-grandmother, and also Oliver and Mari's, three and five times removed, or something of that nature. She's our oldest living relative."

Hoshiko laughed. "I am practically Stella's *only* older relative. At least in Japan. I couldn't stop her grandmother from marrying into an Italian family and moving far from me, but they did honor me in their way by giving Stella part of my name, even if translated to another language."

"Well, then it's really nice to meet you." I extended my fist to touch hers. I estimated her to be sixty in human years, which meant that she was roughly fifteen hundred years old.

She opened her hand, however, for a real handshake. "None of that new nonsense for me," she said. "A handshake is still a better measure of a person." She grinned. "Besides, how else can you tell if they're holding a weapon?"

"Good point." I took her tiny hand in mine. Her grip was strong, her skin dry.

"The life force you carry is strong and healthy. I will do a full exam later, if you wish."

"I'd be grateful, actually." I trusted her without knowing why.

I took a few moments to introduce Blaze, Oliver, and Graeme. Stella warmly shook Graeme's hand. "I've heard so much about you from Anina. I feel I know you and your wife."

He bowed over her hand. "We are deeply indebted to you for caring for our daughter."

"It has been our complete pleasure," Stella responded graciously.

"Where are the children anyway?" I asked.

"Playing in the courtyard. Their nanny needed a rest, so I sent her upstairs." She laughed. "They bug her incessantly since school got out for the summer. We thought we were only keeping her on because of the baby, but she's been a godsend.

Anyway, Marco will be checking on them now, not that they can get into anything dangerous out there with the pool cover closed. We'll call them in to see you after we take these ladies upstairs." She leaned against my brother. "Chris and I feel it might be best for Anina not to see her mother until she at least has a heartbeat."

"I agree," Graeme said. "I admit that I've been worrying about her reaction. She's been through enough."

"It will be all right." Hoshiko put a tiny hand on his arm, and I could feel the tension leaving him. "Let's get them into the elevator."

Blaze was already punching the button down the hall, where he'd rolled Lacole's table, and Chris jumped forward to help Graeme with Valerine.

Hoshiko started to pass Oliver but paused. "You are in great pain," she said, reaching out to him. "I can help you."

He stepped back before she could touch him. We all stared, and he sputtered, "I'm really all right. Please save your energy for Valerine and that other one. I just need to rest."

"He was wounded during the confrontation with the Avowed," I said. "We've been giving him curequick." It was exactly like annoying Oliver not to heal properly so he could direct all the attention to himself, but I suspected he didn't want to look weak in front of Stella. Like most men, he was a little enamored of her. Though she might be centuries old and a relative, physically she was near his own age.

Hoshiko nodded. "He'll be all right." To Oliver she added, "A good painkiller would help you sleep until you're healed."

"Would you like to go to your room?" Stella asked him.

"Um, no. I'll help first." He started quickly toward the table holding Lacole, wincing as his hand hit the table.

Chris met my gaze, his eyebrows raising. I shrugged with a "Don't ask me" twist of my hands.

The infirmary was on the second floor, where Oliver, Dimitri, Keene, Marco, George, and our cook also had suites. The large infirmary space was divided into sections, one of which was basically a glass prison. Blaze deposited Lacole there and secured the door before joining us at Valerine's bedside.

Hoshiko unzipped the body bag and straightened Valerine's head, clearing away gel that had covered her mouth during the ride from the airport. Then she moved down her body, slowly, pausing at her middle. "She saw a healer in—where was it you found her?—New Zealand?"

"No," I said. "One of the Renegades there stitched her up, though. He did a pretty good job."

"It's not that. Her arteries and veins are all lined up and knitting well. It looks like she was helped along."

"I tried a little with her," I said. "Dimitri taught me some."

"He's the best. But I didn't realize you were also a healer."

The room was utterly silent. "I'm not."

"Show me what you did."

"You will have to drop your shield then." The barrier over her mind was as strong as any I'd seen. Maybe stronger. A whirling dark gray that seemed impenetrable.

She gave a slight nod, and the gray disappeared.

Okay, I said in her mind. *I traced her veins, following them like thoughts, and then I sort of adjusted them on the outside with my hands.* I sent the images to her mind, and she observed impassively as I tweaked a few minor veins and a ligament that probably didn't need any help and was too deep for my physical touch to do anything anyway.

After a few moments, she said, "Hmm."

What does that mean? I could see her thoughts streaming past me as she considered numerous possibilities—none of which stayed long enough for me to glimpse their full meaning.

I will need to think on it. And perhaps call a few of my oldest friends.

A loud *thump!* on the closed infirmary door startled all of us. My thoughts flew to the life forces there. Three children and a dog. "Looks like the kids are impatient," I said.

"Go." Hoshiko waved a hand. "I will work better in private."

"Call me before you go into the room with the other one," Blaze said. "She's dangerous."

"I'd like to be there too," I added.

Nodding, Hoshiko lifted her eyes to where Lacole lay beyond the glass like a princess in a fairy tale. "She was poisoned. I determined that on the way up the elevator. A very high dose that completely destroyed her liver and kidneys. I can clean it out and give her a counteragent, but Valerine will awake sooner, so I will focus my attention here first."

Because we were still connected, I knew that Anina was her real reason for focusing on Valerine. She'd grown fond of the child during her stay. "They also need to be checked for transmitters. Graeme too. The electronic grids here will prevent broadcasting, but at some point they'll need to leave."

"How soon will they be conscious?" Oliver asked.

"Or at least breathing?" I didn't need them conscious to examine memory bubbles.

"By tomorrow for both of them. In fact . . ." She went to a cupboard and took a vial, filling a syringe and handing it to Blaze. "If you'll give our guest this counteragent . . . I will get to work." Then she selected another vial and gave a syringe to Oliver. "Take at least four millimeters if you want to sleep."

Oliver nodded his thanks. Blaze took his syringe to Lacole while Stella, Chris, Oliver, and I headed toward the door. Graeme kissed his wife and came after us. As we opened the door and stepped into the hallway, a ball slammed into the edge of the door, disappearing inside.

"Balls in the house?" Chris said, scowling at the kids. "Really? With all the space outside and the workout and play-rooms in the basement, you brought it up here? You know the rules."

"It just got away from me!" protested eleven-year-old Spencer, his round, freckled face serious.

"Not true," said Kathy. "He hit the ball on the door because he wanted you to know we were out here." With her latest growth spurt, Kathy was more than a head taller than her brother, though only two years separated them.

"I didn't mean—" Spencer began. But both kids fell silent as nine-year-old Anina spied her father coming through the door behind us and hurled herself into his arms, sobbing.

He held her tightly, murmuring in Sinaltan. She answered, her words coming fast and low.

"Why don't I show you to some guest quarters?" Stella said to Graeme after several awkward moments. "We have some on this floor. Over this way." She motioned along the hall. "Later, Anina can give you the grand tour."

"Thank you," Graeme murmured.

Anina asked a soft question that radiated so clearly in her unblocked mind that I picked it up: "Where's my mother?" He spoke to her soothingly as they followed Stella down the hall.

"Now, about that ball," Chris said to his children.

"Forget the ball," I broke in. "Come give your favorite aunt a hug. I've missed you guys." I hugged them so tightly they were probably gouged by the weapon bulges in my body armor, though they didn't complain. "I swear you've grown a foot, Kathy. You'll have to eat more so you'll fill in."

"Dad says she eats like a horse," Spencer informed me. "So do I. But I'm not growing much. Stella said boys who get their height later grow taller, and she knows everything on the internet, so I'm glad I'm not growing yet."

"I'm sure you'll be as tall as your dad." His mother had also been tall, but I didn't bring that up. Some days, her loss eleven months ago was still too fresh on their minds. Stella's attention and this amazing house had helped them immensely.

"I'm going to shower now," I added. "And get this thing off." I tapped my body armor. "It's starting to feel like a straitjacket."

Spencer turned to Oliver, who had squatted down and was petting Max. "Will you show us some illusions?" he asked. "Please? I really like the elephant ones you did last time. And the lions. Those were amazing!"

"Oliver needs rest," Chris said.

"How about later?" Oliver held up his hands. "Help me up and walk me to my room. You can tell me which animals you want so I can look them up for later."

The kids each grabbed one of his hands and pulled him off in the direction Stella had vanished. Max whined, but he didn't follow, choosing instead to rub his body along my leg.

"Whew!" Chris said. "They have so much energy that we've decided to do year-round school starting next week, even though both children are already a year ahead. At this rate they'll finish college by eighteen."

"That's a good thing." I started toward the elevator, the squeaking of my boots on the glossy floor sounding louder now that we were alone.

"I kind of like the change in Oliver," Chris said as the elevator doors opened. "Looks like he overcame his fear of dog hair and germs."

"Max has a way of growing on people. I'm a case in point."

"Touché."

I followed him inside. "I think it's a woman. Mari hinted around about him dating someone in New York."

"No wonder he refused to come home." Chris waited until the elevator doors were closed to say, "So about the baby."

This time I was prepared. "Look, don't you think you should talk to Stella about this? I mean, she won't even look at the ultrasound because she doesn't want to know if it's a boy or a girl. And I know you think it won't change the way you look at this child, but it will." I thought of Rose and her brood. "Before we knew about Unbounded, one lifespan was enough, wasn't it? You're going to love this child regardless, so why borrow trouble?"

"Will you look at your own child?"

"I don't think so."

"But you don't know." The elevator opened, and we stepped out into the hallway.

"Ritter and I made the decision not to, but if we change our minds, it's something we should do together."

"Yeah, it's just Stella's been through so much. I thought if I found out and the answer was yes, then I could tell her, and she wouldn't have to worry."

I had no doubt that knowing her child would outlive her would make Stella happy. "And if it's no?"

"Then she'll have time to prepare."

"And it might also be a barrier to her loving that child fully. She'll already be gearing up to say goodbye."

"Of course she'll love our son." His voice was harder now, insistent.

But I knew that it made a difference, because as much as I loved Kathy and Spencer, a part of me died whenever I thought about losing them, and Chris too. The relationship I had with them was far different than the one I shared with Jace. Yet on the other hand, I didn't feel that agony with my parents, so maybe there was wisdom in what Rose had shared with me. Maybe when it was time to say goodbye, it would be all right.

I started walking. "What about having six or a dozen children? Stella has a massive amount of money in the bank, and

I know you're paid ten times what a normal pilot makes. It's not like you can't afford it. You can hire help, and Stella can do what she's been wanting to do for centuries and spend a few decades raising babies. You can love all of them, knowing that at least some will Change."

"So you won't do it." He cast me a black stare.

"I'm not saying that. Just think about it."

"Okay." He stopped outside my suite door. "But you think about it too. Please?"

"I will. But remember, even if I can manage to figure out how to do it, I can't do it on my own, so that means letting a healer help."

"Dimitri will be back soon," he said. "Or there's Hoshiko."

"No, it has to be Dimitri." I'd altered the DNA of an Avowed baby with Mikyn, or at least he'd claimed it was me, and that meant there was a possibility I might accidentally change the baby at the DNA level without meaning to. Because Dimitri was aware of the secret, he could help me avoid doing something that might ultimately take years away from Chris's son.

I sighed with relief when I shut the door on Chris. In the shower, I stood under the deliciously warm water, not even missing the days when I could relax in near scalding water without becoming dizzy or nauseated. It simply felt good to be free of the armor and the worry.

We are safe here, I told my daughter.

My stomach had grown enough in the past weeks that I'd have to ask Stella about new body armor. I looked a lot larger than three months along.

Ritter had texted for me to call when we'd reached the Fortress, so I dropped to the comfortable couch in front of my large flat screen, bringing my knees up to curl my body around our baby. Since the electric grid was active over the house, all signals from phones, computers, or communication monitors went through secured internet connections impervious to back-tracing by technopaths, no matter how skilled. Ritter's face appeared before I'd plumped a pillow between my knees.

"Hey," he said, his eyes lingering over my body in my thin nightshirt.

"Hey."

"How are you and baby?" The pride in his voice almost hurt.

I pulled the nightshirt tight over my belly. "One of us seems to be growing."

"I was just thinking that." But his eyes were on my breasts, not my stomach.

"I bet." I laughed. "Did you know Stella's fifth great-grandmother is a healer?" He did, but I updated him about Valerine and the Avowed prisoner. He had news too.

"Jace met again with your father on the beach. He found out something interesting, though perhaps not really important, but we want you to run it past Graeme. Here, I'll let you talk to Jace directly." He left the screen for a few moments and returned with Jace.

"Okay, it might not be much," Jace said, "but yesterday Stefan made a comment about having people placed inside Mikyn's organization. I told him there was no way because Mikyn was sensing and would know, and he said his people didn't appear to be soldiers, and Mikyn would never know. Then today when we met, we talked about the embryos they'd kidnapped." Jace paused and frowned. "I wanted him to admit what a monster he was for helping them, for trading those kids for money. He said some prices had to be paid for long-term plans, and that he'd lost just as many of his progeny in the beginning as they'd taken from anyone else, or even more. When I asked him why he'd allow that, he clammed right up and wouldn't say anything more. Here's the thing, Erin, I think he's telling the truth, but why would he send his own offspring to Sinalta, especially when he was thinking it might become necessary to blow it up?"

I swung my feet down from the couch. "I don't know, but I hope you can see what's really important to him. He'll use anyone."

"Me, you mean." A look of pain crossed his face.

I wanted to remind him that he had a father who loved him, but I knew it wouldn't make a difference, not now. He was beginning to see for himself that Stefan only cared about his power and control. His heart would need to be broken before it would heal.

Ritter spoke into the silence. "Maybe ask Graeme what it might mean."

"Okay, I'll also have Stella research the records of all the embryos who are now members of the Sinaltan families. We might be able to see if Stefan is telling the truth and where those people are now. But you should know that one of the Avowed who kidnapped Valerine was gifted with combat, and he looked a lot like Stefan. Like you, Jace. He could block his life force completely, so he had good training. I couldn't tell his age."

We all stared at each other for a few moments. "What now?" I asked.

"We're coming back," Ritter said. "Mari can't come for us, but we've chartered a flight and will be there tomorrow. Stefan's made it very clear that he's done negotiating. He wants proof now that we'll help reinstate Tsaoussis and Scala before he'll officially step down from the Triad."

"We won't need him after Keene's voted in tomorrow."

Ritter's face was grim. "*If* he's voted in."

"What aren't you telling me?" I asked, my gaze moving between their two faces. "Has something changed?"

It was Jace who answered. "Just that Stefan believes he has more people still loyal to him and his ideals than he'll need, including Tihalt's actual contracted successor, who currently lives in China doing questionable research in a lab. He's on his way now to New York to join Stefan against Keene's appointment."

"If he'd stayed in China, I wouldn't be nearly as concerned," Ritter added.

"This is Tsaoussis and Scala's fault for freeing Stefan," I growled. "I'm guessing Stefan will withdraw the support and order the successor to stand down if we help him."

Jace nodded. "Exactly."

"Even if Stefan doesn't succeed," Ritter said, "this could delay the vote for days or a week or more. That's the best-case scenario. Worse is that he'll start another war between the remaining loyal Emporium agents and the Renegades."

My heartbeat thundered in my chest. "It'll be a blood bath for both sides."

Ritter nodded. "Right, and in the end, I'm not sure we'd win."

Chapter 13

I'D BEEN SLEEPING ONLY FIVE HOURS WHEN THERE WAS A KNOCK ON the door. I was on my feet instantly, alert and reaching for my weapons before remembering where I was. With the guns mounted on the house and in the trees, we could withstand a major military assault, but I'd been out in the field until recently, and that created a new level of awareness, even without direct combat. My heartbeat steadied, and I mentally checked the baby, sleeping soundly in her blissful innocence.

I knew without asking that it was Hoshiko at the door, and I didn't bother with my robe before answering the door. "Yes?" There might be a little too much eagerness in my voice.

The old lady smiled, the skin at the corners of her eyes crinkling. "Valerine's heart is about to start up again."

"I'll put on some clothes."

"Not yet. After the blood begins to flow properly, it'll take a while before her brain clears. Meanwhile, I want to make sure you're okay. May I?" She indicated my stomach.

"Please."

She motioned to the bed, and I lay down, leaving room for

her to sit on the edge. She placed her hands over my stomach, and after a few moments began smiling. "She's doing very well. Her brain pathways are particularly developed. Have you been communicating with her?"

"Well, yeah, in a way. I mean, she doesn't answer back. But lately, I've been feeling emotions from her. Is that normal? I'm only three months along."

Hoshiko smiled. "I've never taken care of a sensing mother before, but gestationally, she's on par with other Unbounded mothers, maybe even a little more advanced. Compared to a mortal pregnancy, you're already past the fourth month stage. If you continue at this rate, we'll have a healthy baby here within four months."

I sighed with relief. "That's good. I've been really nauseated."

"That will probably end any day now."

"Good." I sat up and started for my closet. "We should go to the infirmary."

"Don't you want to talk about what you did for Valerine?"

I frowned and sat back on the bed beside her. "What do you think it means?"

"I talked with a few friends last night as I sat with Valerine. I believe it means that you have learned how to heal, or at least partly."

"But that's not my gift."

"Maybe, maybe not. Perhaps the old legends are true about some gifts overlapping. Or . . . Dimitri is your father. You might be strong in sensing, but you also have his ability in your DNA. Who knows how much of our gifts are actual learning versus innate skill?"

Shock reverberated through me. This was the last thing I wanted to hear because it meant I was like Mikyn. And not only me, but perhaps every sensing Unbounded or Avowed who also had a healer for a parent. The Avowed had no more healers—Mikyn's father had been the last—so they weren't in danger of creating more seers, but we had at least two dozen among Emporium employees, including those in Russia who were descendants of the former Triad leader Delia Vesey. How many of them had parents gifted in healing? If they knew what they might be capable of, how would the knowledge alter our society?

"Why is that a concern to you?" Hoshiko asked.

Her words brought me back to the present. If she hadn't made the connection, I wasn't going to help her out, but once the reason for Mikyn's ability to foretell a child's Change was more widely known, it wouldn't be long until others began exploring the possibility of being doubly gifted. For instance, Jace came down from Ava's lineage exactly like I had. If he tried, could he start sensing even a little?

"The legends," I said. "Were they always with sensing Unbounded?"

Still sitting on my bed, Hoshiko tilted her head and considered awhile. "The ones I'm familiar with were sensing, but you make a good point. We definitely need to research. It might not be limited to one of the gifts. Even if it is, we know there is a wide disparity inside each ability. I have healers come to study with me who will never understand the human body even as well as you demonstrated last night."

"And what would you say if someone had three abilities?"

Hoshiko stood and faced me. "Do you have a third ability?"

I'd fought like a combat Unbounded in the hotel back in New Zealand—I was sure of it. But had it come from me?

Abruptly, I spun from her and began moving through my taekwondo forms with all the additions and flourishes that Ritter demanded in our daily morning training. Gradually, I increased my speed. *Faster. Faster.* I told myself, dancing across my bedroom and into the adjoining living room and over to the kitchenette, pushing hard. My movements were sure and correct and strong, but my edges didn't blur, and my endurance waned long before my mind was ready to give in.

I stopped moving and turned back to Hoshiko, who stood with a knife in her hands and was backing toward the door. "Do I need to be worried?" she asked, looking exactly like any sweet mortal Japanese grandmother.

"No. Sorry." My chest heaved as I struggled for the breath that never eluded me when I was channeling Jace or Ritter. "But I definitely don't have three abilities, and probably not even two. At least not at the moment."

She smiled and opened the door. "Very well. Glad that is settled. I'll meet you down in the infirmary after you change."

Feeling a little foolish, I watched the door close behind her. Inside, the baby moved, and I put my hand on my stomach. *Sorry for waking you,* I told her. *Just a little exercise.*

"I FOUND ONLY INACTIVE TRACKERS IN BOTH GRAEME AND VALERINE," Hoshiko explained after I joined her a short time later in the infirmary. "The nanites keeping Valerine's inside her body lost power after her death, and during the repairs, her body pushed it out into the curequick."

Graeme looked up from the recliner next to where Valerine lay inside her bag, where he'd obviously been all night. "She deactivated our broadcast signals when we decided to help Erin back in Sinalta. But we didn't have access to turn off the nanites keeping them in. She'll be glad to know it's gone."

"I can remove yours if you'd like," Hoshiko said. "Lacole's was only blocked, but I removed it permanently."

"So how did they find us on the runway in Christchurch?" I wondered aloud, resting my hand on the machete I wore hanging from a strap over my shoulder since it no longer hung properly at my waist. I'd brought it in anticipation of Lacole's interrogation later. The physical talisman was even better than the mental image I used to break through mental barriers, and once Lacole was awake, I might need a little extra push.

Hoshiko's eyes followed my hand. "Possibly an emergency beacon that activated at Lacole's death. Without movement and recharging, her body would have eventually ejected it, perhaps in the plane or in the car on your way here. Blaze is following up on that now. But there's one more thing you should know about Lacole."

Since I was obviously making her nervous, I removed my hand from the machete. "What?"

"She was pregnant. Only a month along. I preserved some DNA, in case we need it, but the baby, of course, died shortly after she did. Her body will either absorb the tissue in the regeneration or expel it in a miscarriage. So whoever did this to her killed the baby as well."

My thoughts snapped back to the hotel room where Lacole had said how easy it was to block the womb when you knew how. She'd clearly hidden her pregnancy from me. "Then she wouldn't reset herself, would she? Not after connecting with the life inside her. The Avowed revere embryos—at least until it's proven that they won't Change."

My question was directed toward Graeme, but it was Hoshiko who answered. "We can only ask when she's awake, but from what I've learned, it seems their worship of life doesn't go very far." I had to agree.

"How much longer?" Graeme asked Hoshiko, reaching into the unzipped bag to rub a thumb over the back of his wife's hand.

"Any time now for her heart to start beating. But she won't regain consciousness until later."

I reached out my thoughts and could see the difference in Valerine. The representation of her unconscious mind was filling fast with water, and the memory bubbles were drinking it in. I could see shadows of thoughts.

"Graeme," I said. "Do you know of any reason why it would be beneficial for Stefan Carrington to have sent dozens of his descendants to Sinalta? I messaged Stella about it, and she says our records indicate that a large number of his children and grandchildren and so forth were transported to Sinalta in the early years after the Senate's agreement with him. The children came from both privately and publicly funded foster care situations. A few of those who looked like teens were already Unbounded because they were involved in experiments that forced an early Change. Meaning they still looked like teenagers, but they age at five times the rate of those whose Change was naturally occurring."

Graeme's face twisted in thought. "I wasn't involved the first few years, and then I was only on the boat after the children and supplies had been gathered."

"I understand that. But what would be the advantage for Stefan? Obviously, the children Mikyn deemed wouldn't Change went to the mines or other work situations. But for those who would Change, or who had Changed early before being taken there, where would they go and why would Stefan want them there?"

Graeme shook his head, still smoothing his wife's hand, seemingly oblivious to the gel covering his own skin. "I can't think of any reason he'd send his own descendants, except if they were causing issues." He made a face. "I mean, if he had dozens to send in the proper age range, it's obvious he wasn't in any kind of a committed relationship, and the children didn't mean anything personally to him."

"He was building an army for his war against the Renegades

up here," I conceded. "But he had to have a reason to send his children to Sinalta, especially if he planned to blow it up if things didn't go his way."

"Maybe they were sleeper agents," Hoshiko said from the head of Valerine's table, where she gently stroked her temples.

I shook my head. "Most of these Stefan would have never met, with the exception of the ones forced to Change early. They would know him, of course. But Mikyn would have been able to sense if they were programmed for destruction." Another thought came to me. "Who actually assigned the embryos to their new Sinaltan families once it was verified that they would Change? Tsaousiss?"

"Statesman Tsaousiss was in charge of the goods we traded. It was Statesman Scala's team that placed the children. Then once the embryos give birth to widen the gene pool, they are free at that point to leave the family for another or be adopted into it themselves."

"So Mikyn and the other two ruling families were at Tsaousiss and Scala's mercy for new genes?"

"Mikyn was hardly at anyone's mercy," Graeme said, bitterness filling his voice. "Each of the families got the same number of embryos to be distributed as they saw fit, but no one can add to their family without the great seer signing off on their future Change. If Mikyn had any preference, he was always given first choice. I know for sure that he took all of those with sensing progenitors because he didn't want any other family to share that gift. Tsaousiss was the same way with hypnopathy. He likes controlling people."

"Tsaousiss just didn't realize that Mikyn can break into people's minds and control the controllers. But that still doesn't tell us what Stefan gained by sending his descendants there."

Hoshiko's hands stopped moving on Valerine's temples. "Maybe you are asking the wrong question. How is leadership determined in Sinalta? Is it limited only to the current ruling families?"

Graeme released his wife's hand and stared at the old woman. "Statesmen are always chosen from the five families. Always. Most people can trace their heritage to one of them, to be sure, but not all. To rule, there must be a blood link or adoption. The families are large enough that it doesn't feel like exclusion, but of course to be voted in, you need more money than everyone else, just like in your own countries. That alone makes it impossible for anyone else to challenge the law."

The bits of information were beginning to make sense, though they were still like interchangeable puzzle pieces I had to fit into place, each interlocking but creating a distorted picture. "If Stefan's descendants were adopted into the families and had children with them, could he also make a claim to belong?"

Graeme leaned back in his recliner, a line of worry creasing his brow. "It doesn't work in reverse. I mean, yes, the children adopted or marrying into the family and their offspring are eligible with the right backing, but not their birth parents."

"Are you sure?" I held his gaze until he shook his head.

"I guess I'm not. But I don't think reverse inheritance has ever been considered."

"So maybe the law doesn't prevent it." I paced a few steps before rounding and coming back to the bed. "I know that Tsaousiss and Scala have no plans to include Stefan in any meaningful decisions once they regain their support in Sinalta, but maybe they won't be able to stop him."

"None of them will be able to return while Mikyn is in charge. Tsaousiss and Scala are on Sinalta's most wanted list." Graeme's hands fisted on his lap. "With Valerine and I being first on that list, of course," he added. "I only hope Stefan's plan somehow includes getting rid of all the ruling families."

Hoshiko emitted a delicate snort. "You still believe Stefan will be easier to get rid of than Mikyn."

"I know," I said. "Hard to believe."

"Mikyn's a murderer," Graeme shot.

"So is Stefan. Look, we need a copy of your laws because we may be way off base here. And I can't just go onto the internet and download them."

"Valerine will know where to find them, but I still don't see how it's relevant. Each family has thousands of influential members, and a lot of uninfluential ones. And they each have hundreds or even a thousand years of experience. A few of Stefan's comparably young offspring added to any of the families isn't going to faze them."

"Right," I told him. "But we have to look into it because it's unusual."

"Stella might already have access to the information," Hoshiko said.

I looked at Valerine and then at the door, debating which might be the most pressing task. I was saved from making a decision when Chris appeared in the doorway, his blond hair on end and a bright grin on a face that looked as if he'd recently been shaken awake.

"Stella's water just broke," he said. "I think we're having a baby!"

Chapter 14

WITH STELLA'S PREVIOUS PREGNANCY, THE ONE SHE'D LOST IN A battle with Emporium agents, she had researched birthing methods and had decided on a water birth. One of the recovery rooms next to the infirmary had been equipped with a large round tub, a king-sized bed, and every other conceivable piece of equipment that might be needed in a birth. Not that she would need anything but the tub. Unbounded couldn't die in childbirth. They never hemorrhaged or had other issues that sometimes made birth dangerous to mortal women. Only the baby was at risk, and with a healer present, that was negligible. Or two healers, rather, since even if I wasn't exactly a skilled healer, I could channel Hoshiko if needed and follow her guidance.

The pain, however, was another issue. The amount of sedative necessary to eliminate pain in Unbounded was often high enough to be a concern to the baby, and the body would fight it all the way. So the best that could be done was to take the edge off. For most Unbounded, that was good enough because a high tolerance to pain was customary. For others, it meant hours of torture.

For Stella, it ended up being four hours of moderate labor in the round pool with Chris and Hoshiko while Kathy and Spencer and I checked on them every thirty minutes. Kathy and I were also there at the end as the infant boy emerged from Stella's body and was guided by his sixth great-grandma into his mother's arms. The entire time, I talked to him mentally, letting him know that he was okay, and connected Stella to his mind as well. By the time he was nursing at her breast, we were all in tears.

"Yes!" Spencer pumped his arm when he was allowed inside after the little family had transferred to a large bed in the room. "I finally have a brother."

"He's perfect," Kathy agreed from her seat on the bed next to Stella. "Absolutely perfect."

I grabbed my machete from a chair, pulled the strap over my shoulder, and thumbed at the door. "I'm going to leave you guys alone now. Call me if you need me."

"Thanks for watching the kids," Chris said. He really meant for being with Kathy during the birth, making sure she was looked after and not frightened so that she could be included. And she had been. Watching them all together in the big bed, I knew that in a very real way the new baby had cemented this family as Chris and Stella's marriage hadn't.

In the hallway after a few deep breaths, I called Ava to let her know about the birth. "I'm sorry I missed it," she said.

"Any news on Dimitri?"

"No. Mikyn is being very coy. I gave him an ultimatum that if he doesn't produce Dimitri, we won't bring Keene back, ever, which will add months if not a year to their journey. Still nothing. And the White House is getting anxious communications from South Africa, Madagascar, and Australia about the Sinaltans. Russia and China have both reached out to Mikyn and have offered them sanctuary, which you know the US absolutely won't allow as long as Sinaltan technology is so far ahead."

"Well, I'm about to see what I can find out from Valerine's memories. Graeme let us know that her heartbeat is back."

"Are you sure it wouldn't be better to wait until she wakes? Otherwise, you'll need to be careful not to accidentally extract a memory we'll end up needing."

"I won't pop any memory bubbles." I started walking toward the infirmary. My own gift was one I felt a lot of confidence in using, at least in that way.

"Put me on the screen when you're with Valerine. I'd like to be there."

"Okay."

"Also, how's Oliver?"

"Still holed up in his room, licking his wounds."

"I wondered why I haven't heard from him. With the debate going on for Keene's position in the Triad, I'd thought he'd request to be there."

"I think he doesn't want us to know how badly he was wounded, because he was the only one of us who was. I'm sure he'll be his annoying self again soon." I hesitated before adding, "He made a good addition to the op."

Ava laughed. "That's what Blaze says. As soon as I can, I'll tell Oliver I'm happy with his work."

"That will mean a lot. I'm going in to see Valerine now. I'll connect in a few." I pocketed my phone and pushed inside the infirmary.

Graeme was there, but this time he wasn't alone. Anina jumped off his lap and came running to hug me. "Thank you! Thank you! For bringing them back. I was sure that they . . .

But look! My mother is still in that sticky gel stuff, but her heartbeat is on the monitor, and it's perfect. Dad says she'll be awake soon."

There was a slight question in her voice, so I said, "She definitely will."

"Wait, if you're here, that means there's a baby, right?"

"Sure is."

"That's amazing! I want a little brother too." Anina glanced back at her father, and he smiled.

"Let's get your mother well first," he said.

She rolled her eyes. "Well, you'd better do it before I get married and have my own baby. I'm only going to be a child for nine more years, you know. In California you're an adult when you reach eighteen. That's when you usually go away to college and have a lot of parties."

Graeme laughed. "Easy. Nine years is still quite a few."

I had a sudden itching to go inside Anina's head to see if too many of the bright pinpoints representing years of life had been snuffed out during Mikyn's testing of her. If so, she might not live longer than her two older mortal brothers had in the mines. Could we somehow reverse that in Anina and the mortals we had rescued from Sinalta? Only time would tell, and right now I had another job.

"I think you can go see the baby now," I told Anina, hoping that none of my thoughts reached my face. "Just go knock on the door."

Graeme and I watched her go, then he said, "Blaze searched everywhere, including on the plane. There's no transmitter that could have led them to the airstrip. Do you think someone in Christchurch could be compromised?"

"I doubt it." I frowned. "Maybe it was a tag on our clothing. We could have been shot with something during the battle. We'll have to check."

His face relaxed. "Of course. That's probably it." He shook his head. "I'm seeing enemies everywhere."

"That's natural after what you've been through. The important thing is that we're safe here." I pulled a large screen from the wall, secured by a thick metal arm, and swiveled it into position by Valerine. "Now if you don't mind, I'd like to see what information Valerine has for us."

"I'll help," he said.

"You know how to do it?"

"Yeah, I know. I may not have learned how to get through mental shields, but the unconscious mind is another story."

"About that." I unsheathed my machete and passed it to him. "This is my talisman. It was given to me in the Mexican jungle by a native, and it's rumored to have special mystical properties."

"Does it?"

I shrugged. "I don't know, but it helps me break through barriers that I ordinarily can't. I imagine holding it and slamming it into shields. Then I keep hacking to make a crack I can slip into. Works even better when I also physically hold it, but it isn't exactly easy to walk around with it on my hip. Or shoulder."

"I guess not, though I saw a lot of people walking around with swords on their backs on our drive here."

I rolled my eyes. "Believers. They like to pretend they're us."

"A strange form of worship in a world gone mad."

"Exactly. My point is that if you have something like this that makes you feel powerful, it can help you break through mental barriers. Even Mikyn's, though he might be on the lookout now that he knows I can get inside his shield. If you don't have anything, I can take you through our weapons locker to pick something out that might appeal to you."

He handed me back my talisman. "I'm not a fighter."

"We're all fighters. Besides, once Ritter's back, he'll insist on training you. Even I have to train every day, and I have a good excuse not to."

"That explains a lot."

"It's survival."

"I understand." His gaze dropped to his wife's pale face. "She said all along it would come to a civil war. I thought we could beat Mikyn without bloodshed, but after these past terrible weeks, I understand that may not be possible." His eyes lifted to mine again, the blue looking dark in the dim lighting. "There are many good people in Sinalta, but I don't believe there is any way to change the government without first destroying what is there and rebuilding the right way." He shuddered and glanced toward the closed door. "I don't envy whoever has to do it. I'm just glad Anina is away from there and that she won't have to live her life as a second-class citizen."

I grinned at him. "Me too."

Once Ava was on the screen, I stepped closer to the table and laid my hand on Valerine's arm inside the gel. Inside her head, I saw a changed world. Her unconscious mind was now a placid lake with water so blue it made my heart ache with its beauty. Not real, just a representation that made sense in some kind of strange way.

Together, Graeme and I dived inside the lake. The memory bubbles beneath the water were now plump and floating— sometimes even bounding—past us.

Unfortunately, there was no way of ordering the memories, or calling up certain ones, unlike the way I could use questions or suggestions to focus thought streams. *Just look for anything she might think is important,* I told Graeme. *Something Lacole didn't want her to pass on.*

I saw many memories of Anina as a baby. A glimpse of Mikyn telling Valerine that Anina, like her two brothers before her, was mortal made me want to cry out with her pain. I didn't see the days she learned of her boys' deaths in the mines, and I was glad.

What about this? Graeme asked.

He waved his hands to send a bubble in my direction, and I moved my metaphysical presence to follow its trajectory. *It's where she placed the explosives on one of the shield generators.*

Not at a junction where automatic rerouting was possible, I noted from her thoughts. And so perfectly disguised that only someone well versed in the shield tech could possibly identify the tampering. If these explosives had gone off under the water, the city would have certainly imploded.

You removed them, right? I asked Graeme. He'd said something to that effect to Lacole at the hotel.

Not me, but Valerine did during the week we were apart after your team left Sinalta. A few moments passed and then, *Unless she didn't remove it. If it's still in place, I'd say that's pretty important, but why wouldn't she tell me?*

Removing it is probably in another memory. But I thought it might be possible that Valerine hadn't removed the explosives and hadn't told him for his protection.

We continued to search, with me waving away anything earlier than six weeks prior. I was careful not to send anything flying too vigorously in case it caused some kind of chain reaction.

Then I saw a flicker of what might be a connection to the explosives, and I followed it, swimming up and over memory bubbles lying between me and my target. There. Inside the shimmering bubble, Valerine was talking to Mikyn on a screen. "I've given you the location of the explosives," she said. "Can't you call off the search? No one is in danger, and the city will be up soon. Graeme and I just want to leave and find our daughter."

"Soon," Mikyn said. "I'm working on it. Tell my great-grandson that I'm doing the best I can."

"Thank you." Valerine cut the link before it could be traced. She sighed and said to herself, "Too bad I don't trust you, old man."

Graeme, look at this. She gave up the location to Mikyn. So he must have deactivated the explosives. That can't be the information she had for us.

He studied the memories. *She told me she'd asked Mikyn to help us but not that she'd given up the location. I wanted her to, though. At the time, I thought that would appease everyone.*

I'm sorry it didn't.

I am too, but it doesn't matter because that other memory we saw of explosives was after this one, and it's not the same location.

Shock reverberated through me as I verified his statements. *So maybe there still are explosives.*

That makes sense. She always insisted that the explosives were our leverage. She didn't want to give them up.

Not even when you insisted.

He laughed. *No, and I'll be the first to admit that my wife is a whole waterway above me in intelligence.*

With an attitude like that, no wonder she was so much in love with him—I had witnessed that love for myself, both back in Sinalta and today in her memories. *Let's go tell Ava.*

You go. I'll keep looking. Because as far as secrets go, it doesn't seem all that urgent now that Sinalta is above water.

I left him and turned to Ava, who was still waiting on the screen, though she was sitting at a table now with a cup of steaming something in her hands. A glance at my phone told me two hours had passed.

"Well?" she asked, setting down the mug. "What did you learn?"

"Two things so far. Valerine showed Mikyn where she'd

placed the explosives on their electronic shields in an effort to clear her and Graeme of charges. Mikyn promised he would help."

"Interesting. He told us they hadn't been located."

"Well, the second thing is that Valerine set more on at least one other location. But I got the feeling she didn't tell anyone about it. Graeme said he'd pushed her to give up the explosives to Mikyn, but she was reluctant. Maybe that's when she placed more."

"Smart woman. They might come in handy, and the fact that Mikyn lied to us is important. Very important."

"I thought so too. But Graeme is still looking."

"What about the empath?"

I looked through the glass where monitors showed Lacole's heart beating now too. "I can check her memories now," I said. "It might be easier if I can find what she's hiding when she's out. Well, provided I can get in. Even unconscious, her shield is strong."

"You'll get in. But who knows what you'll find there. What's Ritter's ETA?"

"Two or three hours. Before noon, I hope. But we shouldn't wait."

Ava picked up her mug again. "Go ahead and have Blaze and Hoshiko help you with her, but only if she's unconscious. If she's awake, wait for Ritter, just in case. Because of the baby mostly. We don't know what else Mikyn might have up his sleeve or what this Avowed is capable of. I regret not being there with you, but I'm still trying to force Mikyn to turn over Dimitri, or to agree to a face-to-face meeting."

"All right." I glanced at Graeme, who wasn't paying attention to me but would hear me on some level, so I'd have to choose my words carefully. "There's something else I wanted to ask you. Something personal."

"Go ahead."

"Chris wants a foretelling to know if the baby will Change." Ava would understand that it was me Chris asked and not that he wanted Mikyn. Graeme wouldn't make that connection yet unless we told him.

Ava sighed. "And so it begins. Before long, people will want a lot more."

This time it was me who understood that she referred to changing a child's DNA. I shook my head. "We can't let it continue." I felt mentally ill as I spoke the words.

Ava's face was now as grim as I felt my own to be. "Agreed."

Mikyn had to die.

But would his death ultimately kill the knowledge of what he could do? Of what I or others like us could possibly do?

Sighing, I called the others. It was time to see what Lacole was hiding.

Chapter 15

THE ODD THING WAS THAT LACOLE'S ACTIVE BARRIER OVER HER unconscious mind was utterly gone, as if being reset had eliminated it and her unconscious mind hadn't replaced it automatically.

"Is that normal?" I asked Ava, now on the screen in the holding area. "I've never investigated any unconscious people directly after reset."

"Usually, there will be at least some mental barrier," Ava said, "even after reset, especially in stronger people. But if she used a hypnopath to help her put it in place, it's possible that influence was also reset. Those kinds of fixes don't usually last long and need to be continually strengthened."

"Good for us, then."

Lacole's unconscious mind, like Valerine's, was a placid lake, but when I tried to dive in, I hit on a silvery something that made me slide across the surface instead of sinking under the water.

"Ah, but she's got some kind of construct in here," I announced not only to Ava but also to Blaze and Hoshiko, who were in the room with me. I was connected to both of them mentally in case I encountered distress. "It doesn't seem very thick, though, so maybe it was also damaged during the reset."

"Can you get past it?" Blaze asked. I could feel a strange sort of heat emanating from his body as he stood alert, ready to incinerate Lacole should she attempt to harm me mentally.

"Maybe." I felt for my physical machete with my fingers, even as I drew my mental version of the weapon. "I'm going to give it a shove. Looks like it might not be covering the entire area."

The construct moved aside easily enough, and I sank into the liquid. Memory bubbles floated toward me. They were inconsequential, from years in the past, and I continued on until I found one more recent of Lacole kissing a man in the hotel room where I'd freed Valerine. I waved it aside, becoming aware of something pressing down on me: the constructs. Since all thoughts and memories were duplicated after a reset, not only in the brain but in the other two focus points of heart and reproductive system, memories were always retained in a regeneration, and I supposed that meant the permanent constructs Lacole had put in her own mind were reassembling as well.

In fact, they had reformed over the surface above my head, and even though it was all figurative, the sensation of enclosure made me feel claustrophobic. I shoved my machete upward to slow down the process and break up the surface above me.

The machete had no effect on the slivery substance except to make it more solid. *What?* I exclaimed silently.

"What is it?" Hoshiko asked.

I sent her the image of the substance, even as I began to hack at it. Vaguely, I was aware of her reporting to Ava.

"Get out of there!" Ava said.

My idea exactly. I was already moving toward an open space some distance away, jabbing the machete up to keep it open.

There, I was above the water, watching the roiling of the metal-like construct grow. No, it was moving upward, and the lake was gone. Sand stream thoughts ejected from somewhere above me. The next instant, I was pushed hard and found myself watching Lacole from the bedside.

Her eyes blinked open in a murderous rage. "You!" she growled, tossing her head so violently that her blond hair, now with inches of new growth, fell into her eyes.

Hoshiko looked at the monitor. "She shouldn't be awake yet. What did you do?"

"She was snooping!" Lacole jerked against the bed restraints. "I pushed her out."

I tested for a shield, and sure enough hers was active now and strong. "Guess she was too close to consciousness." I shifted my gaze to Ava on the monitor. "I should have come in here before we checked Valerine."

"We'll have to do it the hard way," Ava said. "Once Ritter gets there."

"Excuse me. I'm right here. Will someone address me?" Lacole looked wildly between all of us, her bottom lip curled in hatred and fear. Whatever her blocking prowess, those emotions were clearly spilling from her surface thoughts.

I met her furious stare. "That depends on if you answer questions truthfully."

"What questions?"

"What information did Mikyn Zenos want you to prevent Valerine from sending us?"

Lacole glared. "As if I'm going to tell you. I hope this means Valerine is swimming permanently in another ocean."

"She's actually healing nicely, and I've been able to retrieve information from her." I leaned against a set of cupboards near the bed, keeping my voice even. "In fact, I would like your take on it."

Lacole jerked again, rattling the belts that secured her. She sneered. "Swallow a thousand iceberg shards and bleed out while fishes dine on your decomposing body."

"As much as I'm enjoying your colorful Sinaltan terminology, I'm losing patience." I leaned a bit closer. "So let's try an easy one. After your capture, how did your friends track you to our plane even though we disabled your transmitter?"

Lacole hesitated, and for a clear second, I sensed a flash of triumph. "Someone from the hotel got away then."

"Maybe. Possibly more than one." I looked at Blaze. "Any word from that agent we talked to?" I didn't mind giving up useless information if it goaded Lacole into spilling something important.

"They found seven Avowed," he said. "Six are alive or will be soon, and one was permanently killed. They're saving his remains to be identified, though there was fire damage, so identification might not be possible."

Lacole's face blanched at the words. "What did he look like?" The words held a hint of pain that tore at me. I remembered the man she'd been kissing. Her technopath husband perhaps?

"Please have her send me pictures so I can show Lacole and Graeme for identification," I said to Blaze. To Lacole, I added, "Answer the question. How did they track you? We didn't find a transmitter."

She snorted. "How would I know? I've been dead. If you're too stupid to know the answer, then all I have to say is to be prepared because wherever I am, Mikyn will find and rescue me."

"You think you're that important?" This came from the doorway of the glass holding cell where Graeme now stood. "We are inside a veritable fortress that's so protected, the entire US Army would take days to get in. Besides, I'm Mikyn's great-grandson, arguably one of his closest sensing relatives, and look what he's done to *help* me."

"You are a traitor!" Her lips twisted as she strained once more against her constraints.

He stepped into the room. "Valerine gave him the location of the explosives as he requested in a private communication. He was supposed to help us." Graeme glanced at Ava on the screen, and I could see he was uncomfortable with the half-truth we'd discovered from Valerine—though until Valerine awoke, we couldn't prove the second set of explosives was still in place.

"That's a lie. We still have crews searching all possible locations and have found nothing. The electronic shield and the physical one could have blown at any moment, and we've all had to live with that hanging over us. We've lived in fear ever since the topsiders came to our community."

"Valerine told him," Graeme insisted. "And we should be hailed as heroes! We saved the topsiders and helped get Sinalta to the surface. If not for us, you might all be rotting with the fishes."

Lacole's blue eyes could have frozen melting metal. "You are still a traitor. If those explosives had gone off, you would have killed four million people. Mikyn has every right to hunt you down."

"No, he doesn't." Graeme reached the bedside, his arm brushing mine. "We are loyal to our people, not to Mikyn. And he has plenty of real traitors to hunt."

"You mean Tsaousiss and Scala?" Scorn dripped from her words. "Even now, their families are clamoring for their return. You don't know what it's like—all the mistrust and backroom deals going on. We need the statesmen back to unify us, but the topsiders refuse to let them return, so Mikyn must unite us in another way."

Ava and I exchanged a worried stare. Publicly, Mikyn was still adamant against the statesmen's return unless it was in chains, but Lacole's comments seemed to indicate that maybe the hint picked up during our chat with Stefan about them all working together was true.

"How?" Graeme demanded. "How is he going to unite Sinalta?"

Lacole glared at him without response. Across from us, Blaze lifted one brow, indicating that I should say something, but I shook my head. Graeme was getting more out of his cousin than I had. Already it was apparent that Lacole believed the explosives were still in play, so either Mikyn had lied to her, or he knew about the second set. Regardless, there was something more to her statements.

I reached out to Graeme, tapping gently on his mental shield, but his barrier was zipped up tightly—probably a good thing where Lacole was concerned—and I didn't want to distract him now by breaking in.

"Is it the topside healer?" Graeme asked. "Is Mikyn going to make an example out of him?"

Lacole snorted. "Possibly. He's been nothing but a pain." The careless way she spoke told me she was only buying time.

Graeme's face contorted. "You *will* tell me what he's up to!"

I felt him attack her shield, raising something that resembled an anchor from a ship. *No, Graeme!* I said. But it was too late. He'd taken my word about using a talisman, and apparently being forced to live on a ship to help smuggle goods and living children to the underwater city had taken its toll. He bashed through Lacole's shield on his third hit.

And we were in.

Get out! Lacole screamed at him.

Her sand stream of thoughts hurtled past us, hot and furious. But that wasn't the only thing hot. All around us the thick construct material dripped and coagulated like silvery drops of blood. I pushed back, encasing myself in a similar substance, a bubble shield of my own making, but her liquid was already covering Graeme.

Lacole laughed at his furious attempts to free himself. *I have you, cousin. You aren't stronger than me.*

No, but I am. I stepped forward to enclose Graeme in my protective bubble. It was the same type I'd used to protect myself while in Mikyn's mind during the newborn embryo ceremony back in Sinalta, though he'd made no move against me then, and in fact I'd ended up hurting him when I'd learned the truth. Helping Dimitri heal him after was a regret I still carried.

Lacole screamed and attacked, pushing mentally against us. Her silver constructs covered my protective shield and began to squeeze. Flashes of light followed, and for long, tortuous moments, I scrambled to strengthen my barriers, fearing for my sanity and even my child.

Why had I come in after Graeme? I should have waited for backup. Shock and fear flowed from Graeme, further eroding my confidence and somehow fueling Lacole. No, not just his fear but my own. She ate it like energy.

Like energy.

I realized I'd made a mistake in waiting to question her. The wait had only added to my fear and let her feed.

Not from me, you won't. Gathering my strength, I pushed out with both hands, expanding my bubble and sending her dripping constructs to the floor of her mind, where they were greedily sucked in.

How are you doing that? she demanded.

I laughed at her dismay. *You are not as strong as Mikyn wants you to believe. You are not as strong as I am.*

But how can you know . . .? Graeme began.

Because Mikyn would never have taught her enough or allowed her to become powerful enough to destroy him. Of that, I was completely certain. And that meant she couldn't beat me. My thoughts transferred to both Lacole and Graeme instantly without the bother of forming words, and now it was Lacole who desperately tried to protect herself with her constructs.

I set them on fire with a wave of my machete. *What is Mikyn planning?* I demanded.

I won't tell you.

I stabbed my machete purposefully into her thought stream. The sands slammed into it, redirecting, and she screamed, spewing Sinaltan curses that also needed no words or translation. She wanted me to die with my fingers and toenails pulled, every bone in my body broken, and my entrails removed and shoved down my throat.

So ladylike. I sent a mocking laugh to her mind.

I continued to divert the sand stream. A piercing howl filled my brain and my physical ears as well.

"Hoshiko!" Ava barked from somewhere very distant.

"Erin is fine," was the old woman's reply.

And I was. *One last chance,* I told Lacole. *I won't ask again.* I'd told her that back in the hotel room—would she remember?

She let the thoughts come, whimpering in relief as I stepped back. I had my answer, and far more. I clamped down on the shock of the information, though Graeme reeled with it.

And how did your people track us? I demanded, determined to get the rest while I was there.

I don't know. One of my team must have done something. Maybe my husband. Defeat oozed from her like a foul odor.

For what it's worth, we didn't cause your reset, and I'm sorry for your loss.

For my . . . ? Understanding dawned. *You mean for the glob of cells.* The words were a sneer, but she couldn't hide the loss behind them. She'd sensed her child's self as I had mine. She'd felt the heart beating with her own, the essence of innate trust.

Get out! she screamed. "Out, out, out!" The words came both physically and mentally.

She had no power over us, but we were finished here. *Come on, Graeme.* I led him from her mind and opened my eyes to find him clenching my physical arm so tightly that it would leave bruises.

For a full minute, there was silence except for Lacole's tortured sobs. Finally, Hoshiko reached out and gently brought her unconsciousness.

"Well?" Ava said.

"She t-tried to kill us!" Graeme spluttered. "Our minds. Could we even come back from that?"

I unlatched his fingers from my arm. "She doesn't have that kind of power. Fear was our greatest enemy. Somehow, she fed on it. Either Mikyn taught her, or that's why he chose to train her." I faced Ava on the screen. "But we do have a big problem. Mikyn is facing a huge rebel faction in Sinalta called the Unsworn. They have renounced the vow they once made to the Avowed rulership. Most come from the outer ring in the service district." The poor relations, as I thought of them, the ones who survived in cramped conditions while those in the center ring lived in opulence. "But there are many from the middle ring as well. They want equal representation and the freedom to leave Sinalta if they wish—and many of them wish it if the current leadership remains in place. They are rioting in the streets and have damaged some of the ancient buildings."

"As glad as I am that people are waking up to the injustices on Sinalta, it's hardly time for a civil war," Ava said from the screen. "Not with every country resetting their nuclear sights on the city."

Graeme's shoulders squared. "I beg to disagree. Now *is* the time. If we don't remake the government now, we might never have another chance."

Ava considered that. "Maybe so. But the world needs stable leadership in Sinalta to deal with. The sooner the better."

"I agree," I said. "Which I believe is why Mikyn is considering pardoning Tsaousiss and Scala, despite their attempt to murder all of us." As always, anger spread through me at the memory. "He's having problems controlling people without Tsaousiss's mind control since Tsaousiss's successors are not cooperating."

Graeme walked over to a chair near the foot of the bed, sinking into it. "I'm surprised he hasn't already let the Senate grant their request for reinstatement."

Ava shrugged. "Mikyn knows we will never agree to work with them after their treatment of us."

"Unless," I held up a finger, "we have another reason to agree."

"Stefan," Ava and Blaze said together.

"So that's why they got him involved," Ava continued. "He ensures our success in the Triad vote, and we sign off on the reinstatement, which gives Mikyn a stable government and Stefan his freedom to do whatever he can there. Which means they're all in this together."

"You think Mikyn will actually work with Tsaousiss and Scala?" I asked. "Because it's apparent from my conversation that they intend to take control and put him back in his box. And it was also clear to me in Lacole's mind that trusting them is Mikyn's last resort. So how can that make a stable government? Especially with Stefan as a player."

"The Sinaltan government only has to appear stable to the outside." Ava pursed her lips and added, "Mikyn refused to give us the data on the ruling families, so we can't tell if he's been sabotaging them through birth ceremonies, but looking back, I believe he did use us to rid himself of his most powerful competition in the Senate. Then he literally became Sinalta's savior by raising the city from under the water. Even if the statesmen are returned now, he is a hero in the eyes of the people. And I'm sure he's taken steps to retain power over the statesmen once they help him bring order. Maybe he and Stefan have an understanding." Ava tented her hands on the table in front of her. "And now he also has Dimitri for leverage against us."

"There's something else," Hoshiko said, her hand still on the unconscious Lacole. "Erin mentioned that reinstating the statesmen is Mikyn's last resort. If that's true, what is his first choice?"

I exchanged a glance with Graeme and sighed. "It seems so ridiculous that at first I didn't think it would work, but now that we've talked, I'm not so sure."

"It's me." Graeme dragged a hand through his hair. "And Valerine. Now that the city is topside, Mikyn plans to set off some explosives and claim we did it. Then he'll make an example of us. That's why he sent Lacole after us when we ran from Sinalta. He thought we'd discovered his plan. That was the information they didn't want you to have."

"He's going to destroy the electronic shields?" Ava said, blinking in disbelief.

"Not the actual shields." I stared down at Lacole's now-peaceful face. "But close enough to several of the generators to make it appear the shield was the target. Right now the Unsworn are hailing Graeme and Valerine as heroes, but Mikyn's going to target them particularly and gain their support." I frowned. "That's ridiculous, right? Why would they believe him?"

Ava sighed. "They'll believe. If history repeats itself, and I've witnessed for myself that it does, there's always been one way for tyrants and presidents alike to unite the people they've betrayed—give them a common enemy to hate. Most of Sinalta already believes them to be traitors. It won't be hard to convince the rest."

I slid my fingers along Lacole's restraints, checking them. She was still thoroughly out under Hoshiko's ministrations, but it comforted me to be sure she wasn't going anywhere. "They don't need the shields anymore, so why not blow the original shield target as well as any others that might win over the Unsworn? Why risk that someone will find out he's lying?"

Graeme sucked in a breath loud enough to draw our attention. "I think I know. Those shields might have been ready to fail under all that water, but they might be plenty strong enough to keep the world out for a time up here, if Mikyn decides to use their weapons. Maybe he wants a backup in case your government takes issue with the way he runs things."

Like killing babies? My blood froze. "Mikyn could start a world war to get what he wants."

Ava stood, her face set. "We will go to Sinalta today and get to the bottom of this, whether Mikyn agrees or not. When Ritter gets there, I need you both back here as soon as possible. Jace, Blaze, and Oliver too."

"What's the plan?" I asked.

"I don't have one—yet, but we're going to find Dimitri. It's time to take this war to Sinalta." Ava leaned forward, hand outstretched, and ended the transmission.

I nodded, blood now racing through my veins in anticipation. So it would come down to confronting Mikyn, as I'd expected. I was more than ready for it. Grinning, I smoothed a hand down over the bump of my baby. "Looks like I need to go track down some new body armor."

Hoshiko walked with me to the door. "Stella mentioned something about armor for you." The old woman's eyebrows tilted inward as she added, "But there's something more she wants you to do, something about the baby."

"He's okay, right?"

"I believe so." But Hoshiko couldn't hide the puzzlement in her eyes. "She hasn't shared any concerns with me. It's just a feeling I have."

"I'll check in with her." To Blaze, I added, "Start brainstorming ideas. When Ritter and Jace arrive, we have a mission to plan. And whatever happens, we can't let Stefan gain control of the Sinaltan weapons."

"Right," A fireball started in Blaze's hand, hanging at his side as if he couldn't contain his emotions. "Unfortunately, letting Mikyn keep them might be just as bad."

I had to agree.

Chapter 16

STELLA WAS IN THE THIRD-FLOOR SUITE SHE SHARED WITH MY brother and the kids. It was only a few doors down from mine, but I hadn't been inside since their remodel had combined their suites into one, with a large entryway that made the best of the ten-foot ceilings.

"Come in," Stella said, opening the door herself. It had been a few hours since the birth, but even so, I'd expected her to be resting, surrounded by her family, but Chris and the kids were nowhere in sight. She led me to the adjoined sitting room that was embellished with artwork, statues, and furniture that looked like expensive museum pieces. Sometimes I forgot about all the years she'd lived.

"How are you feeling?" I asked as we sat on her very modern leather couch.

"All better." Grinning, she looked down at the tiny bundle strapped to her chest with a wraparound carrier. "He's perfect. I feel . . . Oh, Erin, I should have done this before. All these years I've lived, the men I've known, especially my last husband . . . I shouldn't have let him get the vasectomy. I shouldn't have directed my nanites to prevent pregnancies. The wars, the fighting, the struggles—this is what makes it all worth it." She cradled the baby's head, then ran her hand down his back. "I didn't know, and I should have with all the information at my fingertips."

"Renegades had to hide their babies from Stefan's hit teams," I reminded her. "It was hard to place children for their own protection."

Stella put her arm into the carrier and scooped out the baby, impossibly small, and plopped him into my arms. Involuntarily, my arms tightened around him. I could feel his presence—alive and vital—similar to my own unborn child. He wasn't exactly happy at his sudden change of location because he could no longer smell his mother or her milk. I bounced him awkwardly, sending him soothing thoughts until he seemed to recognize me and decide that I would do for now.

"I want you to see if he'll Change," Stella said.

That took me by surprise, though it shouldn't have given Hoshiko's warning. "Have you talked to Chris about this?" I hoped that was why she was bringing it up.

Stella tucked a length of ebony hair behind her ear. "No, of course not. I don't want him to think it matters that much. But knowing I'm going to lose him and the other kids . . ." She sighed. "I know I can have more children, but I think Chris will be happier knowing I'll have Grant when he's gone."

"Grant? You're naming him after our father?"

Stella nodded. "Yes. And we already called him and Annie to let them know. They're planning to give us a week and then come visit. But about the baby. You can do it, right?"

"You know I need Mikyn or a healer."

Stella tilted her head to study me. "Um, Hoshiko told me about your possible second gift, and this morning, I scanned everything there is in our database and in the Emporium data-base regarding those legends."

"You had a baby this morning."

"That was a lifetime ago." She turned her head, moving aside her hair to reveal a blinking earpiece. "It's not as fast as my neural transmitter, but it works well. Keeping it on low helps my brain from going bonkers without enough input. Even with Grant here, I need that."

"Oh, right." I'd channeled her before, but not for long enough, apparently, to understand her constant need for input.

"Anyway, double gifts have only been recorded for sensing Unbounded, and I'm thinking it might be because they can learn mentally from others about a trait that is already in their genes. I mean, maybe everyone else could also do that via a sensing Un—" She waved a hand. "Never mind. The point is. I think you can do it without help from a healer."

"It's dangerous."

"How?"

"I'm afraid I could hurt him."

She snorted. "Ridiculous. I know you wouldn't. You love him like you do Kathy and Spencer. What is the real reason? What are you hiding?"

I couldn't tell her. If she knew there was a possibility of altering her son's DNA, she wouldn't request it because the consequence of failure would be too high. But in the case that he didn't Change, I wouldn't want her to bear the weight of the what-ifs. No matter how I tried, I couldn't tell her if altering the DNA would be successful, and I didn't know anyone who could.

"What aren't you telling me?" Stella pressed. "I knew there was something. Something Ava wouldn't tell me. What is it, Erin?" Her gaze fixed on me, compelling me to spill all.

"Please don't ask. You have to trust me." I looked down at the baby, smoothing his cheek. "I saw a lot of horrors on Sinalta, and I don't want to share them—I *won't* share them."

I met her gaze again, making a sudden decision. "I'll look and tell you if he'll Change, but please don't ask about Sinalta. Trust me. Trust Ava."

She held my stare as if gouging into my head. I didn't look away. Finally, she nodded. "Okay. Tell me. Will Grant change?"

"First talk to Chris, okay? Because like it or not, this will alter the way you look at your son and maybe the way you look at Chris too. Because being with him, a mortal, does lower your children's chances, even with altered sperm."

She considered that a moment. "I was thinking not to tell him, if it was bad news, but maybe you're right."

If it had been any less important a subject, I might have laughed at the idea of both of them trying to protect the other.

"Don't think of it as bad news," I said. "You wouldn't change Kathy or Spencer for other kids who are immortal, would you?" I kissed the baby's forehead. "You're better off having a dozen more and just seeing what happens."

She smiled. "Did you already say something to Chris about this? Because before he left to take the kids downstairs for yet more ice cream, he asked me when I thought I might be ready to have another one." She grinned. "I'm not sure how long nursing will prevent me from getting pregnant, but I heard tandem nursing isn't all that bad."

I laughed. "I always thought that was for hippies."

"Maybe, and for women who have waited far too long to start a family." She started to reach for the baby but stopped short of taking him from my arms. "Oh, wait. I have something for you. I noticed you've grown quite a bit, and with Dimitri still missing . . ." She rose and moved across the room. "I'll be right back."

Which left me alone with little Grant. He was so tiny and perfect, and even as I watched him, he opened his eyes, large and deep, looking more like a slightly wrinkled old man than my brother or Stella.

The next moment, I was in his head, watching his thoughts hurtle down toward me. Thoughts of milk and cuddling, contentment and curiosity. He wanted to reach out and explore my eyes, but his hand wouldn't quite obey.

Don't worry, I told him. *In a few months you will be grabbing everything.* He might not understand the actual words, but he did get the gist of my thoughts through the images I sent. It was rather amazing to communicate with him this way.

I was standing close to the edge of his thought stream, flowing from the top of his mind stage and disappearing near my feet, and I almost didn't realize it when I drifted inside them. There was no pain or reaction from the baby as there had been with Lacole and my machete when I'd intended injury. The sand simply flowed around me and continued on its journey.

Mikyn and I went upward, I thought, and before I could stop myself, I was diving in an upward direction that soon shifted downward into a glasslike pool, as if up and down had no meaning here. I followed a path of energy similar to how I'd traced Valerine's veins and arteries. My heart thumped rapidly in time with the baby's. Time passed, and yet held still as I delved deeper.

Finally, I was standing on glass in the center of the baby's inner self, staring into a midnight blue sky peppered with tiny dots of lights, some traveling gently while others simply glowed. These were the stars Mikyn had too-often erased in his efforts to alter a child's future. Years of life.

I expanded my thoughts further, and I could see everything at once. Little Grant would have black hair and brown eyes like his mother. He would be taller and more muscular, though, and love flying like his father. He'd hate broccoli and crave salt. He'd be outgoing, brave, and loyal.

At last I saw it, shining out more brightly than any of the stars, one light so brilliant that its burning filled me with joy. Grant was destined to Change. As long as he survived until then, his mother would never have to bury him from natural causes.

"Here we go," Stella said cheerfully, bringing me back to the couch where Grant's eyes began to close, contentment, health, and trust radiating from him.

I looked up at Stella, tears blurring my vision. She tossed the body armor onto a chair and sat beside me. "I know," she said, touching my shoulder. "I can't stop staring at him. Chris and the kids can't either. I practically had to kick them out of here so I could have him all to myself."

"He's really beautiful." Blinking hard, I passed her the baby, who, sensing the change, opened his eyes again sleepily.

I popped to my feet and grabbed the armor. "Thanks for this."

"I had the height adjusted for you," she said. "It should be more comfortable than the last two sets."

"Thanks. If there had been time, I would have gotten my own."

Stella came to her feet. "Maybe next time we won't need them at all."

I laughed. "Hopefully." I was torn between wanting to tell her about Grant and knowing that if I did, it would be just that much harder with the next baby to tell her it wouldn't happen. No, telling her couldn't be my decision but hers and Chris's together.

"I'll let you know about the . . . you know," she said as she walked me toward the door. Her eyes went slightly out of focus. "Guess what? Ritter and Jace are here. I just got a message from Marco."

I thought she might stay behind, but she tucked the baby

into his carrier and came with me as we rode down the elevator to find Ritter and Jace with the kids in the entry hall. Ritter hugged me tightly while Jace tried to grab the baby from Stella.

"No," she said, warding him off with both hands. "You might be immortal, but he's only a few hours old, and you've been traveling all day. You need to wash your hands before you hold him. Who knows where you've been."

Jace laughed. "Okay, okay. Good point." He set a hand on Anina's shoulder. They'd become friends when we'd taken her from Sinalta, and she still seemed to adore him. "We have to leave soon anyway. We're all anxious to find Dimitri."

"Well, first you need the location of the explosives Valerine set on the shields," Stella said. To me she added, "Ava wants her to show you exactly where they are mentally and on the map."

"Is she conscious yet?" I asked.

"No, but Hoshiko says it should be soon. I'll let you know." Stella adjusted her baby's position, her face melting into a smile as he tried to suck his fist.

Chris frowned at her. "Shouldn't you be resting?"

Stella leveled a glare in his direction. "I'm fine. And if I hadn't researched the benefits of nursing, you'd be staying here with Grant while I helped get Dimitri. In fact, maybe I should go with them. I can take the baby, and you can stay with him on Ava's boat. Should be safe enough."

"Really?" Chris asked. "With all that advanced weaponry and the Avowed stealing children? You want to risk our son?"

Stella's glare faded. "Okay, you win. But I'll continue to do what I can from here."

"So," Jace said in the awkward silence that followed. "You named him after Dad. Cool."

My heart eased a little at the words. Jace hadn't forgotten that he had a father who had raised him and loved him. Maybe his heart understood that he didn't need Stefan or his approval.

"Since Valerine isn't awake yet, I'm going to gather my gear." I'd left the armor Stella had given me in the hallway upstairs.

"I'll go with you." Ritter's eyes gleamed with a hungry expression I recognized.

"I'll make sure the plane is ready," Chris said a little uncertainly.

Stella put her arm around Chris's waist and gave him a sympathetic smile. "No need at the moment. Keene will update us with the Triad voting in the conference room at two, which is their dinner break back in New York, and Ava thinks now that it's started, Mari will be able to get away long enough to shift you back to the ship. It was one thing to delay while we waited for Valerine to heal, but Erin shouldn't be parachuting out of a plane right now, and we don't happen to have any Sinaltan submersibles nearby. Even those would take longer than we can afford."

"But how do you know all . . .?" Chris's hand shot out to the right side of his wife's face, where he moved her hair to reveal her earbud. "Seriously? You literally just had a baby this morning."

"*Early* this morning," she corrected. "I've only used it for a bit of research and to stay in contact with Ava. Besides, you knew what I was when you married me." She gave him a slow smile that undid my brother. His arms wrapped around her, and he didn't seem to mind when the kids giggled at his defeat.

"Let's go." Ritter, his hand locked on mine, was patient until we got into the elevator, and then his lips were on me, his hands kneading my back as he pulled our bodies together. He kissed my face and neck, trailing downward to the hollow between my breasts, then up again. I kissed him back deep and hard, wrapping my arms tightly around his neck. He felt so good.

His mental barrier slipped, and I was hit with a wave of

his desire that made what I'd been feeling before seem like a schoolgirl crush. Powerful and all-encompassing. I slid my hand inside his shirt.

Somehow, we made it to our suite before his weapons began hitting the ground. I dropped Stella's armor that I'd swept up in the hallway and pulled off his shirt, nipping his skin with my teeth. He groaned.

"Feels like we've been apart a week," I panted between kisses.

"At least two."

My shirt and pants were next. His body was hot against mine. The mate bond and our desires mingled into something indescribably amazing. We barely made it to the bed.

Afterward, I cuddled into him, my back to his chest. "I know people talk about taking their time," I murmured, "but there is a lot to be said about urgency."

He chuckled softly. "I love you." He pulled me closer, his hand on the mound of my stomach. "Both of you." His fierce emotion for the baby was every bit as strong as his passion for me.

"I love you too."

"We might be late to the conference room." He nuzzled closer, kissing my ear and nibbling on my lobe, his breath creating goose bumps over my skin.

My laugh was low and deep. "I think they're used to that by now." Turning, I kissed him again.

STELLA'S NEW HAND-ME-DOWN ARMOR FIT ME FAR MORE COMFORT-ably than the last set. I began filling the hidden pockets with my favorite weapons as Ritter changed, his hair still wet from our shower. "I know Ava briefed you on what we learned from Valerine and the Avowed empath, but I have personal news."

I told him everything Hoshiko and I'd talked about regarding a possible second gift.

"You think she's right?"

"I can heal at least a bit," I admitted. "But even if I can heal, that still doesn't explain how I was able to fight and move so fast at the hotel."

"Or on the boat when Brenna attacked you."

I frowned. "Yeah, maybe. I think I was harboring hope that was all me. But when I tried it here, I couldn't move nearly that fast, so I definitely don't have the combat ability."

"You had to be channeling."

"Probably. Only it was like I didn't have to break through any shields to use the ability."

"Have you ever noticed it happening before?"

"No, I don't think . . ." I began. "Wait. When we were on the ship, I channeled Mari and Keene after they let me inside their mental shields, but when we shifted to Rio, I saw Mari's numbers, and I don't remember asking to channel her." And I would have asked. Breaking into the minds of those I loved was something I rigorously avoided.

He wrapped his arms around me, smoothing my tense expression with his kisses. "We'll figure it out. I'm sure there's an explanation." Satisfaction emanated from his surface thoughts as he spoke. However it happened, he liked the idea that I was additionally protected by whatever means.

"There's more." I pulled away from him to tuck my ballistic knife into the pocket on my sleeve. "When I held Grant a little while ago, I saw everything that he would become. Everything. He's going to Change."

His eyes locked on mine. "I'm taking it that you didn't tell Stella and Chris?"

"No, but I will if they both agree and ask me to. I hope they don't, but I'm glad to know myself."

"Only because he'll Change. Because otherwise, knowing would be a huge weight."

"Right." He knew me too well. "Are you having second thoughts about looking at our daughter's self?" It was his way of acknowledging that he couldn't stop me if I chose to do it.

"No. We already made that decision. And for all the reasons it's wrong for them to know, it's wrong for us." Even if not knowing was a torture in itself. I blinked hard before I could become emotional. *Compartmentalize, like in battle.*

Wait, was I channeling Ritter? Because his mind was closed to me at the moment.

"If only there were a way to see that altering the DNA would work." I removed the magazine of my .380 and checked the chamber, removing the bullet there, moving as fast as I could. Was that combat fast? "Then trying would always be worth it. We wouldn't be sentencing someone to die early just for the chance."

Ritter's hands shot out, capturing my hands in both of his, my gun pointed downward to the reinforced floor that would stop a barrage of bullets. "Even with knowing they might die early, many would risk it, for themselves and their children. Like the Sinaltans."

"That's exactly why we can't let anyone know. Sinaltans might have become desensitized to murdering their own babies after they're born, but we can't let that madness spread."

"To be fair, that may change now that they'll have more space," Ritter said. "They won't have to enforce their one child at a time law to keep the population sustainable."

"As long as they don't send more children to work in any mines," I muttered. The conversation reminded me that I still needed to look into Anina to see if I could determine whether or not Mikyn had tried to "fix" her. My heart hurt at the thought.

Ritter released my hands, waving his finger in a circular motion, signaling for me to check the gun again. "If only those who have both sensing and healing parents can see a child's potential Change, that'll narrow the pool of potential seers. Maybe even to two—you and Mikyn."

"Only because the Sinaltans don't have any healers." Mikyn had been forcing his progeny to mentally join with him during the baby ceremonies to see if any were able to do it on their own, and he'd claimed to be unsuccessful. Now I understood why.

"Until we gave them Dimitri."

"Exactly what I was thinking." I removed the magazine again and rechecked the barrel of my gun. Even to my eyes, my hands blurred with the motion.

Ritter nodded in approval. "I don't know how you're doing that with my shield up, but you're definitely channeling me. Unless you're connected to Jace."

"I'm not. Grab your gear. For once, we're not late. Let's get to the conference room and then see if Valerine is awake. I want to be ready the minute Mari can help us. Let's just hope Keene has good news from New York."

Chapter 17

THE CONFERENCE ROOM ON THE MAIN FLOOR WAS ALREADY FULL when we arrived. Blaze, Oliver, and Jace sat around the wide mahogany table, and Stella and Chris were heading toward their chairs. Baby Grant was still in Stella's carrier, but the other children were nowhere in sight.

"How's Valerine?" I sank into a leather, high-backed chair next to Jace and kitty-corner to the head of the table, which was left open for Ritter as op leader in Ava's absence. The padded black chair cradled me with a comfort that was almost distracting.

"She woke a few minutes ago," Stella said in the chair across from me. She was back to wearing her neural headset, which blinked as she worked her invisible connections. "They're moving her to a recovery room. You can go up for the information after Keene's update." As she spoke, the retractable monitors set at each place rose and rotated into position in front of us, showing Ava seated at her table on the ship.

"Did you get what you need from Valerine?" Ava asked me.

"Just about to after Keene's update. It won't take long."

"Good. Stella, will you see if Keene's ready?"

"He's ready," Stella said. "Putting him on now." Keene's face appeared on half of the screen as she finished speaking.

"I only have a moment." His face was haggard and his voice weary. "This has turned into a circus. Catrina voted for me, and Stefan voted for my contender, who happens to be the murderer responsible for inventing the forced Changes, by the way. He has what appears to be an official contract, and though it's older and therefore not as valid as mine, Stefan has somehow found an authority who has cast doubt on my papers. Since the Triad vote is a tie, the simple confirmation has turned into an actual election. I'm guessing Stefan anticipated that once we heard about his escape, we'd make the move to install me in my father's place, so he's made sure everyone knows he hasn't given permission for Jace to vote for him."

"Let me guess," Jace said. "He'll let me take the vote if we let him go to Sinalta."

"That's my guess. Because he hasn't yet officially been convicted of any crime, he can still vote. So right now, the Triad pre-vote is tied. That means the vote by the unit heads will be binding, and so far it's a leveraging madness. Thankfully, we've been able to stay caught up, mostly because people believe my father wanted me to assume the position, and they know and like me. Others have a real hatred for forced Changes. But it's a battle. I can spare Mari to take you where you need to go as soon as she gets back from Russia with Catrina's family head, but not for any extended op. As the vote changes, we have only an hour to reverse it, or the other side can call for an immediate final vote." Keene's face darkened. "It's a convoluted system that Stefan definitely rigged to his advantage while he was in charge. In fact, we just found out that a billion dollars were wired to one of the opposing manager's accounts. We'll get the man's vote thrown out, but his successor's bribe might not be that obvious. In fact, I'm sure Stefan let us discover it so we'd know what we were up against."

"Is there a way to force Stefan to appear in person to validate his vote?" I asked.

Keene shook his head. "No, he knows there are too many here that don't want him back, and we refused to guarantee him safe passage because of the unresolved charges against him. So he's evoked some little-known clause relating to unfolding political events and sent in his vote and proof of DNA via his and our representatives, who are also unit heads. It came in this morning. With Mari's help getting people when we need them, I think we'll still win this. Many of those loyal to Stefan still recognize how much better things are now. But with all of Stefan's paid moles in the leadership, it'll take time. If you can do anything to get Stefan off our backs before that . . ."

"You mean like kill him?" Jace ground out.

Keene's smile flashed bright like a signal flare before winking out. "That would work."

"Are you okay if we keep Oliver for a while?" Ava asked.

"I think so. At least for now." Keene looked to the side. "Sorry, guys, they're signaling me. I'll have Mari coordinate with Stella to shift into the Fortress."

"No," Ava said from her side of the screen. "The team will go through the tunnels to meet her at the offsite entrance. I don't want the electrical grid down now with Mikyn's people targeting us. I don't think they'll have the resources here to get inside, but with Stefan involved, you never know. There's enough proof here that he's playing both sides of the Sinaltan issue."

"Sounds good," Keene said. "I'm sorry I can't spare her for more."

"We only need to get to Sinalta," Ritter said. "We can do

the rest. Or even to Ava's ship." To Ava he added, "We still have the transport Brenna used to board, don't we?"

She inclined her head in the affirmative. "Yes. But I'm not sure about protocols for getting in and out of the city from underneath. I've asked for a delegation visit but have thus far been denied anything but electronic communication."

"Graeme and Valerine may have codes or know someone working the underwater gates," I offered.

"That might become an option, but my current plan is to have Mari shift the team directly into the city to confront Mikyn and find out where Dimitri is." Ava set her hands down on the table in front of her. "Thanks, team. Let's get to work." She and Keene disappeared from the screens, which began retracting to Stella's silent command.

As I stood to go, Jace spoke, "If I'm not needed anywhere right now, I think I'll play with the kids until go time." He looked at Oliver and Blaze. "You guys coming?"

Blake nodded and started toward the door with Jace, but Oliver hesitated. "What about the Avowed empath?" he asked. "Is she going with us?" While his dark skin seemed paler than usual, he no longer appeared exhausted, and I was glad that the night's rest seemed to have done him good.

"Why would she?" I asked.

Oliver shrugged. "She seems to be important, that's all. To Senator Zenos—Mikyn. Whatever we're calling him. Thought maybe we could use her as leverage."

I glanced at Ritter as I considered the statement. He was op leader, and it was his call.

"We're not taking her to Sinalta," he said. "But maybe to the boat to wait with Ava. That way, she's near enough if we need her."

"She may not cooperate," I said. "She won't admit it, but she's upset about her baby."

"She was pregnant?" Oliver looked aghast.

I nodded. "At least until her poison or whatever kicked in. The baby, of course, is lost."

"I didn't realize." Something odd came through in Oliver's voice, a hint of an accent, or maybe—could it be grief? I wondered if that meant maybe he'd had something to do with Lacole's reset, even if by accident, but I couldn't think of any time he'd been alone with her except on the ship, and she'd been secure so he wouldn't have needed to protect himself or us.

"None of us knew," I said. "Or we would have been more careful." In fact, had I given her the right amount of sedative? I pushed the thought away and turned back to Ritter. "You think Ava will stay on the boat?" Given how she felt about Dimitri, I wasn't sure.

"It's you or her." He pushed back his chair and rose, grinning a challenge. He knew how much I didn't want to stay behind. "Because we need a backup communication if our coms fail."

"If Sinalta uses their electronic grid to block coms, that would block me too."

He nodded. "It's still a backup. Because if they put up the grid at this point, with the weapons they have, it could be considered an act of war."

"Maybe we should take Mikyn out of Sinalta for our chat," Blaze said from the door where he and Jace had paused to hear the conversation. "After all, Dimitri doesn't seem to be there."

"I've been thinking about that," Oliver said, recovering his composure. He passed Chris and Stella to join Blaze and Jace. "There could be a lockup below the city with electronic grids. They might be invisible to sensing if enough electronics are in place."

"Tsaousiss or Scala didn't seem to think so," I told him.

"Right, so you said, but do we believe them? Or maybe it's something Mikyn added after they left."

"I couldn't find any hint of it, even with Keene and Mari's help."

"Maybe something else is masking it, like the city's nuclear generators."

"Hmm, just a minute." Stella's neural headset blinked more furiously, as if she were calculating something that required all her computers and her attention. Finally, she walked over to Oliver and clapped him on the back. "Nephew, you could be right. I've just run simulations, and it might be possible to hide a small cell behind the nuclear weapons they claim to have—at least if Erin wasn't looking especially at them. And if they have more weapons than they claim, well, that could mean a bigger room."

I half-expected Oliver to make a mocking comment about his great intellect, but he said with unusual self-deprecation, "Just thinking aloud. I don't know much about how sensing works."

"We have to stop the explosions anyway," I said. "That means we go to Sinalta." I felt better, though, knowing that maybe we'd find Dimitri there after all.

Ritter nodded. "We'll meet you all in the basement when we're finished with Valerine."

In the infirmary, Valerine was no longer in a body bag but in an actual hospital bed wearing a tie-on gown. Her eyes were open, and her blond hair, still slick with curequick, had been combed back. Graeme stood over her, his expression eager and relieved as if he hadn't quite believed she could come back from a reset. Hoshiko was nowhere to be seen.

"Welcome back," I told Valerine. "It's good to see you awake."

"Thank you. It's good to be awake. And safe." Valerine gave

us a wide smile. "The healer went to find Anina. I can't wait to see her."

"I'll bet. She's been a little impatient to see you awake." I put a hand on the bulk of Ritter's arm. "Valerine, I'd like you and Graeme to meet my husband, Ritter Langford."

Valerine's eyes ran over Ritter. "I recognize him from the news feed in Sinalta. Nice to meet you." Graeme murmured in agreement.

"You too," Ritter said. "Both of you. But I'm afraid we need some information."

Valerine laughed. "I don't think there is much you are afraid of. What do you need?"

"I need you to show me something," I said. "Can you drop your shield?"

She nodded, and I slipped into her mind. *We know about the explosives,* I told her. *But more has happened since you were out.* I relayed what had occured since we'd found Graeme, including what we learned from Lacole. *We also know that you tried to bargain with Mikyn by giving him the location of the explosives. And that you actually planted two sets.*

Three, she corrected. *But how did you . . .? Never mind. You looked at my memories, didn't you? Graeme told me that was possible.*

You set three sets of explosives on the shield generators? I asked. *And Mikyn doesn't know about the other two?*

I wanted to have a backup, and a backup for the backup in case something went wrong with your team's escape from the city. I was planning on telling Mikyn about all of them, so that everyone could stop being afraid of the city imploding, but when he didn't announce that we'd turned in the first explosives, I knew something was up. I decided not to tell him about the other two. I figured we'd need them as leverage to gain our freedom. I also didn't know if you had been successful in getting Anina from the city. Our intel said you had, but Mikyn might have planted the information.

Aloud, she added, "I know it shouldn't be hard to believe that Mikyn would set us up after he promised me he would set things right, but I thought maybe . . ."

"You were right in coming to tell us," I said. "We're leaving to meet with him in a few minutes. I need you to show me where the explosives are. I need details, and I need to share them with Ritter too. We've studied what we know of the layout, but I'm sure there is a lot we don't know."

"Okay," she said.

Just think of it. Show us, I told her silently.

Ritter had dropped his shield, and I connected him to her thoughts as well. Graeme also joined me on the stage of Valerine's mind.

She took us through the main entrance I recognized from my last visit and down into the depths of the city. *I'll show you a different way in and out after this one,* Valerine thought. *The main will be too hard to get inside.* We went down corridors and even passed through several tunnels through the water.

Here is the first. Valerine's thoughts showed me the explosives on a generator that helped create the electronic shield. *We don't really know how the generators work,* she said, *and we have no more left in storage, which is why we've been so desperate. We can't bypass too many more either without failure.* It was an apology of sorts for her people and their atrocities.

You are not responsible, I told her. *Where's the next?*

She showed us the second location on the main central relay, once again cleverly disguised as part of the wiring.

"Do you have a way to set them off?" Ritter asked. "Originally, you gave Erin a detonator, but Mikyn has that now."

"These two were never set up on a remote. There wasn't time. They'll have to be set off manually—they do have timers.

Keep in mind that if you set them off, it will be the end of the shields. At least until we redevelop the technology to replace them."

I had mixed feelings about electronic shields so powerful that they could protect a dome from collapsing under so many tons of water. They were a technological miracle, but their failure had also caused the death of six million people in Sinalta's sister city. One thing for sure, I wouldn't want to depend on them for my life.

"Look, one more thing," Ritter said. "We want to read the Senate laws about who can occupy the senate seats. Is there a way to get that information?"

"Cherish, the technopath Erin met before, can help you," Valerine said. "She can also set up a meeting with the Unsworn. That's what the underground is calling itself since your arrival in Sinalta. They are growing in numbers. You need to get to them before Mikyn turns them against us and our cause. I can go with you to help."

"No!" Graeme and I said together.

"Anina needs you," I added. "You've done more than your part. I still owe you for my life and the lives of my team."

She met my gaze with a steady stare. "It's me who owes you for Anina. I will always owe you."

I wondered if she'd say the same thing if I told her what Mikyn might have stolen from her daughter. "Let's call it even." I strode to the door with Ritter.

"Wait!" Graeme hurried after us, his blue eyes dark with intent. "I'm coming with you. They're my people, and without me to guide you, it'll be a lot harder. I know Mikyn, and I've spent weeks underground in Sinalta hiding. And let's face it, neither of you are that great with spoken Sinaltan yet. You need me."

My gaze turned to Valerine, but her face showed only

resignation. At some point she and Graeme had already talked about this, and she had agreed. Ritter also seemed resigned to Graeme's presence.

"Okay," I said. To Valerine, I added, "I'll take good care of him."

Graeme started back to the bed. "I'm already packed. I'll wait to say goodbye to Anina when she comes and be right down."

"Take the elevator all the way to the basement," I said. "You can't miss it." We turned to go, but a soft gasp from the bed made us turn around to see Valerine trying to sit up.

"There's one more thing," she said, raising her voice slightly. "Don't you want to know why I contacted you? The urgent information I wrote about?"

The words were disorienting, and I blinked in surprise. "I thought it was because of the extra sets of explosives."

"Oh, no." Her head swung slowly back and forth. "Those were our insurance for getting out, and we're already out. My message was about your healer. In fact, he's the one who told me how to contact you via the message board. I know where Dimitri Sidorov is and why you need to rescue him as soon as possible."

Chapter 18

"WE STILL DON'T REALLY HAVE A PLAN," I SAID TO RITTER AS WE entered the transport Brenna had used to board Ava's ship only a few days before. After Valerine's revelation about Dimitri, the idea of going directly to Sinalta had changed. Instead, a very weary Mari had met us at the Fortress's tunnel exit and dropped us on the boat before shifting immediately back to New York. "What if we can't find Mikyn's transport or Dimitri isn't there?"

"We'll find it," Ritter said, pausing at the base of the ladder we'd just climbed down. "Graeme knows how to track its emissions, and with the Avowed empath onboard, they'll believe us when we say we're there to give them supplies."

I wasn't so sure. Lacole had no idea that Mikyn had hidden Dimitri on a transport that was now trailing the city far enough away not to arouse the suspicion of the various navies accompanying the city to its destination.

"As long as you keep her from warning them," he continued, "they'll accept our offer of supplies, and we'll be able to board. After we rescue Dimitri and take their transport, we'll have a way into Sinalta. Mikyn won't refuse the transport docking, especially if he believes Dimitri has been reset and his life force is too dim for anyone to discover he's there."

"Right. But I don't like trusting Lacole." I didn't add that Valerine's information about Dimitri being tortured had upset me. I had felt an urgency to find him from the beginning, and I had failed him. Still, attacking the transport underwater felt a lot like going into the jaws of the shark without a ready exit. Something was off and had been since before we'd left the Fortress, and I'd made too many mistakes not to trust that feeling.

"Oh, we're definitely not trusting her." Ritter gave me a slow smile that was at once comforting and sensual, and my body responded instinctively. I stepped close enough that our arms touched. Being with him was enough. Together, we would save Dimitri and fix what was wrong with Sinalta.

Brenna's transport was similar to Graeme's only in that it had the top hatch. It was about half the size, and instead of five seats spaced in front of instrument panels in the control room, it had six decidedly more comfortable seats in three rows, similar to the much smaller common transports that most Sinaltans used within the city's canals or on their paved roads. There were no sleeping berths, but the kitchen area was slightly more comfortable and had several seats that folded down from the wall.

Jace led a cuffed Lacole to a seat, and when she tripped, Oliver reached to steady her. She smacked his hands away with her joined ones, muttering a curse in Sinaltan.

"Just trying to help," Oliver muttered.

"You killed my baby," she retorted, surprising me with her vehemence. She'd convinced someone to shave her head before we'd left, so her hair was once again short, and the black freckle above her ear stood out like a stain.

"We didn't kill anyone," I said. Though that wasn't quite true. Blaze had said one of her cohorts had been cut in three at the site, and as yet I hadn't downloaded the images the CIA agent had sent me to get an identification from Lacole. No way was I going to upset her now, in case the dead person was her husband.

Either way, it was hard to feel sorry for her. She blamed us for her baby's death, but the likelihood of her murdering her own child in Sinalta after its birth was at least fifty percent. She wasn't the type to yoke herself to mortal offspring.

Oliver backed away and remained standing against the wall in the cramped aisle space as Jace and Graeme took the front seats, Ritter settled next to Lacole in the middle where he could watch her, and Blaze and I sat in the rear.

"I'm good here," Oliver said when Blaze offered to trade his seat.

"I think there are two pull-down seats there, if you can find them," Graeme said.

"Good thing we really aren't transporting supplies," Jace said, "or there wouldn't be space for them."

Lacole rolled her eyes. "Either way, this isn't going to work. They're not going to listen to me."

"How about *we* don't listen to you?" I fished a strip of cloth from one of the pockets of my body armor.

Ritter took it from me and did the honors. "You try to hurt any of us," he told her, "and you'll not only be in three pieces but a hundred." His voice sent shivers through my heart, and from the way Lacole shrank from him, I knew she felt the same. Ritter could be scary when he tried.

Movement from Blaze next to me caught my attention, and I turned my head to see him staring at Lacole. "What?" I said to him.

He leaned over to whisper, "Just thinking about her reaction to Oliver. She really hates him . . . I mean more than you and me, even. Why do you think that is? Could he have . . . I don't know . . . done something to her?"

"Oliver?" I asked, my eyes going to Oliver, who had found a tiny pull-down seat that looked like it was meant for a child. "I haven't spent a lot of time with him since he's been in New York with Jace and Keene, but it doesn't seem likely. He does seem braver than he used to be."

"Well, I've spent even less time than you have with him, so I'll have to take your word for it."

It was possible Oliver had reset Lacole, and maybe that's why he was acting so strangely now that he knew about the baby. If he had, I was going to lay into him later.

Graeme was busy at the controls, but every now and then, he glanced back at us as if he wanted to ask something. I knew he had questions about how Mari had shifted us so far in a heartbeat. We'd blindfolded Lacole during the shift, and I planned to take the memory of it from her brain later, but it didn't seem fair to expect Graeme to submit to that, not after all he'd done. If he joined us, it wouldn't be an issue, so maybe I'd wait for orders from Ava.

As we dived deeper and headed southeast, I became distinctly aware of tasting seafood and salt on my tongue. I expected the nausea to return with the motion, but it seemed that I was suddenly over that stage of pregnancy. I checked on my daughter, a flutter meeting my silent query. A clear thought came to her mind of a protector and friend. She didn't have a word for it yet, so I taught her: *Mother.* She wouldn't be able to say the word, of course, not for many months, but she'd soon recognize the thought and put it all together in her own time. I gently patted my baby bulge before remembering she'd feel nothing with the armor between us.

I lifted my gaze to see Lacole staring over the seat with icy eyes. I held her gaze in challenge until she looked away.

We caught up to the transport trailing Sinalta in three tedious hours. The transport moved northwest underneath the water at the same velocity as the city moved—less than ten knots per hour, or eleven and a half miles per hour, which was slow for the small hydrogen-driven transport, but an excellent pace for the huge city—at least without Keene's help. The transport was electronically shielded, completely dark to my senses, unlike our own transport.

"Drop your mind shield," I told Lacole as Ritter grabbed her and repositioned her next to Graeme in the front seat. "Graeme and I will make sure you don't send any secret signals to them."

She tried to speak through her gag, so Ritter undid it. "They aren't going to give us any information," she said, "and going in blind would be stupid. They could have a dozen soldiers in there."

"Drop it," Ritter growled, removing the cuffs from her hands but leaving the separate ones on her feet.

Giving him an evil stare that belied the inherent beauty of her face, Lacole dropped her mental barrier. Graeme and I slipped inside. There were more silvery constructs than ever, perhaps hiding information she deemed important, but she didn't attack us mentally.

Only say what Graeme tells you, I reminded her.

I'm not stupid.

With great effort, I refrained from a response.

"Hailing Transport Five-eight-one-six," Lacole said in Sinaltan. "This is Three-seven-nine-two-four-five with a shipment from Mother." Graeme had explained that the first number described the class of transports, with the number one being the most common and therefore usually the longest. Our transport, a class three, was two sizes up.

"Who is this?" said a voice, the meaning of the Sinaltan words coming to me from my connection with Lacole and Graeme. "We weren't warned about a shipment."

"This is Lacole Desoid, special assistant to Seer Zenos. I've enabled visual for confirmation." Graeme had ensured that the tight angle of the camera would show only Lacole, but even so, we'd all positioned ourselves away from her. Graeme was also typing in the translation of the conversation for Ritter and the others, though Ritter, already fluent in several languages, could understand most of it on his own.

A man's face appeared on the screen inside the wall above the controls. He had long, curly blond hair and a cruel twist to his lips. "I heard you'd been promoted. Guess marrying Basiel paid off."

"Feyard, how nice to see you once again on grunt duty," she retorted. "Looks like nothing's changed."

He's Lacole's old boyfriend, Graeme told me. *Before she realized his impulsiveness would never help her ambition.* To Lacole he added, *Say the rest.*

"I have some topsider specialties on board that Seer Zenos thought you might like since you're on such an important duty." Lacole couldn't help the disgust in the last sentence.

A cheer sounded over the com. "Then we are very happy to see you," another Avowed said, pushing Feyard from the screen. "We could use a distraction."

"I hope they have more of that chocolate stuff," a third Avowed said from off-screen. "Much better than any of our desserts."

"We do," Lacole ground out in response to Graeme's urging.

Easy, I warned her. *Tell them we have at least three large servings.*

She did and was met with disappointment. "You'd better have more. Between all of us, that's barely enough for a good taste," Feyard growled. "We'll begin docking protocols." They signed off.

Graeme double-checked that we weren't broadcasting. "So, more than three. Maybe four or five? Feyard is combat, which most likely means there will be one more combat as they generally come in pairs. At least one empath, I'm guessing, probably with some kind of medical training. That's the usual protocol with eliciting information from prisoners." The words seemed so much cleaner than "torture," but we all knew what it meant.

"Their transport will be similar to the one we used in New Zealand," Graeme continued. "We'll dock under them and come out in a narrow hallway at the end of the engine room. They'll want us to hand up the supplies. We won't be invited onboard." He glanced at Lacole. "If she'd been a little friendlier, they might have wanted to share a drink, but as it is, there's not much chance of that."

Lacole smirked, and I tossed Ritter the gag again, which he secured. Then he moved her to the far seat in the middle row, replacing the cuffs on her hands and securing one side to the armrest. Graeme began maneuvering the transport into position.

I reached out to see if I could somehow sense Dimitri even through their electric barrier, but all I felt was a large gap of nothingness. There was no way of telling if he was even on the ship.

Ritter caught my gaze. "We're almost there," he said. I nodded solemnly.

The outer docking took less than ten minutes, but in that time Jace disappeared and returned wearing a blond mustache. "So they don't recognize me," he said as we crowded into the space underneath the hatch. "Graeme says our faces have been plastered all over Sinalta's media stations." He held up a pale yellow beanie. "Blaze or Ritter could wear this. I know not all Sinaltans are blond, but most are, so we might as well fit in." He started to toss the beanie to Ritter but switched to hit Blaze in the face at the last moment.

"Oliver can cover both of us with an illusion," Blaze said, but he pulled on the beanie anyway.

"Okay, okay." A smile tugged at Ritter's face. "Jace and Blaze can take point, but Blaze goes up first to open the hatch and push them back with his fireballs. We don't want to risk gunfire." To Blaze he added, "Just don't burn a hole through the sub."

At Blaze's nod, Jace said, "Why do I not feel comforted that he didn't laugh?"

Blaze laughed. "We'll be okay."

"That's more like it." Jace clapped him on the back and looked almost jaunty as he took one side of the tunnel leading up to the hatch. Blaze took up the other.

Ritter caught my stare. "He's ready for this. You'll see," he said in an undertone.

I still wasn't sure I liked the idea of my rash brother at the front of the charge.

Ritter positioned himself opposite me and behind Jace. I was behind Blaze, with Oliver and Graeme still with me in the control room. They would be the least helpful during this close-quarter assault, except for Oliver's illusions, which he should be able to work from this distance.

"Maybe you can create some holos of supplies," I told Oliver.

"They'd know as soon as they touch them," he said with a hint of customary arrogance that made me smile. "Besides, it looks like Ritter has found something else."

Ritter handed a case to Jace and put another on the floor. "These cases were stuffed in a storage room back there. The one I gave Jace is locked."

Jace laughed. "Perfect. We'll pass it up, and they'll try to unlock it, and then *bang!* Be prepared for dropping Avowed." His anticipation leaked from his surface thoughts and filled me with a strange sense of joy.

Blaze climbed the ladder and began opening the hatch. Jace stood ready to pass him the case.

Here we come, Dimitri, I promised.

Oliver tapped me on the shoulder. "You sure she's secure?"

I glanced behind at Lacole. I was still in her mind because the moment the transports joined and the electronic barrier at the hatch point opened, she'd be able to warn them. If she tried, I'd be ready. "She's secure."

"I'd feel better if I checked."

"Hurry, then."

Oliver went toward her, and Lacole sneered at him before turning her face away, her mind filled with thoughts about her dead baby.

Curious, when she hadn't seemed to care much before about her so-called clump of cells.

Oliver made a hasty retreat. Anxiety leaked from him, completely opposite from what the rest of us felt. I began to wonder if we should leave him behind when we went into Sinalta. Or maybe this was exactly what he needed.

Our top hatch opened slowly with a loud screeching, and the larger transport's underside hatch was even slower and louder. I heard Sinaltan cursing and something Lacole's mind translated as, "Hasn't been opened in years." But finally, we saw two faces staring down at us, both men. They were blocked from my view almost completely from where I strained to peer up because Blaze's body took up most of the narrow space, but I was sure they were the men from the screen, one grinning, the other with a grimace on his lips.

Blaze went down a few rungs and took the case from Jace. He'd almost reached the top of our hatch again when jostling behind me made me turn in time to see Oliver holding a gun. But it wasn't directed at Lacole.

"What are you—?" I started to say.

He fired twice. My ears blasted as the bullets whizzed past me to their flesh target. Flesh, because I heard no ricochet.

"It's a trap. It's a trap!" Oliver screamed in Sinaltan.

Sinaltan.

Behind him, Lacole launched herself onto Graeme's back, trying to choke him with the hard bar between her cuffs, the side that had once attached to the seat somehow free. Her ankles were still chained together, but Graeme was slender enough that she had his waist between her knees as she pulled on his neck.

Furious shouting sounded from the hatch area, followed by a whooshing sound. I reached out to my brother, but his shield was tight. It was the first time we'd gone into battle together without being connected. I had no idea what was happening.

And Oliver's gun was now pointed at me.

Only I knew that he wasn't Oliver.

He fired, but the bullet bounced off my mental body shield. He was slower on the second shot, apparently surprised. It missed altogether as I moved, channeling Ritter's combat ability. Or Jace's. I didn't really know. The bullet slammed into an instrument panel.

Graeme was gagging, so I sent a burst of light to Lacole's mind.

Ha, I was prepared for that, she mocked.

Maybe, but she wasn't prepared for the ballistic knife I sent into her side. Her screams were barely muffled by the gag as she loosened her tension on Graeme's neck. At the abrupt release, his head jerked forward into the metal wall of the transport, but he didn't fall.

Oliver pulled the trigger again, and this time I almost wasn't fast enough. He had fired five bullets, and the Glock carried ten rounds. My mental barrier wouldn't stand up for more than one. Stella's armor could take a few more, but not all five, especially if they were all in my belly.

Heat borrowed from Blaze boiled in my veins as I jumped sideways toward where Oliver had retreated into the narrow space behind the rows of seats. Molten fire encased my hands. I could feel his heart beating, knew exactly where to place the blows. I whipped my hands toward his body from each side as though I carried swords, cutting into his flesh.

And slicing right through.

He fell in three pieces, two large ones behind the seats and his severed head onto the third row. His gun clanged near his body.

Lacole screamed again and stopped fighting Graeme. She collapsed to the aisle. On her elbows, she pulled herself toward Oliver, her blood staining the metal floor behind her. He still looked like Oliver and always would because he could no longer order his nanites to reform his features.

"Basiel!" Lacole cried, the tortured name barely comprehensible under the gag. She grabbed his hand and buried her face into his arm. "Oh, Basiel." It was all she could say aloud, though inside I saw what she'd recently hidden under her constructs, now shattered with her grief.

"Basiel?" Graeme asked, his brow furrowed.

"Watch her," I said, handing him a knife. I had to know what was going on with the others. Calling more fire to my hands, I hurried to the hatch. There was no sign of Ritter or

Jace, but Blaze was on the ground next to the ladder, leaking from two bullet holes, one in his chest and the other in his left leg.

"I'm okay," he said. "Oliver's a bad shot. Go after them."

I shot up the ladder and was greeted by scorched metal walls and a stench of smoke. An Avowed had his face burned off and a stab wound in his chest. Another was laid out with a broken neck.

I could feel the mate bond with Ritter. He was okay, and somewhere up ahead. There were four other life forces, two of which must be Dimitri and Jace. With two Avowed down, my worry lessened.

But how hadn't I seen that Oliver wasn't Oliver? When Mari had come, I'd channeled her without entering her mind, just as I had Ritter earlier, and even his color number had been similar enough that I hadn't noticed anything different. Anything but the uneasiness that had settled into my stomach. Now that I knew, everything clicked into place, from his refusal of treatment to how we were tracked to the runway in New Zealand.

I navigated the narrow corridor in the engine room at a run, not slowing until I reached the cafeteria area where Ritter and Jace held two Avowed at knifepoint.

"Everything okay down there?" Ritter asked.

I nodded and let the lava in my hands dissipate. I would have to explain about Oliver, but not yet.

"This guy tried to radio in a warning," Jace said, pushing his knife into his prisoner's throat.

Jace had him well under control, but I could feel the empath in Ritter's hold trying to break into his mind. I unsheathed my machete and pointed it at him. "Stop that now, or I will kill you." I pounded the mental version of the weapon into his mental shield, breaking through on my fourth try. This guy was strong but obviously not one of Mikyn's preferred trained monkeys. *I mean it.*

His eyes widened. "All right. All right. I stopped."

"Where's Dimitri?" I asked. "The healer."

The empath didn't reply, but his eyes strayed to the closed door of the crew quarters a few paces down the hall.

"They've locked the door from the outside." Ritter motioned to the empath. "Where is the key?"

I saw a clear memory of the empath leaving Dimitri inside after a round of torture. "In his chest pocket."

Ritter retrieved the key. "We won't need you anymore." He jabbed a needle into the empath's neck, guiding him as he dropped to the ground next to the wall. To Jace he said, "Keep the other awake for now, just in case." He opened the door, and I held my breath, wondering what we'd find.

It was worse than I imagined. The room had been sealed like our holding cells at the Fortress, and that meant no way to absorb nutrients. Dimitri lay on the bottom bunk, his once-large frame emaciated to the point of death, though still far from permanent death. The Unbounded protective system meant that he could last for months or even years until his body finally broke down enough to sever all three focus points. It was a long, excruciating way to die.

"Give him all our curequick!" I said, pulling vials from my bodysuit. I passed them to Ritter to begin injecting as I knelt on the floor next to the bunk, sending my mind out to Dimitri's. He was unconscious, the lake representation in his mind barely a stream with half inflated memory bubbles. Worse than I'd expected.

Wake up, Dimitri! I told him.

I sent my mind through his veins, directing the curequick to the areas that had shut down, urging them to repair even faster. Water seeped into the lake. Maybe he wasn't as far gone as I'd thought.

Erin?

The stream vanished, and I could feel him coming around. I stood in his mind in an odd sort of in between, joined with him as I often had while helping him to repair others. Slowly, torturously, the sand stream of thoughts began to run past me, top to bottom.

You're fixing me, he said. *I tried, but it takes a lot of energy.*

What happened?

In a rush, his thoughts came to me. How Mikyn had demanded his participation to impregnate empaths who might give birth to babies that could take Mikyn's place as Sinaltan seer. But as a healer, Dimitri was able to destroy that part of his reproductive system every time it tried to regenerate.

I wasn't going to give them a way to continue to choose which babies to kill. As you can imagine, Mikyn didn't take well to my refusal.

So he obviously planned to continue the baby ceremonies.

Yes, and in multiple locations. He claims to lament the losses, but like Stefan, he believes in a future where Avowed and Unbounded are the majority. I believe . . . I think he is two people inside.

His mind is broken? Insanity in many ways was more dangerous and enticing than flat-out evil

I couldn't fix him. He paused before resuming. *But they succeeded at least once in taking some of my sperm before I realized what they were doing. An empath named Lacole became pregnant. I couldn't . . . I didn't want to murder the child once it had been conceived. It had no fault in this.*

Now all the pieces fit. *The woman was reset. The baby is lost.*

Then what's troubling you? Dimitri asked, stifling the conflicting sorrow and peace my words had caused him.

I showed him everything, including how I'd killed the pretend Oliver and how I could now channel people without being in their minds. *I don't know how or why.*

It's because you can enter their bodies in a different way now, he said without hesitation. *The way I do as a healer.*

Of course! I'd always gone through the mind, but now that I'd learned enough about healing, I didn't need to break through their mental shields. Relief filled me.

I opened my eyes to see Ritter watching us. "Looks like he's coming around," he said, finishing another jab of curequick.

"I am." Dimitri's voice was rough. "Thanks for your help."

"We should have come earlier," I said. "We just didn't know where you were." Seeing the barely healing wounds all over his body, I knew starvation was only the smallest part of his torture.

Dimitri gave me a smile. "I knew you'd find me eventually."

"I'm still sorry."

He rallied enough to give a small snort. "This was nothing. I've endured far worse at the hands of the Emporium." The words reminded me of how little I knew of his life in the thousand years before he'd become my biological father.

I rubbed his hand—gently to avoid causing him pain. "We'll get you back to Ava. But first, we've got a little clean-up to do downstairs. Will you be okay here? We can leave Jace with you."

"I'm feeling better already. Little too much buzz on the curequick, though." He pushed an unused syringe in Ritter's hand away. "Let's hold off on more for now."

"Okay."

We went out to the hallway where Jace had hog-tied his Avowed technopath prisoner and now worked on bandaging Blaze, who had somehow made it up the ladder.

"What happened down there?" Blaze asked, his gaze flicking

toward the engine room. The same question was in Ritter and Jace's eyes. "One minute I was climbing, and the next minute Oliver went berserk."

"It wasn't Oliver." My voice choked on his name. "It was Lacole's husband, Basiel, all along. Ever since we left the hotel in New Zealand. He's a technopath, and when his wife reached out to him mentally to say we'd captured her in the other room, he used his nanites to change his appearance."

There'd been so many holo changes in clothing for Oliver that it might be understandable for me to have missed yet another one, but I should have noticed something. By the time I had, I'd already accepted him as the real Oliver.

I took a calming breath. "He was the one who reset Lacole on Graeme's transport so I couldn't get into her memories. And he was how the Avowed tracked us to the airstrip in New Zealand. He told Lacole who he was when he slipped into the infirmary to visit her, but he didn't know about his wife's pregnancy because he wasn't the father. Dimitri was. Mikyn was trying to create another seer."

Blaze grimaced as he shifted his weight. "That's why she was so angry with him."

"Yes."

She was no longer angry with him now. Her forgiveness came too late for him to care.

"I didn't know they were familiar with using nanites in that way," I said. "Not because they couldn't but because they haven't needed to develop that technology, but either they know all too well, or someone taught them recently."

"It's possible they got the information from Stefan," Ritter said with a grimace. "Or from one of the people he sent there."

Another long pause, and then Jace was the first to ask the question we all wanted to voice: "What about Oliver?"

Silence fell between us. I couldn't speak.

"No," Blazed moaned. "No."

A sob shook my chest as I took out my phone and looked at the message the CIA had sent me. None of the pictures were familiar until the last one that was undeniably Oliver, despite the burns covering three-fourths of his face. He was the only one permanently dead.

Ritter's arms went around me, and I sobbed into his chest. Oliver was really and truly dead, and we hadn't even suspected until the shooting. That hurt more than learning it right away because it meant we hadn't known him well enough—and there was nothing we could do to change that now.

"I should never have let him come along," I said, my voice muffled by his body armor.

Ritter's arms tightened. "It wasn't your call. Ava assigned him and Oliver chose to go. As was his duty. He's been training every day for months like the rest of us."

"He died a hero," Blaze said.

I lifted my face in his direction to see tears in his eyes. "Yes, he was."

"And while something tells me he'd love to have us all sitting around eulogizing him, now's probably not the time." Blaze motioned to Jace for help standing.

The tiniest snort of grief-crazed laughter escaped my throat because Oliver would love to have us all eulogize him—and we'd do it properly when this was over.

Jace leaned over and pulled the larger man to his feet. "You sure you don't want any curequick? Because I have a few more vials."

Ritter and I froze at the suggestion, but Blaze merely shook his head. "I injected some regular old painkillers that will probably be out of my system by the time you get me downstairs. I can't risk another bout with curequick at this stage of my recovery."

"Oh, sorry," Jace said. "I thought that was over."

Blaze started to shrug, then winced. "No one knows for sure how long the addiction will remain in my brain, especially now that I'm not being killed on a weekly basis." Blaze laughed, but I found it hard to see the humor.

Ritter put his arm around Blaze. "Let's get you in with Dimitri for now. Jace and I will go down and clean up and figure out how to get us all back to Ava's ship before we take on Mikyn. Erin will stay up here with you."

I was glad to wait because the last thing I wanted was to see the dismembered body that so resembled Oliver. But I was also sorry for what they'd think when they discovered exactly what I'd done. Because so far only Dimitri, Graeme, and Lacole knew.

But I was wrong about that. Inside the crew quarters, Blaze sank to the floor in the tiny locker space between the bunks and the miniature sink opposite them. "For what it's worth," he said, "there isn't much blood except what Lacole lost. The heat seared the flesh closed on the other."

On the pretend Oliver, he meant. I hadn't felt sick until that moment, and I dived for the sink, vomiting the little I had in my stomach, mostly yellow liquid.

"You did what you had to do," Dimitri said.

Blaze shook his head. "If anyone is to blame, it's me, because I was the one who taught her to play with fire." He quirked a brow. "Seriously, how did you do it? Was it fireballs, or did you figure out how to encase your hand in it like I did back at the hotel?"

It was all so ridiculous and terrible. I didn't know whether to laugh or to cry. I wasn't sorry about killing Basiel as much as I was sorry for the need to kill anyone. "The killing needs to end," I said, wiping my mouth with my fingers.

"We'll make sure of that." Dimitri motioned to me to come

to him and was about to say more when an arm reached inside the tiny room and pulled the door shut. A click sounded as we were locked inside. That could only mean one thing.

Someone else was inside the boat, and now we were all prisoners.

Chapter 19

I SENSED TWO STRONGLY SHIELDED LIFE FORCES RETREATING FROM OUR position toward the engine room. Not our people. I leapt toward the door, pounding hard. It wouldn't budge. I was about to do it again when bony fingers dug into my shoulders, holding me back.

"Stop," Dimitri said, pulling me away. "I already tried that. For hours." He smiled and shook his head. "And that was before most of the torture when I was a lot stronger."

Behind him, Blaze was also standing, his face hard. "Can you reach Ritter?"

I pushed my thoughts out, hoping the hatch hadn't yet closed. Breaking through our captors' shields would take more time than calling our team back—as would trying to cause the Avowed a heart attack or something at this distance with my new healing ability. I could sense Ritter through our mate bond, but his shield was strong, and I couldn't speak to his surface thoughts because he didn't have my ability. Again, breaking in might take too long, and even though Jace's shield wasn't nearly as difficult to get through, he'd be reinforced around Lacole.

Instead, I found Graeme. *It's Erin. Someone has locked us in.* But as I wasn't inside his mental barrier, I was limited to thought speech instead of an instant dump. Speech that was tragically cut off before I'd passed all the information. Cut off before Graeme could open his mind or Ritter could sense my distress through the mate bond.

"I can't feel them anymore," I told the others. "They must have closed the hatch. I did reach Graeme, but I only sent him a few words." Slow, slow words.

Muscles bunched in Blaze's arms as if he was readying to cut through the door with his molten lava. "Can this sub detach without our people closing their hatch?" he asked. Visions of our people drowning as water poured through the hatch filled me with fury.

"Their ship would send a warning first," Dimitri said more calmly than either of us. "They'll have time to close the hatch, or the computer will do it automatically. But they won't be able to prevent the detaching."

A loud clanking filled the transport, cutting off my thoughts and signaling an uncoupling of the two vessels. Hope that Ritter and Jace would save us disappeared.

Blaze slumped, his face pale with pain. "Sit," I ordered. I looked at Dimitri. "You too. Rest. We'll need to heal Blaze as much as possible."

Dimitri sat wearily on the bottom bunk, his body leaning forward so his back wouldn't hit the next bunk up. "Not without absorbing, we won't. Or at least you won't." His eyes dropped to my abdomen.

"Right." I experienced a vivid rush of uncontrollable panic. If left in a sealed room, my body would begin to absorb the baby to sustain itself once I lost consciousness. Then I'd begin on the others and them on me. Survival would go to the strongest, until that one fell to pieces. Already our bodies had absorbed whatever molecules of sea life had been in the air because I could no longer taste it on my tongue.

With effort, I pushed back the useless panic. I was not helpless. I could still break through our captors' mental barriers, and with Blaze's ability, we could melt our way out of the quarters that had now become our cell. It would just take time.

"You okay?" Dimitri asked.

"Yeah." I hated the worry in his dark eyes, but it helped me concentrate on my next move. I was the strongest here, and I needed to take control. "The first order of business is to melt through the seal in this room so we can absorb. I think we can manage that. Then we fight."

"How many can you sense?" Dimitri asked. "I know this room doesn't have an electric grid. Their empath was always trying to get in my mind, even when he wasn't in here."

I hesitated as I double-checked what I'd already determined. "I'm sensing two more life forces besides the two we caught—they untied the technopath, but the empath is still drugged. I don't know if the ones we reset are still here or if Ritter and Jace moved them below on their way down. If they are here, I can't sense them. And I didn't sense the two new ones earlier, so it's possible they have more."

"Blocking that well is hard for anyone," Dimitri said. "I'd bet on a shielded room instead, a safety built into the prison ship from any outside contact. Otherwise, their mental shields would still be strong enough to hide from you."

I hoped he was right. "All of them seem to have strong shields, and it'll be a challenge breaking in at a distance, but I'll get through."

"Three against three," Blaze said. "And a drugged empath who can't get into our minds. I like those odds."

I shook my head. "One against three at the moment. Neither of you is in any condition to fight.

"It took us three hours to get here, so if they're bringing us in, it'll be at least that long for us to get to Sinalta. Or longer, since this time we lose those ten knots per hour they were already traveling toward us." Blaze touched his shoulder. "A guy can heal a lot in that time. The bleeding has already stopped, I think."

"He has a point," Dimitri said. "We might consider waiting and confronting Mikyn once we are back in Sinalta. We won't starve in that amount of time. The baby will be fine."

"No." I made a slashing movement with my hand. "What if they don't take us back? Or what if they wait for a few weeks in the hopes that we'll be too weak to do anything?"

"Mikyn wouldn't risk your baby," Dimitri said.

"Why not? My daughter can't be a seer, and when you think about it, hiding us gives them even more leverage. Mikyn is already complaining about Sinaltan's lack of speed, and he's threatening to tattle to the White House if Ava doesn't bring Keene back to help. She laughed at him, but with me also missing, things might change."

Blaze nodded gravely. "Dad would swim to Sinalta if he needed to get to you."

I hadn't spent enough time with Blaze to be accustomed to him calling Ritter "Dad," but I liked it. "Exactly. And my brother would too. So I say we make a hole to get sustenance and start fixing you." I might not need their backup if I could take the Avowed out from a distance, but at the moment, I had no idea what kind of abilities our jailers had, and we needed to make sure we wouldn't just end up trapped in a sealed room first.

I coaxed a molten ball to life, letting it slide over my hand like a glove, and took a step toward the door. I'd melt my way right through it. *As I had Basiel's body.* Pushing the dark thought away, I lifted my hand to the door.

Dimitri's voice stopped me. "Maybe do that elsewhere and not the door?" His voice was conversational as if trying to calm me down. "Somewhere that doesn't warn them before we're ready?"

I closed my eyes and let the molten hand return to normal, berating myself for not thinking it through. Dimitri was right. I had no idea how many times I'd have enough energy or matter in the room to call the molten ball. Climbing up the ladder to the top bunk, I placed my rear on the edge, hunching and rolling onto it in an attempt to spare my head from hitting the ceiling. The space was tighter than between the other bunks, and I hit the top anyway as I settled on my back. Scooting over, I knocked along the wall, to see if it might be hollow.

"The bathroom is over there?" I asked, trying to visualize.

"Should be," Blaze answered. "If it's the same as the sub we left in New Zealand."

Dimitri shrugged. "My body was far enough gone when they threw me in here that I haven't had to use the bathroom." Which said more than everything else he'd told me about his imprisonment.

I reformed the molten hand and pointed a finger, pulling it along the top of the wall close to where it met the ceiling. My hope was that a line so high might go unnoticed more than a round, fist-sized hole. My finger sank into the wall, melting the metal with barely any resistance.

There was no rush of air, no hiss, but I felt an awakening in my body as it began to absorb nutrients through every pore. The sudden hint of fish and salt on my tongue was more delicious than any expensive, slowly-enjoyed, six-course meal.

I created another line along the ceiling, trying to melt through the metal but not damage the wiring. The double lines made me feel better, even if I couldn't detect a difference in my absorption rate.

I rolled to my side and peeked over the side. "Better?"

Blaze grinned up at me. "Yes." But he couldn't hold back a wince of pain.

"Let's get you fixed up." I climbed down the ladder and wedged myself on the floor beside him.

"Just make sure you're on the lookout in case they revive that empath," Dimitri said.

"I'm watching." With my mind linked to Dimitri's, I traced Blaze's wounds. The bleeding had stopped, as he'd indicated, but his chest wound started up again after I helped his body expel the bullet. I sewed it up with my tiny med kit before mentally knitting veins and muscles, and using my energy to increase his rate of repair. Through it all, he barely moaned. His tolerance for pain had to be off the charts.

I repeatedly sucked in nutrients to sustain my efforts, and even then I tired. Dimitri gave out before I did, but in the end, Blaze rested more comfortably, his leg and chest wrapped with strips of sheets from the cots.

"Give me fifteen minutes, and I can help you too," I said to Dimitri.

His head turned toward me. "No need. I'll be okay now that I'm dining on seafood again."

I laughed. "It's my new favorite meal."

"You know what you have to do now, don't you?"

I nodded. "I'm going to find out where we are and who is on this ship."

After giving myself a few minutes to recover, I closed my eyes and reached out to the life forces. "They're in the control room," I reported. "The empath is still out, but he seems closer to consciousness. They must have given him something to speed up his recovery."

"You can change that by redirecting the drugs," Dimitri said. "Works better if you can lay hands on the person, but you should be able to do just fine in conjunction with your other ability."

That was how it worked for me too. Touching someone always made the mental contact that much stronger. "I'll give it a try," I said.

"Or better yet, stop his heart," Blaze muttered.

Dimitri laughed. "We don't want to call attention to him just yet, but that is an option I used during my captivity, despite my oath to do no harm."

Blaze let out a sigh. "War doesn't count. You know that. Besides, it's only temporary."

Dimitri's nod was weary.

As they talked, I finished redirecting the drugs in the empath and began breaking into the mind of the technopath, whose mental shield appeared weaker than the two others. It was more difficult than I anticipated, but I was determined. Even so, my mind was beginning to weary when the mental version of my machete finally broke through.

"Looks like we're only an hour away from Sinalta now," I told the others after quickly reviewing his thought stream. I'd taken longer than I'd thought with healing Blaze. "But they've been told to hold our current distance and to take avoidance measures if any ship approaches. Ritter and Jace tried a chase, but they lost them."

"So no chance of their taking us to Sinalta." Blaze's voice was flat.

"We aren't waiting anyway." I expected a protest, but they simply stared at me grimly. "I could take them out one at a time," I continued. "But I'm not sure which one has the codes we'll need to get into Sinalta."

Blaze started to say something in response, but I held up a finger as I focused on the conversation in the control room. "They're talking now."

"What about the woman?" asked a female with tightly braided hair who was so decked out with guns and knives that she had to be combat. "She's with embryo." I couldn't feel her emotions or read them on her face, but the question seemed to express concern.

The technopath shrugged. "Seer Zenos says we should open the vents a few times a day."

"Is that sustenance enough for the baby?" the woman asked, glancing between the technopath and the other Avowed, a male, equally decorated with weapons.

He laughed. "There are two others she can absorb if she needs more."

"True," the woman said. "Her body will likely protect the pregnancy. Or will until it can't anymore."

For a full moment, I allowed anger to take me, but only after placing the mental barrier around my womb. My daughter didn't need that negativity.

"Erin?" Dimitri asked.

I opened my eyes, consciously unclenching my hands. "I really, really hate those Avowed. I don't know that we should have saved any of them. The evil runs so deep." I walked to the door, thinking about cutting around the lock. "Let's go."

"No. Bring them to us. Or as close as possible. It'll be easier if we can separate them." Dimitri grinned. "Besides, I'm not altogether sure I can walk that far yet."

"I'm ready." Blaze came to his feet more heavily than he should have.

"Okay." I formed a thought, as if on an imaginary slip of paper, and held it next to the technopath's rushing sand stream. It wavered a second before being sucked in and immediately absorbed into the whole. The thought became his own, but he dismissed it. Some people weren't easily influenced, but usually another nudge or two was all it took.

The technopath only needed the second. "I'd better check on them," he said. "Or at least open the vent. It's been hours."

"What for?" the other man growled. "We're only keeping them for leverage. How we keep them doesn't really matter."

"Well, Seer Zenos seems to have a little bit of a soft spot for the woman. I just want to check."

"I'll go with him," said the female Avowed.

The man grunted. "Just don't open the door. You know they came in armed."

A short time later, a knock sounded. "You okay?" the technopath asked us.

"No. We're not," I said. "We need medical attention. My friend has been shot twice. Do you have any painkillers?"

"Sorry, we're not authorized to open the door. We know you came in armed."

"Can't you just pass in a first aid kit?" I asked. "We'll stand away from the door. And please, can you get some flowing air in here? I'm expecting."

"I can open the vent for a few minutes." A soft, mechanical scraping accompanied the words. "But only for a few minutes. We can't have the healer recovering."

"Apparently, you're scary," I whispered to Dimitri. Which meant they'd learned the hard way that healing gifts could also be used to kill. To the technopath, I added, "Please give me the first aid kit. Both of my friends are in a bad way. We'll lay down our weapons. Don't you have cameras in here? You can check."

The answer about the cameras appeared in the technopath's mind. No, they didn't have cameras, which seemed rather short-sighted for a vessel used as a prison ship, no matter how quickly it might have been retrofitted.

"No. Sorry," the technopath said. "Once our backup arrives, we can take care of them."

I hadn't seen this information in his mind before. "And when's that?"

"Sorry, it's classified." Not really. He simply didn't know because he was awaiting more orders from the Sinaltan Senate—or rather from back channels. Obviously, this wasn't an official op.

The rest of his thoughts upset me more. "They plan to gas us so they can remove our weapons," I whispered to Blaze and Dimitri. "They're going to inject me with a sedative to keep me out." That couldn't be good for my child.

"Screw this!" Molten fire suddenly encased Blaze's hands. "We aren't waiting for more of them. Stand back."

I grinned a little too widely. "Let me show you where they are."

He let his mind shield drop, and I showed him where the technopath stood with the woman in the hallway. *She's combat and the more dangerous threat.* I told him. *So I'll disable him as a distraction and tell you when to go for the woman.*

"Dimitri," I said softly, "what part of the brain controls movement?"

"It's kind of tricky. He might die temporarily if you don't do it right."

"Then show me."

I linked mentally with Dimitri, and together we began tracing the Avowed's neural pathways, my mental connection with both of them making it almost too easy, despite the metal door separating us.

"I'm sorry," the technopath said. "We have to close the vents now." He was definitely not sorry.

No, I'm sorry, I said in his mind. *I can't let you do that.*

Shock reverberated through his mind, turning to terror when he found he couldn't move. He struggled to walk, and we released him long enough to allow one jerky step before letting him collapse.

The woman muttered something the technopath couldn't quite catch. "Now," I told Blaze as she bent over him.

Blaze carved out the lock with his hand and pushed the door open, slamming it into her behind. She was skilled enough to draw her weapon as she fell, but Blaze's fire burned her hand, causing her to drop it. She let out a short scream before he followed with a chop to her vocal cords. Leaving Blaze to secure them, I jumped over her body and sprinted the few feet to the control room.

If I'd had enough nanites in my blood, I'd channel the technopath to change my face to the Avowed woman's, but a direct assault would have to do. I threw myself to the side against the open control room hatch a few seconds before the combat Avowed came rushing through. He detected me at the last moment, but my gun was on his neck before he could defend himself.

"Drop your gun and all the other weapons," I ordered. "One at a time."

When he hesitated, I jabbed a knife into his side, bringing blood. He still refused to comply, but by then I'd broken through his mental shield, our physical connection giving me more strength. I thrust my machete into his thought stream, twisting it. *Now.*

He sucked in a sharp breath, and then his gun clanked to the metal floor. Two more guns, a knife, and three odd-shaped weapons I wasn't familiar with followed. By then Blaze was there, and he cuffed the man before patting him down, discovering another knife, several vials of liquid, a garrote wire disguised as a decoration for his hair, and a heavy ball-shaped device.

Blaze examined it. "Seriously? A grenade? Under the water? You Avowed are certifiably nuts." The man began cursing in

Sinaltan, but Blaze tied a gag around him. "You won't need his mouth, right?"

"No, and I don't even need them close. Let's put them in the crew quarters."

"What about the technopath?" Blaze asked. "What if he mimics . . ."

I was still connected to his mind, and now that I wasn't occupied with the Avowed, I saw that Blaze was thinking about the guilt he felt for Oliver's death. I withdrew from his mind as I said, "He doesn't have any nanites in his blood, so he can't do what Basiel did."

He relaxed. "Good. Let's get these guys taken care of and go find our friends."

I jabbed my gun into the Avowed's neck. "Walk."

Once they were secure, we helped Dimitri to the control room as he was the most familiar with piloting all kinds of craft. He began a careful sweep of the area around the transport. "There's no detectible sub near here," he said. "Can you reach Ava mentally?"

I shook my head. "Even if we managed to disable the electric grid around the transport, I can't do it over that distance without Keene's help. It's just too far. Can we radio?"

"Only if we want to alert Sinalta. They've got a boatload of security here that sends automatic alerts every time we communicate from the ship itself or when we approximate any vessel. Plus, there's an automated program that sends a signal from a predetermined spot every thirty minutes. I'm not sure even Stella could rewrite the code from inside here."

"What do we care?" Blaze said, leaning back in his chair. "They won't be able to catch up to us if we head toward Ava's ship."

Dimitri frowned. "No, but potentially they could blow us up."

"Even at this distance?" I leaned forward to stare at the information on the screen, which didn't make a lot of sense to me because it was all in Sinaltan. Apparently, Dimitri had no such limitation.

"Absolutely, with significant leeway in case we bolt. Which is why I suspect this is how close Mikyn ordered them to come."

I wondered if the Avowed on the ship understood the danger. "Right. Then we need to get to Sinalta as soon as possible. Because I'm pretty sure everyone on this transport is expendable to Mikyn Zenos, including us."

Dimitri nodded. "The world can't know what he has done or intended to do here."

Blaze grinned and sat up straight, forming a molten ball in his palm. "I'm game. Let's go directly to Sinalta."

"The only problem," Dimitri said, "is that even if we take off right after the next thirty-minute check-in, we'll need at least one more before we get to Sinalta, or they'll know we are no longer here." He hesitated before adding, "But I have an idea that might work. We just need a technopath, a few tools, and a lot of luck."

I held up my hand. "I can give you the technopath."

Blaze jumped to his feet. "I'll search for tools."

"Good." Dimitri grinned. "Luck will have to take care of itself. Hurry. Let's try not to get ourselves blown up."

Chapter 20

THE PLAN WAS SIMPLE. SINCE IT DIDN'T APPEAR THAT WE COULD reprogram the system from the transport, I would channel the technopath to track down the physical part of the ship that supported the automatic check-in. Then we'd use tools to remove and eject it and its interconnected location beacon with the hope that it would maintain position long enough to send another automatic blast. By then it would be off course by as much as six miles as the city moved away from it. At that point, we hoped they'd give us until the next check-in to correct course. If they didn't, then at least any missile sent from Sinalta would target the location beacon instead of us.

"Once we're closer, we'll be on the nation's monitors, and they won't risk blowing us up with a missile while the world watches," Dimitri said. "Even if they can hide their missiles like the technopath seems to think they can." He studied the monitor. "We've got about five minutes before the next check-in. It'll probably take longer than that to find what we're looking for and to access it, but we should try to finish at least by the next blast. Because we really have no idea when they might send more information that requires a live response."

"I could force the technopath to respond for us," I said. "But that brings up a good point. Will we still have communication ability after we throw out the automatic response system? Because we'll still need to send codes to get into Sinalta. And they may contact us about being off course."

"We'll be able to communicate. But if they contact us after we expel the location beacon, there will be no way to hide that our live communication isn't coming from the same place. They are genius at underwater communication. But as long as we don't send any communications or call attention to ourselves, we might make it close enough to Sinalta to prevent them from blowing us up when they finally realize where we are."

I didn't like the term "might," but my thoughts skipped past that, racing ahead. "What if . . . I bet our prisoners have phones, or their version of them. Those should work close to the city, right? Even with the electronic grid in place. Just like their communication pads when they are close to other transports."

"Yes, but who would we call?"

"I know one person," I said, thinking of Cherish, the olive-skinned technopath who had forged an ID for me during my last visit. As the only Avowed of color that I had personally met in a sea of blond heads and blue eyes, she might not be all that hard to find, provided I could search a database of numbers and names.

Blaze grinned. "Now we're talking. Let's get to work."

We did, but we were approaching a fourth check-in by the time we found the equipment and were able to separate it from the transport, anchoring it down on a huge passing under-ground canyon before kicking up the transport to full speed.

"Looks like we're at fifty-five minutes to get to the city at this velocity," I said, leaning back in one of the control room chairs and using my borrowed technopath ability to do the calculations on the transport's computer system.

Concern knitted Dimitri's face. "That's cutting it short."

Too short, seeing as we'd have to cut our speed closer to the city so we wouldn't alert them. We had to hope there would be some leeway.

I turned on the phone that I'd taken from the Avowed technopath. It was smaller than those we used topside, but as I looked at certain tiny sections of text, they automatically enlarged so smoothly that reading was possible. It took a few moments for my brain to catch up, but channeling the technopath made it easier. No signal yet. Four million people to search once we were close enough, but the name Cherish might be unusual enough to stand out, and I knew she lived in the city's inner ring and worked with Valerine below the capitol in engineering, which could narrow it further.

"I bet the technopath has a way of accessing information more quickly," Dimitri said, "like Stella with her neural headset."

I snapped to my feet. "Good idea. I'll go see."

"We'll need codes for entry into the city anyway. If they let us get that far." Dimitri looked at the screen. "No sign of any incoming missile yet."

"Unless it's cloaked," Blaze said cheerfully.

I couldn't help grinning at his flippancy. If not for the danger to my daughter, I'd also be reveling in every second of this op.

The technopath tried to redirect my questioning, but I pushed and found the information in his thought stream. His device was like Stella's earbud, but it had more functions than her advanced neural headset. It could even control basic movements of the transport. "I have a friend who's going to love this," I told him. "And I'll be able to find the person I'm looking for in minutes. In the meantime, you'd better hope your leaders don't spot us and shoot us out of the water."

He cursed me unintelligibly through his gag, struggling against his bonds as he lay on the bottom bunk in the crew quarters. I thought it quite fitting that the thin mattress was stained with Dimitri's blood.

"What's your name anyway?" I asked.

He shook his head, but it appeared in his mind: *Caedmon.*

"Okay, Caedmon," I said. "Nice to meet you. Or it would be if you and your boss weren't trying to kill us."

He started to protest against his gag, but I put my finger over his mouth to still the rush. "Mikyn Zenos is a murderer. He has not only sentenced babies to die by telling their parents they won't Change, but he stole years of life from the children he placed in the mines." It was as close as I would ever get to telling anyone that Mikyn could change DNA. "I'm going to stop him." I didn't add that I should have stopped Mikyn when I'd first had the chance because my guilt wasn't anything I needed to share with this man.

I thought about Ritter and Jace and wished that I could disable the electric grid to search for them. But we were likely still too far away.

"Now I need the codes to get inside the gates under the city," I told Caedmon. "Please."

Again came the garbled curses that I couldn't make sense of except in his mind. I took the codes from his thought stream.

"Thank you," I said with a satisfied smirk.

He glared at me, his dire warning resounding in my head: *They'll be reported the minute you go through. They'll have guards waiting.*

WHEN WE WERE TEN MINUTES FROM SINALTA, WE CUT THE ENGINES SO the emissions wouldn't give us away. They would likely already have us on their sensors, along with all the subs and transports belonging to the other nations and their own city, but once we dropped to a crawl and hugged the canyon rising up from the sea floor, we'd be essentially invisible until our final approach. By then we hoped we'd be too close for any action.

Had they already sent out a missile to explode the communication system? We wouldn't know until we tried to use the codes to enter via the waterway gates below the city, at which point we'd trigger some kind of alarm. Or until our transport sailed close enough to any other vessel to set off a warning. Or until someone noticed how out of place we were.

Our odds were getting worse by the moment.

We had to be within mental range of Ava's boat, but we still hadn't figured out how to deactivate the electric grid. However, I was finally able to access the Sinaltan phone system, which used an internal connection wired into the transmitters on the transport's hull, outside of the grid, much like the system at the Fortress. As the system wasn't compatible with ours, it made sense they wouldn't block use of the phones, even on a prison ship sent far from the city.

Using the technopath's gift and his equipment, I found Cherish's number easily and made the call. She appeared on the phone screen, a curvaceous, black-haired woman with a large, hooked nose and elaborately styled hair draped with the customary Sinaltan rhodium and gold. When I explained who and where I was, she looked at me doubtfully. "I recognize you, but how do I know this isn't a trick?" Her prominent lyrical accent sounded a bit like singing.

"Because you and I are the only ones besides Valerine and Graeme who know that you made me a false ID when I was here before. You're part of the underground—the Unsworn, I hear they're called now."

We took the phone to the crew quarters and showed her the tied Avowed, making sure they didn't see her face, but knowing I was still putting her life at risk if we didn't succeed. No doubt the call could be traced.

"Don't worry about it," she said when I stepped back into the hallway and apologized for the danger. "I have contacts who can delete the call log from the network. What do you need from me? We didn't know where they'd taken your healer, so I'm glad you found him."

I felt a slight unease at the words. She had doubted me, but how did I know that *she* hadn't been compromised? I had little choice at this point, so I pushed on. "We have codes to enter the city, but this transport isn't supposed to be in this location. And they may or may not have sent a missile to where it is supposed to be to blow it up."

"I doubt they would send a missile directly," she said. "Not with everyone watching. There are more than forty topside countries represented here. I mean, we do have a kind of visual cloaking technology, but it won't fool radar. More likely, the Senate would send a vessel that appears to be a supply transport but is really loaded with weapons, but that would be extremely suspicious right before a destruction. So my guess is that any explosives they might use are already on your transport. I'd have to check the refit logs to be sure."

Next to me in the hallway, Blaze cursed under his breath. "Of course we're on a death trap. Much easier to explain a ship exploding itself than to send a missile that might be detected and considered an act of war."

Cherish nodded. "It's only a matter of time until they realize you're not where you're supposed to be. They are monitoring everything carefully. So you need safe passage in—and fast.

As much as I'd like to hear what's going on with Valerine and Graeme, that will have to wait. I'll send out a fishing transport for you, but you need to get suited up and out of there now. The suits should be in the cargo container near the bottom hatch."

Suited up? I looked over at Blaze, who nodded and said, "I saw the suits earlier. I'll show you."

"What about our prisoners?" Dimitri asked.

Cherish's face creased. "They were probably dead from the moment they were chosen for that job. I don't believe the seer will want any witnesses to what he's done."

I frowned. "We can't just leave them behind."

"We may not have enough suits," Blaze said. "Even though Dad and Jace took the two Avowed they temporarily killed, there's still four of them and three of us."

"Those transports typically come with five suits, but by law they must have enough for all the people onboard." Cherish's words were reassuring because there had originally been six Avowed, plus Dimitri.

I walked back into the crew quarters. "Get up," I told the prisoners. "We're going for a swim." With our guns to their heads, we freed the feet of the three who were conscious and forced them to walk down the narrow hallway to the engine room.

"Better disable the suit locator beacons," Cherish said in my ear. "In case they escape and manage to report in. And leave the phone on. I should be able to track it this close to the city."

Dread now ate at my insides. "How good are these suits?" I looked down at the swell of my belly under Stella's armor. "I'm pregnant. Or, uh, with embryo."

"Don't worry." Cherish waved a hand. "Think of them more like your spacesuits than typical diving gear. They'll pressurize to match the transport. The suits also have jet propulsion so you can get somewhere safe to wait for us. Now hurry!"

We had reached the engine room, and Blaze shoved a suit at me. "Looks like they are as good at following the law as we are topside. There are only five suits."

Which meant two of our four prisoners would be unprotected.

Dimitri's jaw firmed. "We'll take them anyway. They'll die, but they'll heal once we get them to Sinalta."

Blaze had disappeared and returned with the unconscious empath. "I say this is one of those we don't put in a suit. He'd be more of a problem alive anyway. And one of the combat Avowed."

"The male," I said. He was the greatest danger.

The male in question lunged at me, but Blaze jabbed a sedative into his neck. "You won't remember a thing," he said. To me he added, "How many minutes until check-in?"

"Four and a half."

Unceremoniously, we crammed the two remaining Avowed into their suits, who were willing enough to help us now, and tied their unconscious comrades to their backs before cuffing them again. The technopath was strangely quiet.

"Guess you're wondering if maybe your boss does think of you as expendable," I said. His thoughts protested and raged against me, but he wasn't certain. Not at all.

Blaze took my discarded machete and slipped it into a large dry bag he'd found in the container. He had already opened the hatch, and water lapped gently in the open hole. "You first," he said to me as he strung a line of rope between the Avowed. "Then we'll toss out these guys. This sub isn't going fast enough for us to get separated, I don't think."

I didn't have to be asked twice. With every moment that passed, my daughter was in increasing danger. I'd barely slipped into the water when the technopath's earbud informed me that someone was hailing the ship directly.

I made sure the earbud's transmission to the transport was off before opening the audio with Cherish, which I'd also rerouted through the earbud. "Cherish? Can you hear me? Someone is calling the ship. It seems to be coming from the city, but if it's not, they'll be notified if I respond, and it'll trigger the safety protocols. If I don't respond, it'll probably still trigger the protocols. But I don't exactly speak Sinaltan."

In front of me, the Avowed prisoners appeared below the slowly receding transport. Automatic lights on their suits made them stand out in the dark water. They weren't moving their tied limbs, though, and I realized that Dimitri or Blaze had rendered them unconscious after my departure.

"Send the numbers two-eight-five," Cherish said. "It basically means your output audio is down but repairs will be made in less than five minutes."

I sent the nonverbal message exactly as Cherish told me. Would it buy us five minutes? Ten? I hoped so.

Dimitri appeared in the water ahead of me, followed by Blaze. They used their jets to cover the few feet to the prisoners and pushed them in my direction. "We need to find cover." Dimitri's voice came through my suit's com and not the earbud, disorienting me for a brief second.

I looked around anxiously. Where had the underwater canyon gone? Cherish's comment about the space suits seemed suddenly apropos. Being so far under the ocean was like I imagined it would be in deep space, only instead of endless stars there was an infinite blackness unrelieved by anything but the dim lights on the transport that was ever-so-slowly leaving us behind.

"We can at least turn off our suit lights." I jetted myself closer to the technopath to see if there was an obvious way to do so. The lights weren't bright enough to see from far, but they were noticeable up close.

"I mean because of the explosion," Dimitri clarified.

"I'm really not sure Mikyn will give a destruction order," I said. "Not without knowing what is going on. But I think I might be close enough to tell the ship to pick up speed. I'm still connected."

"Any change may give them a hint as to where you jumped out," Cherish said.

"Well, if they blow us up, they won't know we jumped out," I countered.

"True. But they could just board. I've been wrong before."

I was about to agree, but the baby kicking in my stomach reminded me that I wanted the transport far away from me, just in case. I kicked up the transport's speed from a crawl to a good clip of twenty knots.

A bright light flicked on above Blaze's right wrist. "Look at this," he said. "Button is near the elbow. Turn yours on and see what we can see."

After some searching, our lights revealed a faint line of something in the distance that might be part of the canyon—if it wasn't a killer whale or something equally dangerous. It seemed to be to our left and down, though up and down and left and right seemed to have no meaning here.

We triggered our jets and aimed toward the outcropping. I glanced back to see if I could still see the transport, but it was gone. Now the weight of the black ocean felt oppressive.

"How soon can you be here?" I asked Cherish.

"It'll be a good thirty minutes. We have to follow a fishing pattern so we don't appear too unusual. If you can continue to move away from the jump point, that would help our trajectory appear unrelated to the transport you just left."

"Can they trace our current communication?"

"Only if they know to do so, and they might once they realize the transport you were on was compromised. Either way, there's nothing we can do about phone tracing right now while we're still connected. So just float tight. My friends will be there soon."

We moved forward for a few more minutes, towing our prisoners. I glanced back again to check on them, two in suits, two tied on their backs. It was rather gruesome, but what choice did we have?

At that moment, the water in the distance lit up with a silent explosion, followed by an odd jolt. An instant later, a wall of water slammed against us. I tumbled over and over uncontrollably with the force. I pulled my body into an awkward fetal position, my arms curling protectively around my middle, made difficult with the bulk of the suit. Smaller underwater waves followed, hurling bits of fish, metal, and plastic. But in those terrifying seconds, my mental shield covered my suit, stronger than a rushing bullet. Still I tumbled and spun like an air bubble in a hurricane. The light above my wrist spun crazily as I rotated. Voices sounded through my earbud and suit com, before going eerily quiet.

When the tumbling stopped, the blackness was even more profound and infinite. Panic filled me.

I was alone.

Chapter 21

I BREATHED DEEPLY, GLAD WHEN MY LUNGS INFLATED LIKE USUAL. I pushed out my mind, searching for the others. Gradually, I found life forces, but they were of fishes and other sea creatures. The entire ocean lit up mentally, superimposing upon the dark image I'd previously observed only with my eyes. How had I missed it before? The ocean was full of life and color.

But no humans.

"Hey, guys," I said. "Can you hear me?"

"I can hear you."

"Cherish?"

"Yes. What happened? Your signal changed position rather suddenly."

"The transport blew."

"Are you okay?"

"I think so." And I had to be close enough to at least the unconscious technopath because I could still operate the neural earbud as well as before. "But I've been separated from the others. They aren't coming through on the com."

"Those things have notoriously short range. Can you reach them mentally?"

"Trying that now." Just because I couldn't see their life forces didn't mean they weren't near.

Sure enough, I found Blaze with his mental shield down. "Erin, Dimitri," he was saying over his com.

I'm here, I said in his mind. *We're out of com range. I'm coming to you. Wave your light if it still works so I see you when I'm closer. Keep a look out for Dimitri.*

Aloud, I said to Cherish. "I found one of them. Can you tell me if I'm moving toward the city?" As I spoke, I enacted the jets.

"Yes. You're moving generally northwest but not exactly parallel to the city."

"He's not far."

Yet minutes passed before I saw a light moving in the distance, and Blaze's life force registered clearly from the aquatic life.

I see you, I told him.

"And I see Dimitri," Blaze said, his voice finally coming through the suit com. "He looks tangled in the rope from our prisoners. They're behind an outcropping of sorts. I think he was blown down into the canyon."

"I can hear you now," I said. "I'll reach out to him."

I found Dimitri, who was unconscious. I reached Blaze, and together we went to Dimitri. He was thoroughly tangled in the rope that connected the Avowed, but his suit wasn't compromised. Mentally, I traced his body, finding that the cause of unconsciousness was a severe blow to the head. I could find no similar hurt on the unconscious prisoners, even those unprotected by the suits. "I think something from the explosion hit his head, or he rammed into this outcropping. He'll be okay in a bit."

"Leave it to Dimitri to protect the prisoners," Blaze muttered, trying to untangle the rope. "Here, hold this guy steady while I push Dimitri under his arm."

"Erin?" Cherish's voice came through the earbud. "Are you okay to stay where you are now and can you maintain position? If so, we can pick you up there in about twenty minutes. Now that they've blown the transport, I think you need to power off the phone in case someone thinks to trace it. I'll get working on deleting the records of the call."

"How will we know if it's your transport?"

"We'll send you a message with our lights. Do you know Morse code?"

"I think we can manage that."

"Look for Susie sells seashells by the seashore."

I snorted a laugh. "Okay. Powering down. See you soon." I sent the commands through the earbud but wished I could also toss out the actual phone itself.

Dimitri was waking now and asking questions. I let Blaze explain as I slipped from both their minds and reached out to see if I could contact Ava. But her mind was still too far away, positioned as her boat was on the far side of the city we were still miles from. I grabbed the prisoner's rope to stop them from drifting away.

"Let's get a little lower here," I said. "Just in case."

Dimitri's gaze shifted in my direction. "You okay?"

My heartbeat was definitely elevated, and it was exactly like him to notice. "Guess I never thought Mikyn would actually kill me." Me and the baby, I meant, but they would understand.

A few seconds of silence was followed by Dimitri's calming voice. "You know his secrets," he said. "And because you do, you're more dangerous than anyone."

"I guess you're right." Consciously, I slowed my heart rate, and the anxiety receded. Turning on my jets, I guided myself lower behind the outcropping. Blaze followed.

Questions came from Blaze's surface thoughts about Dimitri's comment, but regardless of how much I trusted my stepson, he'd have to stay in the dark about Mikyn's unreliable ability to change babies' DNA.

The twenty minutes seemed more like hours as we waited to learn whether or not we'd be rescued or recaptured. When the transport did arrive, it came more quietly than expected, trailing an array of fishing nets that were currently empty.

"That's got to be it," Blaze said as outer lights on the transport began to blink Morse code.

THE TWO UNSWORN WOMEN WHO PICKED US UP WERE NERVOUS AS we shrugged out of our diving gear, but they didn't ask us to turn in our weapons. The shorter of the two wore her hair in elaborate braids, and the other had chains of jewelry in her hair, but besides that, they looked like sisters, with their narrow faces, blue eyes, and not just pale but nearly translucent skin. I guessed they had spent more time in their transport than under the lights that had once made up Sinalta's false sky.

We secured the prisoners in their crew quarters, where I convinced Dimitri to save his energy for himself instead of trying to fix the empath and the male combat Avowed, as they would recover without him, if more slowly. That didn't stop him from easing the tension in the Avowed who'd come to rescue us, infusing their bodies with a release of serotonin. By the time we were five minutes from Sinalta's underwater gates, they were smiling.

"Cherish says you might want to mentally reach your friends now," said the woman with braids, "before we enter the city."

My gaze snapped to hers. "Why's that?"

She gave me an apologetic grin that made her seem younger than the mid-thirties I'd given her. "Shortly after the transport you were on exploded, they raised the electronic shield over the city. And just now, they've recalled all transports. We're one of the last to go in."

"I see." I exchanged a wary look with Dimitri. Did that mean Mikyn was expecting someone to attack or that he was trying to block any chance of communication with the outside?

I reached out, searching for Ava, pushing hard up and through the water that separated us. I was beginning to worry that we were out of range when I finally felt her, and I tapped on her shield with a request to enter, as we'd never be able to communicate everything in time with surface thoughts, which were harder at a distance anyway.

Is everyone okay? she asked, her relief palpable.

We are. Except Oliver. I winced internally as Oliver's death hit us both with a wave of grief.

Yes, Ritter told us what happened. The agony and responsibility Ava felt about Oliver was far worse than what I felt, yet at the same time more accepting. Loss was something that had chased her for centuries, and she'd learned how to deal with it.

In a rush of thoughts, I updated her with everything, and then asked, *What about Ritter and Jace? What's the plan?*

Ritter, Jace, and Graeme should be in Sinalta by now. They went in through one of the gates using Graeme's connections. Ava's thoughts hesitated, sending a tendril of dread through my stomach. *But I can't check or see what's happening there because Sinalta reactivated their electronic grid over the city thirty minutes ago. It occurred after we detected an underwater explosion—the sub you were on, I'm assuming. They said it was an internal issue, but that they are recalling all their craft for diagnostic tests. They have left one of their Senate transports below the city outside the grid for official communication, presumably so we won't consider this an act of war, but as of right now, we can't get radio, mental, or any other kinds of transmissions from the city. It's particularly interesting that this happened right after we established radio communication with a group of the Unsworn. There wasn't even time to warn them about Mikyn's plan.*

That was bad, but there was more I could feel her holding back.

What aren't you telling me? I asked.

A few heartbeats passed between us. *Catrina is missing as of three hours ago. Mari and Keene are looking for her now, but so far they have searched everywhere using both their abilities.*

Which means she's being kept in an electronic grid. Or she was dead. But I couldn't say that, not even to Ava.

Right. Stefan is contending that if she isn't found, she will need to be replaced by her successor.

And her vote on the Triad would be void. Stefan had upped the stakes.

Does Jace know?

Yes, and he's understandably upset. He wanted to look for her, but we convinced him that securing Sinalta would lower Stefan's influence on us. But you should know that Mikyn and the Sinaltan Senate have already requested the pardon and rein-statement of Statesmen Tsaousiss and Scala in light of extenuating political events.

And they'll bring Stefan. The idea of him running free in Sinalta and having access to their advanced technology and weapons made my stomach twist.

Exactly. We can't let that happen. We need to warn the Unsworn, and then get ready to take down the Sinaltan shields. Ritter and Jace are working with Graeme on a plan.

I'll find them, I said. *But do you think Keene could help our people could break through the electronic shield? Now that it's above water, the Sinaltans wouldn't be in danger.*

I already asked, and he said it was unlikely in the timeframe needed. The strength in that shield is unimaginable. I'm sorry, no one out here will be able to help you.

We'll be fine, I answered.

I was almost looking forward to the cozy little chat I planned to have with Mikyn Zenos.

WE CLEARED THE GATE CHECKPOINT WITH NO PROBLEM, BUT THE larger size of the fishing transport precluded our entering the main sections of the city. We were directed instead to a docking bay, where we were quickly smuggled out with the fish we had picked up during our short journey back. The sun hung low on the horizon, but we'd gained at least two or three hours from the time zone shift from San Diego. Cherish met us in a large outdoor processing area, draped in a purple toga, silver cords circling her waist, and her kinky hair woven with thin platinum chains. A spotted leather wrap hung from her shoulders like a cape, looking a lot like leopard sealskin. I couldn't blame her. The air was moist and cool enough that I was grateful for my body armor. The electronic shield might be up, but the usual warmth and humidity of the city would likely take some time to restore.

"Susie sells seashells?" I asked Cherish with a grin, pushing past her poorly maintained shield to check that it was definitely her. After Oliver, I had to be sure.

She laughed. "With Graeme working topside, Valerine loved studying your culture, and she created the protocol." Her smile faded. "Or she once loved it."

"She will again," I said, forcing a confidence that was rather battered after losing Oliver. "She's recovering nicely, and she's safe for the time being."

"Glad to hear it. And I apologize for the smelly ride," Cherish said. "And I'm even sorrier for the conditions I'm taking you to next."

"I need to find my friends." I had felt my mate bond with Ritter momentarily after entering the gates, but I hadn't felt him since or been able to connect with him mentally, and I wasn't sure what that meant except that he was alive. I could feel nothing from Jace. "And I have some information for you from Valerine." Now that I had verified Cherish's identity, it would be a relief to warn her about Mikyn's intentions toward the Unsworn.

"I've got a search out for Graeme now. If he's used any of our mutual contacts, I'll hear about it. But we can't stay here. There are patrols now in the city since our demonstrations, so we're not exactly safe." Cherish glanced around her uneasily. Her black skin was paler than I remembered, and I wondered if that was because I was seeing her for the first time under real sunlight, however dimmed by the quickly approaching night. "I need to help you with clothes and IDs if you are to move about the city undetected. I have your hand scan and image from last time, so that will work for you, but I'll need the same from your friends."

"What about these guys?" Dimitri, ever the healer, thumbed at the four unconscious Avowed prisoners, who were in one of the fishing crates.

"Someone is coming for them. Let's go." She ushered us toward a smaller transport that had the capability of navigating the canals separating the three rings of the city and also the roads spanning each section.

"I'm afraid there might not be time for IDs," I told Cherish, hurrying to catch up with her. "There's more than what I told you, but I had to be sure it was you."

"I'm listening." Cherish stopped and folded her arms.

"Valerine gave the location of her explosives to Mikyn privately in exchange for safe harbor, but he didn't keep his word, and he didn't announce that he'd found and dismantled the bomb. Instead, he plans to blow up something important to the Unsworn and blame it on Valerine in order to turn public support—including the Unsworn's. But the intel is several weeks old, and we don't know if Mikyn's plans have changed or what his target might be."

Cherish's face tensed, and her eyes grew wide. "I think I might. And there is still time to stop it, but not from here." Turning, she ducked into the small transport, whose single wide door on the side gaped like the open hatchback of a large SUV. "Hurry and get in."

The transport was slightly smaller than the average minivan but was missing a row of middle seats, which made it seem downright spacious. Each of the three bucket seats and the two front ones were padded and covered with some kind of black leather. We'd barely sat when the door clanged shut automatically.

"So what's the plan?" I asked from the right front seat, which also had driving controls on the dashboard in front of me.

"The Unsworn are meeting at an offsite location to put the last touches on a plan to storm the capitol tonight and capture key personnel when the Senate lets out from one of the emergency meetings they've been calling since the surfacing. Even with surprise on our side, it was risky. Now, it may be suicide." Cherish glared at the road in front of her. "If they kill enough of us and blame it on Valerine and Graeme, who have essentially become our figureheads, the resistance will be over."

"I can't believe that," I said. "Not now that you know the truth. Can't you stop the meeting and go underground?"

Cherish's lips pursed. "If we can get to them in time. But

the location will be shielded tonight, with no communication devices allowed, and anyone else I could call is farther away than we are. With the Senate controlling our media and communication, we have little choice other than to take precautions. We have managed to set up a separate, low-tech radio system to stay in contact with cells in other areas, but the equipment is always in a different location day to day. Besides, if the seer has found our newest safe house, we have a traitor, and that means no means of communication is safe. We have to warn them and clear out our supplies." With that, she fell into a heavy silence.

Our destination turned out to be a tall building in the outermost part of the crowded third ring. Its location seemed to fit as a possible accidental explosion meant for the shield generators, though in reality, the shield tech would barely be scathed. I'd learned a lot about the electronic shields they used over the city, and they were impregnable to all but the natural degradation that had caused the death of their sister city—or direct internal explosion on the wiring.

As we entered the building, several people passed us carrying crates, nodding at Cherish and giving us friendly stares. The safe house, Cherish explained, was part of the fourth floor, with several studio apartments having been combined to create a single larger room. The second I passed into the shielded room, I felt Ritter. He was in the midst of a small knot of toga-wearing Unsworn, looking larger and scarier than all of them combined. He glanced up as I entered, eyes locking first onto mine and then landing on his son. He didn't lower his mental shield, though, and I understood why. We didn't know who we could trust here.

Cherish immediately dove into the group while Ritter strode toward us. "Guess you've saved us the trouble of explaining Mikyn's plan," I said.

Without answering, he swept me up into his arms and kissed me, long and hard. I felt his intense relief from our bond and from his surface thoughts as palpable as my own. "I'm okay," I said against his lips. "We're both okay."

Letting me go reluctantly, he greeted Blaze and Dimitri, and then stayed close enough for our arms to touch as we watched them join the group in the center.

"We've only been here twenty minutes," he said. "Took us time to find the place since it's new this week, and Graeme's been out of the loop."

"And newly shielded from mental intrusion," I said. "This wasn't active when Keene and I were searching for Dimitri."

"They seem well-organized. And Graeme"—he jerked his head slightly toward the group—"is doing really well with them."

I followed his gaze to where Graeme was talking passionately to his fellow Unsworn. He looked different from when I'd first known him. More confident and driven. Back then, his entire life's purpose had been to save his daughter. Now she was safe, but he'd apparently realized that wasn't enough.

"Leaders are made, not born," I said. "He's been pushed hard."

"Guess it was time for him to either break, or lead."

"Where's Jace?" My brother wasn't here, and I felt him missing like a limb.

"Helping move some equipment to safety. He'll be back."

"Cherish thinks they must have a leak."

"Well, if the attack is called off because of our warning, we'll know for sure."

"Yeah, but not who it is. And until we know that, the Unsworn can't meet in person or trust one another."

He nodded and I realized it was because I'd channeled him instinctively, so we were thinking alike. "That's where you come in," he said. "You need to look at everyone here and see who is hiding what."

"I can do that." I kept the weariness from my voice, but he caught it anyway through our mate bond.

"I'm getting Dimitri."

I put my hand on his sleeve. "He's not well."

"He's well enough."

Still channeling Ritter's combat ability, I looked at Dimitri and saw it was true. He was a formidable opponent for anyone, even in his semi-healed condition.

"There's one more thing," Ritter said. "Graeme and I accessed the public Senate files on the transporter tablet, and a case for reverse inheritance of a senate seat is possible. Or rather, there is currently no law against it, as we suspected. Clearly an oversight from long before they began kidnapping children or decided to surface. What we don't know is what that might mean for Stefan. He sent a lot of his posterity here, but we have no record of where they are now. The Unbounded who were forced to Change early and pose as children could still be working for him. You know how he's able to promote blind obedience."

I knew only too well. "Senator Scala should have records, and maybe Mikyn and the other leaders have access to them as well."

"We need to be careful with Mikyn." Ritter's voice was hard. "Just because you share the same ability and you're expecting doesn't mean he'll hesitate to kill you."

The comment didn't necessarily imply that I shouldn't be here, but now was probably not the time to tell him the transport we'd boarded had been blown up, though someone was bound to mention it soon.

"Right," I agreed.

"I'll get Dimitri." He stalked away, less with anger than with determination.

I grabbed a chair and pulled it over to the wall near the door, sinking onto it. The knowledge about Stefan had left me unsettled. Clearly, this was part of his plan to somehow put himself in the Sinaltan Senate. Or one of many plans, if I knew him at all.

I let my hand rest on my sheathed machete as I surveyed the room. It was clean and nicely painted, but the inexpensive furniture and fixtures and the crates of supplies along one wall marked a clear difference between the desperation of the Unsworn and the ancient luxury palace Mikyn Zenos called home. There were a total of just under a dozen Avowed here, including Cherish and Graeme, but that changed as some came and went, obviously moving supplies.

My intrusion into the minds of the first two Avowed was simple, and it worried me that Mikyn and anyone trained by him could effectively hurt these people with a mere thought. We'd have to teach them to protect themselves better.

Strength began seeping into me before I noted Dimitri's approach. I shifted my gaze to his. "I'm fine," I said with a little smile.

"You're exhausted. You need to sleep, or you need me." He placed a hand on my armored shoulder, one thick finger resting on the bare skin against my neck for better contact.

"Okay." But I'd keep an eye on his energy level.

The next two people also gave little resistance, and the four after were only slightly more difficult. And that covered those I didn't already know, except for the short, broad-shouldered young man with a slightly crunched look to his face, who had just broken away from the group to riffle through some of the crates along the wall.

Unbounded genes typically occurred in those with the best chance of survival, and though that didn't mean they were all perfectly beautiful, a squeezed look wasn't customary and often related to a forced early Change. In this case, the tightened features wouldn't have been noticeable enough to call my attention if he hadn't also seemed too young to have Changed and to be in the midst of this leadership group.

I pounded on his shield. It held.

"What is it?" Dimitri murmured, seeing my expression.

"How old would you say he was?" I flicked my chin toward the man.

Dimitri followed my gaze. "Early twenties."

"He's Changed, though, and his mental barrier is stronger than all the rest of these Unsworn combined."

"Empath?"

I shook my head. "He doesn't seem to notice I'm knocking." I brought down the machete a second time.

"And if you channel him?"

I reached out and probed, using my newfound healing ability to enter his body. "Technopath," I said, instantly recognizing the awareness I could now maintain with the electronic devices in the room. If only I'd realized that with Oliver's killer. It wouldn't have brought Oliver back, but it would have saved us much pain.

Dimitri tensed. "Wearing his own face?"

"Yes." Pushing back a wave of grief, I slammed my mental machete into the whirling gray shield for a third time. The tiniest hole appeared. "Okay, I'm in. He's excited about something. About our being here, I think. But I'm not quite sure why."

"To save lives?"

"I don't think so. His thoughts are rather mocking toward the others. Gloating, even."

"A spy."

"Yes. But whose?"

The man hefted an overflowing crate and was coming

toward us, heading toward the door, but I could see that his leaving was only an excuse to make a call. I jumped to my feet, pulling my real machete, and stepped into his path. He hesitated, glancing backward over his shoulder uneasily at the group of people.

"Uh, can I help you?" he said in Sinaltan.

"Put that down," I said in English.

"I'd do as the lady says if I were you," drawled Ritter, who'd moved so fast into position behind the man that I hadn't seen him coming. He spoke in Sinaltan, but I knew the man understood my English. Blaze, his hands shimmering with heat, came around behind me, blocking the door. With his shirt still bloodied and torn, he looked as scary as Ritter.

The conversation in the room died as all the Unsworn focused on us. "What's the problem?" Graeme approached, concern on his narrow face. He also spoke in his native tongue, but for such simple words, I didn't need the technopath's mind to translate for me.

"This technopath is extraordinarily excited about us leaving here without having the meeting," I said, still speaking in English. "He isn't what he seems." I didn't know that for sure, but as I spoke, his thoughts confirmed my suspicion. Though he might appear to be in his early twenties, he'd been forced to Change in a lab at sixteen and was now eighty-six and aging at five times the normal Unbounded rate, like all forced Unbounded, which meant he had been trained for twenty years after his Change by Stefan before being brought here as a kidnapped embryo.

Graeme moved to intercept us. "That true, Niepson?" he asked, his unyielding stare not weakened by the gentleness in his voice.

Cherish took a few rapid steps toward Niepson, pulling a gun I hadn't even noticed her wearing and pointing it at his head. "You betrayed us?"

"If you mean did I pass on information about the Unsworn to Mikyn's spies, then yes." Niespon sounded reasonable and matter-of-fact, as if explaining what was on the lunch menu. "And when Graeme arrived, I passed on the fact that you had discovered what he planned and the fact that we would no longer be meeting here. There will be no attack now, thanks to me."

"There will be no attack because my wife discovered Mikyn's plan," Graeme corrected. "And our Unbounded friends came with me to warn you."

"Well, yes. That's also true, but if I had known about the attack, I would have told you."

"I don't believe that," Cherish growled. "You're a traitor!"

"Perhaps," Niepson said. "But not for the reasons you might think."

"And what might that be?" Graeme was with me now in Niepson's mind, entering through the hole I'd kept open. His voice was deadly, like the calm before the storm. I caught the twitch of a smile at the corner of Ritter's mouth that signaled his approval of Graeme taking control.

"Because now that sea scum Zenos's plans are ruined." Niepson's bottom lip curled in disgust. "Now he can't turn us against each other or convince the people to support him. He'll have no choice but to reinstate Tsaousiss and Scala so they can attempt to maintain the peace."

Shocked stares followed this last announcement.

"If they are reinstated," Graeme said coldly, "that means the Senate forgives them, and such forgiveness after they tried to murder our Unbounded allies is unconscionable. They cannot be allowed to rule again."

Niepson nodded, a mocking smile growing on his lips and making his features appear more crunched. "I agree, and so do those I represent. Tsaousiss and Scala won't be statesmen for long. Once they're here, we in family Scala will deal with our own, as will the Tsaousiss family. We have the votes to get them replaced."

"We, who?" Graeme's voice took on a sharp note. "Who is your leader?"

"Stefan Carrington of the Emporium Triad." Niespon lifted his chin, speaking with a relish that bordered on crazed. "Soon to be our leader in Sinalta as well. He's also my biological father."

"You've got to be kidding," I muttered.

The Unsworn stared at each other uncertainly as Ritter glowered and Blaze's heat became molten lava in his hands. Cherish's finger tightened on her trigger.

"Explain," barked Graeme, his calm vanishing completely.

Niepson looked between Ritter and Blaze nervously, and words began spilling from his lips. "After I was adopted into the Scala family, I helped them place Triad Carrington's descendants in each of the major families, and for the past fifty years, I have been working with them from the inside toward a single objective."

Graeme found the truth in Niepson's mind before I did. "They plan to get rid of all the statesmen and replace them with Stefan's posterity," Graeme said.

"So Stefan can take Mikyn's place through reverse inheritance?" I asked because that was the only thing that made sense.

Niepson shook his head. "That may be necessary in the beginning, but ultimately we will vote to restore equal power to the executive branch of our government, led by the magistrate who will work hand-in-hand with the legislative senate run by the statesmen."

Oddly enough, the tension eased from the people around us. "Isn't that what we're trying to do?" Cherish asked. "The statesmen have had too much power for far too long. If Stefan manages to do what we are trying to do without bloodshed, we will be grateful."

Niepson grinned, relaxing. "Exactly. He knows you would be grateful, and so did I. That's why I joined you. I've waited fifty years for this day."

But all this was only part of the truth I now saw in his mind. "But it's Stefan they plan to put in as magistrate of the executive branch," I said. In truth, it was similar to what Tsaousiss and Scala had planned for him, but only because the position currently held no real power. But once the coup was over, Stefan would be left holding equal power to that of a president in a powerful, advanced civilization who would outlive nearly everyone else alive on the planet. "With his children in the Senate, he will rule Sinalta completely."

"And with the electronic shield still in play and Sinalta's advanced nuclear arsenal, there isn't a nation in the world who can fight them," Ritter said.

I nodded, fighting a desire to run Neipson through with my machete. "We have to warn Mikyn." Because as bad as Mikyn was, Stefan would certainly use his power to continue his centuries-long destruction of the mortal world.

Graeme shook his head. "I don't see a difference between either man. But either way, the only option we have is to destroy the city's electrical shield before they can figure out how to permanently repair them. Doing so will make us vulnerable to attack from topside nations, but it will render any use of our nuclear weapons unviable."

"And how do we do that?" Cherish asked. "You said Mikyn already dismantled Valerine's bomb."

"Yes." Graeme's voice had become so hard I almost didn't recognize him. "But what I didn't tell you is that Valerine placed two more sets as insurance. They don't have automatic detonators, so we'll have to start the timers off ourselves, but it is something we can do."

"No!" Niepson lunged at him. Ritter yanked him back and held him in place.

I leveled a stare at Cherish and said in English, "Valerine showed me exactly where the other sets of explosives are, and if you'll show me a schematic, I can show you." While they dealt with that, I would personally go to Mikyn.

A commotion at the door had everyone turning to see Jace, his eyes excited. "There are two dozen Senate soldiers below. Are we fighting? Or running?"

Graeme exchanged a look with Cherish and several of the other Unsworn. By some silent agreement, they seemed to come to a conclusion. "We fight until we're clear," Graeme said. "And quickly before they send more troops."

Jace whooped as if he'd held back too long.

"What about him?" Cherish asked, pointing at Niepson.

"He's going to take a long nap," I said as Ritter plunged a syringe into his neck.

Chapter 22

"WHO WAS THAT GUY EXACTLY?" JACE ASKED ME AS WE FOLLOWED Cherish and Graeme to one of the secret ladders the Unsworn had built into service conduits inside the walls.

"He's your half brother," I said, unwilling to lie. "One of Stefan's plants."

"Really?" He sighed. "Man, this extended sibling thing is still hard to get used to, even though I must have met two dozen siblings since I started working in New York."

"I know." I hated that he had relatives who weren't also related to me when our whole lives we'd thought it was just us and Chris.

Ritter had started down the ladder, and I put my hand out to go down next, but Jace beat me to it.

"So," Blaze said from behind me. "Now that I've been filled in from the half of the conversation that was in Sinaltan, I have one question. Why aren't we also going after Sinalta's nuclear arsenal? Stefan could cause a lot of problems with access to those, even if he doesn't end up as president."

I'd been thinking the same thing, but behind him, Dimitri

answered, "Because while we want to make sure the Avowed aren't too much of a threat, we can't leave them without protection from countries like China and my dear old native Russia. And even from America. For protection against those powerhouses, they need a fairly big stick."

I sighed. "So we're hoping they'll develop enough political stability and compassion toward mortals that they won't wipe out the world once they figure out how to rebuild their shields?"

Dimitri gave me a thin smile. "Exactly." He pushed past me and started down the ladder.

"You want to go before me too?" I asked Blaze now that we were the only two left. Others were going down the second ladder on the opposite side of the building and more had used the main stairs so we could hit them from all sides.

"No. I got your six."

Once, a climb from such a height would have debilitated me, but now my only worry was that my stomach was getting in the way of the rungs. The baby seemed to have grown a week's worth in the past day.

Below, the fight was already in full swing, with Ritter and Jace moving in blurs, matched blow by blow by the combat Avowed. But the Avowed weren't as well shielded mentally, and as Dimitri and Blaze waded into the battle, I began picking off those fighting the Unsworn, one by one, sending flashes of light to their minds or toying with their main arteries to make them collapse. With the new insight given by the healing ability, I could give them enough arterial pressure to render them unconscious and not damage anything too long term. Because one day when the dust settled, they might still be part of Sinalta's peacekeeping force, and I didn't want them holding a grudge for weeks spent healing and retraining.

"Erin!" Ritter called as a bullet whizzed my way.

I looked to see him suspended in mid-air, which told me one of the Scala family levitators had joined the fray. I found the culprit, a sneering woman with angry blue eyes and a long blond braid too thick to be real. She collapsed as I cut off her blood supply rather abruptly, and it was a bit of a scramble to ease Ritter's descent and that of another Unsworn by channeling her. After that, I suspended two of Avowed soldiers and tried to raise a third, but I didn't have the energy to keep them all up. I let them fall in a painful heap.

The struggle was over in a matter of minutes. Cherish motioned for us to follow them out the back door, where darkness had fallen. "Let's not wait for more to show up," she said.

"Where are we going?" I asked.

"To a place below the city. They won't think to look for us there. At least not at first."

We'd gone half a block when sirens filled the air.

"Looks like they've called a state of emergency," Graeme said. "So it seems that even without an explosion, my grandfather may attempt to unite the people through this event."

Grandfather. I sometimes forgot how closely Graeme was related to the Avowed seer, and I stifled the wave of mistrust that my Unbounded genes sent through my brain.

I *knew* Graeme. Didn't I?

Small groups of people were up ahead on the sidewalk, but Cherish and her friends didn't slow or pay any attention to them. With life layered so tightly here in the third ring, the glow of too many life forces and thoughts escaping from their minds made me nauseated. I ramped up my own shield again, and the many voices dimmed to a manageable level, leaving me open to contact but not vulnerable to distraction or attack.

We ran until we neared the wide canal that separated the third ring from the second, where Cherish told us there was a maintenance tunnel that led under the canal. She took us inside the gated tunnel entrance, nodding at the guard. "One of ours," she explained.

"We left a lot of witnesses who can direct soldiers here," Ritter growled.

Cherish smiled. "Most people in the outer ring are connected with us in some way. They won't say anything, and even if they do, we'll be long gone."

My mind raced with ideas. "Do any of these tunnels intersect with those below the capitol?"

"Absolutely. There are airlocks to get through, one way or the other. Those we planned on using tonight will likely be blocked since that traitor reported back to his people. We'll have to use others."

The air was warmer down below, and soon the little heater I carried in my belly made me long to rip off my body armor. But her health signs were strong, and my body wasn't in distress, so I kept up.

"What does the state of emergency entail?" I dropped back beside Graeme to ask as we paused outside a hatch Cherish was attempting to open with a code.

"Movement by essential people only," he said. "Food, peace-keeping, engineering. And of course the politicians. None of their rules ever apply to them. The rest must stay home." He frowned. "I think it's a move that shows their desperation. Because it's one thing to ask those inside the first two rings to stay home, but in the third ring? Impossible to keep it up for long."

Having seen the poor state of the buildings and felt the thoughts of those in cramped conditions, I had to agree.

"Maybe Stefan is already here," Jace said from behind us.

I shook my head. "How could he have gotten here from Rio so quickly?"

Jace shrugged. "We did."

Graeme inclined his head, lowering his voice. "Jace has a

point. We spent a lot of time rescuing Dimitri. Stefan may not have a shifter, but I assume Stefan has a lot of people and money to make them do whatever he wants. Scala and Tsaousiss also have access to a high-speed transport, or they wouldn't have been able to elude Mikyn's search six weeks ago."

"I hope you're wrong," I said to them. "Because I'd rather confront Mikyn before Stefan gets involved."

"It won't matter." Jace's tone held a darkness I'd never heard before, not even when talking about Stefan. "It ends here. Or wherever I see him again."

The hatch opened and Cherish waved us through. "They've disabled the codes, but I have a backup program. They will find and delete it eventually."

"And then what?" someone asked.

"I'll figure something out."

The new hallway was nothing more than a transparent tube that extended deep into the ocean as it cut across the canal where ships passed overhead during their daily business. It was obviously designed so maintenance personnel wouldn't have to waste time going above to get to the next ring. The hatches, of course, were a safety measure.

We finally stopped in a tiny storage room under the city—a closet, really. One by one, we lost all of the Unsworn except Cherish.

"Where did your people go?" I asked her.

"They are spreading the word that the rally at the capitol is still on." Her statement held a bit of challenge in it. "They know well enough what to do without a meeting."

"I thought you were calling off the demonstration tonight."

"No." A violent shake of her head emphasized her point. "We called off the meeting so Mikyn wouldn't blow us up, but we're still going to the capitol. We don't know how much longer they'll be holding emergency sessions."

"They've already requested the return of the statesmen, and that means Stefan too. So what else would they be discussing?"

She shrugged. "What it's about doesn't matter. They'll all be there, and for once, they will hear us."

Ritter's face was tight with anger. "We can't have your people getting in the way of our mission, and for better or worse, that includes warning Mikyn about Stefan's intentions. He's the greater enemy."

"I don't agree!" Cherish's eyes flashed as she drew herself to her full stature. "You have no idea what we have endured. We appreciate your help, but that doesn't mean we will stop our efforts."

"The Unsworn have a right to be involved." Dimitri placed a hand on Ritter's shoulder, his tone casual and calming. "It is their city, their people."

Ritter sighed as Dimitri's gift released some of his tension. "Okay, yes, but they can't go in at will. They need to wait until the right time, or they'll cause more death." His eyes strayed briefly to me as he spoke.

"They won't get in the way." Cherish handed Graeme something that looked like a radio receiver. "They'll await your call. My people are moving our broadcasters there, so you can send a message with this when you need them. The Senate won't know to block the signal until it's too late." Her eyes narrowed. "Just be sure that you *do* call them. The Unsworn are tired of their control, of their murders of our children, of living off their leftovers. We will not allow the Senate to silence our voices any longer. Already, we have refused to ingest their daily birth control nanites, and we will refuse to sentence our children with testing. This is only the first step."

"That is against the law," Graeme said, even while his face filled with hope.

Their surface emotions were so strong, I found it hard to

focus on my own thoughts, but I did know one thing. "Then you make new laws," I said.

Graeme's gaze shifted to me, his eyes watering and not really focusing on anything. "Yes," he said softly. Then more powerfully he said again, "Yes."

When no one else seemed to have anything else to add, I said to Cherish, "Bring up the schematics for engineering on your tablet. I'll show you where the charges are."

Cherish nodded and began clicking and swiping. When I showed Cherish where Valerine had set the charges, she laughed aloud. "She has chosen the most difficult places to get to, but the very best for permanent disablement of the shield. I would never have seen the possibility. She is truly the best engineer we have."

Was that reluctance in her voice? I glanced at Ritter, and the slight cocking of his brow told me he'd heard it too.

"Is there a problem?" I asked.

She shook her head. "No, it's just . . . Valerine has chosen a particular shield generator on the outskirts that we have no more replacements for, and any rerouting they attempt in that location must be done by hand, so it's the perfect target. The second target is the relay from the middle of the city. From what little I understand after reviewing all the information in our database, the center relay takes input from all the different kinds of generators and calibrates them. Technically the electric shield can function for a time with several missing generators—we know a workaround, but the relay is something far more complicated. It's the only piece that remains strong after all these years, and there is no backup. Seeing where Valerine has placed the charges, I had the thought . . . well, I can't help but think maybe she has learned to repair all the parts of the shield, including the relay. Because it isn't like her to destroy something so . . . well, amazing."

Silence fell over the tiny room as we all shifted our gaze to Graeme. I hadn't seen such an idea in either his mind or Valerine's, but I could have missed it.

Finally, Graeme sighed and gave a short nod. "After the explosion of our second city . . . six million lives lost in that single horrifying instant, Valerine began doing all kinds of research. She believed the failures in all the generators were caused by some center piece—it must be the relay Cherish is talking about. The files concerning its creation were corrupted, like so many of our files that we didn't use daily. She was close to figuring it out, but it was impossible to finish her research below the water. The risk that a test would kill everyone was too great. So we don't know—" He broke off. "I'm fairly certain she could fix it now above the water, if given time. She even has a theory of how we could use the shields in space exploration."

I felt grateful Valerine was safe at our impregnable Fortress. "Mikyn must never know, or he won't rest until he gets her back here."

Graeme sighed. "He knew she was close. It might be why he didn't keep his word to her."

"It was only a matter of time until someone relearned the technology to make the repairs," Dimitri said. "The imminent danger you were in created the urgency. But any shield powerful enough to sustain life underneath the ocean is a serious danger to a world already poised for conflict, so let's make it harder for Mikyn to start a war, shall we?" The words were gentle but had the desired effect of pulling us all back to the moment. We could only take care of that right now.

"Okay," Ritter said. "Let's talk assignments."

"I'm going with Erin to confront Mikyn," Jace said immediately. "That's where Stefan will show up. I'll make him tell me where he's stashed Catrina." Ritter's jaw tightened, and I knew he'd planned to come with me himself.

"Assuming Ava and those battleships out there let him through," I countered.

"Oh, she'll let him through," Dimitri said. "It's her only choice with us here and incommunicado. Unless we can get rid of the shield first."

I looked at Ritter. "You have to make sure the charges do what they're supposed to. You and Blaze and Cherish. Dimitri, Jace, and I will go to Mikyn and distract him until you finish."

The rigidity in Ritter's jaw extended throughout his entire body. "You're not safe with him."

"I think I might be—if he realized Dimitri is my biological father and that I have two abilities like he does."

"Two abilities?" Graeme's gasp pulled my attention from Ritter.

Dimitri put a calming hand on his shoulder. "Mikyn is also a healer, and he's the one who's been holding back the insanity your people have created through years of interbreeding."

"It's also why he's able to tell about the babies," I added. "Because he has both gifts."

Graeme's eyes narrowed. "So all that training and watching to see if one of us could take his place . . . that was just blowing water?"

Blowing water? "If you mean smoke and mirrors, then yes," I said. "Apparently, at least some of those with the sensing ability can learn their other parents' ability as well, even if it doesn't come to them as naturally as the main ability." I didn't add the rest about being able to change a baby's DNA—that was still too dangerous for anyone else to know. But with my parentage, Mikyn would believe long enough that I could also do the same thing, whether or not it was actually true, which I still didn't know for sure.

Graeme staggered a bit, leaning heavily against the metal wall. "I can't believe . . . no, I do believe . . . but . . ."

"It's why he imprisoned me," Dimitri said. "Because I wouldn't give him my seed so he could create helpers and an eventual replacement."

"Then Erin's right." Graeme straightened as if calling on some inner strength. "She will be safe with him once he knows."

"Possibly." Ritter's gaze ran over us, his gift calculating our abilities and chances of survival. At last he nodded. "Will you be able to reach us in case you need Blaze's ability?"

I looked down at the plans Cherish still had open on her tablet. "I'm not completely sure. I mean, distance-wise, absolutely, but the equipment may interfere." It was better to tell the truth than have him detect a lie. As mission leader, he'd make the decision that was best for the team.

He nodded. "Get to Mikyn and be prepared to reach Ava the minute the shields are down. Dimitri is team leader, so listen to him. You all have metacapes?"

"Not Dimitri." We'd chosen the regular bodysuits instead of those made with metamaterials and brought along the capes for occasional use.

Ritter tossed Dimitri a small packet. "Cherish, Blaze, you're with me. We'll need a way to trigger the explosions simultaneously."

"We're going to have to fight our way through to the center location," Cherish said. "It's in one of the main engineering areas in the wealthy district, and it's always heavily guarded."

Ritter's teeth-showing grin looked demonical. "Good."

Blaze laughed and said to me, "Now you know where I get my recklessness."

But I knew Ritter hadn't been reckless since he met me and found a reason to live. His eyes met mine now, as powerful as any touch. *I will do the job and come back to you*, it said.

"You think you can find your way to the capitol?" Cherish

asked Graeme. "We have everything we need for disguises here. Just dig through the crates."

Graeme looked uncertain, so I said, "I've memorized the way out." It was easy while channeling Cherish's ability. The city's layout was perfectly detailed on her tablet. "He can get us from there." Graeme nodded.

I stepped close to Ritter. "See you soon, Your Deathliness."

He pointed at Graeme. "Tell Mikyn that if anything happens to her, I will find him and I will separate each piece of his spine and shove them down his throat one by one."

"I'll do that," Graeme said with equal solemnity.

Jace guffawed. "I'll be sure to tell Stefan, too, when he shows up." He paused and said in a darker tone, "In fact, I'm going to do that to him anyway."

I slugged him in the arm. "Shut up."

Ritter left with Cherish and Blaze as we began dressing in Sinaltan robes that made me feel like a powerful Grecian queen—and I had the figure to match since my body armor gave me a little more bulk. We could have relied on the metamaterial capes to hide us, but they wouldn't mask us completely in the bright lights of the tunnels. Besides, blending in, hiding in plain sight, was usually the best option. I chose a hairpiece that matched my own color but whose texture and precious metal weaving turned me into someone quite different. While rhodium was reserved for the more wealthy, platinum, gold, and silver were abundant for all classes in Sinalta, mined by the children they had stolen or thrown away. Heavy makeup in the currently popular style further differentiated me from the woman Mikyn had plastered all over the media. Blue shadow helped my gray eyes resemble Sinalta's most common eye color.

Jace's own hair was already a disguise, having grown inches since we'd left for Brazil. He let Graeme talk him into decorative chains that he deemed "girly." Dimitri opted to shave his black hair and wear a short blond wig. He added a belted pillow. It was hard to maintain extra weight when your metabolism worked so fast, but some still managed it.

Graeme used a darker blond wig past his shoulders and odd, bubble-front glasses that testified of the Sinaltan's long time under the water. I was fairly certain they'd be useless under the actual sun.

"It's dark now," I reminded him.

"These don't change the vision at all. They only appear to. We've never had much need for sunglasses."

"That's an understatement," Jace said. "Give me a pair, would you?"

"Before we go," Graeme said, "I have a question. What did Ritter mean about you needing Blaze's ability? If we need him, it's unlikely that he'll make it to us in time. He's still dragging a bit with his wounds."

Jace and I exchanged a look, which Graeme didn't miss. "I can tell it means something," he said, "and I know you well enough to know if you attempt a lie."

"Tell him." Dimitri wasn't giving a command but rather his encouragement.

I sighed. "It's a thing I can do. I can borrow other people's abilities if I can reach them mentally."

Graeme considered. "Well, that explains a lot. Do you have to be inside their mental shields to access it?"

"That's the way it began," I said. Then, because it was better for him to know the rest, I added, "At first I thought everyone with our ability could do it, but I've only met one other person with that power, and she's dead. And maybe Mikyn. I've been thinking it could be linked to having two abilities, but there's been no time to test."

"Thank you for telling me. I'll have to give it a try."

"You do that." I hoped by telling him I hadn't created a problem I would have to resolve in the future. "Let's go."

We discovered several bodies as we made our way through the underground passageway, each temporarily reset. Every time, Dimitri paused to check them. At first, I thought it was to help them, but I soon realized he was making sure they wouldn't wake up for at least two hours, and my estimation of him increased. Soon, we began running into lone workmen who weren't reset, or sometimes pairs, and Graeme and I had to maintain constant vigilance to make sure we weren't surprised. But these were engineers, scientists, and support personnel, not trained soldiers. Overwhelming them was almost too easy.

Finally, we reached the hatch that passed under the canal between Sinalta's second and inner rings. But Cherish's codes no longer worked.

"They'll be alerted now," Graeme said, his voice tight.

I reached out, searching for Ritter and Blaze. Fire appeared in my hands, quickly becoming a molten ball. I used it to carve out the door.

"If the tunnel is damaged in the blast, water will flood everything down here," I said.

Graeme nodded. "But only sections. That's why we have so many hatches. We've lived with water a long time and know how to mitigate it."

I was more worried about how flooding would affect Ritter's ability to get to us, but it wasn't a concern I should focus on at the moment.

We made our way to a repair access that was two blocks away from the capitol and should be less heavily manned than the main engineering access below the capitol building itself.

"What's the plan if we're seen?" I asked. With the state of emergency in progress, we were bound to be noticed by any soldiers on the street.

"I'll try to talk our way out of it," Graeme said with a tight smile, "while you three take them out."

"Or," Dimitri said. "We turn ourselves in and let them take us directly to Mikyn."

I considered it for a moment. "We'd have to do it in a way that all of Sinalta knows we're here. Otherwise we might end up in a transport three hours away." I didn't need to add the words, "Like you were before."

"So no giving up." Jace exuded energy, obviously pleased with his conclusion. "The faster we get this done, the faster I'll kill Stefan, and if he's hurt Catrina, so help me *he'll* be the one eating his vertebrae."

"Remind me to thank Ritter for that image," I said dryly.

I took a moment to check on the baby, placing a barrier not only around her but around me because I was her life. I felt vulnerable in a way I never had before. If something happened here today, I could have another child, but not *this* child who depended on me, whose blind trust and acceptance and love came as naturally to her as growing. She was unique, irreplaceable, and I would do anything to save her.

I felt the same about Jace. Of the two, I suspected he might be the one who would be harder to protect. I met Dimitri's eyes, warm and brown and too knowing.

"You could stay here," I suggested. "You're not a hundred percent." I could see that he was drained now, as if he'd transferred all his remaining energy into making sure our enemies wouldn't wake too soon.

Or helping us stay strong and fit.

Since we'd been reunited, I'd grown accustomed to thinking of him in future terms, but nothing was guaranteed.

"Ah, Erin," he said in gentle rebuke. "I've lived a thousand years, which is far more than I ever thought I'd have in my youth. Whatever happens, I have no regrets." He put his hand under my chin, guiding me to meet his gaze. "No regrets."

I slapped his hand away. "Stop that. This isn't some grand farewell that I'll think about when you're dead. I *do* have expectations, and one of those is that you will deliver your granddaughter. So pull yourself together."

He chuckled. "Okay then. But I'm not staying behind."

"Fine. Let's go."

We opened the door to reveal a cobblestone street with ancient houses lit only by equally old-fashioned lampposts. Definitely a wealthy area given the lush vegetation in the yards and the naked statues. Vegetation that was probably completely unused to the colder, moist air it now found itself in.

We made it a hundred yards before I detected Avowed coming toward us in formation. "Soldiers!" I whispered. "Six life forces about half a block down."

Chapter 23

"THIS WAY," GRAEME SAID, LEADING US INTO A YARD WHERE THE deeper shadows of the house would hide us. "Hurry. If they have an empath with them, they'll follow. Our shields are tight, but only Erin isn't emitting a life force."

"I can extend my shield," I offered, "and we could pull on the metacapes. But I think it's too late. They're following us—and fast. So we either run or fight."

"Or pretend we live here," Graeme stepped into the light, whispering a fierce, "They may only request to talk to one of us, so stay back and watch."

"Like we're going to let him tell us what to do," Jace muttered, looking at Dimitri.

"I'll stay with Erin," Dimitri said, sounding amused. "You attack from the other side."

With a nod, Jace shook out his metacape, disappearing under it, and retreated into the dark. I traced his life force as it dimmed to the level of the dozen or so people inside the house itself. I fought the urge to go after him and refocused on Graeme.

"Hey, there," Graeme called in Sinaltan, raising his hands toward the newcomers. "Easy. My friends and I only came outside for a breath of air. It's so cold and heavy compared to underneath the water."

"Don't you know there's a state of emergency?" asked one of the guards. He was definitely combat, but that was true of only two of his friends. One of the other three was an empath, which was how they'd detected us. The fact that he was trying to get into our minds told me he was trained by Mikyn. The other two were something else.

Watch him, I sent to Graeme's surface thoughts.

I see it, he acknowledged. *And I saw what you did to the soldiers with the light back at the safe house. I'll get through his shield and do the same.* Aloud Graeme said, "Like I said, just getting a breath of this air."

"I'll need your handprint." One of the remaining two held out a tablet. *Technopath,* I thought. They sure seemed to have a lot of those in Sinalta. As for the third . . .

I stepped forward, joining Graeme, and put my hand on the screen to buy us more time, hoping Cherish really had programmed an ID for me. Unless he and Valerine had already worked out false IDs, Graeme's print would cause an immediate alert, as would Dimitri's. Jace wouldn't have a registered ID, if they caught up to him.

"Very well," the technopath said, frowning as he compared my image to the picture on his screen.

I tried channeling the last of the six Avowed—and had the sudden compelling urge to burst into song. Ah, he had one of the beautiful gifts which Sinalta had cultured over millennia.

Graeme offered his hand next as I noticed Dimitri positioning himself to confront the combat Avowed. I could sense Jace again, coming around on the far side of the house. Would the empath be able to tell that he wasn't in the house itself?

No warning registered on Graeme's print, so he must have taken care of it before.

"Now you." The technopath motioned to Dimitri.

I met Dimitri's gaze with a message I knew he wouldn't miss. As he stepped forward, holding out his hand toward the reader, one of the combat Unbounded fell as a bullet entered his neck, shot by Dimitri's other hand near his waist. It was a move to be admired, but he was already firing his ballistic knife at the technopath. I broke through the second combat Avowed's mental shield and sent him to la la land. The empath joined him with a burst of light from Graeme. There was only the singer now, his weapon half drawn.

"Don't move," I said, as a gun jammed against the man's head from behind, wielded by my invisible brother. My voice warbled a bit as if I longed to sing the words.

"We have to move." Graeme looked urgently up and down the road. "Someone will have heard the shots."

"Why the state of emergency?" I asked the songbird.

"The Unsworn are going to make trouble," he said, his voice almost as mesmerizing as a hypnopath's, though there was no coercion involved. "And we are going to have an outside visitor."

"Who?"

He shook his head. "We don't know exactly, except that it's an ally who will help make sure we remain a free people among the untrustworthy topsiders. The Senate is meeting about it now." His eyes narrowed. "Wait a minute, I know you." His gaze went to Graeme. "And you."

"Thanks," I said, and promptly sent him into unconsciousness by cutting off the blood supply to his brain. Jace caught him as he fell.

This time we all pulled on our metacapes, keeping to the shadows of the houses as we approached the capitol. Twice more, I sensed life forces coming our way, but this time I extended my barrier to block my companion's life forces, and we were able to distance ourselves before we alerted any empaths who might be with them.

"Let's use that side tunnel," I suggested when we finally hunched beside the public library across from the capitol. "The way we left the last time we were here. With the metacapes, we can easily get there unseen."

"We can't." Graeme's eyes glinted at me in the dark. "After we used it to escape the last time, they've permanently closed it."

"As long as I can reach Blaze, we can get through just about anything," I said.

"Oh, right." Graeme closed his eyes, searching. "I can't feel them. Or Mikyn or the other Senators, but I do feel groups of life forces gathering all around the capitol."

"The Unsworn," Dimitri said.

Graeme nodded. "The soldiers are going to figure out something isn't right very soon."

He was right. If any more people showed up, it would be a veritable bonfire of life forces outside the capitol. It was quickly becoming as congested as it was inside the capitol building near the Senate chamber where they held the emergency session. The chamber itself was blocked from my senses, however, a change from our last visit, and a serious one. It meant I couldn't reach Mikyn mentally or anyone else inside the room to see what they were saying.

"I can reach Blaze," I said. "I can burn our way in."

"We'll have to circle around to get better access to that second entrance." Jace leapt down from the library roof where he'd gone to do reconnaissance. Only his head was visible as he let the hood fall back. "Come on."

I'd taken a few steps toward him when a movement of

life forces inside the capitol stopped me. "Wait. Something's happening."

"You think they noticed the Unsworn gathering?" Jace asked.

"I'm not sure." I stretched my thoughts, trying to determine more. Were soldiers being activated, or was it something else?

"It's Mikyn!" Graeme's whisper was hoarse. "I can't get inside his shield, but I can feel it's him. His bodyguard is weaker. A few more hits—"

Show me! I demanded. He did, and I slammed my way through the bodyguard's already weakened shield in a single blow. I recognized him. The last time we met, I'd rendered him unconscious inside a minute and earned Mikyn's respect and supposed aid. Aid that now appeared to have been lip service only.

From the bodyguard's eyes, I saw that Mikyn looked exactly as I remembered, stooped and gray. He was surrounded by at least four dozen soldiers in the capitol entryway, all standing at attention in strict formation. I narrowed the opening in the guard's shield to a miniscule pinpoint, which Graeme and I could mask from Mikyn and other empaths. It wouldn't stand up to even cursory examination, if Mikyn were to focus on him in any real way, but it might prevent the other empaths around Mikyn from noting anything.

"I want a steady marching formation all the way to the dock," the bodyguard announced as he stood with Mikyn in the midst of the soldiers. "Be alert. Our intel says we managed to avert the Unsworn demonstration scheduled for today, but we never know how the subversives will act."

Mikyn nodded and smiled as if he had made the announcement himself.

Magarete Santiago, Mikyn's assistant, leaned over to say loudly enough for the bodyguard to hear, "Are we sure we can trust Ava O'Hare?" Her round face was drawn with concern. "Just because the Americans signed off on letting the transport come through doesn't mean she's onboard."

"She has no choice," Mikyn said. "And whatever happens, she is not in control here. She can't decide who we give asylum to either."

"Once she discovers her healer is dead, things may get complicated."

Mikyn shrugged. "By then Statesmen Tsaousiss and Scala will have their people in hand, and we can squelch the uprising once and for all. With Triad Carrington's help, I believe we'll find a way to permanently repair the shields. After that, it won't matter what the Emporium or the Americans do. It will be too late."

Magarete nodded and smiled, but there was a tightness in her soft face. Before I could decide whether her thoughts might be worth the added effort of another connection, Mikyn stumbled and winced. Both the bodyguard and the assistant reached to help him.

I'd been wrong, I saw now, using my healer ability, though it was hard at this distance, as if I were looking through a thick window that happened to be the guard's awareness. A sickness in Mikyn made every step slower and more painful, and the flowing robes masked an unhealthy thinness of his body. Something had changed or was affecting him, but I couldn't tell what.

Mikyn looked up at his guard, his eyes catching on him.

He sees something, I told Graeme, pushing him out and letting the guard's shield close. *I don't want him to know we're here yet, so let's watch from farther back. But first, what's wrong with him?*

What are you talking about? Graeme asked.

Never mind.

We chose another guard, well behind Mikyn but still in the group. I'd have to be vigilant.

"Mikyn is heading to a dock," I reported to Dimitri and Jace. "With about fifty troops in attendance. They're going to pick up Stefan. Ava either agreed to let him through, or someone ordered her to stand down." To Graeme, I added. "Any idea what dock they'll use?"

"It's close," he said. "At the end of the street. With that many soldiers, they'll walk."

"Mikyn will go by transport," I predicted. Not to make an impression on Stefan but because he was having issues moving. "Dimitri," I said. "The last time you were with Mikyn, did you notice something wrong with him?" I didn't understand why his Avowed genes weren't repairing the damage.

"Nothing unusual for his age," Dimitri said. "He is aging, though."

"How old is he exactly?" Jace wanted to know.

"He wouldn't say, but my best estimate is about seventeen hundred and forty-five years old."

Graeme scratched at the hair thickening by the hour on his jaw. "I think he might be older than that. Though I'm not sure how much older."

"Well, he appears to be in pain," I said. Maybe that explained the pressure Mikyn felt to find a replacement.

"There's the transport," Jace said as the troops spilled out of the capitol building. "I'm going to fall in behind them." He slipped off the lightweight metacape and began stripping off his toga and the chains in his hair. Beneath the garb he wore the tunic of a Sinaltan soldier. "I freed this from one of the guys we met," he said. "Pulls a little over my own armor, but they haven't been fighting as long as we have, and I don't trust that theirs are bulletproof."

"Come on," I told the others. "Keep your capes on. Let's stay ahead of them so we can look for a chance to confront Mikyn."

Leaving Jace, Dimitri and I hurried forward, with Graeme trailing behind, speaking into his radio. Given the presence of the fifty troops, I was glad of those silent Unsworn now.

I reached out to Ritter to find his shield strong and tight, a swirling blackness that allowed no entry. I tapped on his shield, but of course he couldn't feel me, except for our mate bond, which wasn't the same as communicating.

His shield wavered, and I slipped into his mind. *You should be more careful,* I told him.

You needed me, he said. *You felt closer somehow. I took a risk.*

Well, stop it. I knew I was being ridiculous because I did need him.

Tell me.

Stefan is coming. Mikyn is going to the dock to meet him now. It's not far from the center relay.

We're almost finished at this generator. We'll get there as soon as possible.

Okay. Now put up your shield.

I waited long enough to be sure he complied before refocusing on our race through the city. We had the double challenge of keeping to the shadows while staying ahead of Mikyn's transport and the soldiers, now jogging in unison through the street. The only good thing was that the soldiers patrolling the city seemed to have disappeared.

We soon found the missing soldiers gathered at the dock, waiting in formation. Anticipation surged in my gut. Finally, I would face the people who were responsible for so much death.

And make them pay.

"Strengthen your mental barriers as much as possible," I

told Graeme and Dimitri. "I'll help block your life forces until we get past those soldiers. They'll have at least one empath on the lookout."

I pushed out my shield, layering it over the shields of the others. I was aware of Graeme watching me. He began to help, and I saw that I'd misjudged him. Lack of training was what made him weak. Or lack of necessity, as Dimitri might say.

With our capes tucked carefully around us, we made it past the soldiers' position to several inactive public transports along the water and hid behind them. To the side of the transports a short distance away sat two platforms with metal gates. Presumably, the transports would enter the water there and either sail straight across to the second ring or circle the entire canal, stopping at other landings. But now, like the road, the entire canal was clear of transports, and the calm of the water was broken only by gentle waves likely caused by the western movement of the city.

A third gate, its lower rung brushing the water, angled oddly compared with the previous two. "This one," Graeme informed us in a whisper, "leads down and out of the city to the ocean below, passing the outer subgates that require permission codes. The statesmen likely used a larger transport since they arrived so quickly, but they'll leave it at a subgate like we did, unless Mikyn goes in to get him, which I don't think will happen given the presence of the soldiers."

"Let's get as close as we can." I edged along the transport, darting across the open space to the next one where we had a better view of the ocean gate. The others followed me, and we hunkered down to wait.

A shout rose when Mikyn's transport arrived at the dock. He exited and made his way slowly down to the platform as the water in the third gate began to churn.

"We can't wait for Ritter to blow the shields," I said. "I need to talk to Mikyn before Stefan arrives, or we may never get the chance."

"What about mentally?" Dimitri said.

He meant surface thoughts, but staying here crouched behind a transport not only limited the movement of the others as they stayed to protect me, but also limited my ability to fight Mikyn. I needed to be closer.

"I'll go confront him," I said, standing and smoothing my toga. "Though I will let him know I'm coming so he orders people not to shoot."

"I'm coming too." A ripple of fear came through Graeme's surface thoughts, but he squelched it almost as quickly as I noticed.

"I've got a few things to say to him myself," Dimitri said.

"Don't kill him yet," I warned. "Stefan is the greater threat."

"Is he?" Dimitri arched his brows.

I didn't know anymore. I turned away and reached out to Mikyn. At first, he didn't appear to notice me, so I took out the mental version of my trusty machete. I'd been inside his head once before, but I still didn't know if I'd broken through on my own or if he'd let me inside.

Mikyn! I tapped his shield.

Instantly, I was pushed away, and the sensation followed through to my physical body as I stepped instinctively back. "I'm okay," I said as Dimitri steadied me. "He sees me now."

Erin. Mikyn didn't try to hide his surprise. *Why are you here?*

Don't you mean, how did I avoid being blown up?

That too. Amusement came through the communication.

I let my anger surge over him. My Unbounded genes demanded retribution for the attempt on my baby's life. *Before you try that again, you should know that I'm Dimitri's daughter. And according to you, that means I can tell if a child will Change.*

This time he tried to hide his rush of excitement, but I

caught it anyway. *So you weren't channeling me at that birth ceremony.*

I still think I had been channeling him at the time, or at least partially, but it was better to portray confidence. *No.*

Well, I'm a little busy right now.

I know that. But we need to talk. Are you going to let your men shoot me? Because we will reset all of them, if we must. It was only a threat because there were now at least seventy soldiers, and I wasn't sure the Unsworn would be able to help us overpower all of them. *Besides, if you want to retain autonomy here, you'll want to hear what I have to say.*

Several seconds ticked by. The lights on the gate began flashing.

You have my word, Mikyn said finally.

And what is that worth?

You will have to decide.

I let a moment more go by. *I'm coming out with Dimitri and Graeme Padovan.*

Graeme? A rush of greed came through at the thought, and I looked uneasily at Graeme.

"Maybe you should wait here," I told Graeme. "Mikyn seems a little too happy to know you're with me."

"Because of Valerine," he said. "But she and I already discussed it. No matter what he threatens to do to me, she and Anina will not come here to let him use her." Weariness tinged his voice, but the underlying determination was resolute. For a man whose self-sacrifice had begun with the sole goal of saving his daughter, he had definitely evolved.

Mikyn's bodyguard was saying something to the crowd of soldiers now, and I waited until he'd fallen silent before tossing back my metacape and emerging from behind the transport. The hush over the crowd seemed to grow as we strode over the cobblestone walk toward the platform. I was glad now for the native clothing we wore because it made us seem familiar to the soldiers, less like something they should shoot.

Dimitri put himself between me and the crowd. He couldn't know like I did that there were more people on the other side near the gate itself, though their life forces glowed too brightly to be much of an obstacle to me. I broke through their shields to monitor their thoughts, ready to silence them. There was a limit to the number of people I could monitor at one time, at least without Keene's synergism, so I was relieved when they seemed to bear no personal animosity toward me. In fact, several were largely sympathetic to the Unsworn.

As we arrived on the platform, Mikyn's gaze flicked over Dimitri before landing on me. "You look well," he said. He had a cane I hadn't noticed before, and while he didn't lean on it, his hand fisted tightly over the hand grip.

"I can't say the same for you," I answered. "You are in need of a healer."

Mikyn didn't respond but signaled his aid and bodyguard to give him some privacy. "I see you brought the traitor." His gaze landed on Graeme.

"No," I said. "He came of his own accord. But he is not a traitor to Sinalta, as you are very much aware."

"He made his choice."

"As did you," Graeme retorted. "And you chose to kill."

Mikyn didn't respond, studying me. He looked like a worn but kind grandfather, and regret oozed from him. Regret that meant nothing.

"You're making a mistake trusting Stefan Carrington," I said. "He is here to take over Sinalta, not to help you."

Mikyn shrugged. "He is a necessary evil at this point. I need to reunite my people, and unfortunately, the Tsaousiss and Scala families play a vital role in that. Carrington is only part of the package at the moment." He allowed himself a small grin. "After all, he got your leader to let them through, didn't he?"

"Not exactly. You did that when you exploded the transport I was on and put up the shield. Otherwise, we would have held out against him. You may feel you can keep him under control, or give him a job without real power, but you are talking about a man who has ruled the Emporium Triad with an iron fist for centuries. There is only one person who is responsible for more deaths, and you and I both know who that is."

Mikyn's jaw worked, and for the first time, I caught the scent of his burning anger and ambition. It had been there all along, of course, but the glimpse told me he wasn't the innocent victim he had tried to make me believe he was.

I plowed on. "What you also don't know is that Stefan has been sending you his own progeny for fifty years, including a few early-forced Unbounded that you may have thought were simply those who Changed early. One of those has been placing Stefan's progeny in different ruling families and secretly training them in anticipation of Stefan's eventual arrival. We thought that might mean Stefan taking over one of the seats in your Senate by reverse inheritance, but one of his operatives told us tonight that they have plans to overtake every single seat and put him in as their leader in the executive branch after restoring its power. Whatever Stefan ends up with, it won't mean him taking a back seat while you and Tsaousiss steer your city to whatever end you have in mind. It means him taking complete and utter control. You have a choice here tonight, but tomorrow you may not have any choices."

Mikyn considered that for a moment before turning to his assistant. "Magarete, my tablet!" The round-faced woman brought it forward, her face impassive but her surface thoughts volatile and angry. I'd have to watch that one. She hovered as Mikyn flipped through information on his tablet.

"No," he muttered. "It can't be possible. They are even in my own family."

Dimitri nudged me, and I followed his stare to see that the gate in front of us was rolling slowly upward almost soundlessly. Our time had run out.

I reached out to contact Ritter. He and Blaze were closer than previously, but I could feel exertion that signaled a fight. No way would I distract him. The electronic shield over the entire city was still in place, its strength impenetrable. That meant no help from the outside, either. Jace was here, though. I could feel him in the midst of the soldiers behind Mikyn. If anyone noticed he was out of formation, no one seemed to care.

During my brief distraction, Graeme had stepped closer to Mikyn. "You knew that none of us could replace you," he said in an undertone with enough anger in it to call my attention. "All this time, you knew, and still you made us watch the baby ceremonies."

Mikyn drew himself up to his full height just as a breeze rustled his robes, making him look like some kind of powerful magi. "None of us knows what we are capable of until we are compelled," he said. "I was simply looking for a solution." His eyes went to me as he spoke the last word, and I knew he thought he had found what he was looking for, but I would never take his place.

Mentally, I neared his shield. Would he feel any slightest touch? Or would it be possible that my physical presence would mask the intrusion if I acted slowly? To my knowledge, only one person, Delia Vesey, the former Triad member, had ever entered my mind when I hadn't been aware. It had been a horrifying realization, and since that day, I'd overcompensated by checking and rechecking and rebuilding my shield constantly so that it had become a habit. Mikyn had the power to "see" me if he tried, but would he think to look if I didn't use force? The memories Delia had left inside me before her death when she'd tried to take over my body suggested that maybe I could break him down bit by bit.

We heard the gentle hum of a transport engine now, and we all turned to see one sailing from the tunnel, looking for all the world like those that normally ran through Sinalta's canals and streets. Smaller and less obtrusive than the public transports, though certainly not the most humble.

The transport passed the gates, its wheels descending and locking into place as it reached the dry cobblestones, first the front and then the back. The transport rolled up the dock, turning sideways before reaching our location, and the hatch side door lifted up and out, revealing Statesmen Tsaousiss and Scala, already standing in front of the opening.

A few scattered claps and cheers rose from the crowd, and I realized that not all of these soldiers did Mikyn's bidding. Had he been aware of that, or had these particular soldiers been a condition the returning statesmen had requested?

Statesman Tsaousiss's wavy hair was once again grown out and his gold beard as heavy as a lion's mane. His regal face lifted in disdain as if he was doing everyone the favor of his presence. His toga was a bright red, the white gown underneath short enough to reveal gold sandals. With a gallant gesture, he motioned for Scala to precede him from the transport. She also no longer resembled the woman we'd seen in Rio but was now dressed in full Sinaltan regalia. Her long, white, flowing dress was topped by a rich purple toga with so many folds she had to drape it over her arm in order to leave the transport. Both her body and the high pile of her hair dripped with precious rhodium. No doubt of her status here. Tsaousiss stepped from the transport, offering his arm to her, and she glided from the transport with the air of an ancient Greecian queen.

As they closed the distance to where we stood, Scala's eyes flickered over me, recognition in her eyes, but Tsaousiss didn't appear to notice me in my disguise. Instead, he fixed on Graeme, his nostrils flaring and his blue eyes flat and mean.

Still no one spoke, and it wasn't until they'd almost reached Mikyn that Stefan appeared in the hatchway of the transport, dressed in an expensive black suit with the collar of his white shirt open at his neck. No clapping or cheers now, but a wave of murmurs passed through the crowd, almost like a breath.

A pregnant, waiting kind of breath.

Something's up, I told Graeme, my body abruptly awash with goose bumps. *Did you feel that?*

I did. It's like they . . . they've been waiting for him.

Chapter 24

I WIDENED MY VISION TO TAKE IN THE SOLDIERS TO EITHER SIDE OF THE gate, moving both hands close to weapons: my Ruger and a throwing star. Jace would have my back if he didn't let his passion control him.

And where was Ritter? He wasn't as close as I wanted him to be. But I felt both his speed and Blaze's heat pumping in my veins, so I was ready.

Graeme fingered the radio in his hand, sending a message, I guessed. I continued my subtle assault on Mikyn's shield, peeling it like an onion. His focus was on Tsaousiss.

"Statesman," Mikyn said in Sinaltan, dipping his head slightly.

"Hello, old friend," Tsaousiss responded, but he used a word for friend that I wasn't very familiar with, one that seemed to have a double meaning. "I am not sure of the company you are keeping these days." He sent a disgusted look toward Graeme.

"He will serve his purpose," Mikyn said mildly.

Graeme's surface thoughts roiled at that, but before I could use my healing to calm him, he managed to get his emotions under control. More life forces were gathering behind the soldiers both behind and to our sides, dimmed but still plenty bright for anyone to see who might be looking. Like Mikyn, who stiffened at my side. I knew they were the Unsworn.

"Are you going to ask your friend to join us?" Mikyn's simple question showed none of his tension. "The Senate awaits your presence at the capitol."

Tsaousiss waved at Stefan inside the transport. Stefan turned his face, chiseled to harshness under the hard light of the station's many lampposts. At his brief nod, two men emerged from the interior dressed in full Emporium battle gear, edging carefully past Stefan and leading a small-statured woman I recognized instantly: Catrina Silvaski from the Emporium Triad.

Instinctively, I looked behind Mikyn, catching sight of my brother's furious expression. If Stefan hadn't a clue about the extent of Jace's feelings for Catrina, he was about to discover them. But why didn't she react to our presence?

Stefan waited until his men had visually searched the area for danger before emerging from the transport himself. Again, a wave of murmurs skittered through the crowd, making me uneasy. In fifty years, how much damage could indoctrination with a few dozen well-placed operatives do? I had no answer, but if the uneasy expression on Dimitri's face was any indicator, I was right to worry.

Stefan strode forward, flanked by his men, with Catrina wandering next to him as if by accident. She wore a loose dress with spaghetti straps that was completely out of place in the new moist coldness of the city, but she didn't appear to notice, except to fold her arms across her narrow chest. Her orangey red hair hung loose past her shoulders, curling with the moisture. With the light-colored freckles splashed across her face and her blank expression, she looked more like her physical age of nearly twenty instead of the sixty-nine she actually was.

Catrina? I reached out to her, only to find that her normally strong mental shield was almost nonexistent, and emptiness filled her mind. What was wrong with her? At least she didn't appear hurt or afraid. I tried to check her sand stream and found it surrounded by a curtainlike film of black that resisted my efforts to penetrate. Definitely a mental construct of sorts, and I'd felt this signature before—Tsaousiss. He had done something to her, probably to render her unable to escape or to fight back. Born and bred and raised by a strong community of sensing Unbounded, Catrina should have been resistant to commands from a hypnopath, even one of his stature, and I wondered what else they had done to her first to force compliance.

I wanted desperately to see what they'd done to Catrina and to reverse it, but I needed all my faculties around me. *You see this, Mikyn?* I said, calling him to her mind. *Catrina is an important member of the Emporium Triad, who voted against Stefan earlier today. This is what he does to those who thwart him, even those who are supposed to be his equals. I demand that you turn him over for crimes committed against this woman, members of my family, and so many of my people. He has filled your purpose of bringing Tsaousiss and Scala here.* My disgust toward Mikyn was probably more than I should have let him see, but I was through playing games with monsters.

No response from Mikyn. I peeled away another layer of his shield in the area where I was working. Tension was building, but I couldn't figure out from which direction the danger would come. Even channeling the combat ability, no likelihood appeared stronger to me than any other.

"Greetings," Mikyn said to Stefan as he arrived at our position. "Thank you for bringing back our statesmen."

"It was my pleasure." Stefan's attention barely grazed him before moving on. "Daughter," he said to me, looking as in control as he ever had at Emporium headquarters. "I confess that I didn't expect to see you here."

"I didn't expect you either." Not quite the truth. This had been his goal all along, and Stefan was nothing if not determined.

"I thought the healer was her father." Mikyn motioned to Dimitri.

Stefan laughed, pinning me again with those compelling blue eyes that were so like my brother's. "Well, he could be, I suppose. I ran into a mind raider prior to the time of my illegal incarceration, and the section of memories taken from me included her. However, I do have it from trustworthy people that she is of my blood, and her brother is for sure my son. I had his DNA tested myself."

Mikyn shifted his gaze toward me.

You want proof? I asked. Reaching out mentally, I cut off the blood supply to his leg until it began tingling. He gave a subtle nod, which I knew meant he believed me and not Stefan, which was a step in the right direction.

"What did you do to Catrina?" I asked Stefan to cover the silent exchange. "Kidnapping is illegal."

Stefan snorted. "Does she look like she's under duress?"

"Yes." I met his gaze, unable to stop the rage swelling in my heart. What he'd done to Catrina was only the last in a long line of vicious sins, yet he stood there like some charismatic billionaire running for election.

"Guards!" Mikyn snapped his fingers with surprising strength, and a dozen men shot forward, grabbing Stefan and his two men.

"What's this?" Tsaousiss barked.

"Don't play stupid," Mikyn growled. "This is what we agreed

upon. I told you before that I won't have that man running free in my city. Especially now that I've learned he could use reverse inheritance to take one of our Senate seats and possibly has enough backing to change our whole government. But you didn't know any of that, did you, *friend?* Because you always underestimate your enemies."

"Not this time!" Tsaousiss gave a shout and waved at the crowd of soldiers, but whatever he expected to happen fell short as the few soldiers who moved were quickly subdued by their comrades. Two of the soldiers who had surrounded Stefan pointed their guns at Tsaousiss and Scala instead.

Mikyn's chuckle sounded like a sneer. "And you think I didn't replace your soldiers?"

"Is this really necessary?" Scala said, her face pinching with hatred. "You said you had need of us, and here we are."

"Your families demanded your return," Mikyn corrected, "but that doesn't mean a return to power. They will give me the aid I need now that you are back. That was my deal with them. Whether or not you will face trial along with this traitor" —he glanced at Graeme—"remains a matter for the Senate. But I would urge you not to test my soldiers' patience."

So maybe Mikyn wasn't as vulnerable as we'd thought. I relaxed marginally, but something was tugging on me . . . it was my mate bond with Ritter. I reached out immediately, fearing the worst, but he was all right. In terrible pain but alive.

I'm here, I said, slipping into his unblocked mind.

It's Cherish, he said. *She sabotaged the detonator we set on the first location. We didn't realize until too late. We had to fight her and some of the Unsworn at the center relay. So watch your back. We have to get clear and then we're blowing the relay.*

It is all the Unsworn?

I don't know how far it has spread. She said she believed Stefan was their best bet for freedom. I had to reset her.

Good. I could spare no sympathy for the deluded woman.

I waited until his shield was back up before stepping close to Graeme. "Cherish sabotaged the first location and attacked Ritter and Blaze. What do you know of this?"

He stared back at me. "It doesn't make sense. She's completely loyal to the cause."

"Yeah, but to *what* cause?" Because I remembered the way Cherish had identified with Stefan in the safe house. Had she been working with him all along? Obviously, she hadn't been aware of the double agent in their midst, but Stefan could have used others to plant ideas about him being their savior.

I caught Stefan's eyes then, and the mocking grin on his face grew. He reached over and grabbed the gun from one of the guards, wrenching it from him in a move so fast that no one could stop him. The others fired.

Nothing happened.

Stefan bashed in the guard's face with his own gun. Then hell broke loose.

Half the soldiers around us surged forward, as did all of the hovering Unsworn behind them. Guns fired but were decidedly one-sided as more soldiers discovered tampering with their weapons and fell at the hands of the Unsworn and their own comrades alike. Knives and other weapons emerged, but they were useless against the bullets and the anger of the Unsworn. The fight was quick and dirty.

When the dust settled, I saw Statesman Tsaousiss had been cut in three, his lion beard drenched in blood that was a deeper red than his toga. Scala was also really and truly dead, her white dress stained red, though they seemed to be the only ones who had suffered that permanent fate. The Unsworn, both those in uniform and those in tunics or togas, encircled all of us, looking at Stefan for direction. He met my stare with one of his own.

"Take their weapons," he ordered, gesturing at me and my companions.

Hands ran over us, and it was all I could do to stop myself from fighting back. I could take out at least a dozen with a light flash, but that wasn't enough. Together, the Unsworn and the soldiers who had betrayed their comrades numbered two hundred. I could have kept my shield over me to prevent the removal of my weapons, but that would only make Stefan focus more on me. Even so, the man taking my weapons missed the single throwing star over my breast.

I could hardly breathe. I didn't know yet what Stefan's victory might mean for the Emporium or our friends here and now, but I knew what it meant for the world. Death. Mortal lives being thrown away like kindling in the fires that would follow.

Where was my brother?

I searched for Jace, finding him on the far side of one of Stefan's guards with Catrina. He was holding her hand and talking to her, but whatever she said in response made him flush a deep, angry crimson.

Mikyn was sputtering something, and Stefan focused on him. "Your life will be spared for now, old man, but only because you are the seer, and I need your services."

"I'll foretell nothing for you," Mikyn said. He opened his mouth to say more, but I spoke over him.

"Go ahead. Kill him," I told Stefan. "No one should be able to do what he does. He will only get in your way."

"But . . ." Mikyn began, then stopped. *Oh,* he said in tight communication to me. *You're trying to save my life.*

Stefan looked back and forth between us, his eyes calculating. He suspected something was going on, but he couldn't know that Mikyn had been about to tell him that I could do what he could do. If Stefan even suspected my ability, Mikyn would die. And both our lives would mean nothing if Stefan learned that the ability came from a union between a sensing Unbounded and a healer.

Of course, it wasn't as simple as that. Mikyn had influenced me greatly during the birth ceremony—giving me a crash course in finding a child's center of being. I might never have thought to look there on my own, and even upon discovering it, I might not have realized what I was seeing.

"I may still kill him," Stefan said.

My stomach plummeted as Stefan's gaze turned toward Dimitri. "He's my healer," I said. "I need him for the baby."

"For my grandbaby or his?" Stefan's smile was predatory.

"Please," Graeme said. "Don't hurt our people."

"Are you a statesman?" Stefan asked. At the shake of Graeme's head, he said, "Then you have no need to worry. But things are changing." Stefan lifted his voice and said, "Sinalta was once the greatest nation on earth, and it will be so again. It will be the capital of the world. Beginning with me giving you the continent I promised."

As cheers rose from the crowd, despair fell over me. The Unsworn and weary Avowed had no idea that they were about to exchange one controlling dictator for one that was every bit as evil. Desperately, I began searching the soldiers and Unsworn around me, searching for a gift I could use to get us free. I still had the metacape, my mental shield, and my body armor, but there were too many bodies between me and freedom. If I could find a levitator, I might be able to clear a path.

Dimitri's hand gripped mine. "Get yourself free," he said. "Don't worry about me. I can take care of myself. That is an order."

I nodded because as much as I had come to love my birth father, my daughter came above all else. My duty was to her.

"To the capitol!" Stefan raised his fits in the air to enthusiastic cheers. He motioned for the Unsworn to take us.

As they stepped forward to obey, shouts began on the far side of the station plaza, barely heard above the cheers. Molten fireballs fell into the crowd, and the cheers became screams of pain.

Ritter and Blaze were here.

Soldiers and Unsworn surged toward the conflict but were knocked to the ground as a huge explosion rocked the entire plaza. The water in the canal sloshed, spilling over the sides in impressive waves. Terrified screams filled the air.

The electronic shield was no more.

No time to reach out to Ava. The battle was now or never, levitator or no. I sent a flash into the minds of the enemies closest to me, those with little or no shielding. Two more crashed when I stopped their hearts—a temporary reset at best, one that wouldn't hold for more than a few minutes, but it would buy time. Three others close to Dimitri hit the ground, and we swept up their guns. Smoke and fire filled the air, accompanied by gunfire.

A sudden, powerful blow knocked me backwards onto the ground. But my shield held. The Unsworn who'd shot me fell, revealing Graeme behind him with an Avowed weapon, blood pouring from two different wounds in his body.

I jumped to my feet, only to see Jace delivering a fatal blow to one of Stefan's guards. "I will kill you for what you've done to her," Jace growled, launching himself at Stefan with his sword.

Stefan laughed. "Boy, you think you can best me? I was defending my throne from offspring like you long before your grandmother stole my genetically modified sperm to beget you." The words sounded like a curse, deliberately chosen to remind Jace that his birth hadn't been in Stefan's plan.

For answer, Jace swung hard at Stefan's neck.

Stefan twirled and leapt at the same time, narrowly escaping decapitation. His own sword came out.

Meanwhile, the fight raged around us. I fired my stolen gun, my back to Graeme's, trying to hold off a group of Unsworn. The return fire was only scattered, as if they were afraid of hitting Stefan behind us. I could feel Ritter and Blaze closer now, and the soldiers hesitated, appearing confused about which way to turn and who to fight.

Dimitri was battling Stefan's second guard, which would have been an unfair fight, except Dimitri had done something with his blood supply, and the man was moving more slowly despite his combat ability.

Fire swept through the plaza as Blaze tossed more molten balls. Ritter was a blur, pushing through the soldiers and Unsworn. So many emotions tugged on me—pain, elation, terror, determination.

A scream sounded from my right, and I whirled to see an Unsworn man in a blue tunic launching himself at Jace where he stood like a crazed demon over Stefan, now bleeding profusely on the ground. I threw my one remaining star at the man, slicing into his neck. Jace easily lifted a leg and kicked him away.

Jace stared down at Stefan with a maniacal smile. "Now look who's laughing," he said. His sword raised.

"No!" I shouted, sprinting to cover the few steps between us. As badly as I wanted Stefan gone, I understood how volatile and uncertain my brother's feelings were toward this man who had—however unwittingly—given him life. Killing Stefan would haunt Jace forever.

"I have to," Jace ground out. "He hurt the woman I'm going to marry, and he would kill all of us to save his own skin."

I could feel the sword coming down, down, down.

At the last moment, it slammed into the cobblestones by Stefan uselessly, shattering them. Jace let out a frustrated cry. "I can't," he cried, his words barely audible.

Stefan crowed. "Coward. You are not good enough for my new world." His muscles clenched, and I knew in the next moment he'd be on his feet, and my brother would be dead.

Throwing myself at Stefan, I swung my glowing hand across his torso in a single burning slash. Then I reversed my swing, angling upward to slice across his neck. As my molten hand penetrated his flesh, our eyes met, his showing shock and maybe a little admiration.

"Daught—" was his last whispered utterance as I severed his vocal cords and his head separated from his neck. His charred flesh sizzled, and the burning stench was overpowering. Three separated focus points. Stefan would never again hurt my family and especially my little brother.

"Erin." Jace uttered a hoarse cry and fell to his knees. His chest heaved, and I almost missed the next word. "Thanks."

"It was always supposed to be me." I looked past him, ready to throw a fireball at the pair of soldiers coming at us, but Graeme stepped in front of them and waved them to a halt.

"No more!" he shouted.

His voice rang out over the station plaza, oddly amplified, perhaps by someone with the ability, and movements around us slowed. All except Ritter's and Blaze's, who had neared us, leaving a wide swath of reset bodies in their wake.

Encouraged, Graeme stepped forward, both hands raised with his palms open and out. "Stop! It is finished!" Again the words resounded far too loudly for the space we were in, and I looked to Mikyn's assistant, Magarete Santiagio, who was focused on Graeme intently. It was her, I was sure of it. Soldiers and Unsworn alike faltered. There was no hypnotic cast to Graeme's amplified plea, only a heartfelt appeal.

But it wasn't finished, not yet. Because Mikyn still lived. He sat on the frigid cobblestones near Statesman Scala's head, the decorative chains of her hair brushing his right foot that was half out of his sandal. His chest heaved, but he appeared miraculously unbloodied.

I used my mental machete, breaking through his weakened shield with a single concentrated blow. He barely acknowledged me as I stepped onto the stage of his mind and headed toward his thought stream. I dived up, into it, aware that he trailed along behind me, silent and unresisting.

When I reached the place that was his essence, the stars making up his DNA gleamed beckoningly. They told me he had a love of music and was skilled enough that if he had so desired, in the mortal world he might have become a famous violinist. He had a craving for hot peppers, a birthmark on his left knee, and a genetic tendency toward paranoia. He was definitely Unbounded—or Avowed, rather. Except his beginnings hadn't started seventeen hundred years ago but over three thousand.

What? I thought at the impossibility.

Shame washed through Mikyn. *It wasn't planned. I tried not to. I didn't know how to reverse it. Besides, Sinalta needed me.*

Finally understanding, I recoiled from him in horror. With every failed change that had resulted in years stolen from his victims' lives, he had received the side benefit of extending his. Not in equal measure but in a small percentage that had added up over the centuries.

Never again, I promised.

I reached out and grabbed the brightest star, pulling it to me and squeezing. A flash exploded, brighter than any I'd seen or caused before, as if we were in the middle of a supernova. The brightness was followed by utter inky black that felt oily on my mind.

Dizziness crashed over me as if fired at high force.

"Erin!" Ritter called from what seemed like very far away.

He was coming toward me fast. So was Dimitri. Overhead, I heard the sound of a chopper, and I felt Ava up there somewhere.

Vaguely, I became aware of my body falling on top of Mikyn's physical form as I collapsed into unconsciousness.

Chapter 25

"I CAN'T BELIEVE I WON THE VOTE," GRAEME SAID, SHAKING HIS head as we looked around the ballroom in the Magistrate's mansion, full of supporters who were eagerly celebrating with fruit, cheeses, breads, and wines brought to them by servers. "In this city, sixty-two is barely legal age, especially when so many are in their second millennium. And several of Mikyn's descendants who ran against me have actual political experience."

My fingers smoothed the rich red fabric of the sofa we sat upon. "Yes, but not everyone helped pull down three dictators in a day, was instrumental in raising the city, and led the charge to return power to the executive branch of government," I said, ticking these off on my fingers. "Of course you won. Everyone in Sinalta knows what you did for them, what you risked for them. I am not surprised at all that they gave you the top executive seat, Magistrate Padovan." I gave him the same deferential dip of my head that I'd seen the newly elected statesmen giving each other. There had been a complete overhaul in the

Senate, and not one of the five previous statesmen had been retained.

"Besides," I added after a brief basking in the moment, "you are mentally the strongest of Mikyn's descendants."

"Not strong enough," Graeme said wistful smile. "Certainly not as strong as you . . . or Mikyn." His voice lowered "How is he, by the way?"

"As good as can be expected. He didn't change in his physical age now that he is mortal"—I tripped a little over the last word because I was the one responsible for that—"but he is of course dying at a faster rate than before. His body is no longer even partly healing itself."

"Or glutting itself on the lives of children." Graeme's lips clenched tightly before adding, "The way he did with my sons."

"But not Anina." I glanced around to be sure no one was close enough to hear me. "At least he didn't try to alter her DNA."

He gave a short nod. "There is that. But I am less optimistic about his intentions. He knew we planned to train her to work under Valerine instead of in the mines. Even then, he was courting my wife for her brain."

"Or maybe he had compassion on you." I knew it was strange to have pity for Mikyn, but I did. I knew only too well the inner conflict he'd fought for over three thousand years.

"Possibly. Regardless, it's a fitting punishment for his crimes, and no one except me is aware of how it happened and why." He knew because he'd followed me into Mikyn's mind, and the man had told him as it happened. "And you, of course. Do not blame yourself. He will live out his time here comfortably, which is more than his victims can say."

"We can never tell anyone." I pushed back the urge I still had to wipe the memory from Graeme's mind. He'd proven himself trustworthy. "And stay on alert for any offspring of empaths and healers."

"We will remain vigilant. And for now, let's celebrate the victory we have gained for our most innocent population."

He spoke of what I considered my most personal victory, one made much more emotionally significant as I approached the end of my own pregnancy. In the nearly four months since the Revolution of Sinalta, as it was now heralded throughout the world, no babies had been murdered after their births simply because they would never Change. I predicted a baby boom was coming to Sinalta, and already thousands of Unsworn women were expecting.

Also in those four months, Keene and Jace had taken their places in the Emporium Triad, and, with a healed Catrina, had restored peace. Keene had then turned to helping the Avowed levitators and engineers move Sinalta to its new location, an island in the South Pacific between Fiji and New Zealand. My island, to be exact.

The one hundred and twenty square miles of land left to me by Keene's brother Cort Bagley was the only solution we'd found that allowed Sinalta to retain autonomy without giving up too much in negotiation to a single nation. Sinalta had wanted to buy the island outright with their huge stockpile of precious metals, but I took an interest instead in their future exports, wanting nothing to do with what I thought of as blood money from their forced-labor mines, now defunct, of course. It would be enough space to begin a new nation, but Valerine Padovan was already looking into creating a larger land mass or more floating cities like Sinalta.

"Ah, there's my lovely wife." Graeme placed his hand briefly over mine before standing to meet Valerine, who was coming toward us, hand-in-hand with Anina. Both looked radiant in their gowns and togas. After months of jeans and shorts, Anina had balked a little at the costume, but in the end, she decided that dressing up wasn't all that bad, especially when Kathy and Spencer had dressed up with her.

As Graeme kissed his wife, I awkwardly pushed my swollen body up from the sofa. Ritter came up beside me, his arm going around my body, covered only by a toga. No armor for once.

"I missed you," he murmured in my ear.

"You did the rounds?"

"Of course I did the rounds, but either all the Unsworn have thrown their support behind Graeme and the new statesmen, or they have gone underground."

"We gave them what they wanted. Maybe they aren't lying somewhere in wait."

"There are always fringers who aren't satisfied. There will still be trouble."

I smiled at his pessimism. "Then Graeme and the others will deal with it. Anyway, I'm more worried about the former ruling families. They're too used to being gods here, even among their own people."

Graeme turned around, obviously hearing our exchange. "Funny you'd mention that. It brings me to something I have been meaning to ask both of you but didn't feel I could before we knew the election outcome."

"We're listening," Ritter said, kneading the muscles in my back that still ached no matter how fast my metabolism worked to alleviate my discomfort.

Graeme glanced at Valerine, who nodded in encouragement, telling me that whatever he was going to say, she already knew and approved. "I'm going to need help here," he said. "Not only with sensing and learning more about my ability but also in figuring out how to help my people learn right from wrong while living free in a democratic republic instead of a dictatorship—which is what they are used to, regardless of the pretense perpetuated by my predecessors. My first plan is to enlarge representation across Sinalta, including adding mortals to our Senate."

"That's going to take a few more years of deprogramming," Ritter said, his eyes lifting to the celebrants. Besides Graeme's daughter, Anina, the only mortals here were servers.

"Or more," I said.

Already the Church of the Unboundaried had added a sect of worshippers honoring the Avowed, and the Sinaltan media was eating up the coverage. The Avowed loved being hailed as gods by the lesser mortals. Both sides needed to stop.

"Your first step needs to be fulfilling your promise to pass a law releasing all the former kidnapped embryos who Changed and are still interspersed among the families," I added. "In the interviews Ava and I've conducted, nearly all of them want to leave Sinalta, with their children and spouses, and while they have been given some monetary recompense, nothing has been done about their release because of the election. Also, while the Senate did release the kidnapped mortal children from the mines before we brought Sinalta topside, there has been no recompense for them or for the families of those who died there. That recompense needs to be very generous."

"You're right, and the fact that I didn't lead with the need to help them is exactly my point. We *will* end up passing the required laws, especially as it is part of our agreement with you for raising the city, but it's not like any of the new statesmen will consider that a priority. Four out of the five have strong roots in the leading families, and together they still have a lot of control. That means I will need people I can trust who aren't out to benefit themselves. Not only do I need security without local ties, but I need an advisor with immediate access to people in the Emporium so that we can work together for a common goal." His eyes pinned mine in a personal appeal. "You help me see all sides of the issue. You and Valerine, but she doesn't have the right security clearance for everything." His gaze widened again to include Ritter. "Isn't there a topside proverb or something that says if you save a life, you are responsible for it?"

"No," Ritter said, his voice slightly aggrieved. "Have you been talking to Jace? That's only urban legend."

Graeme chuckled. "Of course it is. Still, in a very real way you are responsible for raising Sinalta, and for its revolution. Things at your Emporium are under control at the moment, but we are still on the edge and will be for quite some time. So I thought maybe you two would consider staying to help us. We are the new frontier, after all." His smile widened. "I'm not saying forever, of course. But maybe a half century or so. You have the time."

I looked at Ritter, not as surprised at the job offer as I might have been had Graeme not asked him to supervise security throughout the Senate reorganization and election, which agreement officially concluded today. "What do you think?"

Ritter lifted his hands in front of him, his wide shoulders rising in a gentle shrug. "I do have a few ideas that would help. We've made a good start, but changing this society is going to take time, and we'll need to give a few kicks in the pants along the way. I've also been thinking that with your advanced technology and the combined efforts of our scientists, we may be able to figure out how to feed the world or eventually expand into space." He paused for a heartbeat before adding, "I have the feeling this is where the future begins."

An entire mouthful of statements, but it meant Ritter was bored with a world that was now more peaceful than it had been in all the generations of his long life. I understood the feeling. We were made to explore and push and move mountains. And he was right that being here could be important for the future of humanity. But I wasn't sure this was where I wanted to raise my child.

Where the future begins.

I opened my mouth to speak when a rush of liquid began down my leg. I met Ritter's gaze. "Sorry. We'll have to pick this up later. Our baby is coming."

MY LABOR WAS SHORT AND INTENSE, WITH NO TIME TO GET TO A Sinaltan birthing center. It didn't matter. A lush guest suite in the Magistrate's mansion was everything I could have wished for my daughter's birth. Ava was there, and so was my mother, Annie Radkey, who had shifted to Sinalta with Mari and Stella. Dimitri was also at my bedside, soothing my pains, though not enough, according to Ritter, who was experiencing a goodly amount through our linked minds.

"Too much for you, Your Deathliness?" I asked with a mocking raise of one brow. But I knew that wasn't the real issue because he was used to pain from both wounds and torture, far worse than childbirth. It was knowing *I* was in that kind of pain that made him crazy because there was nothing he could do to change it.

"Can't you give her something more?" Ritter asked Dimitri.

"I'm fine," I said at the same time Dimitri said, "There's really no time. She needs to push."

So I bore down.

It didn't matter that I felt torn apart. I was connected to my daughter, and surprisingly, she was taking the pressure very well. She was excited to see the light and meet the people I'd been introducing her to over the past months. Well, not in so many words, but her curiosity and anticipation were certainly real enough. She held on to my mental presence in a way that made me feel as if she were already in my arms.

It won't be long now, I assured her.

I shared each emotion and sensation with Ritter, so he could also feel our daughter. The contractions intensified. The pressure grew on her head. My nails bit into Ritter's hand as I pushed, my back pressing against his chest as he supported me on the bed. My mother offered me ice chips. Ava rubbed my feet.

Then my baby's head was through, and the pressure cut drastically. I felt Dimitri's finger tugging under her arm as if he touched my own skin, guiding her to turn and emerge the rest of the way. He pulled her up onto my chest, and she was finally in my arms, and I could barely see her through the tears.

Ritter hugged us both, and I saw he was crying too. His emotions were so large that they filled me up, and I had to partially close off the feedback from his mind. He'd waited centuries for this little one, and in comparison, I had only thought about children for the last few of my thirty-two years. Besides, I needed to focus on experiencing the new sensations around me as seen through the eyes of my daughter, who admittedly was perfectly content to nurse and sleep. Not much change from when she was inside me. Yet.

In the next few days, we had a steady stream of visitors who wanted to honor the first child born since Sinalta had come to its final resting place in the South Pacific, though she would be far from the last. These visitors were fielded by my parents, or more particularly my mother, who was excited beyond measure to be visiting the famed city of Sinalta that was on all the news channels. She even gave interviews to a few lucky reporters.

When Valerine finally enticed my parents away to see the sites of the city, Ritter and I found ourselves suddenly alone with our new bundle in our guest-suite sitting room. Ritter held her in the crook of his arm, and she looked tiny against his bulk. He'd already bought her a one-hundred-year-old sword from the best artisan in Russia, a mirror of the one he'd bought me, and no less than two handguns, a ballistic knife, and a dagger. The weapons were his love language, and I didn't have the heart to tell him that the taekwondo workout schedule he planned to start when she was a year old was likely too soon. Who knew? Maybe it wouldn't be.

"What are we going to name you?" he asked in a voice that wasn't exactly baby talk but was so gentle it might as well have been.

We'd been going back and forth on names, calling her each for a few hours, but nothing had stuck.

"I have an idea," said a small voice.

We looked up to see Anina Padovan in the open doorway, twirling her long blond hair around a finger. "Come on in," I invited.

"I wasn't eavesdropping," she said with a tentative smile. "I was trying to get away from my new tutor."

I laughed at her expression before remembering why her parents hadn't sent her back to school where she would be one of the few mortals in her age group. The Unsworn had welcomed back the children they had been forced to place in servitude, but the prominent families of Sinalta were not as willing to allow them to learn alongside their own offspring, who were destined to Change. Things would be different in the future, of course, as new babies would be raised and loved before their parents knew their future, but for the time being the prejudice remained. It was just as well. A special school would give the older children the attention they needed to make up for the lack in their education, and we still needed to find a fix for the years Mikyn had stolen from them.

"Then shut the door quickly," Ritter said to Anina with a

chuckle. To me he added, "They take education way too seriously around here."

I blinked at him. "This from the man who has already interviewed sixteen part-time nannies worldwide about their ability to teach phonics?"

"That's different."

"Sure, it is." I beckoned to Anina, who came forward, looking reverently at the baby.

"Her hair is so dark and beautiful," she said. "And her eyes."

I smiled. "Thank you. We think so too. So what was your name idea?"

"Raya," she said. "She was the first Sinaltan Magistrate, and it was cool because that was thousands of years ago when everyone else in the world except the Avowed treated women like . . . uh . . ." She frowned. "Well, like mortals."

"It's a beautiful name," I said uncertainly. But did I really want to name my child after a Sinaltan ruler?

"She had so many children, but two turned out to be mortal," Anina rushed on as if sensing my reluctance, "and when they put the dome on the city, she helped them and a lot of other mortals leave. She saved them from being . . . well, you know. Slaves."

I was liking the name better and better. My gaze caught Ritter's. "We can try it out," he said. He stroked the baby's cheek. "Hey, Raya Radkey-Langton." The alliteration was a bit of a mouthful, but since Unbounded custom generally didn't have women taking their husband's name upon marriage, we'd agreed to hyphenate.

Whether it was the roughness of his finger on her vernix-softened cheek, the tone in his voice, or because she felt some sign from me, she reacted with a mental image of contentment and satisfaction which I shared with Ritter.

"Raya, it is," I said to Anina. "And thank you."

She glanced toward the door. "Thank *you* for hiding me."

"Would you like to hold her?" Ritter asked. At her nod, he patted the sofa. "Sit up here between us."

Anina's reprieve didn't last long. My parents soon appeared from touring the hydrogardens, bringing Valerine, Graeme, and Dimitri with them.

"So here's where you're hiding," Valerine said to Anina. "Your tutor is looking for you."

"My goddaughter and I have been doing the important work of naming the baby," I interjected. "Everyone, I want you to officially meet Raya Radkey-Langton."

A soft sigh escaped Valerine's lips. "Perfect."

"I love it," my mother agreed. Dimitri and my father nodded their approval, though I suspected they were simply glad they didn't have to keep figuring out what name we were currently using for the baby.

"Now let's see how the new outfits we found look on her," my mother said. She took Raya to her changing table, where even my father fussed over her, making me laugh.

"Okay, you've had your reprieve," Valerine said to Anina as my mother reached for another outfit. "If we go now, I think we'll have time for a bowl of ice cream to help you study." Grinning, Anina skipped out of the room with her mother.

"So . . ." Graeme said after a few moments. "Dimitri has agreed to stay until we can get a few more healers to come from Europe. Are you ready to sign on too?"

Ritter draped an arm over my shoulder, a question in his eyes. I knew what he wanted me to say, but I still felt unsure.

"Before you decide," Dimitri said, "there is something you should know. Something Graeme and I each discovered but that tie in together."

This sounded serious. "Oh?" I asked.

Dimitri looked at Graeme, who in turn glanced backward

at my parents, who appeared oblivious to our conversation. "I was looking into my genealogy," Graeme said, "and Mikyn's by default, of course. I discovered that Mikyn's father died when he was only eight. Turns out he was raised by his grandfather, who was a hypnopath. The records aren't clear, but somehow, his father ended up dead and his mother married her former father-in-law."

I thought about that for a moment. "That might explain why Mikyn wasn't a very good healer—because his father wasn't around to channel and learn from—and why he was so good at controlling everyone with his empathic abilities. But are you saying that some of us might have the potential of accessing more gifts in our lineage? That Mikyn may have done so with his grandfather?"

"Possibly," Graeme said. "Perhaps by first channeling those gifts until the ability awakes in their genetic makeup, and channeling may be limited to empaths with a healer parent, so that narrows things down drastically. But that's not the point."

"What he's trying to say," Dimitri's voice showed an uncustomary impatience, "is when I personally examined Mikyn's failed attempts with the idea of reversing the shortened life spans, I discovered that his method of altering babies' DNA was imperfect. Think of it as tossing a bomb to get through a lock when you could simply turn a key—if you could find it. I believe the children were damaged during the failed attempts because he wasn't properly trained."

Graeme nodded in emphatic agreement. "In Sinaltan history before Mikyn became seer, there were far fewer instances of failure, and while the resulting mortals were enslaved, there's no record of their lives being shortened."

Dimitri paused to let that sink in. "Erin," he began again after I'd had a moment, "we think it's possible that with what we've learned from Mikyn and can learn from Sinaltan history, we might be able to figure out how you can safely turn the key in most of our descendants. Maybe not those who are already born from several generations of mortals, but at least our first generation."

"And not shorten any lives," Graeme emphasized.

My heart raced. Until that very moment, I hadn't been sure about staying in Sinalta, so far away from my family. But this new information could mean everything, especially for my daughter. I could pull in scientists to study the pattern of a Change, healers to determine how to apply it, and Keene's synergism could propel us to our full potential. I couldn't wait to get to work.

"Okay," I told Graeme, "I don't know for how long, but I'm in."

Ritter jumped up and pulled me into a hug, his laugh loud enough to make my parents look our way. "We'll stay," he confirmed, "but I'm taking at least the next month off. Paternity leave, you know."

I sputtered a laugh at the idea of him hanging out in the nursery for a month. "Right," I said. "Then maybe it's time you learned to change a diaper. Because I'm going to be busy changing the world."

Or pushing it to Change. Literally.

This was going to be fun.

TEYLA BRANTON GREW UP AVIDLY READING SCIENCE FICTION AND fantasy and watching Star Trek reruns with her large family. They lived on a little farm where she loved to visit the solitary cow and collect (and juggle) the eggs, usually making it back to the house with most of them intact. On that same farm she once owned thirty-three gerbils and eighteen cats, not a good mix, as it turns out. Teyla always had her nose in a book and daydreamed about someday creating her own worlds.

Teyla is now married and has seven kids, so life at her house can be very interesting (and loud), but writing keeps her sane. She's been known to wear pajamas all day when working on a deadline, and is often distracted enough to burn dinner. (Okay, pretty much 90% of the time.)

Teyla has worked in the publishing business for over twenty years. Teyla also writes romance and suspense under the name Rachel Branton. For a free ebook and more information, please visit http://www.TeylaBranton.com.